# DESCENT

First published in Great Britain in 2024 by Literacy Club Publishing



Cover illustrations by Assina Rana
Instagram: @sinaart.r



Paperback ISBN 978-1-916848-08-5
eBook ISBN 978-1-916848-09-2

# Acknowledgements

Abu Hurayrah (may God be pleased with him) reported: The Prophet Muhammad (peace and blessings be upon him) said, "He who does not thank the people, is not thankful to God."

– Sunan Abu Dawud 4811

All praises due to God for allowing this book to come to fruition.

I would like to express my deepest gratitude to everyone who helped make this book a reality, no matter how big or small:

To my editor, Eduardo Hormazabal, who went above and beyond in his role. To Assina for her immaculate cover design. To Zahrah for developing my writing skill and knowledge of journalism. To Tukeer for his endless belief in me.

To my beta readers, Yusuf Oxford for his deeply insightful critique of my story, Uthman for his amazing knowledge of worldbuilding and wonderful suggestions to improve my writing, and Ahsan for being who he is – a mentor, a role model, and a dear friend.

A special thank you to Halima, who helped build this story from the ground up and develop the characters

And to Sayf – only one thing can be said: You made me an author.

I only wish that I remember you all in my prayers as often as I remember myself.

*Dedicated to my family and my chosen family*

*And to my students – be leaders of your generation. Be the change you want to see*

*Written in Java*

# Contents

# 1
# Kyung-tae

*There was definitely a struggle,* Kyung-tae thought, analysing the layers of snow. What else could explain overturned industrial-sized bins a few minutes from an isolated restaurant? It was a strange area to start up a restaurant. There was next to no foot traffic. There were four bins, each one for a different type of waste, two of which had been knocked over. The deep layer of snow was disturbed, and not by footsteps leading from the diner to the bins. It was as if something was being dragged through the snow. Or someone. Someone who was thrashing about, struggling to escape. Kyung-tae could just barely make it out due to fresh snow beginning to cover it up, but he was sure that there was a path made in the snow leading directly into the epicentre of the struggle. One of the girls who went missing, Kim Sun-jung - he was certain that she had been kidnapped.

He scanned the ground for traces of evidence, but the new layer of snow made it difficult to decipher much. He continued searching. Searching for cars, traffic cams, anything that could have recorded the area when something glinted in the corner of his eye. Underneath the large dumpster lay a pile of fine see-through crystals. They had a very faint blue tinge to them that only showed up when he looked at it in certain ways. What was it, useless junk? No...no it couldn't have been. This was different - he hadn't come across anything like this the last time it happened. He took a small plastic bag out of his pocket and scooped a sample in.

As he took note of the lack of cameras to aid his investigation, the wind howling in his ears and biting at his nose led him to make his way to the front of the diner so that he could question the owners. The wind grew stronger, blowing his hair over his eyes. He ran his hands through his hair, slicking it neatly over to the side.

A large neon sign with English letters protruded from the roof. Using all he could remember from his poorly taught high school English lessons, he attempted and then failed to read the letters. A bell rang above his head as he entered. Rows of maroon leather booths were seated to his right, between each one a rectangular white table with laminated menus spread across it. As he marched across the chequered tiling floor, up to the long sky blue counter, he peered through the kitchen door on his left which was slightly ajar. Two men in black t-shirts and long aprons were having a heated discussion. One was young and the other a fair bit older. A tingling sensation spread across his lips as the warmth of the room brought his sense of feeling back into them. A beaming young lady stood behind the counter. She had bleached blonde hair tied up in a bun and a plastic sheen to her cheeks.

"Welcome to Jimin's Diner!" she said. "What can I get for you today, sir?"

Kyung-tae showed his badge and her face dropped.

"Detective Oh Kyung-tae," he said in a dull tone, "I'm here about Kim Sun-jung. I have a few questions."

Her smile flickered on the verge of returning.

"She's not here at the moment, do you want me to pass on your details when she next comes in?"

"Her family reported her missing."

"What? Oh my, poor Sun-jung." She gasped, placing her hand on her chest, "and here I was annoyed that she hadn't come into work today." She slapped her palm across her forehead. "Silly me."

Kyung-tae looked around the empty restaurant. Only an older couple sat in a booth in the corner.

"Well," she continued, "we don't know anything about that, so I don't think we'll be much help. But thank you for coming by!" She beamed.

"Were you here two nights ago?"

Her face dropped again.

"I don't work the night shift like she does. Last I saw her, we had a passing conversation when switching shifts. That was a while ago."

The argument in the backroom got louder.

"And you didn't notice anything unusual?" Kyung-tae said, pulling a notepad and pen out of his pocket. He flipped it open, putting the pen to the paper. "Maybe in the way she acted or anyone strange she may have been speaking to?"

She shook her head.

"Apart from the odd customer pining over her every now and then, no. But she's a nice girl, you know, not one to hang out with strange men."

The shouting in the back had quietened.

"And those strange men; you see any of them lurking about?"

"Not that I can remember. Why do you ask?," she said, as her lip began to tremble, "do you think one of them could have hurt her, or worse?"

In a flash, the older of the two men came bursting through the kitchen door. Kyung-tae unconsciously jerked his right foot back, shifting himself into a fighting stance.

"What you think you doing?" The man bellowed. "You trying to cause trouble?" Why was his Japanese so broken? Was he foreign? It would make sense with him running an American themed restaurant. Kyung-tae could sense the eyes of the only customers in the building turn towards them as he held up his badge once again, stopping the man in his tracks.

"Calm down, sir. I have some questions for you regarding Sun-jung."

The waitress slapped the man's arm.

"Hey! How could you not tell me about Sun-jung? Is this why you asked me to work evenings this week?" She slapped him again, causing the man to recoil his arm. "Have you got no decency?"

"Her parents call, and I say I don't know anything," he said, looking over his recoiled shoulder, "what am I supposed to tell you?"

"You could have told me that!" She scowled. "Why wouldn't you let me know her parents are worried about her?"

The man threw his arms in the air.

"Are you my boss or am I yours?"

"Sir, you better settle down," Kyung-tae said, raising his voice, causing the man to calm himself somewhat.

"She's too big headed," he said, pointing at the waitress and then turning to her, "you not even close with her."

"Sir, just answer my questions as I ask them," Kyung-tae said, holding up his palm, "are you the owner?"

"Yes, Lee Ji-min. But I don't know anything. She left when her shift end and I close up one hour later."

"Where are all your cameras? I didn't see any outside, or in here for that matter."

"You think I'm rich? We small business, we don't have money for cameras. Now you go," he said, walking out from behind the counter and gesturing towards the door, "we can't help you."

Kyung-tae held his hand out, to stop Ji-min from pushing towards the entrance.

"Mr Lee, I think it's important for you to know that I've already looked into your business." Kyung-tae was grateful that Woo-young had already done a lot of groundwork on this case. He wouldn't have had any more leads at this point if he hadn't.

"What?" he said, in a venomous tone.

"There are a whole lot of financial discrepancies. Surely there's some money somewhere that could have gone towards cameras?"

Ji-min began pushing him towards the door, shaking his head.

"I don't know what you talk about."

Kyung-tae stood his ground, stopping Ji-min from pushing him any further. He grimaced as he realised that he didn't have the strength to move Kyung-tae.

"I'm no businessman," Kyung-tae said, closing his notepad, "but with what's written on your financial reports, there's no way that this business should still be standing. You're supposedly making a loss every year." Ji-min stood quietly, as did the waitress, who watched with worry in her eyes. "You've fired so many employees, but you've still got money going out to them? Are you telling me that's just out of goodwill?"

"You talk nonsense! Get out!" he yelled.

"You aren't from here, are you?" Kyung-tae said, "I've never heard of a Korean man who speaks Japanese as poorly as you."

"My grandparents go America after war," he huffed, "I don't know why they so stupid. America is crap."

"Well, I don't know how things work in America, but in this country there's something called tax fraud." Kyung-tae leaned towards him. "And it's damn serious. If you have any information on Sun-jung, I suggest you let me know now."

Ji-min lightly pushed him away.

"Y-you don't know what you talk about." His hand was jittering as he waved him away dismissively.

Kyung-tae stood back up straight.

"I'm going to be keeping a very close eye on you. I'm giving you a week to get your business in order, or I will be calling in an auditor."

"Whatever," he said, pointing to the door, "now get out."

"You should be thanking me, sir," Kyung-tae said as he turned towards the door, "fraud will get you a minimum of five years in jail. I'm saving you from that."

As Kyung-tae exited, the bell ringing above his head again, the backdraft of the harsh air blasted him in the face. After walking a few paces, the bell behind him rang again. He turned to see the waitress jogging up to him.

"Hey," she said, "my boss isn't in trouble, is he?"

"He still has time to save himself," Kyung-tae said, turning to walk away.

"Wait," she said, halting him yet again, "how long have you been investigating this case?"

"Not long."

"How much have you found out? Are there any people you're investigating?"

"Sorry," he said, holding up his hand, "You're not privy to that information."

"But what about suspicious evidence, you found any?" she asked eagerly.

"Like I said, I can't disclose that."

"Have you questioned her family? Who knows, maybe her family wasn't the best and she ran away or something. She's an adult, she has the right to do that."

Did she not understand a single thing he was saying? Her continuous chattering mixed with the icy temperature caused a clamping sensation to form around his head. If she was going to talk, the least she could do was say something useful. Starting with that suspicious boss of hers.

"Your boss," he started, "do you like him? Is he good to you?"

"Sure, he's pretty cool, especially when it comes to customers," she said, instantly distracted by the change in topic. She seemed pretty dim-witted. "When we're dealing with money, though, he's totally strict. If we mess up with that, he starts thrashing about like a caffeine addicted customer who has to wait too long for their food. Why do you ask?"

"This is a confidential conversation. He won't know about anything you say to me."

"I swear there's really not much to say. He came to the country two years ago for a better life. It's only natural he gets that serious about his money."

"And has he ever been so annoyed to the point where he'd hurt someone?"

"What?" She gasped. "No way, he would never. He's a control freak, not some kind of barbarian."

"I see."

Kyung-tae ended the conversation there and he walked off, since she no longer served a purpose to him.

All the painstaking buttering up he had to do with Detective Woo-young was worth it. Doing a month's worth of his paperwork meant nothing in comparison, especially considering the six months of his own that he already had to catch up on. Hopefully Lieutenant Kim wouldn't find out that he was working on the case. Kyung-tae scoffed. Desk duty for two weeks - that's what he got for being the best detective in the precinct? Over what, late paperwork?

After about five minutes of walking, he checked the time on his phone. He had seven missed calls.

*Crap, I'm late for my own wedding.* Kyung-tae spun in the opposite direction and dashed off, paying no heed to the slippery surface below him.

# 2
# Yu-ra

*My teacher had her house raided last night, but the soldiers didn't arrest anyone. Although she said "the soldiers didn't choose to arrest anyone." Maybe something did happen? She gave us all books to take home this morning. She said to keep them and hide them from other people. I'm not sure why she wants us to keep them, but I love reading them, so I'm happy to.*

*I heard from a friend that there's a man in the next village who is trying to recruit Koreans to resist the Japanese. But I hear he's light-skinned, so it's pretty obvious that he is a Russian spy, if you ask me. Maybe that's why they raided my teacher's house, to be cautious? Maybe they found something suspicious. I've seen posters around explaining what disgusting acts the Russians get up to. I'm glad the Japanese are protecting us from that. During the raid last night, they mixed our flour and wheat. I don't understand why they would do that. It must have been an accident because it took my aunt forever to separate them. Sometimes I hear they do strange things, like when my classmate said they ruined his books. I guess they would never do anything like that to me, because I haven't done anything wrong.*

\- *Tuesday 15th November 1910*
*Diary of Baek Sun-hwa*

Baek Yu-ra poured herself a piping cup of coffee at the table of refreshments at the edge of the conference room. One of the other interviewees stood beside her waiting for her to make space.

"Oh, sorry," she said to him, smiling politely. He nodded awkwardly but remained silent.

Yu-ra sat back down at the long table in the centre of the room with the rest of the candidates - men and women all around the same age as her or older, all dressed in suits. Yu-ra opted to wear a long, loose-fitting dress which matched her headscarf in colour, with a structured blazer on top. The room was spacious and well-lit, with large windows allowing natural light to filter in. Along one of the walls was a whiteboard with some markers, and a projector was mounted on the wall opposite. After a few moments, the interviewers, a man and a woman in similar attire to the interviewees, looking to be in their late thirties, entered the room. They took a seat across from them, an inviting smile spreading across their faces.

"Let's get on with these interviews," the man said. "Obviously there is more than one opening, so take a breath and just do your best. You can just call me Min-ho. And this," he said pointing to his co-worker, "is Myeong-hee."

"Remember, this position is for interns," Myeong-hee said. "We're not expecting you to have the solution to everything and ten years of expertise.

"So, who is Baek Yu-ra?" Min-ho asked excitedly.

"I am," Yu-ra said, raising her hand, "nice to meet you."

"Oh," Myeong-hee said, both of their smiles suddenly washing away, "you're not what we expected."

"I get that a lot," she said meekly.

As the interview started, each candidate received a different set of questions. It seemed an unusual way to host a group interview. Yu-ra sat quietly listening to each candidate's questions. They were asked standard questions such as why they decided to pursue journalism, how they stayed informed about current events and news trends, what previous experiences they've had, and how they would manage tight deadlines. All questions that Yu-ra had prepared for and found easy to answer. Then they came to her.

"How do you approach building relationships with sources and conducting interviews, especially when dealing with difficult subjects?" Min-ho asked with a bored face, "And considering your background, it may be even more difficult for you regardless of the subject."

"Uhh," Yu-ra started, "could I have some time to process the question?"

"We're on a tight schedule here," Myeong-hee said, tapping her watch, "just get on with your answer."

"Oh. Well…" Yu-ra trailed off.

"Well?"

"Um," she started, "In my experience, building trust and rapport with sources is essential to conducting meaningful interviews and uncovering important stories. When dealing with difficult subjects, I approach each interaction with empathy, respect, and sensitivity. I make a concerted effort to listen actively, ask probing yet respectful questions, and create a safe space for sources to–"

"Okay, that's fine, you can stop there," Min-ho said.

This process went on for a few more rounds. The other candidates would receive questions such as their approach to writing stories and how their values aligned with the company's. And then they would arrive back at Yu-ra.

"Given the increasingly polarised media landscape, how do you navigate your own political biases and ensure that they do not influence your reporting, especially on contentious issues?"

"When covering stories that may involve powerful individuals or institutions, how do you navigate potential pushback, threats, or legal challenges to your reporting?"

"Journalists often bear witness to traumatic events. How do you cope with the emotional toll of covering such events while maintaining objectivity and professionalism in your reporting?"

Similarly to the first question, she was cut off halfway through answering these.

At the end of the interview process, they explained that they would get back to the candidates by the end of the day. Yu-ra contemplated on her way back to her university. All things considered, she was proud of the fact that she was at least able to answer such difficult questions, and she hoped that they would see that.

Back in the study space at Maehwa university, she stared at her laptop and pushed her circular rimmed glasses further up her nose, ready to begin her assignment. But her phone buzzed before she could even start typing.

*We're sorry to inform you that you have not been chosen for the position of intern. Unfortunately, your values do not align with ours and we can not take you on due to this fact.*

*Figures,* she thought. *Why would you expect anything different?*

She took a deep breath of the warm fragrant air, the pleasant discord surrounding her quietening as she put some headphones on over her headscarf. As soon as she put them on, the hum of her music amplified, and the high-tempo hip-hop beats began to blare. She stretched her arms forward and cracked her knuckles. She laid her fingers on her keyboard then hammered away, everything outside of her field of view melting away into the background.

VRRMMMPP VRRMMMPP- The monumental yet somehow empty table she sat at in the centre of the room, quaked and Yu-ra almost leapt out of her seat. She was so engrossed in her typing, for over half an hour, that it shocked her out of her state of concentration - a state she wasn't able to get back to.

The bustling of Maehwa University was lively, which of course was only natural considering it was exam season. She looked around the room. Friends were chatting, catching up on the latest gossip, study groups were helping each other learn difficult topics, people were collaborating on group projects and presentations. Study pods packed out the room – circular, back to back, sofa-like booths that were arranged in rows. Each row consisted of a different colour and the warm lighting made it even more homely. She shoved her phone away and got back to typing, pounding at the keyboard, her fingers moving so fast that passers-by would just see a blur. Or at least, that's what it felt like.

VRRMMMPP VRRMMMP, VRRMMMPP VRRMMMPP, VRRMMMPP VRRMMMPP- Her phone buzzed until the vibrations merged into one continuous rumbling.

*"Oh my God, leave me alone,"* she thought. *"This better not be about last minute wedding prep."*

She detached the magnetic box from the back of her phone causing the charging symbol to disappear from the top right corner. She slid the top and bottom edges apart, which elongated the screen, and swiped down the top of the screen.

*12 messages from Min-Ah,* it read. Yu-ra grinned as she opened the message.

*OMG gurllll check this out.*

*I was emailed this ad for KNS.*

*They're running a competition and the winner gets a PAID INTERNSHIP at the station.*

*Likely to be offered a full-time role if they're impressed with the intern.*

*This is HUGE, you have to apply.*

*Woman, check your messages.*

*This is so exciting!*

*Hey.*

*Hey.*

*Hey.*

*Hey.*

*Hey.*

*Check your damn phone.*

Competition for an internship? It was hilarious to even think she would ever have a shot at it. Yet, it was still an excuse to talk to her best friend. She tapped the phone icon next to her name. It rang for a few seconds and then stopped.

"Well, hello to you too," Yu-ra said, unable to contain the glee in her voice.

*"Yo,"* Min-ah said monotonously.

"I'm not in the mood to talk about job hunting right now."

*"Another one?"*

"Yeah."

*"Either way, you're going to lubb thif, trush me,"* Min-ah replied whilst clearly stuffing her face with food. *"It's completely blind hbhring."*

"What?"

Min-ah swallowed her food.

*"Blind hiring."*

Yu-ra closed her laptop, turning her wheeled chair away from it. Unconsciously, she edged forward on her seat.

"...I'm listening."

*"They don't need to know any background information about you. They won't even know what you look like until security checks are done and you've got the job."*

"Sounds too good to be true. But okay," she said, turning back to the table. "How does this competition work?"

She slipped her laptop into her bag and slinged it over her shoulder.

*"You submit a real piece. That's it. If your story gets picked, they hire you!"*

Yu-ra gasped sarcastically.

"You mean they actually hire based on skill? No way is this real."

*"It's real enough. Time to shine, girl. At long last, you can bloom into that beautiful little flower I raised you to be."*

"Gee whizz, thanks mom." She giggled. "I'll be sure to make you proud."

*"Just be glad I've already got a job lined up, I'm in half a mind to go for it myself. You wouldn't stand a chance."*

Yu-ra sighed.

"Can't wait to see you tonight."

*"I can't believe I haven't seen you in four months. But don't worry, I'll be there extra early. InshaAllah, as you say."*

Yu-ra chuckled quietly.

*"I'll help you with your story when I see you."*

"I'll just use some of the ones I wrote back in high school," she said, absent-mindedly using her feet to twirl her chair in circles, "I won't need any help."

*"Hey! Talk nonsense like that to me again, I dare you."*

"What did I do?" she whined.

*"You know damn well. That's it, I'm coming down early, I'll meet you on campus. This is a once in a lifetime opportunity. I know you're good, but you don't have real experience, and that sets you back a mile."*

"Honestly, I would love to, but I have to be home by four," she said, unconsciously rolling her eyes. "In fact, I may as well start making my way now."

*"What happened to half five?"*

"My mom is being over the top and making me come home extra early for the wedding."

Yu-ra stood up from her seat, adjusting her blazer and slipping her glasses into its case, before setting off down the long winding corridors, through the foyer and out the automatic doorway.

*"That sucks."*

"Yeah," she said.

Her boots crunched with each stride as she ambled across the snowy plains and down the grand steps at the entrance to the university.

*"I'll keep your spirits up so you can handle dealing with your family and I'm ready to beat down your husband if he does anything to tick me off."*

Yu-ra giggled.

"Oh, come on. Just because I didn't date him, doesn't mean I made this decision lightly. He's a good guy. And his mom is friends with my parents. She's literally the coolest. I'm sure you'll love them."

*"You're not marrying his mom. That doesn't mean anything to me,"* Min-ah said in an uncharacteristically serious tone. *"I'll go along with it for now, but I've always got my trusty crowbar in case you need me to break his legs. Just give me the word."*

"Thank you, I'll use this gift you've bestowed upon me wisely."

*"Alright, I need to get back to work. My lunch break is almost over."*

"Okay." She sighed. "I'll see you later."

As Yu-ra traversed the illuminated streets, she passed through a market area, filled to the brim with vibrant stores. Her chest tightened slightly as she ended the call, a pin prick burying itself in her chest. The spirited passers-by and sparkling stores enveloped her, and their eyes were drawn to her. Was this enough to negate the black vacuum yanking at her from within? No, it added to it - the loneliness. Yu-ra shook her head, Min-ah would have her neck if she knew what was going through her head.

The tip of her nose was starting to drip from being in the cold for too long and her bag was weighing down her shoulders. A burst of images ran through her head of what it would be like to win an internship at the biggest broadcasting station in the country. She would make history.

As she meandered through the streets, she discovered that she was not in fact making her way home. She was actively scouting. Searching for something. Searching for any story that could be remotely interesting.

The number of stores began to slowly decrease, until soon she found herself in a residential area. It wasn't the most pleasant area – the street sloped upwards and garbage mountains peaked beside the houses on either side of the road and all the way up the incline. The white bricking was damaged and there were red maze-like designs below the windows. The triangular tiled roof looked old and worn down. It must've been an area untouched since even before the 1900s. It was all purely Korean housing. It was so cool! How had she not been there before? It was surprising that it even existed. She took out her phone and started collecting pictures.

She was nearing the top of the incline when she overheard two men speaking on the next road over.

"Please, just give me another week. I'll have all the money by then," a man whimpered.

"I'm getting real sick and tired of hearing goddamn scum like you tryna weasel your way out of your debts," a grouchy voice replied.

Yu-ra peeked around the corner. A quivering man down on his knees, in a torn suit and mussed hair, was looking up at a hunky bald thug with an irritated look in his wrinkled eyes.

She hid behind a nearby lamppost and watched the scene unfold. As her hand flew to her mouth, the bulb of the lamppost lit up above her head. This was almost too perfect. What was he? A loan shark? An investigation into a loan shark injecting his vein of money into a local naive community to coerce some sort of power over them. It was definitely a story worth submitting. A flurry of thoughts rushed through her mind; all of the tedious tasks that this project would entail.

"I swear, I almost have all of the money," the man on his knees wailed. The thug threw his fist into the other man's face, causing him to tumble over as he gripped his cheek in pain.

*Worrying about that now won't get me anywhere.* She shook her head. It was time for action.

Yu-ra quickly dialled the number for the police after seeing that the man's lip had split, and his cheek had begun to swell up. She told them what was going on and where she was, the woman on the phone seeming all too familiar with the area. She switched to her camera app after ending the call, pointing it towards the two men and hit record. She figured it could make for a great story.

"All that yapping just sounded like you saying you ain't got my money," the brute said, "and you know what happens when I ain't get my money back."

The man on his knees gripped onto the thug's leg.

"Please, I'm begging you. I can give you a down-payment now if you let me go get my money. I'll have the rest by next week."

The thug slipped his hands into his pockets. Cocking his head to the side.

"Sure, I'm cool with that."

"Wait," the man said, looking up at him with a glint of hope in his eye, "really?"

"Yeah, sure. Why not?" The brute patted him on the shoulder, causing the man to recoil slightly. "One condition though."

"Y-yes. Name it," the man stuttered, "I'll do anything."

"You just have to choose."

The glint disappeared from the man's eye.

"Choose?"

"So, what'll it be? You, your wife, or your son?"

"What? I don't- I don't understand."

"You're real slow on the uptake ain't ya? I'm letting you decide whose legs I break." The thug kicked the man's grip away and leaned in close to him. "Or would you prefer I break them all?" he said calmly, a sinister smile on his face.

"My wife," the man blurted, "definitely my wife."

Yu-ra's jaw plunged towards the ground. She must have misheard him, surely? The thug howled with laughter.

"You ain't much for loyalty, are ya?" he said, gripping on to the man's elbow. "Well get up, you gotta direct me to that dear old lady of yours."

As he said those final words he turned towards Yu-ra, whose figure was hidden solely by a slim lamppost.

Her eyes shot open and she spun around, leaning her back on the lamppost. As the crunching footsteps got closer and closer to her, her pulse beat heavier

*Stay calm. Stay calm. You can handle this.*

She lifted her phone back up and pointed it towards the buildings until a man, exhaling an air of confidence that was clearly unwarranted, stepped into the frame, towering over her.

"Hey lady, what do you think you're doing?"

"I'm sorry?" Yu-ra said, attempting to keep her voice from wavering as she put her phone to her side.

"That ain't no answer," he said, stepping closer. The whimpering man stood a little ways away from them, simply observing, wringing his hands together. His gaze shot to the ground as Yu-ra glanced at him.

"Oh, what am I doing?" She smiled nervously, and then flipped the loose part of her hijab over her shoulder as she reclined against the lamppost. "I'm just hanging out. You know, doing me. Living my best life as they say."

"As who says?"

"You know…they."

What the hell was she even saying?

"Are you messing with me right now?" He turned towards the other man, gesturing towards her. "Is she messing with me right now?"

"I-I'm not messing with you," she said, lifting her phone back up. "Can you just let me get back to my photography, please?"

"What photography?"

"I'm taking pictures of these buildings." She paused momentarily. "For an art assignment."

"You're using these crappy buildings for an art assignment?" He laughed, throwing his head back. "Good luck with that. I'll leave you to it." He took out a business card from his pocket and handed it to her, winking, "here's my number if you ever need any extra help on an art assignment."

Yu-ra's stomach began to somersault as she fought back the urge to upchuck everything she had eaten that day. Even men with a hatred for her would still hit on her if they had the confidence for it.

*"Li Feng,"* it read. A Chinese name. The man snapped his fingers at the suit and took a step away to walk off. But Yu-ra needed to keep them there. The police still hadn't arrived. What was taking them so long?

"But wait, mister," she said, rushing up to Li-feng, looking up into his eyes, "how can you help me with my assignment?"

"Just give me a call later and we can discuss it - over some dinner and a couple drinks."

This was an avenue to keep him talking.

"Where would we go? I like barbecue," she said eagerly. "Can you take me there?"

"Pfft, typical," he muttered under his breath.

"What was that, mister?"

She fought to keep her brow from shooting to the sky.

"I said sure, whatever you want, missy."

"Great! When should we go? What time? Do you have a car? Can you pick me up?" she said, stepping closer with each question.

"I ain't got time for this. We can decide the details later."

She hesitated for a moment and then grabbed his arm. As she did so, a shiver ran down her spine while she prevented herself from recoiling away.

"Oh no, I just remembered I'm only free tonight." Her voice began to waver, but she pushed through it, continuing to blurt anything that came to mind. "And my daddy always says I'm really picky, so maybe we should decide now. Do you have any recommendations? Maybe we can do other stuff too. I adore karaoke. Have you ever been? It's amazing, you're going to love it if you come with me."

"For gods' sake," he grumbled to himself. "Lady, I think you got that scarf wrapped around your head too tightly because clearly it must be cutting off the circulation to your brain if you're this dense."

"Dense?"

She would've balled her fist had her phone not already occupied the space.

"I ain't that interested in you. And word to the wise, men don't like clingy girls."

"But wait!" She racked her brain for a way to stop him. "Who's that strange man over there? Is he okay? He looks hurt."

Li-feng put his hand on her shoulder and she immediately jerked her body away, but his grip was too strong for her to actually move.

"I'd appreciate it if you mind your own business, there. Nothing good is gonna come outta you sticking your nose where it don't belong."

Yu-ra took a deep breath before continuing.

"Maybe we should help him. Mister." She waved him over to them. "Are you okay? Do you need to go to the hospital? That looks like it hurts."

He looked over to Li Feng, seeming to silently ask for confirmation on what to do.

"No, I'm fine," the suited man said in a solemn tone. "I just slipped on the snow. It doesn't hurt at all. We should be going now. Thanks for your concern."

"Wait, I have some wipes and plasters in my bag. Let me just get them out."

"Don't worry about it. We should really be going now."

"C'mon, it'll take two seconds." She began digging through her bag. "Do you guys live around here?"

"Okay, listen here, bitch," Li Feng said, shoving her and sending her toppling into the pile of snow behind her. The melting snow underneath her began seeping into her clothes, as she pushed herself up off the ground and lost any sense of feeling left in her hands.

"Excuse me?" she said, raising her brow sharply.

"I've had enough of you," Li-feng said. "You better beat it. I won't be responsible for what comes next."

"That's not a very nice way to speak to a lady, or anyone in fact. I'd like you to apologise."

*What the hell are you doing Yu-ra? Is this worth you keeping them here for a few more minutes?*

"Tough shit. We don't always get what we want. Now beat it, bitch. I ain't afraid to hit a woman."

Yu-ra's anger finally bubbled to the surface. It was worth it.

"Oh, you think that makes you strong? Do you feel powerful, knowing you're physically stronger than helpless women?"

"Matter of fact, I do." He chuckled.

"You know, just a word of advice," Yu-ra scoffed, "don't try and flirt with strangers. In fact, stay away from the entire female species. We don't like chauvinistic pigs."

"Chauvinistic?" he cocked a brow.

"Yes. No one likes a misogynistic a-hole. Your mom never taught you how to be a gentleman? Or did she get sick of having a scummy, self-absorbed, shit for brains son like you and leave?" she yelled.

"Oh-ho, the bitch seems to have some bite now, does she?" The smugness on his face infuriated her even more. "Last chance. Or you're asking for it." He cracked his neck in an attempt to be intimidating.

"Go on then, tough guy, hit me. I dare you," she said, dropping her bag onto the pile of snow she just fell in, "unless you haven't got the sack for it.

And judging by how much you seem to be overcompensating, I'm guessing you genuinely don't have anything down-"

THWACK.

A wave of light-headedness came crashing into her, sending her tumbling to the ground. A high-pitched ringing dug into her left ear and a warmth grasped her cheek, followed by a sharp stinging pain. The icy wind pummelled like a million tiny palms, leaving a red-forming bruise that did her no favours.

Li Feng bent over.

"That was me going easy on you. If you get into situations like this in the future, you should really learn to hold your tongue, missy. Not everyone is as gentlemanly as me."

Yu-ra brushed herself off as pushed herself up off the ground, her jaw clenched as she tried not to think about her stinging cheek. A faint police siren hollered in the distance. All she needed was a minute or two at most. Adrenaline coursed through her veins making her body tremor as she plotted her next course of action. There was no need to keep holding back.

"Hey, asshole," she said, stumbling towards him, "learn how to hit." Yu-ra drove her knee straight into his groin and he let out a girly shriek and collapsed, spluttering on the ground. Before he could get up, she thrust her boot into his jaw, a crack echoing down the empty streets. She turned to the man in the suit, his jaw hanging open. "What are you doing? Let's get out of here before he gets up." She grabbed his sleeve and they both hobbled away.

They ran around a nearby corner and stopped to take a breath, her hands trembling as she dropped them to her knees, and her heart racing. They could still hear the thug groaning and the police sirens closing in. She checked the time and her eyes shot wide open, even more so than earlier. It was scarier than when Li-feng saw her. *5:45pm,* her clock read.

"You really, really shouldn't have done that." the man in the suit said, catching his breath.

"What?" she said in between heavy breaths.

"Do you realise what he'll do when he's able to get up?"

"A thank you would've sufficed."

"Were you the one that called the police too?"

Yu-ra stood up straight.

"Yes, as any concerned citizen would."

He threw his arms in the air.

"I had everything under control! Look, thanks for getting me out of that situation, but next time stay out of things you don't understand, for their benefit and for yours."

The police had finally arrived on the scene and were lifting Li-feng up from the ground.

"I need to get out of here," the man said.

"What? You can't leave," she said, grabbing onto his sleeve. "You need to give your statement to the police."

He flung his arm away from her.

"No, you can stay and do that if it's so important to you."

"I can't, I really have to go." She turned and began rushing away before calling back at the man. "I'm *extremely* late for something important and I'd rather be in trouble with the police than have to deal with my mom's antics."

Her wedding began in less than an hour. Who knew what her mom would do when she got home. She waved down the police to get their attention, so they knew the man in the suit was there, and off she dashed back across the snowy plains, trying to hail down a cab.

# 3
# The Wedding

"C'mon, let's go, let's go!" Kyung-tae's mother echoed through the house. "What's taking so long?"

"I'm almost ready. Stop badgering me, ma," Kyung-tae called back from his barebones room. All it contained were three books strewn on one of his bedside shelves, a small plastic lamp on the other, and a cheap wooden wardrobe against the back wall. His bedsheets were precisely aligned atop his king-sized mattress. He finished tying a knot on the black and white striped band which was holding his loose matching skirt against his waist. Afterwards, he threw on his long black half-coat to finish the look of his formal kimono. Neatly slicking his hair back to one side before slipping out into the living room, not a sound was made from his feet on the soft carpet. Plush furnishings adorned the space and a generously sized, well-worn couch sat at the room's centre. Nestled nearby, an elegant armchair, its upholstery a gentle shade of cream, beckoned with open arms. Kyung-tae wanted nothing more than to just sink into the furnishings and fall into a deep slumber at that moment.

Kyung-tae crept up behind the giddy woman in front of a six-foot standing mirror; she was adorned in her fanciest clothes, a pale blue kimono with a floral skirt and a matching scarf, loosely wrapped around her head.

"Okay, I'm ready, ma," he said, tapping her on the shoulder.

"WUAHHH!" His mother screamed, flinging herself away from him. "What did I tell you about doing that?" she said, turning to him and slapping his arm.

"To not do it," he muttered, pouting a little.

"So why are you doing it?"

Kyung-tae scoffed.

"There's literally a mirror in front of you. It's not my fault. Can we just get this over with?"

"Always rushing around, even on your wedding day." She sighed, brushing down his lapel. "Can you just enjoy the moment. How many of these are we ever going to get?" She locked her watering eyes with his.

"Not this again," Kyung-tae said, slapping his hand across his forehead. "Ma, it's not like I'm going to disappear and never visit."

"That's what they all say."

"Who's they?" He moaned. "I'm your only child. What are you even talking about?"

"All I'm saying is that Yu-ra will do anything I ask her to, especially break your heart."

"You're supposed to be happy today," he said, taking her hands in his. "Can we skip all the unnecessary emotions, please?"

"Who said I'm not happy?" she scoffed. "The only thing making me sad is your haircut. But marrying the girl I've planned for you for years? How could I not be filled with glee?"

"The day's not over yet, who knows what'll happen," Kyung-tae muttered.

Her palm shot out from her side and, almost autonomously, without so much as a single deviation, zipped into his arm with a deafening thwack.

"Don't make stupid jokes like that with your stupid deadpan face."

"Ow," he said, rubbing his arm, "everyone knows I'm incapable of making jokes."

"It's a mystery how you even got this girl to like you. Black magic, I'm guessing?"

"I used all my famous charm," he said, with a click of his tongue and a wink of his eye.

"Oh, of course," she said, raising the back of her hand to her forehead, "how could I forget that trademark charm of yours?"

"It didn't work though, so I told her I was your son and she swooned." Kyung-tae couldn't contain his rising smile, proud of his quick wit.

"Flattery can get you a lot from me," she said, before running her fingers through his hair, fashioning it into something more photogenic, "but not enough to let you out of the house with your hair like that. You have to take pictures today. Honestly, what is with you and trying to look like that Jinmu?" She slapped his arm once again. "And don't even think about rolling your eyes at me."

"I wasn't going to." He huffed. "Let's just get today over with. We're late as is."

"And whose fault is that?"

"Obviously everything's always my fault," he said as he linked his arm with hers and guided her towards the door before they both slipped into their shoes and left the house.

When they arrived at the wedding hall, much to their surprise, Yu-ra's family had yet to. Great chandeliers hung from the ceiling and guests were seated at round tables covered in white cloth and bouquets of flowers. The chairs were decorated with ribbons tied in bows. There was a head table situated at the other side of the hall with fashionable curtains hung behind it, and a three-tiered cake set to the side. It looked quite respectable, he decided. He and his mother waited at the head table, greeting everyone who came up to him and directing them to their seats. Majority of those guests were in traditional Japanese dress.

"I could be doing much better things with my time than greeting these people I'm barely acquainted with," Kyung-tae whispered to his mother.

"Shh," she snapped, "stop being a brat."

Across the bustling of waiters, the rush of people hopping between tables picking at whatever starters they found, and the distant relatives coming up to pinch his cheeks, he noticed his bride-to-be entering the building. No one else had seen her yet, but his keen eye picked her out the moment she stepped foot into the room. She stood at the entrance of the hall, taking in the sites, a dumbfounded look plastered on her face. She was a simple girl with a simple nature. And that simple nature of hers shined, even through the obnoxiously extravagant and unusually puffy dress she wore and the goofy way her upper lip rested above her glinting teeth. She was garbed in a puffy red skirt and a matching robe, with a white lapel. On her sleeves were a few golden strips sewn in and a flowery pattern was embroidered into the robe. She also sported a matching, stylishly fashioned hijab. As others began to notice her, a throng of guests rushed over to greet her. She grew a shy smile before speaking with them. Her smiles came as quickly as they went, deep indentations forming on the corners of her cheeks each time, and between each guest her demeanour reverted to her usual mild bemusement. But, that wasn't to say her smiles were faked. Sincerity oozed from every single one of them. She was genuine. And she was simple.

The rest of her family - her father, mother, and brother, arrived at the entrance, the slew of guests leaving Yu-ra for a moment to greet them. Her hesitant eyes wandered until they met his. They gazed at one another, neither one waving nor showing any sort of emotion towards each other, though she flickered on the verge of a smile. It was as if they were both waiting for the other person to react first and then the other would follow suit. And as such, there was no reaction from either of them. They stared for just long enough to make it uncomfortable, until fortunately the guests returned to her.

After getting through the horde of teeming guests, Yu-ra finally arrived at the head table and gave her greetings to Kyung-tae and his mother. Her family was still lagging behind her by a few guests. Now that she was closer, he noticed her make-up was a lot heavier than he was used to seeing her in. Though even he had to admit it was stylishly done.

Upon greeting his mother, Yu-ra smiled a smile he hadn't seen on her yet that day, as though she was suddenly full of life. She wrapped her arms around his mother and hugged her tight.

"Mrs Oh!" Yu-ra squealed. "How have you been?"

Yu-ra had a southern twang that crept into her accent, something she hadn't lost since she moved away from her hometown.

"I'm a lot better now that you're finally here!" she replied in a warm tone before gesturing to Kyung-tae. "How could you leave me in this one's company for this long?"

"Ok, thank you," Kyung-tae said as Yu-ra began chuckling quietly. His mother kissed Yu-ra on both of her cheeks before pulling back from her, yet still keeping hold of her shoulders.

"Oh wow, aren't you just the prettiest bride I've ever laid eyes on. I've never seen such a dress before. I love this floral embroidery!" She said, rubbing the strips sewn into the loose sleeves.

Yu-ra blushed.

"It's called hanbok."

"Oh! I know this," his mother said, excitement still ringing in her tone. "This is one of those dresses that they used to wear back when we were an independent state. How did you even find one of these outside of a museum?"

"It was passed down through my family," Yu-ra said. "My grandmother wore it on her wedding day." Yu-ra gave an energetic little twirl before settling down.

"Well, I'll tell you what, you look like a princess straight out of a fairytale! Too bad you had to settle instead of marrying a prince."

"Thanks again, Ma," Kyung-tae mumbled. "Don't know why that was necessary."

"You are too kind, ma'am," Yu-ra said, curtseying.

"You've never been this excited to see me," Kyung-tae interjected a little louder this time, poking the shoulder of his mother. "Maybe you should be the one marrying her."

"Oh I wish!" Yu-ra said. "Have you seen her? She's an absolute stunner!"

"And she's definitely too good for you," his mother added.

They both pointed finger guns at one another.

"And men are trash!" they chanted in unison, before bursting into laughter.

Kyung-tae nervously joined in with some quiet laughter of his own, not knowing what else to do.

He cut his laughter short the moment he saw the rest of Yu-ra's family get through the guests. Her father stood a few inches shorter than him but had an admirably full beard, something he had tried and failed to achieve. He was adorned in a similar attire to Yu-ra, except the robe piece was not nearly as long, stopping above his knees. Strangely, her mother, a spitting image of her daughter, who donned an annoyed look in her eye, wasn't wearing anything similar to them. Neither was her skinny, awkward teenage brother, with eyes shrouded by his bushy mane. Instead, they opted for traditional Japanese dresses similar to the rest of the guests.

Kyung-tae paced towards them, then presented his hand to Yu-ra's father. He offered to get them some of the complimentary drinks that came with the venue package, but Mr Baek quickly dismissed the idea, clearly in a rush to get the marriage process begun as soon as possible. Yu-ra's mother greeted him. However, similarly to Yu-ra, she was more excited to see his mother. Her brother, Hyun-woo followed closely behind his mother like a lost puppy.

The two families reconvened at the table and another man came to join them - the Imam, a teacher of religion from the only mosque in the city, dressed in a gleaming white Arab gown, and a waistcoat donned over it. Though he looked young, his thick, bushy, greying beard suggested otherwise, and he gave off an air of accomplishment. His smiling eyes instantly softened the hearts of those he approached.

Greeting them with blessings, and hugs for the men, he asked them to congregate around the table for them to begin the sermon away from prying eyes. The men put half of the chairs on the other side of the table so they could sit in a circle. Then, the Imam began his speech.

"Brothers. Sisters. Why are we here today?" he started. Without waiting for a response, he said, "we are here for a union. A union of people. One in which we are forming not just a bond between two families," he said, lifting a finger, "but a bond between two souls." He lifted a second finger.

Kyung-tae kept his eyes on the Imam, not daring to even glance at Yu-ra.

"Yes, through marriage you gain completion of half of your religion," he continued, leaning forward and his voice growing sharper. "But you gain much more than that. You gain a companion for life. A companion that will be there for you through thick and thin. Your spouse will become like a garment for you." The Imam paused again, letting his point settle before raising the intensity of his voice once again, emphasizing each syllable. "Your spouse will become like a garment for you." As he repeated those words, Kyung-tae felt a stir in his heart.

"There are a lot of struggles that come with marriage," he continued, "and you will surely face a few of them, as would anyone who gets married in any sort of manner. Having to adjust to each other, the other's family, or their lifestyle may very well pose a challenge."

The Imam began to itch his head nervously. "You should ask my wife. She struggles to eat my cooking once a week." Some giggles were heard from the women, and her father smiled at the lousy joke. "But there are also many blessings that come with marriage. Blessings that far outweigh the struggles. And in those times of struggles, just remember these blessings you have been given."

The Imam held the bridge of his nose as he looked down, his voice beginning to croak. "And subhanAllah, your spouse is one of your greatest blessings. The number of times my wife has lifted me up when I was at my lowest..." He wiped his eyes as he trailed off. "I thank Allah every day for what He has given me. Many people believe the wife is there to benefit the husband, and that there is a clear power dynamic in a relationship such as this. That simply isn't the case. Each of you have your own rights that you are entitled to, but more than that, you must remember that marriage is a team effort."

Kyung-tae looked at Yu-ra's parents as they aggressively nodded their heads in agreement. He then looked to his mother beside him, who nodded much more softly. He placed his hand on her knee as he returned his eyes to the Imam who continued with his monologue.

"The only way to win at marriage is to always be there for each other, communicate when there is a problem, work together, as a team, to solve issues. Only then can you keep moving forward and keep improving your relationship.

"Now, bearing that in mind moving forward, I understand you want to keep the mehr private from anyone outside of the family and that this gift has been given already?" Kyung-tae looked to his mother, and then over to Yu-ra's father, unsure of whether he should be the one speaking. Her father noticed him looking around and decided to speak up.

"Yes, that's correct."

"Very well," the Imam continued. "Now you are the father, giving your only daughter away, correct?"

"Yes," he replied.

"Now, when accepting the marriage, saying it once will suffice but it is also common practice to say it three times. So, Mr Baek, do you accept the marriage of your daughter and this man?"

"I accept," Mr Baek said.

"And do you, Mr Oh Kyung-tae, accept the marriage between yourself and this woman?"

Kyung-tae's eyes once again escaped to his mother. She nudged him in the side with her elbow, a little too roughly.

"YES!" Kyung-tae blurted out. "Sorry. Yes, I accept."

"And finally, do you accept the marriage between yourself and this man, Miss Baek Yu-ra?"

"I accept," Yu-ra said.

"Now if the couple and the two witnesses can sign the contracts here, you will be married."

Kyung-tae waited for them to go first. Her father signed first, after which her younger brother signed, and then she did. She held the pen out for Kyung-tae to take. Holding his hand out underneath hers, she placed it in his hand, her fingertips brushing against his skin. That minimal physical contact was enough to make his brain functions freeze for a split second, and the pen fell out of his hand. Fumbling around, he attempted to retrieve it. He must have looked like a complete buffoon, because when he stood upright, Yu-ra looked as if she was hiding a grin by pressing her lips tightly together. Pausing before putting pen to paper, his mother pointed to where he needed to sign. He looked at her then back at the papers before proceeding to write his signature. Then, underneath, he dated it - sixth of December, two-thousand-and-ten.

"And now," the Imam said, "you are officially husband and wife. May Allah bring countless blessings and happiness to your marriage, your families and all of those here today. May it be a means of you bettering yourselves and entering into heaven. Ameen."

"Ameen," they all repeated.

Following the intimate ceremony, they arranged the chairs so they could sit across from each other. Kyung-tae across from Yu-ra, and their mothers to their side. The Imam went and brought his wife back with him to sit at the end of the table after Kyung-tae offered that they be seated with them. Waiters brought around trays filled with an array of different types of sushi to start off with. Kyung-tae picked up the serving chopsticks and put some on his plate, after which he returned the chopsticks to their original position. His mother nudged him in the side once again.

"Ow. What did you do that for?" he whispered. She gave him one of her trademark stern mother looks and used her eyes to direct him to the empty plates in front of him. Yu-ra's father had already started serving the food to the other three people on his side of the table. Realising what she meant, he jumped out of his seat. Across the table, Yu-ra's mother was whispering in her ear and before Kyung-tae could pick up the serving chopsticks, Yu-ra had already taken them up herself.

"What would you like?" Yu-ra said, with a soft smile. "Everything?"

Kyung-tae looked to his mother for help again, and she once again gave a stern look.

"I can do that, don't worry," he said as he held his hand out for the chopsticks.

He then asked Yu-ra's mother what sushi she would like and put a generous helping onto her plate. He then did the same for Yu-ra and finally his mother before returning to his sitting position and picking up his own chopsticks.

Yu-ra and Kyung-tae ate in silence whilst their mothers caught up, eating at regular intervals. His mother must have noticed the silence between them because she started nudging him again.

He jerked and stomped his foot.

"Will you stop already?"

She was clearly done with trying to get him to act appropriately seeing as she started the conversation with Yu-ra herself.

"So how is your studying going Yu-ra? I hope the wedding prep didn't distract you too much."

"Well, women are natural multitaskers, right?" Yu-ra said.

Kyung-tae cleared his throat and finally spoke up.

"This venue is nice. You did a good job planning this, Yu-ra."

"It wasn't all me," she said, hinting at both his mother and hers. "I was in charge of the food, though. What do you think?"

Kyung-tae's mother had redirected her attention to Yu-ra's mother, now that her job was done.

"Yeah, it's good," Kyung-tae said, popping another salmon nigiri in his mouth.

"Have you tried all of them?" she said, gesturing to the array of sushi.

"No, just the one."

"Oh my God, you have to try this specialty roll. I created the recipe myself."

Yu-ra used her chopsticks to pick up a colourful sushi roll that was almost the size of her palm and placed it on his plate.

"Yeah..." Kyung-tae trailed off as he stared down at his plate, "I'm good."

"No, seriously, try it. I created this concoction during a trip in Europe for my university course. It was an absolute hit."

Some waiters had arrived at the table and had set out an array of noodle soups.

"I believe you," Kyung-tae said, moving his head so his view was no longer blocked by the waiter's arm.

"What a great use of your time, that was," Yu-ra's mother chimed in.

"This journalism nonsense is what's going to get you into heaven, isn't it?"

Kyung-tae flicked his eyes to her mother and back to Yu-ra who was now deeply rolling her eyes.

"Seriously, I'm completely happy with this tuna nigiri. It has a good level of protein, carbohydrates, and omega-three fatty acids."

"Yeah, well mine has mango in it. Does yours?"

"And what type of mango is it? Is it fresh, or from a can filled with syrup?"

"A can," she said, frowning, "but who cares? The flavour profile is unbeaten."

"I've got a question for you, because I get this reaction a lot," Kyung-tae said, adjusting his chair and leaning forward on the table. Everyone around him seemed to blur as his vision tunnelled with Yu-ra at the opening on the other end.

"Go ahead," she said.

"Why do you eat?"

"What?"

"Why do you eat? It's not a trick question."

Yu-ra raised her brow, making a face at Kyung-tae as if he was a complete idiot.

"So I don't die. Same reason as every other human on the planet."

"Exactly," he said, snapping his fingers, "we eat for sustenance."

"Ok, so?" Yu-ra replied, narrowing her eyes at him as if he had just uttered completely useless information.

"So, if I'm eating for sustenance, and I'm trying to be the most efficient about it, this tuna nigiri is the most nutritionally balanced item on the tray. Why would I throw off that balance to try your concoction, as you put it?"

"Oh, you're one of those," she said, rolling her eyes again, "a robot."

"Let me run a scenario by you. I've created this super dish that packs in every single nutrient you need." He gestured to the empty plate in front of him. "It tastes somewhat decent, maybe even good. You're telling me that you wouldn't consider eating it for every single meal for the rest of your life?"

"You would eat dry toast for every single meal if it had enough nutritional value, wouldn't you?"

"Yes," he replied without missing a beat, "But you haven't answered my question."

"Oh my God, you actually are, aren't you?" She giggled. "You're a robot. Show me your motherboard. I think you need some rewiring."

"Ok, let me adjust my approach. What are the factors you take into account when deciding on what to eat? There's nutritional value, cost per unit of volume, ease of preparation, and of course taste."

Yu-ra slapped her hand onto the table, the bouncing metal chopsticks beside her clanging together.

"You've even changed your language into robot language! Who speaks like that!?"

"Now, now," he said, waving his hands to calm her down, "the point I'm trying to make is if it tastes good, it tastes good. Why then do I need to experiment with dubious concoctions such as this?"

"Oh, you did not just call my food dubious," Yu-ra said, struggling to hold in her giggle as she mimed rolling up her sleeves.

"Your diet is simply a scientific equation," Kyung-tae said, as a figure in the corner of his eye became more prominent. "You plug numbers in, and it tells you what requirements to meet. Makes being healthy so much easier."

Kyung-tae's view disengaged from Yu-ra as the tall and bulky figure came into view with his shorter, slim-figured daughter beside him.

"I'm gonna make you eat your words when I fatten you up," Yu-ra said, rubbing her palms together with a sinister smile.

"Sorry, hold that thought," Kyung-tae said, holding his index finger up to pause Yu-ra.

He leapt from his seat and made his way to Yu-ra's side of the table, waving the two figures over - Mr Choi and his daughter Chun-mi. As they arrived at the table, Kyung-tae couldn't help but relish in his admiration of them yet again. Mr Choi's presence demanded attention and respect. Even at his age, his clear dedication and discipline had manifested into his broad shoulders and bulky, yet chiselled physique, perfectly filling out his attire. His rugged exterior was enhanced by his badass silverfox hair and different coloured eyes. He was nothing less than the very definition of masculinity.

"Mr Choi, sir!" he said, shaking Mr Choi's hand. "I really appreciate you and Chun-mi being here today."

"What kind of mentor would I be if I didn't show up to your wedding?" Mr Choi said, waving his hand dismissively before returning it to his other hand behind his back. "I'd like to formally congratulate you on your marriage."

"Thank you. I'm sorry I couldn't convince my mother to let you be there for the ceremony. She was adamant on it being immediate family only."

"Nonsense. What your mother says goes. Sung-jae couldn't make it today, I presume?"

"He said he had other business to attend to," Kyung-tae said, a small frown crossing his lips, knowing he could have done more for the situation. "Ah, this is my now wife." Kyung-tae gestured to Yu-ra.

She stood up and waved politely.

"It-it's nice to meet you," Yu-ra said, getting out of her seat and staring up at Mr Choi with a mystified look dancing on her face. "I'm Baek Yu-ra."

"Heterochromia," Mr Choi said, "That's the word you're looking for."

"Sorry?" Yu-ra asked but looked away sheepishly as if she had just been caught committing a crime. "I'm Choi Jinmu. This is my daughter Chun-mi." Mr Choi gestured to the beaming, pale skinned woman in the tight-fitting silky-black kimono beside him. Her straight black hair was almost equally silky.

It was impossible for Kyung-tae to deny the obvious allure Chun-mi had. She carried herself with immense confidence and a magnetic smile that played on her lips, which drew people to her like moths to a flame. Her plain charisma enchanted everyone around her, as seen by the hordes of men around the room that leered in her direction. Yet, Kyung-tae never truly understood why people were enamoured with her. Perhaps it was due to the fact that he knew her while she was an acne ridden teenager and knew all of the flaws she hid from everyone else.

"It's nice to finally meet you," Chun-mi said to Yu-ra, bowing. "Congratulations on your marriage. I pray the gods will bestow many blessings upon it."

"Thank you very much," Yu-ra replied, putting on a polite smile. "May I ask how you're acquainted with Kyung-tae?"

"You could say we're childhood friends," she said, punching Kyung-tae in the arm lightly. "My father met him on a case and introduced us."

"Case?" Yu-ra asked.

"He used to work for the police force," Kyung-tae said, "before he retired."

"Ah!" Yu-ra said, perking up as if she had just solved a riddle, "you must be the family friend that got Kyung-tae into detective work."

"He was a bit of a troublemaker when he was younger." Mr Choi chuckled haughtily, "He just needed someone to set him straight, that's all."

"Yeah, that's all I needed," Kyung-tae said, smiling to himself. "Anyway, it's good to see you Chun-mi."

"You too good to spar with me these days?" She jabbed. "With your skills, I wouldn't be surprised if you get put in a hospital one day."

Kyung-tae wanted to explain that it was a choice to never spar with her again, but they wouldn't understand his reasons, so he faked a chuckle.

"Yeah, probably," was what he settled with.

"And Mrs Baek," Chun-mi said in a velvety voice as she stroked the sleeve of Yu-ra's dress, "can I just say, I absolutely adore your dress. May I ask where you got it. I'm loving the whole vibe."

"Sorry, it's a family heirloom," Yu-ra said, shrugging her shoulders. "Couldn't tell you because I've never seen another like it."

"That's a shame. My wardrobe could use some sprucing up. Of course I'd want a more toned-down version than what you have on."

"Well you rock a kimono better than anyone I've ever seen," Yu-ra said, smiling warmly. "I'm afraid you'd show me up if you had one of these."

"Oh please," she said, waving her hand dismissively, "you're the bride here. Don't put yourself down."

"Mr Choi, sir, there's something I'd like to discuss with you," Kyung-tae interjected. "Shall we leave the women to get acquainted and go somewhere with less people?"

"Yes," Chun-mi answered, "you boys go have your private discussion. I'll get to know Yu-ra. After all, she's family now."

"Very well," Mr Choi said, gesturing for him to proceed, "lead the way."

Kyung-tae half-waved to Yu-ra before walking off with Mr Choi. They stepped out into the foyer, the noise from the hall turning to a quiet muffling. Grand stairways with golden railings were laid out on either side of the doorway to the hall leading up to a second floor which was rented to another party.

"What is this about?" Mr Choi said.

"This," Kyung-tae said, pulling out a little plastic bag from his trouser pocket. The bag he found in the alleyway.

Mr Choi's eyes widened ever so slightly, then he raised a brow.

"Remember that missing persons case I led last year?" Kyung-tae continued. "Another one has sprouted up. So I took the lead on it."

"This isn't some kind of redemption thing for you, is it? It won't give you what you think it will."

"I'm just doing my job." Kyung-tae shook the little bag he was holding up. "Have a look at what I found at the scene. Ever seen anything like it?"

Mr Choi took the bag out of his hands, examining it closely as he stroked his chin.

"Business as usual, even on a day such as this. Respectable." He handed the bag back to Kyung-tae. "I can't say that I have seen anything like this. What did forensics say?"

"Nothing yet."

"Trust your intuition. You've got enough experience for at least that much. I suggest a stakeout. How about we go together, like we used to when you were still a trainee," Mr Choi said, squeezing Kyung-tae's shoulder with his large hand, "tomorrow. They'll return to the scene of the crime at some point."

"Really? I would never have thought that," Kyung-tae said, tucking the bag back into his pocket.

"Maybe you haven't been around long enough to see it for yourself, then," Mr Choi said, his expression darkening. "They're like daredevils out for some sick thrill. They don't fear the system, and with good reason." A wave of anger crashed on his face as he raised his tone. "When all is said and done, you know who's left to pick up the pieces? The ones who suffer the most? The innocent civilians!"

"Yeah," Kyung-tae muttered, "I know."

Mr Choi calmed himself, lightly breathing out.

"Sorry."

"Tomorrow, then?" Kyung-tae said.

"Agreed. But apart from work, how are things?"

"I'm doing great. It's my wedding day, how else should I feel?"

"Come on, son. I know you," Mr Choi said, squeezing his shoulder once again. "You don't have to pretend that you're okay with all of this."

Kyung-tae hesitated.

"You should get to know Yu-ra a bit more, she's a good person."

Mr Choi paused momentarily.

"Very well," he said, dropping his hand from Kyung-tae's shoulder.

Kyung-tae and Mr Choi walked back to the busy hall, looking for Yu-ra's parents on the way. He was going to be seeing them a lot from now on, naturally, so the first thing he wanted to do was introduce them to Mr Choi when he had the chance. They met her father but Kyung-tae's mother interrupted them and took him away from them.

"Have you seen Yu-ra?" she asked, her eyes darting around the room as if scanning the environment.

"I left her with Chun-mi," Kyung-tae replied as he let himself be dragged toward the head table.

"I can't seem to find her. Her friend Min-ah has been looking for her for a while and it's getting late."

"Call her phone," he said with a calm demeanour.

"She's not been answering," she said, dropping her grip on his arm and beginning to pace about.

"Bathroom?"

"Not there. I'm starting to get worried."

"About what?" he said as he grasped her shoulders, holding her in place. "It's her wedding. Where is she going to go?"

"I don't know, but don't you think it's strange for the bride to be missing at her own wedding?"

"How hard is it to spot a woman in a bright red puffy dress? You think she went outside for a smoke? Talking to all these people must be stressful."

"Don't get snarky with me, boy," she said, shooting her index finger into his shoulder.

"Fine." He sighed. "I'll look for her. Go sit down and have some cake before it gets finished by all the guests."

His mother took up a slice of cake on a paper plate and left to go sit with some guests on a random table. He dragged his feet to the head table where Chun-mi still sat, eating some cake and texting on her phone. She looked up, beaming from ear to ear and brushing her hair behind them.

"Hey, finished your business with my father?"

He looked down at her plate.

"I know," she said, "I never eat this stuff, but it's your wedding. I thought I'd indulge myself a bit, just for today."

"Sorry, I can't catch up right now," he said, shaking his head. "I need to find my wife." Her smile dropped, and he could have sworn, for just a moment, she wrinkled her nose in disgust. But it disappeared so quickly that he was sure his mind just played a trick on him. "Where did she go?" he asked.

"I don't know. She just left all of a sudden without saying anything. No one can find her? Was it my fault?" she said, her lower lip trembling.

"Don't worry, you didn't do anything wrong. I'll find her."

Kyung-tae left her to finish her cake and took out his phone to call her himself. No answer. So on went his imaginary detective hat and he began working the case of finding his missing bride.

# 4
# Chun-mi

*Guess what? I've officially finished my training! I am now a respected soldier of the Japanese empire. And even bigger news? They've recruited me into a special ops unit! Are you proud of me? They said I have the potential to become a squad leader one day and maybe even aim higher. I'm doing good, right?*

*-Letter #15*

Yu-ra fought to hold back an escaping giggle as she feigned anger, rolling up her sleeves. Kyung-tae implied her food was rotten! The absolute nerve!

"Oh, you did not just call my food dubious!" she said, but in reality, she felt the conversation had taken a nice turn. They had gotten past the initial deafening silence that accompanied every interaction they had ever had. At first, she had been baffled by his rudeness, but later came to the realisation that he may have just been oblivious to the social etiquette of accepting what you're offered. Her contemplation led her to the conclusion that Kyung-tae's passion was refreshing. It was passion for nonsense, but passion nonetheless.

Kyung-tae's eyes disengaged from Yu-ra quite abruptly as he stared behind her head and suddenly, the bustling of the crowded hall rushed back into her ear canals

Suddenly leaping out of his chair and coming over to her side of the table, Kyung-tae greeted a giant sullen man, shortly followed by his beaming daughter. Choi Jinmu and Choi Chun-mi.

It was his eyes that immediately caught her attention. For a moment, she had thought he might be wearing coloured contacts, then she remembered there was a condition where a person's eyes may not be the same colour. An icy blue eye sat beside a twilit brown one, like two different sides of his being - one basking in light, and the other shrouded in darkness. His steeled gaze fixed on Yu-ra was telling - telling of a man who gathered everything he needed to know about you from that one look. Yet, Chun-mi was quite the contrast to him. Her doughy eyes teased you, rolling over you then playfully maintaining eye contact with you. But Jinmu - his hardened stare weighed up whether you were worthy of his respect, all within a matter of seconds.

"Heterochromia," he said. "That's the word you're looking for."

"Sorry?" How did he know the exact word she was trying to recall? She struggled to decide how to react. *Well, I'm sure he gets it all the time,* she thought. But there was something about the confidence with which he spoke that suggested he read far more than he let on.

Chun-mi's self-assuredness differed from Jinmu's, but it was there nonetheless. Her traditionally confident aura was much more overt. For instance, the way the fit of her flashy, silky kimono was just a little too snug, making Yu-ra a tad uncomfortable with her brushing up against her new husband.

Yu-ra was soon left alone with her and Chun-mi's perky smile immediately relaxed. It was a little awkward at first, being alone with a stranger whose only connection to her was Kyung-tae.

"I was just about to go look for my friend," Yu-ra started, standing up from her chair and straightening out her dress, "do you want to join?"

Chun-mi gestured her hands in a forward motion, allowing Yu-ra to take the lead.

"So, I popped into the wedding upstairs before coming in here," Chun-mi said, following closely behind the bride, who flashed her a polite smile, as she navigated her way throughout the maze 9oof tables. "They did a beautiful job. I'm thinking you should've hired the people who did theirs."

What did she mean by that?

"Sorry, what was that?" Yu-ra asked, in between greeting guests at the table she had stopped at.

"I was just saying I spoke to the decorators upstairs," Chun-mi leaned in closer to her, presumably so that Yu-ra could hear her over the other guests better "They're really well known. I heard you guys got a quote from them too."

"Oh, right. We just decided to go with someone else." Yu-ra shrugged.

"It was a financial issue, right? You know, you could have just asked me. Kyung-tae's family; I would have been delighted to help. And I know he's good for it."

What a peculiar way to begin your very first conversation with someone. What was she getting at? Yu-ra decided to ignore it and change the subject.

"Kyung-tae mentioned your father before we got married but I don't think he ever mentioned you," Yu-ra said, as she moved onto the next table of guests. "You grew up with him, then?"

Chun-mi pouted in a cutesy manner that garnered her the interest of the guests at the table they were at.

"I kind of want to go back upstairs too. It's so much more fun than this."

Did she hear her right? Why would anyone say something like that to a bride? Especially one they had never met before.

"Sorry, I don't think I heard you correctly." Yu-ra itched her head as she put on the politest smile she could muster.

"I said this wedding is boring." Chun-mi spoke a little louder than before. She definitely heard her correctly. Seemingly paying no attention to what Chun-mi just said, the guests Yu-ra just greeted continued to gaze at Chun-mi in awe.

A friend of Kyung-tae's would never say something like that about his wedding. He was robotic, but he knew how to control his tongue. The people he surrounded himself with would be the same.

"It's a little too big to feel intimate, right?" Yu-ra said, keeping up her warm smile before continuing her way around the tables. "So it just feels like dinner with strangers."

"No, I mean the party upstairs had drinks, dancers, pop music. Do you guys just eat and go home and call that a celebration?"

"We don't drink," Yu-ra said, as she moved onto the next table. She was under the impression that it was common knowledge that Muslims don't drink. "And since we're not segregated, it wouldn't really be modest for us to dance in front of each other."

"So, because you don't drink, you're just going to ruin the fun for all of us?" Chun-mi said, with what Yu-ra realised was the most forced smile stretched across her face. It just didn't look like it took much effort. "What, we can't drink around you because of your beliefs?"

"I didn't say that," Yu-ra replied with a raised brow as she stopped in her tracks. "It's just wrong for us to encourage drinking so we made the decision to not pay for it. You can do as you please."

"Oh, good," she said with a sigh of relief, placing her hand across her chest, "Because some people snuck some drinks in from upstairs."

Yu-ra's mouth opened, but nothing came out. What was she even supposed to say to that? Should she go tell Kyung-tae? She didn't even know if it was true. What would they do even if it was? How would they find out who did?

"I need to go find my friend," was all she could muster up, as she made a beeline for the entrance. She was sure Min-ah hadn't arrived yet. It would surely have been much easier to find her if she was there.

"Sorry, I'm conveying what I really want to say in the most convoluted way," Chun-mi added as she effortlessly slipped between tables and kept up with Yu-ra, "and it's coming off as passive aggressive. I apologise."

Yu-ra slowed down. Maybe she did get her intentions all wrong.

"Ah, don't worry about it," Yu-ra said, looking over her shoulder at her as they continued towards the entrance, "I'm sure you just couldn't find the right words. A lot of people have trouble articulating themselves well when they don't have time to decide what they want to say. We did just meet after all, so you probably have a bunch of questions."

"You're right, I just needed time to articulate what I really meant," Chun-mi said, as she gripped Yu-ra's shoulder and, with an unbelievably strong force, spun her around so that they were facing each other. "The truth is, if you're going to steal my man, the least you could do is provide me with alternatives, be it alcohol, or better men. You've provided me with neither. So where do we go from here?"

"Excuse me?" Yu-ra said, almost slack jawed from her brash statement as she rubbed her shoulder where Chun-mi had gripped her. She could tell that Chun-mi meant to harm her considering she could feel it even through the heavy padding of her dress.

"I thought forced marriages were a thing of the past," she scoffed, "yet your backwards religion still enforces it."

Some of the guests on the table behind them, men that had unsurprisingly become enamoured with Chun-mi, had begun to take notice of the rising tension between the two. Struggling to keep her jaw from locking in place, Yu-ra continued to unnecessarily defend herself.

"No one was forced into anything. We both agreed to this." Creases formed in her forehead as she wrinkled her brows. What was going on? "I'm confused. You are Kyung-tae's friend, right?"

Chun-mi turned her nose up at her.

"You heard me right. It's unbelievable. You're okay at best. And I'm much more than just his friend. For him to choose to marry you when I'm right here is an impossibility that I refuse to let you perpetuate."

Blood was now rushing to her ears as she crossed her arms, the uninvited gaze of the male guests behind them discomforting her.

"Beauty isn't all there is to life."

"That's what ugly people say to get them through the day." She smirked a devious smirk which told Yu-ra that she was beneath Chun-mi.

"Speak the truth, spade!" one of the younger men at the table called, garnering a choir of laughter from the rest of the table. "Don't let those ugly spades push their agenda."

Chun-mi gave a smile and a wave towards them, causing them to begin fumbling over each other. Were they drunk? They must have been the people Chun-mi was referring to earlier. And why was she smiling at them? Sure, Yu-ra was used to being called a spade, but she'd never just accept blatant sexism with a smile.

"Besides," she said, turning back to Yu-ra. "I have much more than my beauty. I thought there'd be something substantial for him to choose you over me. But it was just as I expected. His mother forced him into it. How dare you steal what was rightfully mine with your filthy thieving hands?"

Yu-ra scowled at her. She wanted to put her in her place, curse her out and make her feel small. But she couldn't. What good would it do to cause a scene with one of Kyung-tae's closest friends? They might have even been more than friends, possibly romantically involved. Maybe that's why Kyung-tae never mentioned her. And the way these guests were acting, she wasn't sure they'd even take her side. Clearly some of them hated being there already considering the drunk haze they had put themselves in.

"I don't want you at my wedding, please leave. I'd rather not have a heated argument with you."

Circling around her, Chun-mi leaned in, her soft oriental fragrance filling the air as she smiled sinisterly. Her pleasant scent seemed only to exacerbate Yu-ra's already built-up frustration.

"I can see you seething," she whispered, like a devil on her shoulder. "Let it out. Do me a favour and tear me a new one. Maybe throw a few punches too. I've been wanting to let off a little steam recently."

Maybe she should let it out. Who cares if no one took her side? She barely cared about seventy percent of the guests.

No. She wasn't some random thug threatening her on a deserted street. It would lead to a million different problems. It seemed as though Chun-mi could manipulate any conversation she wanted to. Most importantly, what if Kyung-tae's mother stopped seeing her the same way? She couldn't risk it.

"If you won't leave, then I will be the bigger person and leave myself."

Chun-mi laughed, the first authentic reaction she had had in their conversation.

"Go ahead, be the bigger man or whatever. You definitely look like one."

One of the drunk men choked on his drink as he burst out laughing, an orange liquid splattered all over the table.

"Ewww," one of the other men taunted as they realised the shower of liquid had come from the man's nostrils.

"That spade's getting put in her place," he said through coughs, as he clapped his hands at Chun-mi's comebacks.

Another man on the table cupped his hands around his mouth.

"Shoot back, spade!"

"Oh crap, isn't that the bride?" one of the men said, smacking the arms of the two guys beside him. "Stop it, you idiots," he hushed.

"I'm leaving," Yu-ra said as she attempted to escape the horrid woman.

Chun-mi held her hand out before Yu-ra could pass.

"Just remember you mean nothing to Kyung-tae. Your marriage is a sham and you can't handle a man like him. It's going to crash and burn sooner or later." She winked at Yu-ra. "And I'll be there to pick up the pieces."

Yu-ra pushed past her arm, hurrying away.

A numbing pain, caused by her continually locked jaw, had found its way around her skull as she frantically searched for something to relax her. She swept up a plate, piling on three slices of cake before storming out of the room through a back door hidden to the unobservant. Beside the exit was a concrete staircase leading up to a small balcony on the second floor. Trudging through the unbroken snow, she climbed the staircase and sat down. There was a party on show through the second-floor window.

An unsympathetic chill began to pierce through her dress, biting at her behind. What looked like some professional dancers were performing in the middle of the room. A few people sat at the open bar and others were all clapping in unison and encouraging the performers. The temperature outside cooled off her burning ears, and stuffing her face with cake definitely relaxed her. But she soon found herself shivering from the cold and annoyed at herself for not bringing a coat to the wedding.

She didn't want to go back inside and have to see Chun-mi again. Who knew if she could control herself upon seeing her stupid smug face again? The thought of her made her heat up again and she started stuffing her face more forcefully. Distracting herself with food didn't seem to work as well as she thought it would. What Chun-mi said continuously replayed in her head. *Your marriage is a sham.* Even Min-ah didn't believe she chose to marry Kyung-tae of her own accord. Did she really marry him because she wanted to? Come to think of it, Yu-ra couldn't pinpoint any single moment in her past where she felt that Kyung-tae was the be all and end all of her romantic journey.

After finishing her food, she folded up the paper plate in her hands and tucked her arms between her legs for warmth. She could no longer feel the tip of her nose and her fingers had stiffened a bit. Looking up at the city skyline, she admired the picturesque scene laid out before her. The towering skyscrapers, the neon lights - the architecture was impressive. It really was beautiful from afar. It was a shame what they had to lose for this. But nobody else really cared anymore.

A few minutes later she heard the door creak below her and watched as her husband poked his head out. Upon seeing her, he stepped outside and walked up a few of the steps, stopping a couple metres away from her.

"Hey," he said, leaning back against the wall.

"Hey," she responded monotonously, though she felt a pinch in her chest that told her she wasn't unhappy to see Kyung-tae

"Ma was looking for you. I think one of your friends is here and was asking for you?"

"Which friend?" She sighed, looking off into the distance.

"I think her name was Min-ah."

Her face lit up. She threw her arms in the air, her paper plate escaping her hands as she did.

"Min-ah's finally here? Oh shoot!" she said as she noticed her plate about to fly away.

"Are you happy or unhappy about her being here? Because I am perplexed by your choice of words."

Yu-ra fumbled about on the staircase as she just managed to grab the paper plate before it flew away.

"Sorry. Anyway, what are we doing out here? Let's go meet her."

Kyung-tae's brow twitched in obvious confusion before settling.

"By the way, why were you out here in the cold? Ma was worried about you."

"That's just like her," she said, chuckling to herself. "She's such a sweetheart." Yu-ra paused momentarily before continuing. Causing an issue between Kyung-tae and his family friends on their wedding day wouldn't go down well, she decided. "I just needed to get away from the hustle and bustle for a couple minutes. It was a lot to deal with."

"I thought as much." He took off his large outer robe and held it out to her, his toned forearms now exposed as the sleeves of his underlay only went just below the elbow.

"Here."

"What's this for?"

"It's a coat, you wear it."

Yu-ra tilted her head quizzically.

"Are you sure it wasn't you that was worried about me?"

"No, it was my ma. Besides, are you really making fun of a husband caring about his wife?"

"Haha! You care about me!" she giggled in more of an unhinged tone than she was comfortable with letting out. "I caught you out!"

Kyung-tae shook his robe at her.

"What are you, an owl? Why are you looking at me like that? Just take the jacket."

Yu-ra realised she still had her head cocked and straightened it out. She still didn't understand why he was offering her his robe when they were about to go back inside but decided not to question further. She took it off him and pulled it tightly closed around her. He had never shown this much concern for her before. She guessed it was probably his mother's doing. Before walking down the steps, Yu-ra's gaze landed on the faint scar around Kyung-tae's throat.

"Hey. I've always wondered, how did you…" she trailed off. No, it wasn't the best time to ask something so personal. A scar like that could have come from a very traumatic experience. "About Chun-mi, how long have you known her, again?"

"Around fourteen years now, I think," Kyung-tae said as he opened the door. "Why?"

Yu-ra hesitated.

"It's nothing, I was just wondering."

He stood to the side, allowing Yu-ra to walk ahead of him. She gave a polite smile as she passed by.

# 5
# Stakeout

*The individuals subsequently attacked Mr. Oh Jae-min, the father of the household, while questioning him about alleged debts. Unfortunately, Mr. Oh succumbed to his injuries and was pronounced deceased upon my arrival at the scene.*

*- Case Number 1996-2786*

"No whisky tonight?" Kyung-tae asked Mr Choi as he unclipped his seat belt and re-tucked his white shirt into his trousers. "Thought that was your go-to stakeout drink."

They had just arrived at their stakeout location, a fair distance away from the toppled over bins that Kyung-tae had seen yesterday. Though he didn't feel confident that they would achieve anything that night, he decided it was best not to bring it up. Mr Choi switched off the engine, the van falling silent.

"I quit a while ago," he said.

"Oh," Kyung-tae said with an uncontrollable swivel of his head towards Mr Choi, purely out of surprise. "Well, congratulations on the feat. How long has it been?"

With what Kyung-tae felt he picked up on as a subtle solemnity, Mr Choi cast his gaze towards him.

"I haven't touched a bottle since..." Mr Choi trailed off then directed his attention back to the scene of the crime. "Anyway, I'm taking a page out of your book. Maybe it'll save my health."

Kyung-tae lowered his leather seat back into a more comfortable position, rummaging around the snack bag in the back until he took out a sizable chocolate bar. His eyes remained glued to the bins as he opened the wrapper and took a bite.

"Yep, I'm so healthy."

The snow had melted considerably since the night before, making it much safer to drive, and making the stakeout possible. Kyung-tae pressed the engine button and turned the heat up. Cold air blasted at them for a half a minute before the air began to warm. They had been there so long that Mr Choi's musk had taken over the whole van. He directed his attention to Mr Choi, who was still sitting upright, staring out of the window, as straight faced as ever.

"So, is marriage living up to everything you expected?" Mr Choi said.

Kyung-tae shrugged. "I guess. It hasn't really hit me yet."

"You've grown up a lot. I still remember the moody thirteen-year-old that would get into fights with kids four years older than you."

Kyung-tae chuckled to himself. "I've calmed down enough to be able to settle down now, at least."

"And I must say," Mr Choi said with concern beginning to infiltrate his tone, "your wedding was an unusually extravagant experience."

"I never wanted a wedding that big either."

"You don't get much say when taking into account another family's requests. Especially when you're the man in the relationship."

Kyung-tae sat up straight, adjusting his seat as he went.

"It wasn't them. My mother always wanted to have a big wedding for her daughter. Too bad she got stuck with me."

"She doesn't feel that way."

Kyung-tae watched Mr Choi through the rearview mirror. His eyes were empty as he said those words without missing a beat.

"I know. I just didn't want to be the cause of more grief for her." His shoulders deflated as he shifted his gaze to his side mirror. "She's been through enough because of me. You know about the things I used to say to her when I was a teenager. If you weren't there to set me straight, who knows how bad it could have turned out."

"You can adhere to what you want without causing grief for someone else."

Kyung-tae looked back into the rearview mirror. Mr Choi's eyes were still the same.

"I guess I never thought about it like that because she's my mother. But it's fine, I just wanted to make her happy."

"Take solace in the fact that you're a good son. There are plenty of people out there who mistreat their parents," he said, glancing to his side. "Some people leave and never speak to their parents again." Patting Kyung-tae on the shoulder, he continued. "Just don't throw your own happiness away for the sake of hers."

Kyung-tae searched through the bag of food for one of the tastier snacks, the crinkling of packets crackling through the quiet air. He took out some chocolate caramelised sticks and handed them to Mr Choi. A band of pigeons had flocked to the bins and began pecking at the rubbish littered at the scene as the two men in the car begin nibbling at their respective food items.

"Are you absolutely sure this isn't a waste of time?" Kyung-tae asked. "There's no guarantee these people will show up."

"Have I ever led you in the wrong direction, or given you reason to doubt me?"

"No. Of course I trust you, but what's the game plan here?"

Mr Choi began twisting the ring on his left hand.

"The substance you found, something so strange wouldn't be there, where something definitely happened, without it being important. Call it an experiential hunch. If I'm wrong, I'll give you fifteen thousand yen."

"Well, now I hope they don't show." Mr Choi raised a brow at Kyung-tae. "Sorry. Bad joke," Kyung-tae blurted.

Time passed by slowly as they watched pigeons flutter onto the scene and away. A few people walked by and stared at the bins, a few paid no mind.

"There was a time I was working on taking down a drug cartel," Mr Choi said. "These people were the scum of the Earth. They weren't just selling drugs, they were formulating and creating new ones, with no regard for side effects or even safety measures. Some of the drugs they made would spontaneously combust, cause entire buildings to burn down, and they would still sell them to anyone who was willing to pay."

Kyung-tae watched the rearview mirror again. Life had flushed into Mr Choi's eyes for the first time and creases formed at his eyebrows. He thought for a moment that Mr Choi was reliving his glory days as a detective before he realised that the life that had filled him was in the form of hatred.

"So, for months of my life, this was my sole case," Mr Choi continued. "I made a few arrests, which kept my case going, but they were all low-level street dealers. Constantly I would hit brick walls and more and more drugs found their way onto the streets and into schools. I had the captain and the superintendent breathing down my neck to get results and my wife was pregnant at the time. She would be calling me up non-stop while I was tailing people, on foot chases, staking places out. Splitting my time between work and her needs was more physically draining than the entirety of my military career." His expression darkened as he looked away. "But being there for your wife is its own reward and I'd do it all again. Then after months of leads drying up, I got lucky. I spent all my time staking out the usual drug spots, places they *knew* the police had their eyes on, and finally I caught wind of a supplier. I tailed him, followed him right to a whole cargo full of cocaine and heroin they were bringing into the country. So I took him down, everyone that was there, and anyone I could get him to sell out."

The van fell silent for a few moments before Kyung-tae finally spoke.

"I've never heard this story before. How come you've never told me?"

"I never told you because it's never been relevant before. I also didn't want my experiences to taint how you see your job or how you work." The blood seemed to almost drain from his face while his grip slowly tightened around the packet in his hand, and the sticks inside began to snap. "The story doesn't have a happy ending." He paused momentarily. "But the point is, when I was down to my last straw, the stakeout helped me a lot more than any other method."

Kyung-tae looked down at Mr Choi's hands, still clamped around the packet.

"Was this when your wife was pregnant with Chun-mi?"

"Yes. Raising a five-year-old while pregnant and her husband not being around enough was quite the ordeal for her, as you can imagine."

A few chattering people passed by the bins. Posture immediately straightening up, he edged forward on his seat. But then they exited the scene, and he slumped back.

"While we're on the topic of wives…" Kyung-tae began.

Mr Choi turned to him.

"Are you going to tell me yours is pregnant?"

"What?" Kyung-tae blurted. "God no! We've not even held hands yet."

"I see," Mr Choi said, a sliver of a smirk lifting up on his cheek.

"I'm just having…" Kyung-tae shook his head. "Rather we are *both* having a bit of trouble adjusting to the new lifestyle."

"It's been one night. How much trouble could you have you already run into?"

Kyung-tae put his head to the dashboard.

"It's been so unbelievably awkward. It was never like this before."

"Before what?" Mr Choi asked. "I didn't know there was a before."

Kyung-tae lifted his head back up.

"Before we got married. Say we would go to get coffee for example. Sometimes it's hard to be totally honest with your parents there listening to every word, right? So it would be me, her, and her brother, and we would go to learn more about each other to see if we were compatible. It wasn't awkward at all."

Mr Choi began to nibble on his snack again.

"And what's changed now?"

"When we're around other people, like at the wedding yesterday, we can talk to each other relatively okay. But when we went to our new home, we didn't speak a word to each other," he said, rambling on, "and then we had to share a bed because we've just barely got the essentials and in the middle of the night, she… she kicked me. Right in the stomach."

Mr Choi furrowed his brow and the corners of his mouth twitched downward.

"She did what?"

"It wasn't her fault. She didn't mean to. She said she freaked out because she forgot she was sleeping next to me. I didn't want to make it more uncomfortable for her, so I left and told her I had some work I needed to do. Ended up sleeping with my head against the kitchen counter."

Mr Choi's demeanour began to soften, and his stiff shoulders relaxed somewhat.

"What do you think the problem is?"

"Maybe it's just a big change for both of us, is all."

"You're not wrong. To me it sounds like the type of relationship you have has shifted, and with that shift came a change in how you act around each other. Before marriage, you didn't see each other in a romantic light. Or at least you didn't, I wouldn't know if she did. And now that the marriage is real and you are romantic partners, you feel awkward because you are now seeing her in that light."

Kyung-tae itched his head.

"I understand what you're getting at… I think."

"Think of it this way - the way you two are behaving around each other is how my wife and I were when we started dating. We knew each other throughout school but, once we started dating after we graduated, we would tiptoe around each other with our words and would act as if we barely knew one another."

"So how do I fix it? I don't want to tiptoe around my own home."

"Time. You'll slowly become more comfortable with each other. Just don't force yourself to have feelings for a woman you don't care for. There are more compatible women out there, some may be closer than you think."

Kyung-tae looked at him for a moment, faintly raising his brow before stopping himself.

"You know I'm in this for the long haul, right?"

"I understand. But if things don't change with time, there's clearly a deeper issue at hand."

Kyung-tae sighed.

"Yeah, I know. You're right. But I'll make it work. I'm never going to find a woman my mother likes as much as her."

"There you go again, bringing up your mother when she has nothing to do with the situation," Mr Choi said with a sudden shift in his tone, as if he had been holding this back for a long time. "I know she's your mother but she's not always right. You don't have to follow whatever she chooses. You let her choose your religion and now you're letting her choose your wife even if she's not right for you."

Kyung-tae turned away. He had heard similar notions from Mr Choi before, but for some reason, this time it seemed to bother him. Fortunately, Mr Choi was distracted by movement at the bin. A man had entered his vision. He stopped to lift up the bin and then went on his way.

"Damn it," Kyung-tae said as he gripped the side of his seat and began to squeeze.

Another half an hour passed until they saw more people. And then another forty minutes after that until Kyung-tae saw a familiar face with a cheery grin plastered on. The waitress from the diner was embracing a man with what looked like a thin scar under his right eye, her head leaned on his chest. A gang of people in jumpsuits followed a short distance behind the two. The affectionate couple went on their way, but the gang stayed behind. This was it, what he had been waiting for. He could feel it in his gut. And his eyes then confirmed it. The men shoved the bin to the side and began emptying out the bags. After rummaging through the garbage, they began putting everything back into the bin. Kyung-tae tugged on the door handle and stepped a foot outside.

"Stop," Mr Choi said in a sterner tone than usual. "Where are you going?"

"I'm going to arrest them," he said, directing his attention back to Mr Choi.

"What about the plan?"

"We don't know if tailing them is going to work. I'll arrest them and interrogate them, and they'll lead us straight to the girl."

"You don't know that," Mr Choi said, grabbing onto his arm.

"We don't have time to waste on what we do and don't know. Anything could happen in that time," Kyung-tae said, pulling his arm back. "They could kidnap more girls, or they might end up selling the girls they already have. We can't risk it... *I* can't risk it."

"There's seven of them!"

"Then back me up!" Kyung-tae hollered as he slammed the car door behind him and sped off towards the gang of hoodlums.

Seven of them. What was his plan? No. There was no time for a plan. He just needed to incapacitate them as fast as possible. Kyung-tae checked his back pocket. Only four zip ties. It would have to do.

"Hey!" Kyung-tae called out, marching towards them. "You looking for something?"

They all turned, but only two of them stood up.

"You got a problem with that?" the man in front said.

"Where's the girl?" Kyung-tae said, anger flooding his voice.

"What girl?" the shorter man in the back said.

"All I want is to know what you did with the waitress Kim Sun-Jung," he said as he arrived at their feet. "We don't have to have a problem here and I won't arrest you if you help me. You can make this all go away."

"Arrest me for what?" the front man said, chuckling haughtily. "We're helping clean up the streets!"

"I can arrest you for anything and keep you in holding as long as I want, if I have reasonable suspicion. Don't test me," he said sternly.

"I don't know anything about no waitress. Now, if we ain't got a problem here, you better step to it," the front man said, placing his hand on the detective's shoulder.

Kyung-tae breathed out softly.

"Let's try this again," he said as he slammed his shin into the back of the man's leg, collapsing him to his knees. "Tell me where the girl is," he yelled, grabbing the man by his collar.

Unsurprisingly, everyone else stood up.

"You should know my friends here got no problem with putting you in your place, lawman."

"Fine by me," he whispered.

Kyung-tae flipped him onto his back and fastened the zip tie around his wrists. Gripping the rest of his zip ties in his right hand, the other six charged at him. He kicked the first in the knee, feeling his knee-cap shift underneath his shoe as he buckled over. Grabbing his arm, he flipped him over his shoulder. Kyung-tae dodged what seemed like a speeding dart, as a fist brought a blast of air that rushed past his ear. Whipping the same man's face with the zip ties in his hand, he propelled himself into the air and spin-kicked him to the ground.

Without losing momentum, he tackled the next person, rolling over him and returning to his feet. But, turning just a fraction of a second too late, a punch to the gut tore the wind from his lungs. Looking up to see a fist flying towards him, he blocked it just in time, a shock running down his forearm from the colliding bones. From the other side came another fist, gripping a short blade. A sharp pain sliced into his cheek as Kyung-tae hurled his body away.

Kyung-tae saw Mr Choi strolling towards them in the distance.

"Could use some help over here!" he called out as loud as his breathless body allowed him to.

Blood slowly began to trickle down his cheek. With no more than a moment to catch his breath, he blocked a punch from the woman to his side. Though, unable to react fast enough, her knife tore across his thigh. Kyung-tae rolled to the side and swept her legs out from underneath her. Backing up, with his hands out in front of him, as those on the ground got up, one of them cut the restrained man free.

"I have my reservations about fighting a woman," Kyung-tae said through heavy breaths, "but that was just rude."

Mr Choi had finally arrived, but before they noticed him all seven of them charged towards Kyung-tae. The first swung. He dodged, launching a kick to the man's stomach. Using all his momentum, he spun, jumped in the air and drove the back of his other foot down into his jaw, knocking him unconscious. The sound of the zipties whipped in the wind as Kyung-tae parried two punches and a knife coming at him. One of them dove at him, slamming into his ribs and causing Kyung-tae to tumble over. They saw their opening and began pummelling him from every direction. One of them stood on his wounded leg, the excruciating weight travelling down his entire vein as Kyung-tae muffled his shout of pain.

Mr Choi finally got their attention as he flying-kicked one of them to the ground. They stopped pounding on Kyung-tae and turned to their new foe.

"Let's get this over with," Mr Choi said to Kyung-tae, while rolling up his sleeves. "You've gotten lazy."

"You guys should give up while you have a chance," Kyung-tae said, catching his breath as he stood up. "You're no match for him. Save yourselves the pain."

They paid no heed to Kyung-tae's words and charged at the older man. Mr Choi stopped a kick from the first man with his bare hands and then flung his heel straight down into his chest. The woman then rushed at him with a knife. Kyung-tae grabbed the man closest to him, twisted his arm and shoved him to the ground. He heard three different cries of pain as he cuffed the man he took down. But just before he stood up, another cry of pain was heard. But this one was more of a gruff bellow and the voice very familiar.

Kyung-tae's heart sank to his stomach when he looked up. No, no, no. This couldn't be right. It didn't make sense. Mr Choi was unstoppable, the best fighter he had ever seen. One of the thugs slid a knife out of Mr Choi's side. As he fell to the ground, blood began leaking through his shirt. He charged through the remaining thugs and slid across the ground, stopping at Mr Choi's side. The thugs picked up their unconscious friend, dragging him with them as they ran off. Frozen, Kyung-tae couldn't decide what to do. If they got away, he might never get another lead. But if he left Mr Choi… Mr Choi could…

"Sir!" Kyung-tae yelled, shaking his mentor by the shoulders, "Sir! Are you okay?"

Mr Choi was staring up at the sky, heavily breathing in and out at a slow pace.

"I'm going to get you to a hospital," Kyung-tae said as he ripped his jacket off and tied it around the wound, pulling it tight to increase pressure, "don't worry."

"Job first," Mr Choi huffed. "There's more at stake than me losing a little blood."

Kyung-tae lifted him up off the ground.

"Forget about them. I have all I need." The adrenaline drained from Kyung-tae's body as they hobbled to the car.

# 6
# Visit

It was a busy day and the subway station was brimming with commuters. Though every day was a busy day, and the high-speed trains were always near full, today was especially packed. Kyung-tae slipped through the crowd, pulling a Yu-ra who was pushing through the bystanders to get on the train. The rows of suited men narrowed the wide carriages. Many of those seated, elderly and pregnant women, were adorned with special priority badges. Managing to find one of the thickly cushioned seats empty next to an elderly lady, Kyung-tae let Yu-ra sit down while he gripped the edge of the headrest for stability. The lady eyed Yu-ra before edging closer to the window. People were still piling onto the near full train.

Kyung-tae tapped his wife atop her head as the train began to move.

"Hey, I wanna ask you about something," he said, "but it might sound weird."

"Ask away," Yu-ra said, rubbing her hands against the knees of her skirt.

"How come you're not covering your bruise with makeup anymore?"

Yu-ra took a quick glance at him.

"That does sound weird to ask."

Briefcases of standing men and women punched into each other before settling into a stillness. A low humming surrounded the carriage as the train moved into terminal velocity.

"I don't mean it in a bad way, I promise. You're very pretty without it of course. Prettier even." Kyung-tae's grip slipped just a tad from the increasing amounts of sweat on his hands. "Why even wear makeup at all when you're that pretty without it, right? It's insane how pretty you are. How is it even possible to be that pretty, you know?"

Yu-ra's shoulders subtly began to bounce as she wrapped her hand around her mouth. Was she... laughing?

"Is this your mother talking again?"

Kyung-tae released his grip from the headrest, no longer needing a stabiliser.

"What? I don't- no, I was just wondering because you were wearing it pretty thick at the wedding, and then you did a one-eighty and barely wear it. It's just curiosity."

"Relax, I'm not interrogating you," she said, staring up into Kyung-tae's eyes, before glancing away soon after. "It was my wedding, I wanted to look my best. And it's kind of suffocating to wear makeup over it right now."

"Oh," Kyung-tae said simply, "fair enough."

"I like how we have matching wounds now," she said, waving her hand around her fading bruise.

"Except I didn't get mine from tripping over. I just hope people don't think we got into a fight with each other."

"It's like we're wearing couples clothing."

"Ah, so this is what they mean when they call people power couples," he said blandly. "It makes so much sense now."

She looked up at him but again, couldn't keep her eyes fixed in one place. "Huh? No. Do you actually not know what a power couple is?"

Kyung-tae itched his head awkwardly. "Looks like my jokes aren't hitting the mark today."

"That was a joke? Honestly, I had no clue."

"Don't worry about it. I don't think anyone has ever found me funny apart from my ma."

She placed her hand on her chest, pouting at him a little.

"Aw, don't you just live the saddest life. I'm pretty sure your mother doesn't find you funny either. Next time tell me when you're making a joke and I'll laugh, I promise."

"Deal," he said, holding his hand out to her. She took hold of it lightly and shook. "I'll calculate the funniest joke possible. Prepare yourself for the laugh of a lifetime."

Yu-ra nudged his thigh with her elbow. "I will genuinely buy a screwdriver one day and rewire you. Even if I've never studied anything to do with machines."

A smile crept at the corners of Kyung-tae's mouth as he looked away.

The train jolted to a stop, causing Kyung-tae's balance to falter. His abdomen knocked into Yu-ra as he stumbled over her, but he quickly held onto the headrest of the seat in front of the elderly woman. The woman smiled at him and nodded. He stood up properly and gave a small smile in return, noticing Yu-ra rubbing the top of her head on his way down.

"Sorry, you okay?" Kyung-tae asked. The train started moving again, soon jetting off.

"I'm fine, thanks" Yu-ra said, but was still rubbing her head. "Do you have a metal sheet under there or something?" she mumbled. "I didn't think you were actually a robot."

"What?"

"Nothing," she said, shooting a polite smile to him, "by the way, are you ever going to tell me how Jinmu ended up in the hospital?"

"It's a little hard to explain, maybe some other time," he said, staring off into the distance of the carriage. After the intake of new passengers from the last stop, it seemed to be causing an issue with passengers by the exits.

"But he's okay, right?"

"He'll be fine in a couple days. You can ask him when we get to the hospital," he said, looking back down at her.

"About that," she said slowly, tightening the grasp she had on her knees as she stared at her feet. "I really don't think I should come."

"Why not? He'll be so grateful, and it's important that you get to know the people important to me."

Yu-ra overtly hesitated then looked up at him.

"Is Chun-mi going to be there?"

Why did Chun-mi come into the conversation? She wasn't the one injured.

"Of course. Is that a problem?"

“No, it's great,” she said, casting her gaze back to her shoes, “but, three's a crowd.”

“I am absolutely certain that they don’t mind. If you’re still worried, I will put all weekend aside to visit your parents. We can even stay over there.”

He looked back down the carriage, the commotion on the other end seemed to have moved up towards them, passengers were bumping into each other more rigorously.

“No,” she said abruptly, “we don't need to visit my parents.”

Why was she being so difficult? He partially knew what he was getting into when he decided to get married, he guessed. Glancing at her, he noticed her right leg bobbing rapidly.

“It's only fair that I visit your family if I'm asking you to visit mine.”

“No, just forget it.”

“Well, why not? I'm doing my best to find a compromise here.”

“Because I said so,” she said, flashing a glare at him.

“That doesn't sound like much of a reason,” he said, taken aback by her look.

“Well it's reason enough, so just drop it, okay?” she said firmly.

Kyung-tae took a moment before he spoke. This was going nowhere any time soon.

“Okay, dropping it.”

“I don't want to cause too much trouble. I'm overloaded with assignments anyway. Life's hectic at the moment.”

Kyung-tae sighed softly as he looked down at her.

“Hey, I really am sorry that we couldn’t have a honeymoon trip. My work is just really important right now.”

“Don't be. I wouldn't have been able to go,” she said, feigning a small smile but quickly looking away again.

“Maybe we can have one when we know each other better,” he said, placing his hand atop her head and lightly shaking side to side, “when it's less awkward.”

"Oh wow," she said, pushing his arm away, "so the awkwardness is out in the open and everything now."

"Where do you want to go? Maybe we'll do one trip to your place and one trip to mine."

Yu-ra opened her mouth to respond, but the commotion that had begun down the carriageway barrelled its way towards them. The standing passengers began tumbling over one another, yelling out as a burly, bald man bullied his way through the crowd.

"Well, well, well, if it ain't the spade that got me arrested," the man hollered.

Yu-ra shrank into her seat as she clutched the arm of Kyung-tae's coat. A tingling sensation ran down the back of his neck. The train made its stop and then moved off again, meaning they missed their stop. Though it was a minor irritation in comparison to how this man's presence made Yu-ra feel. The stampeding man stopped right in front of them and leaned over her, putting his hand beside her head, sending another tingle down Kyung-tae's spine.

"I got a bone to pick with you, missy," he said, excruciatingly close to her.

Immediately taking a hold of his shoulder, Kyung-tae shoved him back an arm's length away.

"I'm going to need you to take a step back, sir," Kyung-tae said. "What do you want?"

The man thrust Kyung-tae's arm away, scowling at him.

"None of your goddamn business!"

Many of the passengers turned towards them, but the elderly lady cowered against the window. Yu-ra took a card out of her pocket and slipped it to Kyung-tae. A business card. Why she had that on her, let alone at all, was beyond him.

*Li Feng.*

*Any loan, any time.*

So, Li Feng was his name.

"What, ya need someone else to fight your battles now?" he sneered at Yu-ra. "Where's that feisty girl from the other day? I liked that version of you."

Some of the passengers slid open their phones, some unfolded their phones, and they all started recording the scene. Kyung-tae put his arm out in front of Yu-ra.

"It is my business," he said sternly.

"This your boyfriend or something? You might wanna keep him in check. I wouldn't wanna break his arm on account of you, missy," he said, laying the back of his hand on Kyung-tae's shoulder.

"He's my husband," Yu-ra said, finally, her voice erring on the shaky side.

Li Feng erupted into a cackling fit.

"Word to the wise, friend," he said, "she was all up in my business the other day. I don't think she's the wife type. Get out while ya can, 'cause she's gonna be taking you for every penny you got in a few months' time."

"My marriage is none of your concern," Kyung-tae said, allowing Li Feng to keep his hand on him. "Now, tell me what you want."

"Hey, I'm just giving you a little friendly advice. Unless you're into that kind of stuff," he said, holding his hands up defensively, "no judgement from me, friend. People are into all sorts of weird things these days. You know, I've been seeing a bunch of folks who ain't sticking by their spouses, lately." He began to itch his chin. "Or is the correct plural spices? Spouci?"

Kyung-tae glanced down at Yu-ra in confusion, who shrugged in response. Her skin had reddened and her grasp on his coat had tightened.

"Since when does assault only land you a few days in jail?" she said with more confidence in her voice.

"Ha! You think I actually got arrested? That little weasel would never sell me out, and there was no one there to confirm your story."

"Well then I'll call the police again and make sure you get arrested this time."

"Go ahead. Just know that shiner I gave you ain't nothing compared to what you got coming," he chuckled, before rubbing his fingers at her. "Or you could make it all go away, with a little paper. Well, more like a lot-tle"

"So you were the one who gave her that bruise?" Kyung-tae interrupted, a sly smile on his face. "I was hoping she would tell me what really happened herself."

"Yeah, and what of it?" Li-Feng said, puffing out his chest. "I'm a feminist, I'd punch any man or woman. Call me the poster boy for equal rights."

"You just confessed to assault."

"Look, friend," Li Feng said, putting his hand on Kyung-tae's shoulder again and closing his grip. "I ain't got no problem with you, you ain't gotta make this worse for yourself."

"The problem is, I have a problem with you."

Kyung-tae thrust his fist into Li-Feng's nose with a crunch, causing him to grunt in pain. Yu-ra flinched as Li Feng stumbled back, masking his face with his hands. Observing the blood dripping from his nose, Li Feng flew into a rage, launching his fist at Kyung-tae. With little space to move, Kyung-tae just managed to block the incoming punch and seized his wrist. Twisting it behind his back, he booted the back of his knee to knock him down. Keeping his tight grasp on the wrist, he retrieved a zip tie from his back pocket.

"You're under arrest for assault," Kyung-tae said as he cuffed his wrists.

"You ain't got no evidence," Li-Feng cried out, as physical tears began to form on his eyelids, "you can't do shit!"

"A confession is as almost as good as any evidence. It helps that there's so many witnesses to corroborate that confession, countless cameras recording, as well the victim agreeing with the confession. Now, sit quietly."

Li Feng obviously didn't sit still and tried with all his might to break out of the ziptie. His wrists reddened as the plastic scrubbed against his skin.

"Hey," Yu-ra whispered, her voice no longer having an ounce of shakiness, "guess it pays off to have a robot husband. That punch must have hurt."

"I see what he meant now. You care more about him than me. The punch hurt my hand too, you know."

"Oh my God, stop," she whined, yet made deep eye contact with him.

"Are you okay, though?"

"Yeah, I'm doing just fine," she said, a grin spreading from ear to ear.

Kyung-tae couldn't help but smile back, her immensely hazel eyes sending chills down his spine. He had never seen hazel eyes so stunningly bright. And it was bizarre that he had never taken notice of her eyes before.

The train slowed and Kyung-tae tapped Li Feng with his foot as it came to a halt.

"Get up. We're going to the hospital before I take you in. We gotta go back two stops."

"I'm feeling a bit woozy," Li Feng said drowsily. "Do you mind cutting this crap off my wrists so I can maybe lie down a bit."

Kyung-tae turned to Yu-ra.

"I'll see you at home tonight."

"Okay, I'll see you later."

Kyung-tae shoved Li Feng along to the train in the opposite direction, countless eyes turning at them. After they reached the correct stop, he pushed him further through the crowds of commuters, out the station and down the streets that were lightly dusted with snow. They soon arrived at the hospital, the automatic door sliding open for them. Stale air wafted up his nostrils, sweet hints of alcohol, sour hints of sweat, and the bitter taste of disinfectant all mixed together. Keeping his hand on Li Feng's shoulder, they made their way to the reception. Kyung-tae was signing his name on a visiting sheet when he heard droplets tip tapping on the desk. The receptionist turned around from what she was doing, placing some tissues in front of him. Blood had trickled over his lips, droplets falling off his chin and onto the pile of tissues.

"I apologise, ma'am," Li Feng said, turning to show his wrists, "I'm in a bit of a bind here, so I couldn't stop myself from bleeding out all over your desk."

"I'm sorry about him," Kyung-tae said. "I know this isn't a walk-in clinic, but can anyone spare a minute or two to take a look at him? I'm taking him into custody after I visit a patient."

"I'll see if anyone is free," she said.

"Appreciate it, ma'am," Li Feng replied in a dazed state. "I think this twerp mighta brokeded my nose. See, I can't even formulated sentences proper-d-ly."

Tugging him back to the half empty waiting area, Kyung-tae pushed him down into a vacant seat, tossing the tissues onto his lap. He sat next to him as they waited for a doctor or a nurse to appear. Spraying her desk with something that added to the overpowering smell of disinfectant, the receptionist wiped down the whole surface. Soon a nurse came through the door and shortly behind him followed Chun-mi. The nurse kneeled in front of Li Feng while Kyung-tae stood up to greet Chun-mi.

"Hey, pretty boy," she said, beaming as she mussed his hair, "new haircut?"

Kyung-tae unconsciously jerked his head away.

"Pretty boy?"

"It's a compliment."

Kyung-tae ran his fingers through his hair before the strands swooped back down either side of his forehead. He wasn't used to having his hair so, what he felt, messy. He would always neatly slick it to one side, never having to feel his hair on his face. But, Yu-ra really liked the new style.

"This is how my hair was on my wedding day, so I don't know what you mean. Anyway, how's your dad doing?"

"He's a lot better. I just got him to settle down. I can't thank you enough for getting him here so fast." She lightly jabbed him in the shoulder. "What would we do without you?"

"My God!" Li Feng exclaimed. "I think I'm in love!"

"I'm flattered, sir," the nurse replied. "But could you focus on answering my questions?"

"No, not you. Her," he said, his eyes bulging as he gawked at Chun-mi, who brushed her hair back as she glanced at him. "The gods have blessed me today. Hey, twerp, you gonna introduce me or what?"

"I have a favour to ask," Kyung-tae said, motioning his head towards Li Feng. "Can you watch him just while I'm up there with your dad?"

"Sure thing, but you have to let me take you out somewhere fun in return for helping my dad."

"That's not necessary. He's my family too."

"Well it's either that or you take me out in return for looking after this guy."

"No, really it's okay."

"I insist. I'm not taking no for an answer."

Kyung-tae knew that she really would keep asking until he said yes. But it didn't feel right to spend a night out with just her. They weren't teenagers anymore. Maybe Yu-ra would be happy to join? It would be a nice way to integrate her into the family after all.

"Ok. I'll get back to you. I'll have to see if I can find time."

"I knew it!" Li Feng called. "Women don't cheat unless their men are already cheating. It's your fault your wife's such a spade."

"What's he talking about?" Chun-mi said, raising a brow. "He knows Yu-ra?"

"Long story. Forget about it," Kyung-tae said. "I'll ask Yu-ra if she is available and then let you know if we can come."

Chun-mi's eyes flickered with an array of emotions, but not one stayed pinned down.

"Ok. I'll get back to you if I have any free days. I'm generally quite busy, unfortunately."

The nurse stood up and turned to Kyung-tae.

"His nose is fine, just a nosebleed, albeit a bit of an extreme one."

"Thank you," Kyung-tae said.

The nurse turned back to Li Feng.

"Just lean forward for me. Oh, guess you can't pinch your nose since you're cuffed." The nurse twisted the tissues up and put them up his nostrils. "Breathe through your mouth. Put some ice on it later and it'll be fine."

"Thanks doc," Li Feng said in a nasally tone, shuffling to the side to get a better look at Chun-mi. "Now could you both leave me alone with the pretty lady."

With the plethora of encounters Kyung-tae had experienced of men hitting on Chun-mi, he knew she had to be extremely sick of it. It must have happened even more often when she was alone. But from the corner of his eye, Kyung-tae could have sworn he saw Chun-mi smirk.

Kyung-tae followed the nurse back deeper into the hospital. He split off from him and, as he walked down the confusing white hallways, the scent of disinfectant became weaker, replaced by the smell of old, and urine, and blood. As he passed by each open door, he heard machines beeping at varying speeds. And soon, he found himself at Mr Choi's personal room. He knocked before walking in and seeing Mr Choi sitting on the side of a bed layered in thick chequered blankets. He was slipping his arms through the sleeves of the shirt that Chun-mi had brought with her. His build was just as intimidating as the day he met him. A little less defined, sure, but even more brawny. The streaming light from the two-metre-wide window behind him illuminated just how large he was. Though he had a few more scars than that time - across his chest, his abdomen. In addition to the excessive number on his back. His side was bandaged up, but a few specks of blood still reached the surface.

"You look different," Mr Choi said, beginning to button up his shirt.

Kyung-tae brushed his fingertips against his hair.

"Just trying something new."

"It's not very neat, now is it? What if you're in a fight and your hair blows into your eyes."

"That's a good point. I didn't really think about that," Kyung-tae said as he itched his temple. "Are you going somewhere?"

"Home," Mr Choi said gruffly.

"What?" Kyung-tae furrowed his brow. "You can't, you need rest. Need I remind you that you got stabbed yesterday?"

"I'm fine. You're acting like I've never been stabbed before."

"So? Chun-mi paid a lot of money for this room, and you need the rest."

Coughing aggressively, Mr Choi lightly held the side of his abdomen.

"I'm not going to sit here and pretend I'm sick just to waste the doctor's time."

"Pretend you're sick? Look at you. They almost got you in the liver!"

"They didn't. And I have work to do."

Mr Choi stood up, tucking his shirt into his trousers.

"What work? You've been retired for eight years."

"Retired from police work."

Kyung-tae sighed.

"I know you have a billion battle scars, but I've never seen you get one with my own eyes. And I just want to make sure you recover properly."

"They patched me up. They did their job, and now I'm fine. Therefore I can leave."

"There's no talking you out of this is there?" Kyung-tae said, resigning his hands to rest on his hips.

"No. I can take care of myself."

"At least let me call ma. She can come over every couple hours to check up on you."

"No. Not only do I not want you inconveniencing your mother, she wouldn't want to either."

"Why wouldn't she want to?"

"Just do as I say."

Kyung-tae took a step back and held his hands out for Mr Choi to lead the way. He knew better than to think he could win an argument with him. Mr Choi combed his hair back before he exited the room. Kyung-tae followed him out and back down the hallways.

"What's the update on your case?" Mr Choi asked, holding his side as he navigated his way through the hospital.

"I tried to track those people through the waitress from the diner, but she claims she has no idea about them. I pressed really hard, but it didn't end up being fruitful."

"You did all this yesterday? When did you get time?"

Kyung-tae shrugged nonchalantly.

"After I brought you here, I went back to work."

"In the evening?"

"Yeah. Didn't get home until one in the morning yesterday."

"Alright. Good work so far. Keep me updated."

As they got closer to the reception at the entrance, a familiar husky voice bellowed in pain. Kyung-tae sped up and happened upon a scene similar to what he expected - Li Feng rolling around on the floor, hands still tied behind his back, blood and mucus streaming from his swollen nose. Chun-mi pressed her heel into his back to stop him from rolling around.

"Calm down, you baby," she mocked, leaning over him. "I didn't hit you that hard."

"If my nose weren't broken before, it for sure is now," Li Feng whimpered. "Twerp!" he cried as soon as he spotted Kyung-tae. "Call me a doctor!"

"Someone is already on the way," the receptionist said.

"What did you do!" Kyung-tae called out as he slowed to a stop in front of Chun-mi.

"He tried to escape, so I stopped him. You're the one who told me to watch him." She shrugged.

"His wrists are bound," he said, rubbing his temples in minor frustration, "wasn't there an easier way to restrain him?"

"Not any that were as fun." She smirked, pressing her heel further into his back, causing him to yelp in pain.

"Hey, twerp," he said through heavy breaths as he looked up at Kyung-tae. "Remember how I said people are into weird stuff these days? I feel weirdly okay with this."

"What are you, a masochist?"

"Probably. Whatever that means."

Mr Choi stood behind Kyung-tae, stiff shouldered and hands clasped behind his back.

"Do I need to be concerned with what's going on?"

Kyung-tae waved dismissively.

"I've got everything under control. And so does Chun-mi, clearly."

A doctor arrived and took in the scene, rubbing his tired eyes before approaching this new patient of his. As Chun-mi removed her heel from his backside, Kyung-tae heaved him up by the cuff around his wrist.

"No! Please!" Li Feng cried. "Leave me with her!"

"Dad, I see you're up and about after I told you no," she said, ignoring Li-Feng.

"As stubborn as ever," Kyung-tae said, then gestured to his perp. "I've got to deal with all this that you've left me with. Can you take him home?"

"I'm glad to see you two are still getting closer," Mr Choi said, a ghost of a smile crossing his lips, "family is everything after all."

Chun-mi rolled her eyes again but still beamed at Kyung-tae.

"You piece of crap!" Li Feng yelled. "You bow down in worship when that goddess smiles in your direction!"

The doctor pressed down on the plastic bandage-like wrapping around his nose and Li Feng crumpled up his body in pain again.

"Your nose will be fine in a week or two. Don't remove this cast. It will realign your nose without the need for surgery. Take two of these antibiotics every morning and night to reduce the swelling." He began to scribble on a notepad. "Here's your receipt for the treatment. You can pay at the front desk."

"I ain't got any money. You mind covering for me, twerp? You know, seeing as this is all your fault."

Sighing deeply, Kyung-tae pressed the bridge of his nose.

"You mind covering this for me?"

"Sure," Chun-mi said before making her way to the front desk to pay the bill.

"Sh-she paid for me." Li Feng sniffled, tears now streaming down his cheek. "THIS WOMAN HAS A HEART OF GOLD, EVERYBODY! TELL THE WORLD OF HER HEROISM AND HER BEAUTY! SHE IS TOO PURE FOR THIS DIRTBALL OF A PLANET!"

"Quiet down, sir," one of the nurses passing by called.

Mr Choi and Chun-mi bowed before they went on their way and Kyung-tae simply waved in response. As this occurred, Li Feng fell to the floor, arm stretched out to Chun-mi.

"Wait! At least tell me your name, my queen!"

A crushing weight began pinching at the bridge of Kyung-tae's eyebrows as he heaved Li Feng up by the arm and dragged him out the door.

****

Down in the basement of the precinct, a tall spindly scientist with pale bony fingers and a large beard slid a tray of vials back into their slot in a wooden cabinet. The metallic table clinged and clanged as he tapped his skeletal joints against it, waiting for his appointment to arrive. Like the teeth of a comb, he ran his fingers through his beard to straighten it out as he eyed the stainless-steel door that was painted a pale shade of blue. The room was cramped and dimly lit, furthering his annoyance. He sat down in his wheeled chair and moved closer to the door. It seemed this detective he awaited thought he had nothing better to do than complete last-minute jobs overnight for him. And now he couldn't even be bothered to turn up on time.

A slim man with a nice haircut burst through the door, a single droplet of sweat dripping down his forehead.

"What's the news doc?" the detective said, resting his weight on the table.

"Are you making fun of me?" the scientist said, his bushy eyebrows turning almost parallel out of frustration.

"What?" the detective asked earnestly.

The scientist banged his bony fist against the table.

"Just because I've been a university student for the past twenty years without finishing my PhD does not give you the right to make fun of me!"

"I-I didn't know that. I don't even know your name."

"Exactly my point!"

"What?" the detective said, shaking his head, seemingly as a reflex.

"You heard me!"

"Ok, then I apologise. What's your name?"

"Stop wasting my time!"

"You're the one not answering my initial question!" the detective snapped, slapping himself in the forehead. "We could have been done with this interaction two minutes ago."

"I don't like you." The scientist sneered, narrowing his eyes.

"Yeah. I can tell," the detective said, hands on his hips. "Can we get a move on?"

Swivelling off his chair, the scientist began circling the room with his hands clasped behind his back.

"I will finish my PhD soon. I just need to get the last set of results."

"Thank you for that information, but I didn't really ask. So, could I just get the information on that substance?"

"It's because the microscopes at the lab keep breaking down!" he bellowed, pointing an index finger to the sky. "I certainly have not been tampering with the equipment to hide the fact that I can't get any meaningful results."

The detective paused, analysing the shifty eyed man.

"Have you been tampering with the microscopes at your lab to hide your lack of meaningful results?"

"NO! I just said I have not!"

"Well, I couldn't care less as long as you haven't been tampering with my results. So, tell me what you found."

The spindly scientist slid a brown envelope across the metal table. Kyung-tae tore open the top and slid the file out onto the desktop.

"I don't know what it is. I've never seen a compound such as this. I do know this though – it is highly combustible."

"How do you know?"

The scientist pointed at his left eyebrow, the corner of which was singed.

"Experimentation," he said simply.

"So you don't know the chemical make-up of it? Or what it would be used for?"

"To me, it looks like it could be a makeshift explosive. What they would need to explode, I have no idea."

"That part's my job."

The door burst open again, another detective ploughing through the entrance. This one was a stout man with a goatee and short spiky hair. As he approached them, the man was wringing his hands together and biting his lip.

"Woo-young?" the first detective said, twisting his body to face the entrance.

"I've got something to tell you," the new detective, Woo-young, replied nervously.

"Spit it out then, boy," the scientist said, achieving a confused look from both detectives.

"There was a body found frozen in Han River," Woo-young said.

"Frozen?" the detective replied.

"Well, the girl they found, they say she matches the description of Kim Sun-Jung."

"What?"

"They haven't confirmed it yet, but they're doing a DNA test now. I just thought I'd let you kn-"

The detective shoved past Woo-young towards the entrance.

"I'll go confirm it myself," he said as he kicked the door open.

****

Driving in these conditions would be dangerous. The train system was much more reliable, but hell if that was going to stop him. Kyung-tae slipped a key off the hook for one of the undercover cars. Striding straight past the booth to sign out vehicles, he slipped into the car that his key unlocked - a sleek, Japanese, silver sedan. After strapping himself in, he zoomed off.

After a few slips on the road and a stop for Woo-young to send him the coordinates, Kyung-tae finally arrived at the riverside. The bridge above it was lit up brighter than the entire city skyline and the river completely frozen over, except a small inlet near the edge of the river from the old sewage system that was cracked open - the place where the body was found. A private ambulance was near the river, the driver conversing with the beat cop who was the first to arrive at the scene. Bolting down the steps and across the grand concrete pathway between them, Kyung-tae called out before the driver could close the back of the ambulance.

"Wait!" he shouted, pulling out his badge. "Detective Oh. I need to see the body you found."

Kyung-tae dragged the sheet halfway down from the corpse's head. The short black, now soggy hair matched every image he had of her. The thin eyebrows, the deep brown eyes, the spotted skin, they did too. But her eyes, they were lifeless. Her skin was a pale blue, and her entire body, head to toe, was stiff as a bone. He pulled back the sheet entirely off her face. River water still leaked from the corners of her mouth and Kyung-tae's eyes began to burn from the liquid film beginning to coat them. Jaw tightening, he crumpled the sheet in his fist.

Too slow. Too slow. He was too slow, yet again. It was all his fault. No matter how hard he tried, he was still too slow.

He flung his other fist at the ambulance wall but then pulled his fist back just before he hit it. Loosening his fist, he simply placed his fingertips against the wall.

What was the point in being angry? He just needed to be better. He couldn't protect her. He couldn't protect any of them. It wasn't his first instance seeing corpses. Far from it. But this one in particular twisted his innards. Kyung-tae kept his sight on the girl's face, his vision slightly blurring. There was no denying it, her face was engraved in his mind. This was the corpse of Kim Sun-Jung. The corpse of the girl that he was tasked with saving.

# 7
# Takemi

Yu-ra rubbed her sighing eyes. After three and a half hours of constant typing, her net total work had amounted to absolutely nothing. One loan shark with no follow up on what happened to him? Who would care about that? Kyung-tae booked him, but who knows how long that would last. And that booking had nothing to do with the loans in the first place. She was too involved for that to be a story. Everything she wrote only felt average, and average wouldn't cut it.

Her vision slightly blurred as she dropped her hands, the harsh lighting of the library stabbing at her weary eyes. The second floor of the library was a dedicated study space, decked out entirely with smooth, polished wooden desks accompanied with long overhead lamps that spanned the length of the desks. Yet, the floor was entirely empty, save herself.

She was getting nowhere with this story. This Li-feng character obviously wasn't working alone. A meathead such as him would likely be nothing more than a debt collector. He wouldn't have the funds to provide the loans himself.

Yu-ra packed her things away and slugged her bag over her shoulder. Strolling down the stairs of the empty second floor, she passed through the aisles of thick oak shelves, brushing her finger along the rough ridges worn into the spines of the books. She wasn't looking for anything in particular. Maybe she was hoping something would catch her eye, or for something to give her inspiration. But more than anything, she just liked the sound of the covers tapping against her finger. She knew traipsing around the whole city day in and day out was going to burn her out faster than going to university did, but walking helped clear her head.

Oh, of course! The solution was so obvious. It came to her as she arrived at the library entrance and then a few minutes later a street market. Li-Feng was a meathead who needed someone to tell him what to do! If she found out who this leader was, it was bound to prove her investigative prowess. She could probably uncover a whole network of loans.

Dangling paper lanterns criss-crossed the cluster of backstreets she traversed, and a myriad of restaurant signs jutted out of the buildings shrouding her. She figured a good way to start her investigation would be to find out if anyone else was having trouble with debt collectors. And the area that she found Li-feng was sure to be the best place to start.

A group of rowdy men passed by her on an uncrowded street, and she turned away, withdrawing herself. She attempted to enter one of the restaurants but a large closing sign blocked her path, her soles scraping against the ground as she broke her momentum. The gang took notice, but Yu-ra had sped off towards the next road over before she could even catch a glimpse of them.

Continuing through the array of side roads, she made her way towards the main streets. No one had been around for quite a few blocks, but every now and then she would hear the sound of shuffling snow getting closer. Did that gang of men follow her? No, that was an unreasonable assumption. Yet, even after reassuring herself, the uneasy feeling from when they had passed her still hadn't left.

She quickened her pace. The shuffling also quickened. Definitely not a coincidence. Yu-ra doubled her speed, almost breaking out into a sprint. But the shuffling didn't stop. It had gotten so close that it was almost adjacent to her. And then it stopped.

Her peripherals fell silent as she slowed herself. Was she imagining things? Glancing back to reassure herself, she collided with a narrow immovable object. Yu-ra's behind slammed against the ground as she slid back a short distance. A sharp pain jolted through her tailbone and immediately began to throb. A leather gloved hand fell in front of her face but she peered past it to see a figure in a forest-green wooden mask eerily cock its head. There was an absence of facial features on the mask, no nose or mouth. The eyes were thin and long, and seemingly purposeful cracks traced from the forehead across them, reminiscent of a battle-worn helmet.

Another crack slashed the space in between the eyes. Yu-ra tried to force her body to shift away but she was frozen in place.

The figure crouched down, hand still reaching.

"Wanna hang out?" it said with a soft, muffled voice relaxing her ears.

"W-what?" Yu-ra stammered.

A southern twang crept into the figure's accent which sounded bizarrely familiar.

"There's an arcade nearby, we could go play some video games." Messy silver bangs hung over parts of the forehead of the mask. It was as if their mother forgot to brush it when she dressed them in their long flowing hooded jacket. The rest of their clothes were oversized too as if wearing their older brother's clothes because their father told them they'd grow into it. "We can play Dancing Fever 3 or maybe do some karaoke. I know you'll love that."

"H-huh?"

The figure finally pushed up their sinister mask, their hair brushing back with it. It was a woman, a tall one. Her sharp eyes and jawline were not what she was expecting to see. Maybe it was the worn eyes, but she didn't think she would look so mature. Examining the woman's eyes a little more closely, she felt a familiarity with her. But it wasn't possible, surely. She couldn't be who she thought she was, right? How would she even know where to find her?

"Takemi?"

"Yes! It is I, in the flesh!" she bellowed, followed by a manic laugh, "your favourite person in the world!"

Yu-ra slapped her hand away.

"You scared the crap out of me, you idiot!" she said, picking herself up off the ground and wiping her now wet hands on her knees.

She massaged the base of her spine, just barely easing her back pain.

"What'd I do?"

She wasn't speaking Japanese anymore, reaffirming she was the Takemi she grew up with. Yu-ra began speaking in Korean too.

"How long were you following me for? Like fifteen minutes straight? You'll give me high blood pressure, you idiot!" Yu-ra pulled Takemi in and hugged her tightly. She was warmer than she thought she would be, given her cold aura. "I missed you, you giant baby."

"Following you?" Takemi said, pulling back from her with a sudden sullen face. "You bumped into me." Before Yu-ra even had time to react, Takemi cut in once again. "Wait, I lied. Before you run off again, it was me."

Yu-ra sighed as she massaged the bridge of her nose.

"How did you even know where to find me?"

"Oh please, I just need to look around for a girl with a scarf on her head."

"There's more than one Muslim girl in Korea."

"Not that I've ever seen," Takemi said, shrugging.

"That doesn't mean they don't exist. I could have been anyone. How did you really find me? You didn't even know I live in Seoul."

A faint siren had begun to holler in the distance.

"I wasn't joking about the arcade, by the way. Let's go right now."

"Answer my question."

Takemi took her wrist and pulled her along in the direction she was walking.

"I told you already."

"No, you didn't," Yu-ra said, yanking her hand back, "and don't grab me like that."

"I'm like one of those sniffer dogs. I'm good at finding stuff."

The siren whirred even louder, accompanied by flashing lights that ricocheted from wall to wall.

"And why did you choose now to turn up? Are you on a military break?" she babbled. "Are you stationed here? Why come here and not go back home? This is so weird. I haven't seen you since we were teenagers." Takemi took her hand and started jogging towards her destination. "Where are you taking me? Hey, are you even listening?" The siren had gotten ever closer. Yu-ra yanked her hand away again. "Stop! You can't just drag me around the city as if we've seen each other in the past six years. Where are you taking me?"

Takemi finally turned to look at her, albeit sheepishly.

"I need your help to lay low."

"Lay low? From whom? For what?"

Takemi scratched the back of her head.

"I, uhh, kind of quit the military."

"You quit," Yu-ra said, pinching her furrowed brows, "your mandatory enlistment?"

"I deserted," Takemi said, twisting the tip of her shoe into the ground.

"Are you crazy?" she blurted. "Isn't that an extremely severe offence?"

"Shh!" Takemi said, throwing her palm over Yu-ra's mouth, "worse than you know."

Yu-ra tugged Takemi's hand away.

"You know I'm all for sticking it to the man, but please tell me it's not because you're still in your phase of quitting everything halfway through."

"No."

"Are you lying to me? Please do not lie to me right now because I will actually slap you."

"I couldn't take it anymore, okay!"

"What do you mean?"

"I just couldn't take it anymore, okay?"

"Takemi," Yu-ra said with a frown as she placed her hand on her shoulder, staring up at her darkening expression, "what happened?"

"How about this!" she said suddenly perking up, as she pointed her index finger to the sky as if a lightbulb switched on in her mind, "if you beat me in a round of Street Kings Twelve, I'll tell you what happened."

As Takemi nudged her with her elbow playfully, Yu-ra realised where they were, looking up at the bright arcade sign.

"Whatever," she said. "I wanted to get out of the cold anyway."

Takemi bolted towards the back of the arcade as soon as they had entered and Yu-ra jogged after her as fast as her relatively tiny legs would let her. When she arrived, Takemi was already engrossed in the game that she had challenged Yu-ra in. Astounded at the constant combos she was landing, Yu-ra caught her up on the struggle to find a graduate job since Takemi had gone silent. She had never known Takemi to be secretive, so it was strange that she wasn't being entirely open about her experience with the army. In fact she always had the problem of talking too much. She could never keep her big mouth shut. It was probably the reason Yu-ra was one of the few people that actually stuck with her for so long.

After Takemi had played a few rounds, she finally challenged Yu-ra. She offered Yu-ra a few practice rounds, but it didn't seem like she would ever reach the level of Takemi, so it didn't feel like there was any point to that. Her strategy would be the same regardless of how much practice she had: spam buttons randomly. Unpredictability was her best weapon.

The round began and Yu-ra immediately began slamming her fingers into every button she could find, while simultaneously shimmying the joystick in all directions. She managed to land a barrage of hits on Takemi's character, but Takemi very quickly saw what she was doing and carefully set in motion a precise combo that knocked her down to half her health. Takemi then began jumping aimlessly around the stage. Yu-ra took this opportunity to begin spamming again and somehow managed to cut her down to zero health.

"Woo!" Yu-ra blurted, jumping up and down with her arms in the air, "eat that!"

"Alright, you win," Takemi said in an unusually calm manner. Another thing that Yu-ra wasn't used to seeing.

"I do."

"Before I was drafted," Takemi said, lowering her head as she leaned back against the machine, "I would always hear about how you can choose how you serve after initial training. General, military police, civil servant, even military band if you have the necessary skills. Sounds great, right?"

"Yeah," Yu-ra said, smiling, "you could finish your whole eight years serving your country and never have to put yourself in any danger."

"And why would the job require anything particularly special from me?"

Takemi sighed. "I don't know, maybe I tried too hard in training, maybe it was natural talent that I never knew I had, but something made me stand out. They assigned me to an elite special forces team, and for a while I loved it, just hanging out with my squad, training day in and day out. Then they shipped us out. Taiwan."

"What made serving in Taiwan particularly hard? It's not like they were shipping you out halfway across the world. Everyone shows utmost respect to the Japanese military, especially in Taiwan."

"That's what I told myself too. They taught us at school that all the colonies are at peace, after all. For the most part, that's true." Yu-ra kept a close eye on her as she continued on. "We got our first assignment, a rising faction of rebels. We dealt with it swiftly, but the way we dealt with it...something felt off. Then we got our second assignment, and our third, and our fourth, fifth, sixth, seventh. The point is sooner or later, it got to a stage where I just couldn't take it anymore, so I got up and left."

"Still, deserting seems like an extreme reaction. You couldn't hold out for one more year?"

"With all due respect, and that's none, you've never served. And you sure as shit didn't serve my time."

"Alright, calm down," Yu-ra said, waving her down. "I just didn't understand the depth of the problem."

"Well, now you have an inkling. That should be enough."

"Okay. We'll figure something out for you."

They began playing Street Kings once again, but the rounds went nothing like the last time. Yu-ra barely managed to land any hits.

"So, will you help me hide from the authorities?" Takemi asked.

"Don't worry, I said we'd figure something out for you, didn't I?" Yu-ra said, trying her hardest to concentrate only on the game in front of her. "If you're staying in Seoul it might be a bit tricky but one of my friends may be able to give you a place to stay."

"Where are you staying now?" Takemi asked, her head turning in all directions, "university dorms, or with your parents still? Let me crash with you for a while."

Yu-ra chuckled.

"I don't think my husband will appreciate me bringing home some random woman."

"Random?" Takemi said, her hands falling still. "Husband?" she said with even more shock in her voice. Yu-ra took this opportunity to batter her opponent into the twilight of her health bar. "BRINGING?" Takemi yelled.

"What's wrong with you?" Yu-ra said, slapping Takemi's arm. "Shut up."

Takemi averted her gaze back to the video game, continuing to play as if nothing had happened. "He might be fine with it, but it would be pretty bad for me to put a strain on the relationship only a couple days after getting married."

Takemi stopped looking at the screen, her character proceeding to get beaten to a pulp, leading to a victory screen.

"Wait...HUSBAND?" she blurted.

"I see you're finally caught up with the conversation."

"What?" she cried. "Who in their right mind would ever marry you? Is he ugly? He has to be ugly, come on."

"He's just some guy."

"Some guy?"

"A family friend, kind of."

"No, I'm a family friend. Who is this guy? How did you meet him? Why don't I know him? How long have you known him? What are his real motives? Because I seriously can't understand right now."

"You're asking too many questions. Also shut up, I'm a damn catch. All you need to know is that I met him through a family friend and we've known of each other for almost a year."

"A year is not long enough."

"Who gets to decide it isn't? Different people progress at different speeds."

"I thought you were more independent than this."

"How does choosing to get married take away your independence?"

"You know what marriage is like, you become a servant for your husband's family."

"His family isn't like that."

"How would you know? You've only just got married. People change once they get comfortable."

"I just couldn't stand living at home anymore, so maybe I rushed the process. So sue me. It doesn't change the fact that he's the first decent man I've ever met."

"I'll make that decision for myself. I don't think any decent person would be trying to get something out of you, and he definitely is."

"Yeah, a wife."

Takemi looked away, pondering for a moment.

"I could kick his ass."

"What?"

"You heard me," Takemi said, punching Yu-ra's shoulder.

"I don't see why he would get into a fight with a girl, but no you couldn't."

"How…how dare you?" Takemi bemoaned. "Organise the fight, I'm begging you. I'll prove it to you right here and now."

"What is up with you?" Yu-ra said, raising her brow. "You could not take my husband in a fight, so keep dreaming about it."

"I'll follow you home and when he arrives, I'll break his nose and tell him I only did it to prove you wrong."

"I'm being deadly serious. He took down a guy almost twice his size, today. It was insane!"

"That guy was probably a wimp. I'd wager my life savings that even you'd drop him."

"Well...I did do that. But that's beside the point. My husband is as tough as a rock," Yu-ra said, patting Takemi on the cheek condescendingly.

"Really? You're calling him 'my husband' to people, now?"

"What do you want me to call him? The guy I'm living with whom I happen to be married to?"

"I want to know the name of my nemesis."

"Nemesis? What are you, a cartoon villain?"

"He's my nemesis, not the other way around. He's the villain."

Yu-ra mussed her hair.

"Whatever you say, kiddo."

"ARGH!" She rubbed her head in frustration. "I'm being serious. I'll mess him up."

"Okay, you can have whatever opinion you choose. I'll just believe in the facts."

"Yu-ra!" she whined, "I'm a grown adult. You can't bully me anymore."

"Oh my, you should see his muscles," Yu-ra said, fanning herself with her hand. "His forearms are so toned."

"Ew, stop! I don't want to know about his body!"

Yu-ra finally stopped holding back her chuckle.

"Relax, I'm joking."

"Wait, does that mean you've seen him, you know..." She gave her a suggestive look.

"What?"

"...without a shirt on?"

Yu-ra slapped Takemi's arm.

"Ew, no! I told you I was joking. Calm yourself, please. Besides, have you never heard of a t-shirt?"

Suddenly another siren interrupted them, one that was so loud that it must have been coming from the same street that they were on.

"We need to go. Now." Takemi said, sliding her mask down. "Follow me."

Takemi led her deeper into the arcade, weaving through the masses of consoles, until they found the fire exit. They crept through the alley towards the next road over, but someone called out to them, causing Yu-ra to freeze up. Takemi took her arm and pulled her along.

"Ms Tsukuda, it'd be in your best interest to stop there," the voice called out. Takemi halted and turned to see who was speaking.

"You know me?"

"I do. I'm surely the only one in the world who truly does. You're a celebrity to me, Ms Tsukuda. My saving grace, my salvation, my hero. You, you're an integral part of my investigation."

Yu-ra finally turned around. A prosecutor's badge hung from the neck of the very tall, traditionally handsome man in question., He wore a plain grey suit that looked a little baggy, which was unusual since everything else about him was precisely measured, down to his short haircut. Behind his rectangular glasses, his shifty eyes were taking in everything around them, but they never settled on Yu-ra, as if she was of no concern to him.

"Listen pal, I can't help you with whatever you think I can. If there's anything else, find me during my office hours."

"You seem to have misunderstood me, Ms Tsukuda. You don't get a choice in this matter. You're under arrest."

"Take a couple steps back," Takemi muttered.

The prosecutor's eyes finally settled on Yu-ra, his hands outstretched as if calming a wild animal.

"Woah there, ma'am. You should stay still. You're under arrest too."

"What?" Yu-ra's voice cracked, a look of puzzlement on her face.

"What?" Takemi echoed.

The prosecutor's gaze shifted back to Takemi.

"You were harbouring a criminal. Granted there's no arrest warrant out for her, but she is a criminal."

"Sir, whatever business you have with Takemi, I promise you I'm not involved. I'm just an old friend of hers who happened to bump into her."

"If that's the case then you should have nothing to worry about. A simple investigation will sort everything out."

"Sir, please, I'm just a student from Maewha university. I can show you my id."

"Don't worry, Yu-ra," Takemi said. "Everything will be fine."

Takemi stuck her wrists out towards the prosecutor, who watched carefully, eyeing everything he could about Takemi in a matter of seconds. Then he stepped forward.

"Before you do what you're about to do, just remember you're endangering more than just yourself."

Takemi looked back at Yu-ra, worry wrought on her face. She dropped her hands, turning around, and the prosecutor took up her wrists to cuff her.

"Sir!" Yu-ra said, starting to get annoyed, but more anxious than anything, "I really didn't do anything wrong. I don't know what you want from me."

"Ma'am, the sooner you cooperate, the sooner I can set you free. If you are as innocent as you claim, that is." Yu-ra sighed. What else could she do, apart from co-operate, in a situation such as this? She held her wrists out and the prosecutor bound them together. "What's your name?"

"Baek Yu-ra."

"Well, Ms Baek, Ms Tsukuda, you have the right to remain silent. You have the right to have an attorney at the trial, if you are prosecuted. You do not have the right to see an attorney before trial or have one present during interrogations. If you cannot afford an attorney, one will be appointed for you."

# 8
# Kim Sun-jung

*Dispatch strongly advised Mrs. Oh to remain hidden and to maintain communication until law enforcement arrived on the scene.*

*- Case Number 1996-2786*

As Kyung-tae scoured the riverbanks and the bridge above, a female detective investigated Kim Sun-jung's body. Everything he found led him to one undeniable truth. There were no signs of struggle, her skin, though shrivelled, was flawlessly intact, suggesting that no harm came to her while she was alive. There was also no trace of anyone being present with her. After spotting some nearby cameras, he tracked down the local footage from which he discovered her trajectory. She wasn't pushed, she didn't jump, she simply stepped off. All of the signs… it wasn't a murder. He would have to wait a couple hours for the autopsy report, but he knew that it would just act as an official confirmation for what he had already found. It was suicide. Was it worth going back to that spindly man for that? All of this open space, an empty bridge, and yet there was nothing there that could suggest anything but suicide.

*Why are you still doing this job? If you keep failing, wouldn't it be better for you to quit? Surely if you weren't there to make these mistakes, they wouldn't occur. Just quit your job. You hate it anyway. You hate seeing dead bodies. You hate having to see battered and bruised wives. You hate having to see thieves and drug dealers get away scott-free.*

*No. You can't quit. What does it make you if you have the capability to protect people and you choose not to?*

The endless thoughts wrapped against the walls of his skull. Though he had no reason to march there, his destination made itself clear - the diner that Kim Sun-jung was employed at. And thus, his legs carried him there autonomously.

A new waitress that Kyung-tae hadn't met was at the counter. He asked for her to call the waitress he had met the other day.

"Well, isn't she popular with the men," she quipped before walking into the kitchen to get her. They both came out from the back and the new waitress went off to attend to the influx of customers.

"Hey there, Detective Oh, was it?" she beamed. "Anything I can help you with?"

"We found Miss Kim." Her smile dropped and a befuddled look crossed her face. "I'm sorry." Her confusion disappeared into a frown, and her eyes began to water. "We found her drowned in the Han River."

She gulped but her eyes stopped watering.

"Drowned?"

"Drowned. All the evidence points to suicide."

"That's horrible. I didn't think she would be capable of such an act."

"Neither did I. You probably know this, but Miss Kim had a nice family, loving parents. They were stricken with grief the moment she went missing. A decent number of people rallied to find this girl - this student, working a part time job at a shabby, exploitative restaurant. A job is a job for students, doesn't matter where it is, so I don't blame her for working here. She even helped out in the community on occasion. A regular role model. Someone with a future. So her character, to me, doesn't seem like a suicidal one."

"Well, that's the problem with mental health," she said as she mindlessly played with her hair. "You can never tell how bad it is for someone."

What an odd reaction.

"Just out of curiosity, who was that man you were with the other night?"

"What man?" she said, dropping her hands.

"The one you were with last night."

"I wasn't with anyone," she said innocently.

"You sure? You weren't with a guy in a leather jacket, medium length brown hair?"

"I'm sure."

What? Was she blatantly lying? Why would she lie about that?

"That surprises me, because I'm certain I saw you with a man. He had his arm wrapped around you. I'd have thought someone like that would be memorable."

"Oh… him," she said monotonously.

"Your memory seems to have come back all of a sudden."

"I barely know him." She shrugged. "I completely forgot about our interaction."

"You seemed pretty cosy to me."

"I met him at a bar, and we hit it off. If it goes anywhere, it won't last. He's a bit of a playboy, if you ask me."

"I didn't. And I don't care about him. You were with a gang of people who were searching for a substance I found."

"Never heard of no gang with us."

"And your boyfriend? How's he involved with them?"

She shrugged again.

"Ain't my boyfriend and I don't know who 'them' is."

Once again the manager came bursting through the door. Perfect timing.

"You get out my restaurant, right now!" he yelled, pointing at Kyung-tae, instantly grabbing the attention of all the customers.

"Mr Lee, just who I was hoping to see."

"You love causing problem, don't you? Get out or I call your superiors and tell them to fire you!"

"Last time I came here asking about Miss Kim, I was awfully suspicious of you. I just want to apologise for that."

"What me? You call me awful?"

"No. I mean I thought you were involved with Miss Kim's disappearance."

"You crazy!"

"And I'm apologising about that. But you didn't fix your financial reports, did you?"

Mr Lee's angry demeanour softened, almost into one of fear.

"I-I did. I don't know what you talk about."

"You understand that it's my duty to bring you in, yes?"

"I-I…" he began to fumble over his words.

"You have the right to remain silent," Kyung-tae began as he motioned for Ji-min to turn his back towards him. Ji-min backed away slightly, much to Kyung-tae's annoyance. Immediately, he lunged for the back of Ji-min's head and slammed it down onto the counter, holding him down as he cried out. The room filled with gasps and the waitresses cowered behind the counter.

Continuing to read Ji-min his rights, Kyung-tae enclosed a zip tie around his wrists and pulled him out of his own restaurant.

# 9
# Sung-jae

*I'm tired of this. Tired of writing about mum day in and day out. Tired of running into her disapproving gaze at every corner, silently judging every move and word spoken. The fact that she traps me in the house like a mouse in a cage, never trusting me to go out alone. Dad still isn't taking my side. And that's fine, because now I realise. I realise that no one really has my best interests at heart. I can rely on nobody but myself.*

*- Tuesday 9th September 2008*
*Diary of Baek Yu-ra*

Yu-ra wriggled her left wrist, trying to find a more comfortable position for her cuffed hand attached to the long dressing table at the foot of the hotel bed. The fluffy red carpet soothed the soreness of her feet from all the travelling she had done that day. A rich floral scent had been dispersed into the air from the jasmine air freshener sitting above her head. There was no doubt that the bed linen also smelled just as sweet. The sensual aura of the room was quite discomforting given the context of her situation. Why a hotel room and not a jail cell? What was more disturbing was that the prosecutor and Takemi must have been in the room next door for over forty-five minutes at the very least.

Suddenly, a sharp click echoed as a card slotted into the door, followed by the distinct clunk of the handle turning. The door crept open, and the prosecutor's head poked in swiftly before he entered the room entirely. He strode across the floor and settled himself firmly at the foot of the bed, though his legs tucked back with a hint of awkwardness. Yu-ra's gaze remained fixed on him, anticipating.

"I guess I'll go first," he said, holding his hand out to her. "Prosecutor Choi Sung-jae, pleasure to make your acquaintance."

"As I've said countless times, I didn't do anything wrong," she said, ignoring his hand. "I wasn't harbouring her. I only bumped into her an hour before you. Wrong place, wrong time, that's all it was."

He slipped her phone from his pocket, presenting it to her.

"I'll give you some time to make a phone call. However, there won't be any bailing you out of this. I'm afraid you got caught up with a very high class of criminal."

Wrinkles formed on the bridge of Yu-ra's nose as she swiped her phone back and tossed it into her bag.

"I don't need bail. A simple investigation will prove me innocent, so get on with it." Yu-ra pressed her feet into the carpet more to stop her legs from showing any signs of trembling. "And if this takes too long, I will be going directly to your superiors," she said with an upturned nose.

Sung-jae chuckled at her comment.

"While I commend you on the effort, Ms Tsukuda has attested otherwise. She told me all about your plans to hide her away."

Yu-ra raised a brow.

"She said what?"

"She was tough to crack," he said, standing up as his shifty eyes darted around her before settling. What was he looking for? "But once I found out how to sweet talk her, her mouth ran like a river. She sure is talkative, that one."

"Yeah," Yu-ra said, eyes narrowing, "she doesn't know when to shut up."

Sung-jae crossed the room and gazed out of the large window.

"I've had a look at your record. Baek Yu-ra, single, Maewha University student, comes from a working class family." He turned back to her, crossing his arms tightly. "I feel as though I can trust you."

Single? Had her marriage certificate not already been processed?

"You can!" Yu-ra blurted, almost jumping up before the tug of her handcuff made her settle back down, "so, listen to what I have to say - I'm innocent! I-n-n-o-c-e-n-t. You know what that spells, right?" She raised her free hand to her cuffed one and began to clap sarcastically beside her head.

"Yep! You've got it, INNOCENT!"

"Believe me, I don't want you to go to jail. You've got no prior offences and it's going to spoil your record and your whole life."

"Then let me go."

"I'm prepared to offer you the same deal that I offered Takemi. A clean slate. Anything done in the past is wiped away and forgotten, for both of you. I will even help Takemi stay hidden from the military."

"I want a lawyer."

"I'm afraid that you don't have that right, Ms Baek."

Yu-ra sighed, taking a momentary pause.

"It's Mrs."

"Ah. Right. Well-"

"And my husband is a decorated police officer." Yu-ra's jaw firmed as she cut her eyes at him, "so this is my last warning for you to tread lightly."

"However you think that will play out, it won't end up in your favour. He has no sway over a verdict. It would actually end up being both career and social suicide for you to go to court."

Yu-ra scoffed.

"Like I'm going to believe you."

"Right. Well, as part of Ms Tsukuda's confession, she happened to have part of a voice recording with you," he said, taking another phone out of his pocket. He waved it at her, then tossed it onto the bed, "a damning recording. It's an open and shut case, I'm afraid."

"What? You're lying. There's absolutely no way she would ever have something like that."

Gliding over to the bed, Sung-jae retrieved the phone. After a few seconds of fidgeting, a familiar conversation played out from the device.

Yu-ra's head sank. Six years really did change a person. Perhaps it was the time that changed her, or perhaps it was the time spent with the Japanese military that turned her into a schemer.

"Whatever it is that you want from me," she said softly, "I can't help you. I really wish I could."

Sung-jae sat back down on the bed, just as upright as before, but planted his feet firmly in front of himself.

"I just need some eyes and ears I can trust. If Ms Tsukuda would sell you out so quickly, how can I be sure that she won't sell me out just as easily?" Yu-ra remained silent. "On top of that, Ms Tsukuda has been working within the criminal underworld for quite some time now. I can't be certain where her loyalties lie."

"It couldn't have been that long. She's been in the military since she was sixteen."

"She deserted a few years ago - only served two and a half out of seven years."

"So, you're saying she's been a criminal for the last three and a half years?"

"As far as I can tell."

What was she to do? Was it true that Kyung-tae wouldn't be able to help her? Was it true that if she involved him, it would hurt him? Kyung-tae was an honourable man, even if she told him not to help, she had a feeling that he would be okay with character assassination if it kept her safe. She couldn't let that happen to him.

The recording said she would help Takemi, but there were never any specifics. If she had yet to go through with it, would it really hold up in court? This man was a prosecutor? What purpose would he find in lying? And if he really did believe she was an innocent person, would he really involve her in a criminal investigation? Maybe it was the only way he could get her out of jail time legally.

"I don't have to do anything apart from make sure Takemi doesn't lie?"

"You, Mrs Baek, are going undercover with her," Sung-jae said, clasping his hand as he sat forward. "Takemi has the hard job - she needs to find a way to disrupt the entire distribution and supply line, as well as helping orchestrate opportunities for me to step in. With your help, Mrs Baek, I'll be able to take down one of the largest crime syndicates in the country."

"And this is the only way for me to go free?"

"I'm afraid it was the only solution I can think of without the effects staining your record."

Yu-ra sank down again.

"You can drop the honorifics," she said, defeated, "just call me Yu-ra."

"You see, Yu-ra, the problem with this gang is that it is very hard to identify members. The only sure-fire way to know is that they babble in a foreign language to each other."

"How am I supposed to get undercover with this gang? In case you haven't noticed," she said, gesturing to her headscarf, "I stick out like a sore thumb. I'd probably be attacked on the first day."

"You're going to stick close to Ms Tsukuda. She clearly cares for you and she certainly has the skill set to keep you safe." Sung-jae held his hand to his heart. "I wouldn't ask this of you if I thought you were in any danger whatsoever, believe me."

"And when do I get to walk free?"

"As soon as I have ample evidence to take in the head of the syndicate, as well as his supplier," he said, pulling a set of keys from his pocket. "You get to walk, and so does she. Free as a bird."

Yu-ra pondered for a moment. Although she had no choice but to comply, this was an opportunity. Going undercover with a gang that speaks a foreign language and a mysterious figure supplying them? There was no way she wouldn't get the internship with a story like this. It may even be her way into a real and permanent job.

"If I do this," she said, shifting to a sitting position on her knees, "do I get full permission to use all the evidence I find to write an investigative article?"

"Ah, right, you're a journalism student. Very well," he said, getting up and walking towards her, "you can release whatever materials you want once the case is closed. But understand this - you will be responsible for your own actions and safety outside of what I ask you to do," he said as he uncuffed her.

Yu-ra massaged her wrist as she responded grimly.

"I've always had to be responsible for myself."

"Then we have a deal?"

He thrust his hand forward. Ignoring his hand once again, she nodded.

"Deal."

Sung-jae awkwardly put his hand back in his pocket. Yu-ra pondered over whether to call Kyung-tae to pick her up but decided against it on account of the questions he'd have about her being at a hotel.

Shortly after collecting her things back from him and signing a contract he had written up, they exited the room. Sung-jae went into the room next door, and then promptly returned with Takemi. As he led them to his car down in the underground car park, Takemi nudged Yu-ra. She shrugged her touch off as Takemi called to her in a hushed tone.

"Hey, what happened?" Yu-ra increased her speed a little, enough to catch up with Sung-jae. Takemi jogged after her. "Hey, are you going to answer me?" She nudged her again. "Yu-ra." She nudged her a few more times.

"Will you stop touching me!"

Sung-jae glanced at her and she looked away out of embarrassment.

Takemi continued to poke and prod her all the way to the car which Sung-jae had entered.

"Yu-ra!" Takemi yelled, before Yu-ra could get in the car too. "What did I do!?"

"You know damn well what you did!" Yu-ra snapped.

"I really don't."

"Oh, please," she scoffed, "do you really think I'd let you off that easily?"

Takemi flailed her body and stomped her feet like a three-year-old.

"Yu-ra!" she cried, almost on the verge of tearing up.

"For God's sake, what is wrong with you?" Takemi's lip trembled at her words. "Do you remember in fifth grade, when everyone in class found out what happened with your parents? That they…" she lowered her voice, "left you. You became an easy target to the ruthless kids that were easily shaped by the parents who raised them to hate anyone that's different. But who was it that shielded you? When the name-calling started to get physical, who stepped in? Who took on all the heat by telling everyone she was Muslim?"

"You did, Yu-ra."

"And in high school, when those guys found out that you're mixed race and wanted to use it to incite violence towards you. Who stopped them from spreading it?"

"I...I didn't know about this. What happened?"

"Well, it was me, and it-it's not important how I shut them up. What's important is that I always stand by your side. And now I'm hearing that you recorded our conversation of me offering to help you and you use it against me? Are you serious?" she hissed.

"No, you don't understand."

"What don't I understand? Please tell me, because from my point of view, this situation is very clear cut."

"I-I'm not stupid, I promise." Yu-ra raised a brow. "I wasn't supposed to record our conversation. I still had my device running from earlier in the day," she said, pointing her thumb at the driver's side of the car. "I only remembered about it when he threatened you. I thought it would get you out of trouble if he knew that you hadn't actually done anything apart from said some words and just happened to bump into me. Clearly that didn't work."

Yu-ra scoffed at her but still pondered upon her words. It didn't make sense that she would sell her out willingly, and she was stupid enough to misread how a prosecutor would react. Maybe she was telling the truth. Her logic, though weak, kind of made sense.

"Alright, alright. Forget it, just get in the car."

"I need your help to get out of this mess," Takemi said.

Yu-ra looked over to her before walking towards the car.

"I need to get home before my husband gets worried about me being out late."

She sat in the back of the car, after which Takemi followed suit and sat in the passenger seat at the front.

****

The warmth of Yu-ra's home enveloped her, the wooden floorboards somehow feeling softer than the icy pavements outside.

"Assalaamu 'alaykum," she called out as she slipped off her shoes and into some indoor slippers. She didn't know if anyone was in, but she had developed a habit of saying it whenever she entered her house, a good sign that her new apartment was starting to feel like home to her.

"Wa'alaykum assalaam," Kyung-tae responded quietly.

*Oh, I guess he is in.* She peered past the wall blocking her from seeing the rest of the living room. Kyung-tae was sitting on the couch, an empty and grease-stained bowl in front of him, as he stared into the black abyss of the switched off TV. After slipping into her pyjamas in the bedroom, she meticulously tended to her teeth in the bathroom. Emerging refreshed, she returned to the living room to find Kyung-tae still lost in thought and his gaze fixated on nothing in particular. Kyung-tae had always been a bit of a weird and slightly boring person, but something felt off. She walked over to the kitchen counter and looked over her shoulder at him. His face was neither happy nor sad, but somehow in a different way to his usual emotionless face. He clearly wasn't worried about her getting back in so late.

She turned back and eyed the spotless kitchen, searching for something she could quickly whip up.

"In the microwave," Kyung-tae muttered.

"Oh, you made enough for me?" she said. "You didn't have to..." she trailed off.

Why did she say that? Kyung-tae raised a brow.

"What?"

"Sorry. I just meant thank you."

She turned on the microwave, allowing her food to heat for a minute and a half before deftly removing it with her fingertips and placing it on the counter behind her. The aroma of sesame oil and a medley of spices filled the air as she pulled her sleeves over her hands and cradled the bowl, making her way to the couch where Kyung-tae sat. With the remote retrieved from the low-risen wooden table, she switched on the TV and began scrolling through the options until she found the true crime documentary she desired. Yu-ra stirred her rice with a spoon, hastening its cooling process. Kyung-tae remained in his seat despite his evident lack of interest in the unfolding documentary.

The documentary began to tell the story of Doctor Hayashi Emiko, a senior member of Japan's Endo Laboratories, who were front runners in many different scientific fields. Emiko was in charge of the microbiology department. And one night, she was found murdered in an alleyway, her blood sprayed against the wall her body leaned on. The documentary flashed between black and white re-enactments of the scenes and coloured interviews in the present. Kyung-tae winced ever so slightly at the murder scene.

"You mind if I ask," he said, turning to Yu-ra to get the go-ahead, "Any particular reason you wanted to watch this?"

"Sorry, do you want me to turn it off?" Yu-ra asked, snatching up the remote from the table.

"No, I was just wondering, why do you want to watch so many documentaries about women being murdered at night? This is at least the third time this week."

"If you want me to be completely honest with you, I don't actually know. But clearly something keeps bringing me back. Maybe it's the mystery of it all," she said with faux awe in her voice, waving her hands about like a magician. With a slight nod, Kyung-tae acknowledged what she said. "Do you not find it interesting?" she asked, to keep him talking rather than out of genuine curiosity.

"I've seen enough of this in my life," he said in a gruff tone. "I'm sure I have plenty of stories that are more interesting."

"Okay, Mr hot-shot detective," she said, crossing her legs on the sofa and turning towards him, "tell me who was behind this case."

"What case?" he said, tilting his head to her.

"The one on the TV that we've been watching for the past fifteen minutes, dummy."

"I don't know. It's barely started… d-dum-dum."

Yu-ra's eyes crinkled with amusement as a giggle bubbled up at the endearing attempt to mimic her.

"I'll give you the next thirty minutes to give me your final answer."

"And if I don't answer?"

Yu-ra rubbed her chin in contemplation.

"You have to buy me a dessert tonight."

"And if I answer wrong?"

Yu-ra rubbed her chin again, more aggressively.

"You have to buy me a dessert tonight."

"And if I answer right?"

Yu-ra rubbed her chin even more aggressively.

"I'll let you know if we ever come to that bridge."

"Sure, let me know after you get friction burns on your chin." Yu-ra dropped her hand in embarrassment as Kyung-tae shook his head, smiling coyly. "How did I get myself into this? I just wanted to know why you would watch something like this. Wouldn't it make you more paranoid at night?"

"What can I say?" she said, shrugging. "Girls are just a bit incredibly insane."

"I don't disagree with you."

"Oi!"

"You're the one who said it first," he murmured.

The documentary continued to unfold, displaying the tyrannical atmosphere Emiko imposed at the lab, regularly firing people, lowering salaries if mistakes were made, giving mere pennies for severance packages. Many laws were broken during her reign, but it never would catch up with her. She lived the life of a Queen, with a husband who would do anything for her. He was surely the only person on the planet who wasn't filled with contempt for her.

"Thanks for dinner," Yu-ra said, after placing her empty bowl back on the table in front of them

"No need," Kyung-tae responded, his eyes remaining fixed on the television.

"So," Yu-ra started. She hesitated, then shook her head. "You seemed kind of out of it when I got home. Everything okay with you?"

"Did I?"

"Yeah, you were just staring at a blank TV screen."

"I was just lost in thought. I just do that sometimes."

"Oh. I see…"

The documentary continued to describe a short vacation Emiko had taken alone while her husband kept tabs on the company and more importantly a new hire that was quickly making a name for himself. Within a month he was already just two levels of authority below Emiko, and he was sure this new employee was going to usurp her. A few weeks later, while only those two were around, there was a small explosion in the lab. The building had to be cordoned off due to the highly toxic chemicals that had been released, and it caused massive setbacks to all projects within the building. Someone had to go down for this, and there was no way Emiko would let it be her…

"It's the husband," Kyung-tae whispered, leaning over to her.

"Did you say something?"

"It was the husband. He's the murderer."

"That's crazy. You're crazy!" she hollered, bringing her hand soaring through the air and then slapping him on the knee. "The husband has barely played a role in the story."

"Ow," he muttered as he pushed Yu-ra's hand off his knee, "Just watch it play out. There's been scenes of tension between her and her husband throughout."

"He clearly loves her more than anything in the world. Why would he ever hurt her?"

"He does love her more than anything, but she doesn't, which is fine. It's normal for one spouse to be more in love than the other. But his love is an obsessive one. He'll do anything for her, like being a spy when she strangely goes on an expensive vacation by herself. And if the day ever comes that she doesn't need him anymore, he'll lash out."

"Like a crime of passion?"

Kyung-tae snapped his fingers.

"Exactly! You're pretty smart."

"You only just realised?"

"I've always known."

"You're cute," Yu-ra chuckled as Kyung-tae just barely revealed a blush at the statement. "Well, my gut feeling is to stick with the employee that's out for her position. She did get him fired and completely ruin his career."

The story played out further. After an extensive autopsy, they found that Emiko didn't die from bleeding out. She had been poisoned with a toxic substance first. A substance which could easily be found at the lab she worked at.

"See," Yu-ra said, nudging him with her elbow, "the employee had easy access to the poison and slit her throat to cover it up and make it look like a normal murder."

As they watched on, it was revealed that another body was found, with the same chemical poisoning. There was a connection to Emiko's death, but what was it? A little digging revealed that they were romantically involved.

"And there we have it," Kyung-tae said, his mood a lot brighter than before. "Emiko cheated on her unstable husband. He found out and killed them both, and then he tried to make it look unrelated by covering it up with a knife wound. I win."

The show then confirmed his deductions.

"Oh wow, you do indeed. How did you know so early?"

"I could tell straight away that their marriage wasn't what it seemed on the surface. She was detached from her husband, and he was too attached. So that would have been the first thing I looked into. It was more of a guess because of the missing information of the affair, but it's something that's relatively easy enough to find out."

"I see now why you're the detective."

"You're not a bad sleuth, yourself. My second choice would have been the employee. But to be honest I don't know how he didn't realise sooner. It was so insanely obvious that she was betraying his trust."

"I guess when you're that close to someone," she said, as memories flooded her mind. Memories of the many friends that weren't really friends to her. Memories of her parents, her mother… "sometimes you just don't want to believe that person could do anything to hurt you, intentional or not."

"I guess that makes sense…" he trailed off and the room went silent for a few moments. "So, what do I win?"

"Drumroll please," Yu-ra said, waiting for Kyung-tae to commence tapping on the table. When he didn't move, she started it herself. "You get…" She drummed at the table a little faster before coming to a stop and flinging her arms into the air in celebration. "To buy me a dessert!"

A chuckle escaped Kyung-tae.

"Should've figured."

"You laughed! I got you to laugh!" she squealed in glee. "You're not really a robot, I knew it!"

"I think my wiring is just frayed." He laughed.

Yu-ra smiled at Kyung-tae warmly.

"What?" Kyung-tae asked. "Is there something on my face?"

"Yeah," Yu-ra said, still smiling as Kyung-tae brushed at his face with his fingertips. She moved his hand away from his face. "A pretty cute smile. You should smile more, it's nice."

Kyung-tae's smile lingered faintly, yet his gaze held a puzzled expression as it roamed across Yu-ra's features. It was then that Yu-ra's words dawned on her, her grip tightening before she quickly released it and her ears flushing with heat. Unable to meet his eyes, her cheeks ignited with the same heat from her ears. She drew in several deep breaths, endeavouring to regain her composure.

"Okay fine," she said, "since I did *technically* lose the challenge, I'll do you the honour of coming with you to get my dessert. How does that sound?"

"Sounds perfect," Kyung-tae said, a smile brushing his lips. "I'll go grab our coats."

"Can you grab me one of my hooded ones? I can't be bothered to put my scarf back on," Yu-ra said, using his shoulder as leverage to lift herself up to a standing position before collecting the bowls on the table. "Let me wash up and then we can go."

# 10
# A Fire

*Despite his courageous efforts, he was subdued by the assailants, who subjected him to further violence, including the use of a wire to inflict injury to his throat.*

*- Case Number 1996-2786*

Kyung-tae shoved his hands into his deep pockets. He really needed to buy a pair of gloves. The sun had broken through the clouds, bringing a little bit of warmth with it. Hopefully it would finally melt all the snow that had built up over the past two weeks. The light winds ruffled his hair causing it to flow over his eyes, a problem he had quite often since he began to style it differently. Although it wasn't something particularly annoying. Kyung-tae trudged along the busy sidewalks, checking his watch every now and then.

The walkways thinned out as did the pedestrians, and so did the... snow? Kyung-tae raised his head. The snow had melted considerably further up the street and the water had begun to flow down the gradient of the road. As Kyung-tae stepped closer, the air warmed, and the closer he got, the more his nostrils itched. Something was burning. Plastic?

A wall of heat, rushing out from a modestly sized warehouse, knocked into him. Based on the melted snow surrounding the warehouse, the heat had clearly originated from there, but there was nothing else in sight to suggest so. There was not one iota of a spark in sight. As he stumbled closer, his eyes began to burn, his vision hazing.

Kyung-tae pulled out his phone and dialled the number for emergency fire services.

"Hello, fire service," the operator chirped in a high-pitched voice. A weird response from an emergency service.

"Hi, my name is Oh Kyung-tae," he said in between heavy breaths. "I think there's a building on fire near me."

"You think there's a fire?"

"I can't see it, but I can smell it and feel it."

Suddenly the tone of the operator changed to a deep one filled with fury. Almost as if the fire was coming from the other end of the line.

"Sir, this is the emergency helpline," they growled. "Smelling something burned isn't a good enough reason to use this line."

"No, you don't understand," Kyung-tae said as his voice cracked and he took more breaths between each word, "please listen to me. There's so much heat coming from the building, I can't even get within a couple metres of it and I can smell burning plastic and I feel like I'm inhaling the fumes from that and my eyes are burning and I can barely see at this point and..."

"Sir, calm down. Calm down and take a deep breath," the operator said, reverting to its chirpy tone. "It's going to be fine. I need you to stand as far back from the building as you can. Can you tell me where you are right now?"

Kyung-tae looked around for any road signs but couldn't see anything useful.

"No, I don't know what street I'm on. I can't find any sign. Can you track my phone?" Kyung-tae said, gasping for breath as his chest heaved. "I'm sorry, I'm really starting to freak out. Which is weird for me because I don't freak out," he babbled, beginning to hyperventilate, "and that's making me... freak out... even more... Do you understand?"

Black spots attacked his vision.

"Sir, you need to calm down. Stay on the line and we'll track your..."

The darkness shrouded more of his vision as he relinquished control over his limbs. Knees buckling, he collapsed onto the ground. His hands numbed as his phone slipped from his hands. On the other end of the line, the operator still spoke.

"Sir, the fire brigade are on their way. Stay calm and focus on..." was the last thing he heard before he blacked out.

****

Kyung-tae awoke to something patting his face. Skin. Fingers? A light pounding sensation made itself known at the back of his head.

"Sir," a male voice said, "are you okay?"

Swatting the continuous patting away, Kyung-tae lifted his head before opening his eyes, the pounding worsening.

"I'm fine," he said, realising that the patting came from the man at his side.

He was cloaked entirely in reflective, waterproof, silver garments that looked as if they were made from foil. He adorned a matching helmet with a yellow symbol of the fire brigade at the front.

As he stood up, blood rushed to his head, causing the pounding to become even more prominent and his balance to wobble. The fireman extended his arms around Kyung-tae, ready to catch him should he stumble.

"Are you sure? You don't look so good."

"What happened?"

"That's what we'd like to know. You called us, we got here and all we found is a burnt down building and you passed out."

"I called you?" Kyung-tae said, furrowing his brow in confusion. "Oh right, I called you. What happened was… there was a lot of heat. And I remember feeling really lightheaded. And that's about it."

The fireman returned his hands to his side.

"What's your name?"

"Detective Oh," he said, smoothly retrieving his ID from his wallet and presenting it.

"There was definitely a fire here, detective," he said, pulling out his notepad and flicking to a specific page. "The whole warehouse is almost entirely burnt down. But when we got here, the fire must have already been put out by the half-working sprinkler system."

"I don't remember a fire."

"You don't seem to remember much at all."

"Did you find the source?"

"Not yet, we're still looking. Security tapes are blown to hell."

"I'll help."

As they entered the concrete building, water dripped from the busted pipes along the top of the walls. Puddles collected in pockets of uneven ground, reflecting the blue sky through the burnt open roof. Half burnt plastic littered the floor.

"Hey, Tae-jun!" a fireman called out to the two men, "check this out."

Kyung-tae followed Tae-jun to the back of the warehouse, near a pile of toppled over crates behind a plastic table that had fallen to the ground. A viscous colourless liquid was splattered across the ground.

The fireman that called them over kneeled down next to the liquid.

"This isn't water from the sprinklers."

"That's a given," Kyung-tae said, the fireman raising a brow at him in response before taking a matchbook out of his pocket.

"It's not normal gasoline either," Tae-jun said as he lit a match and dropped it on the liquid, a blueish purple flame erupting from the ground.

"What am I supposed to be looking for?"

The fireman ignored Kyung-tae, pulling a torch from his belt. Then, as the fireman pointed the light at the flame, by some bizarre occurrence, the flame disappeared.

"Wait, what just happened?" Kyung-tae said, taken aback. "Did all the gasoline burn up?"

The fireman turned the torch off and the flame returned.

"It's methanol," Taejun said.

"Meaning?"

"It looks invisible in certain light. But that also means that this was clearly arson. Why else would a room be painted in it and lit up?"

"Meaning," Kyung-tae added, "the person who did this was smart and had easy access to the chemical compound."

The fireman who found the methanol held something out to them.

"We also found this."

Kyung-tae inspected it. A greasy metal lighter with an engraving that was half melted off. It looked like an animal of some sort, though he couldn't tell what.

"You didn't think to show us this straight away?" Kyung-tae said, snatching it off the fireman. "This is the key."

# 11
# Home

Kyung-tae plonked his tall pile of paperwork on his kitchen counter with a loud thud. Yu-ra came out of the bedroom as he slumped onto the couch, resting his arm across his eyes.

"Hey, you okay?" she said, shuffling her slippers across the floor. Kyung-tae lifted his arm off his face but continued to stare up at the ceiling for a moment before answering.

"Yeah."

"What's this?"

Kyung-tae raised his head and saw Yu-ra standing at the counter, eyeing his paperwork.

"Just work stuff," he said before putting his arm back over his eyes.

"Have you prayed Isha yet?"

Kyung-tae sprang to his feet.

"Nope, not yet."

"Okay, Captain Couch Potato. Let's pray."

Kyung-tae narrowed his eyes at her, then he shook his head, deciding not to highlight his confusion at her comment. Yu-ra went into the bedroom and came back out within a minute with a headscarf on.

"Whenever you're ready, good sir," she said, lowering her head slightly and raising her hand in a gesture to proceed.

After their prayers, they lingered on the floor briefly. Kyung-tae stood before her, settling himself at the kitchen counter. He flipped through the top folder from the pile, casually discarding it onto the counter where it skidded to a halt. Repeating the process with another, then two more, a pulsing sensation throbbed between his eyes, prompting him to massage the bridge of his nose.

"So what kind of work stuff is that?" Yu-ra said, sidling up to the counter.

"Paperwork," he replied, flicking through another folder.

"That's a lot of paperwork."

"Yep."

"You on a deadline?" she asked, taking off her scarf and tossing it onto the couch behind her.

"Yep."

"How can I help?"

"Yep."

"Pardon?"

Kyung-tae looked up at her.

"Sorry, what did you say?"

"Were you even listening to me?" she sneered playfully, throwing her hands on her hips.

"Y-yes," he stuttered.

"What did I say then?"

Kyung-tae did his best attempt at a doughy gaze, in an attempt to look sympathetic. Yu-ra huffed audibly, her arms falling from her hips in resignation.

"What do you need to do? Type it up?"

"Yes, but-"

"Do you know how I got the nickname Bullet-hands Baek?" she said, coming over to his side of the counter. "I'm the fastest typer in the East. Even your robot brain wouldn't be able to comprehend my speed."

Kyung-tae waved the back of his hand at her in a shooing motion.

"I'm not going to ask you to help, so just go away, you nuisance."

"Good thing you aren't asking then. I'm telling you I'm going to help. You talk, I'll type. We'll be done in no time, I promise."

"This is my work to deal with."

"Ah so this is how you want to play it. Okay. Here's my counter argument," she said, sitting beside him, "I will poke you until you give in. And remember, I am called Bullet-hands for a reason."

She prodded him in the shoulder as Kyung-tae began typing, ignoring her. She prodded him again. And again. And a couple more times before he pushed her hand away. He began typing faster.

"Hey, hey, hey," Yu-ra started, "aren't you just so bored? I'm so bored that the only thing that's going to relieve my boredom is doing someone else's work. Isn't that just crazy? I'm crazy, right?"

"Yeah, you are. Now go away."

With both hands raised, Yu-ra drew in two deep breaths. Kyung-tae glanced over at her, suspicion furrowing his brow. She launched into action, unleashing a flurry of finger jabs that pummelled his chest, arms, and back. With each attempt to deflect her assault, she swiftly redirected her finger jabs to new targets.

"Will you stop?" he blurted.

"You know what you must do," she said in as deep a voice as she could muster, which unfortunately caused her to cough violently, a small amount of spittle landing on the arm she covered her mouth with. "But no, seriously," she said back in her normal tone. "Gimme it."

"No," Kyung-tae said with clear annoyance in his voice. "If you're bored, go to sleep."

"Okay, that's it. I'm calling your mother."

Kyung-tae rolled his eyes.

"Sure thing."

Yu-ra left the room and came back three minutes later. She walked back up to the counter and held out her phone.

"She wants to speak to you," she said.

"You did *not* actually call her," he said, with a deadpan expression

"I did," she replied triumphantly.

Kyung-tae took the phone and put it to his ear, greeting his mother on the other end to which she did not respond.

*"What's this I'm hearing about you ignoring my daughter-in-law?"*

"She's my wife, not your daughter-in-law."

*"She's whatever I say she is. Don't forget that you never would have married her if it wasn't for me."*

"Don't I know it," Kyung-tae muttered, rolling his eyes. "Ma, do you even know what's going on? Why are you taking her side?"

Yu-ra fluttered her eyes at him in the most annoying manner he had ever seen.

*"Excuse me? Do I need to know every detail about your life for you to listen to me? I raised you better than that."*

"Ma! I've got work to do and she won't leave me alone. My work is my responsibility, not anyone else's. If anything, you raised me too well."

*"You listen to me, boy. That woman is the best thing that could have ever happened to you."*

"I wouldn't say that," Kyung-tae muttered.

*"You better do everything she asks you to and more, or I'll come down there and beat your ass with every slipper in your house."*

"Ma!"

Yu-ra giggled at his outburst, clearly able to tell she was on the winning side of this argument.

*"And then I'll go home and bring back every slipper from my own house and beat your ass some more."* A silence grew between the two as Kyung-tae looked up at Yu-ra who was still standing at his side, waiting for her phone back. Did she hear everything his Ma said? *"Did you hear me, boy?"*

"I heard you," he responded without delay.

*"Okay, then. Now, do you want any food? I've made kimchi fried rice here."*

"No, it's fine, we've got plenty of food here. I'll try and come over this weekend."

After saying goodbye, Kyung-tae hung up the call and handed Yu-ra her phone back.

"What'd she say?" Yu-ra asked, to which Kyung-tae cut his eyes at her before pivoting his laptop towards her. "Yay," she said in a monotonous tone, before sitting down next to her husband. "Nice to know there's at least one woman you're afraid of."

"First of all, I'm afraid of all women." Yu-ra giggled at his comment. "Secondly, there's like six weeks' worth of work I need to catch up on, so if you're committing to this, you're committing to the entire thing. So, if you want to back out, say now, or forever hold your peace."

"Don't worry about me. I'm one tough cookie. More importantly," she said, resting her elbow on the counter and leaning on her hand as she looked at him, "how did you end up with six weeks' worth of work? I thought you were more organised than this. Unless you lied to me before we got married."

"I didn't lie about anything," he said, cutting his eyes at her again. "I've just had a lot of cases recently, and I felt it was more important to solve those in a timely manner than waste time trying to write up paperwork. Before I knew it everything piled up."

"Ah," she said. "Makes sense. Okay, let's get to work, my boy. We've got a long night ahead of us."

"Please don't call me that."

"Oh. Sorry hubby bubby."

Kyung-tae let out a deep sigh. It was so deep that it felt as if he was excavating the depths of his soul with each breath.

"*Please* stop."

"Sorry."

As Kyung-tae sifted through his initial case, he launched into a detailed explanation of the document's contents to Yu-ra. To his astonishment, her fingers moved with such rapidity that he found himself increasing his speaking pace to keep up. He watched in disbelief as Yu-ra became fully engrossed in her typing, absorbing his words effortlessly and transcribing them onto the screen. Uncharacteristically quiet, she worked diligently, and within the span of an hour, they had ploughed through two weeks' worth of the daunting pile before Kyung-tae. Setting aside his latest folder, he refrained from reaching for another, struck by Yu-ra's unparalleled efficiency.

"I see now where you got your nickname," he said. "You're really something."

"Thanks," she said, smirking.

"Why are you helping me?"

"Uhh, you're welcome?" she said in a tone filled with sarcasm.

"Sorry. Thank you for your help," he said. Yu-ra beamed at his remark. "But genuinely, why help me with my own work? It's not your problem to deal with."

"I just sort of wanted to help, I guess," she said, shrugging.

"Well, I guess that's good enough for me. Let's take a ten-minute break before we carry on."

****

A few hours before dawn, Yu-ra had finally helped Kyung-tae finish all but one of his cases. The stiff joints in her hands protested with each keystroke. Drowsiness had overcome her, eyelids beginning to droop, and a dull throbbing at the base of her skull whispered to her, *why in the world did you offer to do this?*

Kyung-tae rested his elbow on the counter, leaning his cheek on his fist as he smiled at her.

"Do you want to go to sleep? I can finish up here. There's only one left."

*Oh, that's why.*

"No, I said I would stick this out," she said, rubbing her eyes, "and I will."

"If you say so," he said, sitting back up straight and opening his last folder. Yu-ra cut her eyes at him. That was too quick to move on. He could have at least asked her if she was sure. Wait…was she crazy?

As Kyung-tae flicked through his notes, detailing the unfolding of the case, Yu-ra recorded every microscopic aspect of what had occurred and when it had occurred, down to the exact minute. She discovered a newfound appreciation for how observant he really was. Her tired eyes began to feel less so the more he spoke, and as the pain in her fingers faded, it was replaced by an aching in her heart - an aching directed at Kyung-tae. She knew being a detective could be a tough job, but it still seemed like too much for one individual to handle. And yet he still showed so little emotion, as if unaffected. Maybe that's how you had to be to handle the job, to realise that some things are just out of your control.

"At fifteen-thirty hours, the victim's body was reported to be found frozen under the Han River. Officer Ji was the first on the scene. DNA evidence confirmed the victim's identity as..." Kyung-tae hesitated and Yu-ra glanced at him, her eyes riddled with concern. This was the first time she had seen him hesitate in his speech since they started working on his paperwork. "As the missing Kim Sun-Jung at fifteen-fifty hours. At sixteen-fifteen hours, the body was removed and transported to the city morgue for an autopsy. The autopsy report was received at oh-nine-hundred hours the following morning, Tuesday ninth of December two-thousand-and-ten." He picked up the autopsy report, a brown envelope with an opening at the top. Taking out the first sheet of paper and just barely slipping the top edge out, reading it and slipping it back in. "Conclusion: victim known as Kim Sun-Jung had committed suicide." He hesitated once again. "With no external influences. Case closed."

Yu-ra paused her typing.

"Is that the first time you looked at the autopsy report?"

"Yeah, why?"

"Doesn't it have more information you need to note down?"

"No. It just confirms everything I already know. And we've typed it as such."

"Oh."

Yu-ra finished up formatting the document appropriately, saving the document as Kyung-tae got up out of his seat.

"You all finished there?" he said.

"I was finished before you even stopped speaking, kiddo."

Kyung-tae threw his hands up in defence. "Ooh, look who's outshining the rest of us mere mortals" he mocked.

Yu-ra's gaze softened, the corners of her lips flickering in a downward motion. "I'm sorry."

Kyung-tae shook his hands aggressively in dismissal. "I was joking. I thought I was being more obvious this time."

"No, not that," she said, shaking her head solemnly. "I'm sorry about a lot of these cases. They must have been hard to deal with."

"It's just a part of the job." He shrugged. "I'm used to it by this point."

"Are you sure?"

"I'm fine."

"Cause you know…" Yu-ra paused, the temperature of her nape rising as she looked away. "You can always talk to me about anything," she muttered.

"What would I talk about?"

"I don't know, I don't know," she said, looking back towards him, "just…sometimes it can help to talk about things. Things that may haven't exactly been the best experience."

"I'll keep that in mind in the future. But seriously, don't worry about me."

"I'm not, I promise. I'm just saying, I'm always willing to listen. And it's always a good thing if I learn more about you."

Kyung-tae began piling all his folders back up and then stood up to grab a bag at the side of the counter. As he slipped the folders into the bag, Yu-ra tapped him on the shoulder "When you were given this last case," she said, "how did it feel to find out she… committed suicide?"

"I wasn't assigned the case," Kyung-tae said, still looking into his bag. "I bargained with another detective for it. Some of that paperwork we did was his."

Yu-ra itched at her head. He had that much paperwork and he chose to do someone else's?

"Why?"

"I was more suited to the case and would be able to solve it faster. Whole lotta good that did."

"But doesn't your boss decide that?"

"He does. But I just thought he made the wrong decision."

"And did he?"

Kyung-tae put his bag down and finally looked back at her.

"Look, no matter what happened, I would have fought for this case."

"But why?" she said, gazing at him earnestly. "Didn't you say it didn't do any good."

"Because I was the right person for the job."

"But why? Was it that important that you be the one to solve it?"

"Yes!" he blurted.

"Why?" she said, unphased by his outburst. "With this much paperwork to do, surely you had your hands full?"

"I just… needed to handle this case, okay?"

Yu-ra looked him in the eyes, his stern gaze penetrating her soul. Her eyes wavered.

"Sorry," she said, shaking her head, "I'm sorry, I was being rude. I shouldn't have pushed you about it."

Kyung-tae sighed, then sat back down in his seat beside her, clasping his hands together on top of the counter.

"It happened about two and a half years ago. I hadn't made detective yet, but Mr Choi pulled some strings to get me my first case. It was a missing persons case, which is a really rare occurrence in this country, so I was incredibly lucky to be given the case. Now let me tell you, working with Mr Choi?" Kyung-tae said as his mouth curved up slightly. "He was amazing. It wasn't him solving the case, he let me lead and just nudged me in the right direction when I was stuck."

"You must have learnt a lot from Jinmu," she said, keeping her eyes off him to avoid making him feel awkward.

"Yeah, I would've never been suitable for police work without him. He filled a hole..."

Kyung-tae trailed off and Yu-ra examined his eyes. Filled a hole? What was he talking about? His dad? All she knew about his dad was that he had passed away. He never really mentioned him otherwise. She contemplated whether to ask him about it since she had absolutely no idea what he was thinking, but then decided against it.

"So what happened during this case?"

"I was actually on a roll. I arrested a few guys who were involved. But for every arrest, there was so much red tape, I couldn't gather the evidence I needed." He sighed. "And there was this one guy who I knew, I *knew* he was behind the kidnapping. But I took my time to gather enough evidence, tailed him back to his hideout."

Yu-ra felt an ache scratching at the chambers of her heart. She had never seen him even the slightest bit vulnerable. He barely even showed emotion on their wedding day.

"And then?"

"I found enough evidence to at least open up a new investigation on him. If I took him in, then and there..."

"Why didn't you?"

"I was too…scared."

"You? Scared?" she chuckled.

"Yes."

Yu-ra's face dropped and she reverted to a serious tone.

"What were you scared of?"

"Of not being able to take on a whole gang of people. I could have called for backup, but there was no crime happening. I didn't have Jinmu with me and I was afraid of being wrong. So I took the evidence back with me. In fact, I almost got caught by them, I knocked over a pipe that was leaning against a wall. They came to see what it was but obviously I was gone by that point." Yu-ra couldn't tell if he was done with his story, so she waited and listened. "We caught the guy who did it." His almost sullen tone told Yu-ra this wasn't a happy outcome. "Three days after he had already murdered the girl who had gone missing."

Yu-ra covered her mouth with her palm.

"That's horrible."

"It wasn't just three days after the murder. It was three days after I decided to not take him in. If I just…" Kyung-tae began twiddling his thumbs. "If I just acted instead of being too scared to do anything, I would have saved her life. If I just hopped over the red tape. I would have disrupted a whole trafficking ring."

"And you just don't want that to happen to any girl ever again. Is that why you took the case?"

"Something like that. But it did happen again. But it's fine. Like I said, it's just a part of the job."

Yu-ra didn't know what to say. Anything she could possibly say wouldn't make a difference to him. Anything she could logically think of to console him, she was sure he had already told himself. How do you console someone who doesn't let anything get to him? So, she did the only thing she wanted to do. She put her hand on his closed hand, his skin cold under her warm grasp. She opened up his palm and interlocked her fingers with his. Kyung-tae looked over at her, but didn't say anything.

"Your hands are freezing," she said.

"I get that a lot."

"Who have you been holding hands with for them to tell you that?" she said as she raised a brow, her grip tightening.

"No one," he laughed softly.

Kyung-tae's hands had warmed up a bit, but so had hers, to the point that it started to get clammy. She pulled her hand away and wiped it on her pyjama trousers.

"Sorry, my hands got sweaty." Kyung-tae laughed again then moved to get up, but Yu-ra stopped him. "Hey, I didn't say I was done," she said, grabbing his hand again and forcing him to sit back down.

"Okay." He shrugged as the room fell into silence for a few long minutes.

"Hey," she said, unconsciously rubbing her thumb into the back of his hand, "I need to tell you something… something about Chun-"

Suddenly the tranquil atmosphere was shattered by the intrusive clamour of Kyung-tae's phone ringing.

"Sorry, hold that thought," he said before he answered his phone and greeted whoever was at the other end. "What? Another one? Where?" His hand slipped out of her grip as he furrowed his brow and narrowed his eyes, as if trying to untangle a perplexing annoyance. "That's the third fire today, and on the other side of the city," he continued, his expression then morphing into fatigue. "This is definitely serial arson," He steeled his gaze. "Did you find a lighter there anywhere? It's got a very specific design. No? Alright I'm coming now."

Kyung-tae cut the call off, jumping out of his seat.

"Going out?" Yu-ra asked, slumping in her chair.

"Yeah, sorry, I've got to go. Work stuff."

# 12
# Park Ny-ron

*And to those who elect to enact their own commercial undertakings, infantries or kings, the Angel of Death will be upon you. And thus, this ethereal harbinger of fate passes his judgement.*

- *The Contract*

Yu-ra stood before the imposing wooden door before her, her gaze fixed upon its grandeur. Its dark mahogany hue swallowed the feeble lighting and intricate patterns embellished the surface, spreading from the centre like veins. She had never seen an office door this large. Then again, she had never really been to such a high-class restaurant before. How she had gotten this far within the gang was beyond her. She was already meeting the boss, two floors above the kitchen of a public establishment. The dim light cast a grimy pallor upon the door. She itched at the tender space below her ring finger and took a few deep breaths alongside to help her pacing heartbeat settle. Drawing in one final steadying breath, she swiftly knocked.

*You can do this,* she said to herself. *You've got your backstory ready and plenty of acting experience...from school…eight years ago.*

The door creaked open and a man in white shirt and a black Kevlar vest welcomed her into a well-furnished room. Green leather armchairs formed a half-circle around a chestnut coffee table. Three girls in tight dresses filled some of the seats, and two men filled the other two as they conversed quietly between each other. A fabric sofa sat on the other side of the table. Considering they were on the second floor, the ceiling was abnormally high. As Yu-ra took in the sights, she noted a few portraits hanging on the wall of women wearing similar dresses to what she wore on her wedding day. They were pre-empire art pieces. How did they get a hold of something so rare? Sat on the edges of the room were tall white vases with narrow necks and wide bases. Faint blue dragons painted the sides, but the bottom edges had become discoloured and chipped.

As she approached, the faint scent of cigarette smoke permeating the air intensified, leading her to the figure seated before her. Clad in a sleek blue leather jacket and snug trousers, the man exuded an air of effortless confidence. Before him, a series of screens, previously alive with activity, fell into darkness at his command to which he set a remote control down upon the polished wooden counter. In an instant, a door slid seamlessly over the screens, transforming the once vibrant display into a nondescript wall.

Where was Takemi? She had made it clear that she would be there. What if something went wrong? The microtracker planted in her bloodstream wouldn't save her from any danger.

The man in the leather jacket spun his chair around and began inspecting her, head to toe.

"Who the hell is this and why is she in front of me?" he said, clearly annoyed, yet his velvety smooth voice portrayed a different idea. He had a thin healed scar under his right eye, and coppery hair that looked fiery under certain lighting. "I've got enough crap to deal with already and now I've got strays walking into here?" he yelled at the men behind her.

"Yo," Yu-ra drawled, snapping her wrist at him, as she casually slouched her posture, "You good, cousin? I'm just out here trying to snatch up them sheets, you know what I'm saying?" The man's grimace seemed to darken as Yu-ra continued to speak. "So, what's the saying, then?" she said, standing up a bit straighter due to the lower back pain caused from slouching, "...you know what I'm saying?"

The man stared at her for a few uncomfortable moments longer, then his gaze moved past her.

"Has anyone seen my baseball bat?"

In a heartbeat, Yu-ra straightened herself into an impeccable posture, with the utmost composure and poise.

"Sorry. Kim Yu-ra," she said. "Kim Cho-ji's cousin."

The man waved away the gang member that had picked up his baseball bat behind her.

"My condolences," he began, his voice a bit calmer as he bowed his head. "Park Ny-ron. But again, why are you here?"

"I want to join your service, so to speak…"

"Why, so you can find Cho-ji's killer?" he said, lifting his head up and then leaning back on his chair, "enact your own version of justice? We have our own way of dealing with our problems, and it doesn't involve you or anyone here."

"Maybe I do want to find the killer. Maybe I want him to pay-"

"Oh we'll find out who stabbed him, and we'll make them pay, I promise you."

"But that's not why I'm here. Cho-ji taught me everything I know about this business. I just need the work." Ny-ron paused, his gaze piercing through her. But, he didn't speak. Not knowing what else to do, Yu-ra continued with her planned backstory. "It…it all started when some Japanese guy asked me to get a hold of some smoke for him because he knew Cho-ji worked for you guys-"

"I don't care about your story," he said, cutting her off as he stood from his chair. "I think you might actually fit perfectly with us. You see, we're the same. We're both oppressed by our own people."

Yu-ra knew what he meant. She had heard similar sentiments from countless people before. She decided to ask him anyway.

"What do you mean by that?"

"Our own people, Korean people, stand with our colonisers. And if I stand against them…" With lightning speed, he pivoted, snatching the TV remote before whirling back, flinging it like a bullet across the room, narrowly missing the ear of one of the seated men. "I'M THE ONE WHO IS CAST OUT!"

Yu-ra's heart leapt from its position, just as she did. Suddenly, Ny-ron placed his hands behind his back, similar to how her father would when he traversed his own home. The archetype of a wise old man. Then, as someone brought him back the TV remote, he paced back and forth in front of her. When he received the remote, he pressed a button and the wall slid back open, followed by a slideshow displayed on the screens. The first screen displayed simply showed a map of Korea.

"How am I the crazy one?" he said, flicking to the next slide and continuing to pace. The map of Korea expanded to include the top half of the land formation that was previously missing. "When the Japanese literally stole half of our land and forced all of those people into the southern half of the country. And here we are, acting like they've gifted us this half of the country rather than them stealing half."

"Oh," she said, simply.

He didn't say what she thought he would. She actually agreed with him. Never had she met a person outside of her hometown that shared her anti-colonialist mindset.

"I mean surely, just surely," he said, changing the slide again which caused the whole map to go red, "if the time ever comes where they want to, they'll take the rest of our land and kick us out. Leaving us with nowhere to go, right?"

"Are you…pitching to me?" Yu-ra said, raising a brow. Why was he saying all of this to a stranger?

He stopped in his tracks and turned to her.

"Oh, you're right. I don't need to. Because like I said, we're the same. I'm oppressed by colonised Koreans, and you," he said, looking her up and down, "your people force you to cover up without your own say."

Yep. There it was. Their go-to line. Though it didn't seem a useful idea to argue at this particular moment.

"You're right. I share your values. Thank you for the opportunity," she said, placing her hand on her heart.

"But," he said, raising a finger and stepping towards her, "joining won't be as simple as that."

Yu-ra unconsciously took a step back but before she could take another, something dropped down from the high ceiling and slammed against the ground, a small gust of wind slightly blowing the tail of her scarf.

"AAAHHH!" she screamed as a shiver ran down her spine and she jolted sidewards, her head cowering beneath the shelter of her arms. As her pulse quickened and her breaths matched its pace, a sudden eruption of laughter filled the room. Amidst the cacophony, there was a familiar giggling. Slowly lowering her arms, her curiosity piqued. Turning, she beheld a figure adorned in a forest green mask, a dagger twirling effortlessly through the air as they hopped from one foot to the other. Takemi.

"Were you up there that whole time, you freak?" she snapped.

"He likes to climb things." Ny-ron chuckled. "This is Cheonsa. He's the one that makes sure that our turf stays our turf."

"Cheonsa?" she said, raising her brow at Takemi. "As in angel?"

Takemi zipped behind her and wrapped her arm around Yu-ra's neck, holding her dagger to it with her other hand.

"AHH!" Yu-ra cried as she grabbed onto Takemi's arm to stop her pressing the knife against her neck, "what are you doing!"

"Wait," Ny-ron said, holding his hand up, "you know Korean?"

"What? You don't?" she said in Korean, struggling to raise her voice with Takemi's arm around her. "I thought you were supposed to be keeping our culture alive."

"Oh, I speak it," he said, replying in Korean, "but most of our guys struggle."

"My hand's getting tired here," Takemi said, also in Korean with a voice unsettlingly distorted through a voice modulator while waving her dagger in front of Yu-ra's face.

"Eh," Ny-ron shrugged his shoulders. "Go ahead."

All the other gang members had blank faces.

"Wait!" Yu-ra screamed.

Ny-ron instantly keeled over in laughter. After rolling around for a minute, he stood up.

"I'm just messing with you," he said, wiping away an imaginary tear. "But, there's your first lesson. Break the rules and death will be upon you."

"So I'm in then?" Yu-ra said, still struggling against Takemi's arm. Ny-ron paused before nodding at Takemi who then lowered her hands and backed away from Yu-ra. She slid her dagger back into its sheath attached to her lower back.

"We have a process. You need to prove you can do the job first. We have a delivery due at four pm. You'll go with one of our men."

"I'll go," Takemi said.

"What happened to you staying neutral?" Ny-ron said.

"This place is a drag. These guys just sit around smoking and playing cards."

Ny-ron stepped away from Yu-ra, beckoning Takemi to join him.

"This shit's beneath you," he said to her quietly. Takemi remained silent, staring at him. Ny-ron began to write something down on a slip of paper and then handed it to Yu-ra. "Fine. This is the address. Make sure you're there by four, not a minute later."

"Thank you," Yu-ra said. "By the way, your Korean is terrible. It sounds like you're speaking it in a Japanese accent."

Ny-ron chuckled.

"That's cute. Only one girl gets to be snarky with me like that. I'll allow it this time."

He waved her away and Takemi led her out of the room.

Yu-ra and Takemi navigated the restaurant down two flights of stairs until they found themselves in a basement. They entered a dark tunnel that was formed in the back wall of the basement and after about fifteen minutes of walking finally arrived on the other end. A large open warehouse floor splayed out in front of them. Rows of tables were set out like conveyor belts, topped with piles of plastic and mountains of faint blue crystals. Along each belt stood cascades of workers. She noted how everyone could be seen packaging drugs, and a few handling weapons, mostly knives and lead pipes. The ones handling the drugs were syphoning the crystals into small plastic packages. One of the men packing wore a dull white jumpsuit. Yet all the other workers wore grey.

"Hey, who is that?" Yu-ra asked, discreetly pointing to the man as they crossed the warehouse floor.

"I don't know," Takemi said, "just a packer. Why?"

"So he's not got a special role?"

"No."

Yu-ra looked closer at the man's jumpsuit. There were spots of grey decorating the cuffs of his sleeve, and also… red? Was it actually the same jumpsuit as the others but bleached? That could explain the dull white colour. But why would he bleach his clothes? He must have been hiding something.

"Can you find out for me? I have a suspicion."

"Let's focus on the job at hand."

They soon exited the warehouse through the front, out onto the cold streets. Though the warehouse temperature was only mildly warmer.

"How do you do this every day?" Yu-ra asked. "Do these guys even know you're Japanese?"

"No, but does it really matter?" Takemi said. "I'm a neutral entity."

"I don't think that Ny-ron guy sees you like that. Since he sees himself as oppressed."

"You don't feel the same way as him, do you?"

"You know I do. But you were raised in my neighbourhood. You're not the same as them," she said, shoving his shoulder playfully. "Regardless of that, there is absolutely no way that I am dealing drugs to people. So, where do we go from here?"

"Don't worry, Yu-ra, I've got this under control. This is going to be fun!" Takemi cheered as she grabbed her mask and slipped it off simultaneously as she threw her arms in the air. "I never thought I would be working with you."

Takemi skipped along the street and so Yu-ra soon found herself running to keep up with her.

# 13
# Traces

*The home invasion and subsequent assault resulting in the death of Mr. Oh and injuries to his son are currently under investigation by law enforcement. While the son's condition remains stable, there exists the possibility that he has incurred a lasting scar. The suspects involved have been apprehended and are in custody pending further legal proceedings. The Oh family is encouraged to seek support services and counselling in the wake of this tragic incident.*

*Officer Choi Jinmu*
*JN-2378*
*Jongno Police Department*

*- Case Number 1996-2786*

"Hey, you got a minute?" Kyung-tae said, tapping two fingers on Woo-young's desk.

A chorus of ringing phones echoed across the station floor, and the subsequent clacking of keyboard keys punctuated the air.

Woo-young glanced at him before letting out a sigh.

"Yeah, what can I do for you?"

"What, no witty response for me today?"

"Guess not," Woo-young said, shrugging.

"You got that paperwork for me?" Kyung-tae said, extending his hand.

Swivelling his chair toward him, Woo-young gazed up at him as he leaned back.

"You know what, don't worry about it. I've got it covered."

"No. You're not doing this," Kyung-tae said firmly as he bobbed his hand up and down to gesture the handover once more. "I don't want your pity."

"What? Pity?" he spouted, his voice taking on an increasingly uncomfortable high pitch. "No way. I just decided that I can do my paperwork myself."

"Don't play games with me. I know what you're trying to do."

"And what's that?" he said, reverting to his normal tone.

"You think I need some sort of respite because Kim Sun-jung committed suicide. But you know what? Her committing suicide has nothing to do with me. If she really wanted to do it, she would have found a way no matter what."

"Maybe you're right. But it can still affect you, and your ability to do the work."

"It comes with the territory. Now give me the damn files. We made a deal. I keep my word."

"Fine." He sighed, handing over a small pile of folders. "Here."

"Have you found your missing girl yet?"

"I'm working on it. I think I've got a lead, but it's a stretch at best. At least we know they're not connected to each other now."

"Let me know if you need any help with it." Kyung-tae turned away to leave but swivelled back around. "Hey, one more question. You worked in narcotics, right?"

"Yeah, a couple years ago. Why?"

"Can a drug burn up and leave absolutely no residue behind?"

"What are you talking about? Everything leaves a residue behind."

"Yeah, maybe you're right."

Kyung-tae returned to his desk and dialled in a number. The phone rang a few times before Mr Choi finally answered.

"*Hello,*" the voice said through the phone speaker. "*Who is this?*"

"It's Kyung-tae. I'm calling from my work phone."

"*Ah, I see.*" Kyung-tae waited for a moment before realising Mr Choi had nothing more to say.

"Are you healing up okay?"

"*Chun-mi is taking care of me. Is this what you called for?*"

"Yes..." Kyung-tae waited for another response but none arrived. "No, I have a question about a serial arson case that I stumbled onto." He waited once more. "Three warehouses burned down, and I found a lighter in two of them. And I'm guessing the person who did it is smart."

*"What makes you say that?"*

"The flames were invisible in certain lighting because it was caused by methanol. But that's not what I called to ask about. When I was outside of the warehouse, I started to get extremely paranoid and began to hyperventilate. But that's never happened to me in my life."

*"Did you say you found some lighters?"*

"Yeah, at two of them. Not the third."

*"It sounds like that's going to be the thing that carries the case forward. Don't lose sight of that."*

"But again about what happened to me-"

*"You just inhaled too many fumes."*

"But the paranoia-"

*"Are you thinking drugs were burning?"*

"Yeah, some people react to narcotics by becoming paranoid."

*"Have you done a blood test?"*

"No, I'll get that done. But the problem is that I couldn't find any trace of a drug anywhere around. Have you ever heard of such a drug that leaves absolutely no residue behind anywhere?"

*"Not to my knowledge. I think you may have missed something."*

"I'm starting to think I did. I'm going back to the last warehouse again. If drugs really are involved, then so is a criminal enterprise, and criminals love to return to a scene of a crime, right?"

A chortle came from over the phone.

*"You learn quickly. Good work, son. Looks like you don't need my help after all."*

Kyung-tae couldn't help the smile that spread across his lips.

"If you say so."

*"Do you know who owns the warehouse?"*

"I'm working on that."

*"So you're working on another case. I take it you found that girl, then?"*

Kyung-tae caught himself hesitating.

"No... she took her own life."

*"Are you..."* Mr Choi's voice was filled with concern but then he paused, longer than his normal pauses. *"Very well. Unfortunately, these things happen. Don't carry it with you."*

"Yep," Kyung-tae replied instantly.

*"Well, if there's nothing else, I'll be off then."*

After Mr Choi ended the call, Kyung-tae sighed as he put the phone down then tapped his finger against the top of the handle absentmindedly for a few moments. While closing all tabs open on his computer, a vibration buzzed in his pocket. He slipped his phone out. 'Spouse' was displayed on the screen. A grin unfurled on his lips.

*"Hello-salaamualaikum,"* Yu-ra blurted as he answered.

Kyung-tae chuckled to himself.

"Walaikum-assalaam."

*"You okay?"*

"Yeah, I'm okay. What's up?" he said, as he looked up to see Woo-young gawking at him, his mouth agape. Kyung-tae then realised the expression that was still plastered on his face, so he immediately relaxed all his facial muscles leading to a look of disdain from Woo-young.

*"I've got this investigation assignment and I was hoping you could help me out."*

"I didn't realise I had any expertise to offer."

*"It's actually right up your alley. So imagine this - there is a suspect in an investigation and the suspicion comes from the fact that you know that they've bleached their clothes."*

"What's being investigated?"

*"The context they've given us doesn't really explain, so we have to figure it out."*

"That sounds weird. Where does the suspicion come from, unless you're already searching for something?"

*"I know, right? It's weird. But if I had some inclination as to why someone*

*would bleach their clothes it might make a lot of sense."*

"Well, commonly it tends to be that they bleach their clothes to remove evidence. You know, stains, DNA residues and what have you."

*"So, things like blood?"*

"Yes, that could be one scenario. The question then becomes where did the blood come from? No one would use bleach to remove their own blood."

*"Yeah, that makes sense. Okay, next question, I want to know if there are any ways you can tell when someone is lying."*

"Oh, I can definitely help you there," Kyung-tae said as he logged off his computer and got ready to leave the precinct.

# 14

# The Drop

Yu-ra glanced at her watch. They had reached the designated drop point, nestled beneath a quaint bridge by the canal, five minutes ahead of schedule. She had questioned why they were doing a drug deal in such an obviously shady place, but apparently both parties were certain that authorities wouldn't interfere in any of their business. Which begged the question; why not do it somewhere more comfortable then?

After a discussion with Sung-jae, she was more at ease with going through with the deal. Takemi wasn't completely sold on the idea but Yu-ra had made an executive decision that they would simply alert Sung-jae to the buyers and he would arrest them and keep the drugs as evidence.

A short distance away, Takemi, lurking around her car, gave Yu-ra a thumbs up before unsheathing her daggers from behind her back and beginning to juggle them. Yu-ra shot her a stern look and shook her head disapprovingly, though she wasn't certain if she had caught her gaze as the girl continued to juggle unabated.

Suddenly, she swiped both daggers out of the air and bowed in a showman-like fashion before putting her daggers back in the sheaths. A small giggle escaped Yu-ra and Takemi lifted her mask up to reveal a bright smile.

"*You ready?*" Takemi's voice came through her earpiece.

"Born it," Yu-ra said. "Hey, you know I was thinking about that guy with the washed-out jumpsuit."

"*Yeah?*"

"Kim Cho-ji's killer hasn't been found, right? But who's to say it was an enemy that murdered him?"

"*Are you trying to say it wasn't a rival gang? Because everyone else believes it is.*"

Suddenly Takemi yanked her mask back down and discretely pointed past Yu-ra's shoulder. Spinning on her axis, Yu-ra was surprised to find no one there. However, after a few seconds more, footsteps approached followed by two slim Japanese men with buzz cuts coming around the corner on the opposite side of the bridge. Yu-ra glanced back at Takemi one last time before they came to a stop in front of her. One of the men stood firmly before her, while the other stood behind him with his hands behind his back. She turned her nose up at them, trying on her best glare.

"What's with all the funny faces?" the man in front said.

"Sorry," Yu-ra said, relaxing her face. Immediately realising she was being too polite, she leaned to one side and crossed her arms nonchalantly. "Anyway, you got the money?"

"You got the stuff?"

"Yeah, I got the stuff."

She retrieved an airtight plastic bag, no larger than the span of her palm, from the confines of her pocket and then displayed it. It was filled with miniscule blue tinged crystals. The man tilted his head towards his friend, who handed him an envelope of money from his jacket pocket before returning his hands behind his back.

"It's all there." Retrieving the envelope from the man, Yu-ra opened it and flicked through the notes. She counted forty-eight thousand yen. He was telling the truth. "You guys are really ragging us dry these days. Is this drug really worth this much?"

"I don't decide on the price, but you won't get this drug anywhere else. So if you don't want it, I can find another buyer easily."

She hoped that what she said was true because she completely made that up in an attempt to sound confident. Never had she seen a drug such as this, so she must have been right, considering the high price.

"Don't be so hasty. This stuff is no joke, you got yourself a regular customer."

"That's good to hear," she said.

The man's friend finally dropped his hands and went to tap him on the shoulder when suddenly Takemi yelled out.

"Hey!"

Sprinting towards them, she unsheathed one of her daggers and hurled it towards them. Whipping past Yu-ra's ear, it buried itself deep into the left shoulder of the man in front and swiftly yanked him to the ground as he cried out in pain. After abruptly being shoved out of the way by an immense force, a scream fled from Yu-ra's lungs. Falling to the ground, Yu-ra slid a very short distance away.

Takemi feigned a kick to the friend's head, the man attempting to block the kick with his arm. But Takemi quickly dropped her leg and swept his feet out front underneath him, knocking him to the ground.

"Take- Cheonsa, stop!" Yu-ra cried as Takemi pounced on the man with the knife in his shoulder and tore it out of him, causing the man to cry out once again. Flipping the dagger in her hand, she drove it into his neck. The screaming had finally stopped, but only to be replaced with a sputtering cough as crimson spilled from the victim's lips. As Yu-ra stood, Takemi removed herself from the prey she had already caught and then skipped towards her new target. Kneeling down beside him, she pounded her fist into his face, drawing blood from his nostrils.

"STOP!" Yu-ra yelled, though Takemi continued to pummel the man. Her dagger then revealed itself. Yu-ra had to do something. She had to stop this. Darting at her, she shoved Takemi as hard as she could, causing her to wobble to the side before quickly regaining her balance. The writhing man tried to wriggle free from Takemi's grip.

"What?" Takemi said, looking up at Yu-ra.

"What are you doing?" she yelled in Korean, shoving her again.

"I'm making sure we don't deal drugs to them. Isn't this what you wanted?" she replied innocently in Korean.

"No it's not! Does this look like something I'd want? We had a plan!"

"Your plan had holes in it."

Yu-ra grabbed onto the man's arm and tugged him, but to no avail. She couldn't pull him out from Takemi's grip.

"Move!" she said, slapping Takemi's hand. "You're not going to hurt this man anymore."

Takemi sighed before letting go. Yu-ra pulled the man to his feet and held him steady. A gash ran through his cheek and his eye had swelled up considerably.

"What do you think would have happened if they got arrested as soon as we dealt drugs to them? We'd just go about our day and no one would find out? It would get linked back to us immediately."

"You don't think I thought about that? Why do you think we decided Sung-jae would have arrested me too? And we would have made a plan of escape."

"Which wouldn't have worked. This will keep your cover and put you in their good graces."

"You're a flipping psycho!"

Takemi stood silently for a moment. Yu-ra couldn't tell what she was thinking with that mask covering her face. Suddenly Takemi gripped the man's jacket collar with both hands.

"I'm letting you go out of the goodness of my heart," she said, reverting back to Japanese.

"Yes, sir," the man whimpered.

"If you mention this to anyone," Yu-ra said, adjusting her position so that she could hold the man up better, "I won't stop him next time. Do you understand?"

"Yes, ma'am!" The man cried, as blood and mucus streamed out of his smashed face.

"When you get back to your boss, you tell him that he," she said, pointing to the dead man, "pulled a knife on me, and Cheonsa intervened. He let you go because you were never part of the plan."

"Okay, I promise I'll let my boss know that!" He cried, clasping his hands together and shaking them in a begging motion.

"This can be beneficial for you," Yu-ra continued. "We're willing to make amends."

"W-what?" the man stuttered.

"You know this has nothing to do with the Koreans. Cheonsa is a neutral entity. However, we can make some compromises. The next five shipments that you order from us will be completely free just for you."

"Make it ten."

Takemi seized the collar of the man again.

"Who the f-"

"Done!" Yu-ra said cutting Takemi off.

"Can I go now?" the man whimpered.

Takemi pushed the man to the ground and he scrambled away from them, scurrying out of sight.

"I'm glad he forgot about this," Yu-ra said, pulling out the plastic packet of crystals. "You really need a better way to keep peace. Violence won't always work."

Retrieving her dagger from the dead man's neck, Takemi wiped it clean before sheathing it. She then pulled out her other dagger and took Yu-ra's right hand in hers.

"What are you doing?" Yu-ra said, pulling back slightly.

"We need to make it look like you defended the gang. They pulled a knife on you. I went to defend you and you fought them off to make sure they didn't get away with stealing the drugs."

"Okay? So how are you going to do that?"

"Like this," she said, digging the tip of her blade into her middle knuckle. Yu-ra yelped in pain as she sliced across it. As she clamped her hand over her mouth to muffle her screams, Takemi sliced the knuckle at the top of her index finger too. A burning sensation flared up on her hand as blood began to drip down her knuckles. Takemi then put the knife to her cheek.

"Wait!" Yu-ra yelled, pushing Takemi an arm's length away. "Kyung-tae will see this and ask questions."

"Let's do it somewhere he won't see then."

She lifted up Yu-ra's sleeve and pressed the knife into her forearm and pulled away, causing Yu-ra to grimace as the stinging, burning sensation travelled from her knuckles to her arm. As the blood began to drip from her forearm, she began to contemplate whether this story truly was worth the trouble.

# 15
# Date Night

Finally finding a moment to sneak away from Takemi and go to the bathroom, Yu-ra called Sung-jae. The room, gleaming in pristine white, had its tiled floor sparkling under the gentle glow of the lighting. A row of spotless countertops housed paper towels and automatic soap dispensers that were precisely arranged. Above them, mirrors hung in perfect alignment, offering crystal clear reflections. She entered one of the stalls, not a creak coming from the door. Sitting down on the closed lid of the toilet, the weight of the phone caused the aching of her bandaged hand to become more prominent. She lightly massaged the fresh fabric bandage she had just wrapped tightly around her forearm, the pain of which seemed to have dulled with only a little blood seeping through, drying on the surface. The ringing stopped, followed by a confused greeting from Sung-jae.

*"Hello?"*

"I need to talk to you," she spouted.

*"Is this a secure line?"*

"What? I don't know." She huffed. "What does that matter?"

*"Just because these people are from a gang, doesn't mean they're not intelligent. For some reason they seem to have access to an incredible number of resources. They could easily be listening to our conversation."*

"Fine, whatever. But I need to talk to you now," she said, changing to a whisper mid-sentence.

*"And it can't wait till you're in a safe place?"*

"Takemi is dangerous. You need to arrest her. For her own good."

*"Has she sabotaged the investigation in any way?"*

"The deal didn't go through, that's why we didn't call you earlier to pick them up."

*"So, you didn't need my help after all. I don't see an issue here."*

"It didn't go through because she murdered one of the buyers and she would have murdered the other if I didn't stop her." Sung-jae remained silent so Yu-ra, now rapidly bobbing her leg up and down, continued. "She said it would help me get in with them if it looked like I solved a problem for them. She cut my hand up and everything. What am I going to tell my husband?"

*"Did it work? Did she get you in?"*

"Yes, it worked."

*"She did well. I'm surprised at her. Didn't think I was so convincing."*

"She what?" Yu-ra said, planting her foot firmly on the ground to stop her leg from shaking. "You're defending her? Aren't you a man of the law?"

*"Do you think I care about one petty junkie? I'm working on bringing down an entire syndicate. This drug that they're peddling is some dangerous stuff. If it breaks out to the masses, we'll never contain it."*

"I don't care. If this is how this is gonna be, I don't want to do this anymore."

*"What part of our deal ever made you think you have a choice in this? Your alternative to this is jail time."*

"Then I'll take the jail time," she seethed through gritted teeth. "I can't sit by and watch my friend unaccountably commit these crimes."

*"It took me a very long time to set up this investigation. Do you want to know why?"*

"No," she said bluntly.

*"I'm not convinced that I can control Takemi. There's no rhyme or reason to anything she chooses to do. But it seems to me, she now has something she cares about."*

"That didn't work. She murdered someone."

*"But it did work. You stopped her from killing two people."*

"So what if I did? Does that mean I should forgive her?"

*"I don't give two craps if you forgive her or not,"* Sung-jae said, raising his voice in clear annoyance. *"Do you think I'm your therapist? I'm not here to give you relationship advice."*

"She did something wrong and she needs to pay for it. Is this what the law stands for in this country?"

*"Enough!"* he yelled. *"Have you never heard of the greater good? We're finishing this investigation,"* he said more quietly, though his voice more than a little stern. *"I told you what would happen if you're arrested. It won't just be you that's hurt. Your whole family will be shunned. You said you had a husband who's a cop, right?"*

"Yes."

*"He'll be fired or mistreated so much that he'll quit himself and have nowhere to turn. Think about your actions before you do them."*

Yu-ra clutched her skirt, tightening her grip.

"I don't feel safe around her."

Sung-jae audibly sighed.

*"She's proven multiple times that you're the only thing she cares about. Maybe you're the only one that can stop her from doing anything worse."*

"It is not my job to save her."

*"But maybe you can."*

Yu-ra paused for a moment, pondering on how to respond, when a sudden banging on the door caused her to jump out of the seat. She quickly cut off the call and shoved the phone in her cardigan pocket.

"J-just a minute," she called out.

"Are you ready?" came Takemi's voice through the door.

Yu-ra quickly pressed the toilet flush down and washed her hands in the sink beside her before shoving the door open, Takemi hopping back in response.

"Yes."

"Ny-ron wants you back here in two days. He says he needs to decide where you'll be useful."

As the two exited the bathroom, they came upon a scene of at least fifteen gang members awaiting their return. They all began clapping and whistling.

"What…the heck is going on," Yu-ra said, body frozen.

"They're applauding your actions," Takemi whispered. "I said it was you who saved us from being ripped off. These guys really hate the Japanese, so anything that causes them grievances is worth celebrating in their books."

"Yu-ra! Yu-ra! Yu-ra!" they chanted.

****

"Woo!" Yu-ra squealed, bouncing up and down lightly on her toes. "This is going to be so fun!"

"Yeah," Kyung-tae smiled, "it can be quite exhilarating. Jinmu took me once as a form of training and I've been a fan ever since."

The gentle rustle of leaves in the cool breeze whistled in Kyung-tae's ears, occasionally accompanied by the soft whinnies and snorts of the horses behind them, the sound heightened by the shelter of the stable they stood under. Off in the distance, the barren meadows were muted in tones of brown and beige, dotted with twisted leafless trees. Across all of it, two moustachioed men guided their horses, bridles in hand, towards the couple. One of the workers was stout and chubby with a cheery grin and the other was tall but grimacing the whole way towards them. The faint smell of saddle leather and hay, mixed with the earthy aroma of damp soil in the air.

"It was nice of your cousin to get us this for the wedding," Yu-ra said, after settling down. "I didn't think you'd be up for it."

"If it wasn't set up for a particular date, I would've second guessed coming. But I've done this a few times. I enjoy it."

"Wow, you can actually have fun? When did they install that setting?"

"When they installed the setting that allows me to recognise an actually good joke. As you can see, my body is not reacting with a haughty chuckle."

"Woah," Yu-ra said, turning to him in faux shock, though keeping her hands deep in her pockets, "it's like that, now?"

"Yeah," Kyung-tae said, smirking lightly, "it's like that."

The clip-clopping of hooves arrived closer to them and as such so did the moustachioed men with their respective horses. Both horses were dark brown with well-kept manes.

"Mr and Mrs Oh," the cheery man said. "I'll be the one training you today. You can call me Ma-reu."

"Well uhh Ma-reu," Yu-ra said, "let's uhh go!"

"She's a little excited about this," Kyung-tae said. "I have some experience with this, so we can get straight into it."

The grimacing man strutted away into the stables, muttering something to himself about having to work on such a cold day.

"Don't mind Ru-ji," Ma-reu said, "he's been in a sour mood ever since he left the womb."

After Kyung-tae mounted his horse, he looked across to find Yu-ra struggling to climb hers.

"Need some help?" Ma-reu asked.

"I'll help her," Kyung-tae said, hopping off his saddle and making his way to Yu-ra. "It's okay, Ma-reu, you can go relax. I can teach her." He turned to Yu-ra. "I'll hold you steady. You just focus on getting your leg over the saddle."

"Okay," Yu-ra said.

As Kyung-tae gently grasped Yu-ra's forearm, she winced, snatching her arm away. What was that?

"Are you okay?" Kyung-tae said, puzzlement riddling his features.

"Yeah, sorry. I just needed to itch my nose," she said, suddenly scratching at her nose. "Hold my hand."

Kyung-tae followed the order, taking her warm hand in his.

"What are these?" he asked, lightly rubbing the plasters across her knuckles.

"I hit my hand on the kitchen counter in the morning, started bleeding."

"You're really clumsy, aren't you?"

"Yep."

Yu-ra finally managed to get her leg onto the other side of the horse, and Kyung-tae returned to his, easily mounting it once again. Kyung-tae began trotting his horse in circles around her. After seeing this, Ma-reu nodded affirmatively at Kyung-tae and then returned to the stable to meet his coworker.

"Ok, student Yu-ra, are you ready for your lesson?" Kyung-tae said.

"Yes, teacher Kyung-tae," she said, nodding with determination.

"First thing's first, straighten your posture, keep your shoulders back and your heels down." Kyung-tae stopped his horse in front of hers. "Like this."

"Like this?" Yu-ra said, following his instructions exactly as he described.

"Perfect, student Yu-ra. Now, just stay relaxed and keep a light but firm grip on the reins." After Yu-ra followed suit, Kyung-tae continued. "Now onto the basic cues. Listen carefully. You're going to use your legs and seat to get the horse to move, stop, and turn. Don't start whipping the horse with the reins."

"Why in the world would I do that?" Yu-ra said, shaking her head at him in disbelief.

"I know what you're like."

"What-"

"Don't interrupt me, student!" Kyung-tae said, holding his hand out and turning his nose up at her.

"You ass," Yu-ra muttered.

"Silence!"

"Can we just carry on with the lesson?"

"Yes," he said, returning his hands to his reins, "anyway, to get the horse to start walking, gently squeeze your legs against the horse's sides."

Yu-ra did as she was told and the horse took up a slow gait.

"Oh my God!" she squealed. "This is too fast for me! How do I get it to stop? Stop, boy!"

Kyung-tae began chuckling lightly.

"I told you to relax your body. Let your body move with the horse."

"Then what?"

"Then enjoy it," he said, trotting his horse beside hers.

"If you want to turn, use the reins to lightly apply pressure to that side of the horse's neck and slightly shift your weight and legs to guide the horse.

"Like this?" she said, turning towards Kyung-tae's horse.

"Yes." He laughed, moving his horse away from hers, "but turn the other way."

"Oh, sorry," she said, turning the other way. But as she did so, she winced once again. What was up with her? Was it something he did?

"Are you sure you're okay?"

"Yeah, I'm fine," she said, correcting her posture immediately.

Kyung-tae shrugged it off.

"Okay, let's walk down to the other side of the field."

As they traversed the field for half an hour, Yu-ra engaged him in small talk, asking him about his current case, to which he concluded that he hadn't found any solid leads yet. Although it definitely wasn't a cold case.

"Your dad called, by the way," Kyung-tae said. "He wants us to come down."

"When?" she asked.

"Any time on the weekend."

"I can't. I'm super busy."

"Oh right, how is that assignment going?" Kyung-tae asked.

"Assignment…? Oh right! That assignment. It's going well. I have some ideas for it that I need to write down."

"You're getting pretty good at this. Let's speed up," he said, showing her how to with his legs as his horse moved into a light gallop. The increased wind speed began to blow his hair back. "Just be ready to slow down by lightly pulling back on the reins."

Yu-ra matched her horse's pace with Kyung-tae's, but visible discomfort crossed her features as she sped up. Was it the horse riding that she was finding difficult but didn't want to say anything?

"So, my assignment," she said as she got used to the speed.

"Oh right, what is the assignment even about?"

"We got some information about a murder, but with a massive lack of evidence. There was one piece of evidence which stood out to me which was the bleached clothes."

Yu-ra winced once again. Something was definitely wrong.

"Woah!" he called out, pulling back on his reins and slowing his horse to a deliberate walk. "Slow your horse down, like I just did."

Yu-ra slowed her horse and Kyung-tae caught up to her.

"What's wrong?" Yu-ra said.

"You tell me. There's clearly something going on with you."

"What do you mean?"

"Is it the horse riding? Are you finding it painful? We can stop the lesson, you know?"

"I'm fine. I'm doing well aren't I?"

"You're doing amazingly, but that doesn't change the fact that it looks like it's causing you some kind of difficulty. Stop. Stop your horse," he said as he halted his own, followed by hers.

"I promise you, I'm fine," she said innocently.

Kyung-tae eyed her.

"No, we're getting down. At the very least, we're taking a break."

As the words left his lips, a sudden surge of surprise rippled through him. Why was he so adamant? He had never been one to force a decision, and especially not with Yu-ra. What had changed? And why did he feel an uncomfortable pang in his chest every time he thought she had any discomfort?

Yu-ra stared at him, and then a smile formed on her face. And the longer she looked, the wider it grew.

"What?"

"Thank you."

"What for?"

"It's nice to know how much you care. I really do appreciate the concern."

She winced once again.

"Are you sure you're okay? I don't care if we use up the rest of the time to relax, as long as you're okay."

"Okay, maybe my shoulder does hurt a bit. But trust me, I'm fine to do this."

"Do you want to get on my horse and we'll just ride together?"

"Boy, you're really worried here, aren't you?"

Why was he so worried? She had made it clear that she was capable of riding the horse herself. And discomfort aside, she was doing pretty well with it. But every time she felt discomfort, Kyung-tae felt responsible because he could stop it at any point.

"Yeah, I'm worried," he said with concern filling his eyes. "If I can stop this, doesn't that make me responsible if you get hurt?"

"This isn't because of you. You can't stop me riding this horse. And if you're really worried, then just make it your life goal to keep me happy." She grinned.

"Sounds like a fair trade deal," he determined.

"Okay then, teacher Kyung-tae," she said, "back to the lesson."

"Well, student Yu-ra," he said, his subtle smile returning, "this is the part where I show you what you'll be capable of if you follow your ambitions and practise hard!"

Kyung-tae moved his horse into a trot as he circled her once, and then reversed, circling her backwards. He then stopped and reared the horse, lifting its two front legs in the air. The wind rushed against the back of his head and he tightened his core to maintain his balance. The horse returned its legs to the ground and Kyung-tae grinned at her.

"Show off," she said, giggling.

"Okay, student Yu-ra. For our next activity, I will gallop around the field and you have to catch me. Ready?"

"No. You need to let me practise galloping first."

"Go!" Kyung-tae called as he raced off.

"HEY! SHOW ME HOW TO GALLOP FIRST!"

# 16
# A Scuffle

Yu-ra maintained a sizable distance from Takemi as they walked through the compound. They journeyed past the rows of packers lined up across fifty thousand square feet of concrete. Park Ny-ron, stood atop a platform to the side and eyed them for a moment before continuing to bellow out names. As each name was called out, a packer would walk past them and line up at the platform. Before they exited the compound, Yu-ra took one last glance to see those who had lined up following one of the guards to Ny-ron's headquarters. Rumours had spread amongst the packers that there was infighting and that someone within the gang had been the cause of Kim Cho-ji's death. Obviously this had reached Ny-ron considering his current course of actions.

A sleek silver sports car awaited them outside the building. Sprinting up to it, like a leopard pouncing on its prey, Takemi leapt and slid across the hood of the car, landing flawlessly on the other side of the car.

"Yu-ra, did you see that?" she called out, bouncing up and down, as Yu-ra maintained her pace all the way up to the passenger side of the car.

"No," she said before opening her door and sliding into her leather seat. Before her head had fully entered the car, she glimpsed Takemi's head drooping.

A deafening silence filled the car as Takemi sped down the wide-open streets. In all her years around Takemi, she couldn't remember a single moment where they ever sat in silence. Takemi turned to her, her eerily bare mask still on. How could she even see with that stupid thing on? It was surprising that they hadn't been pulled over yet. Did she ever take a second to think about what she was doing?

"Sorry we had to make this detour," Takemi said. "Duty calls, you know."

"So if your justice system is so flawless, how do you still get turf wars occurring?"

Takemi slowed the car to turn into a side road.

"It's not a turf war. it's a racist scuffle."

"Ha! Scuffle. Brilliant use of the word."

"The Koreans built their gang upon hatred for colonisers. what do you expect? You can't burn the hatred from their hearts by just imposing new laws." Yu-ra looked out the window but continued to listen. "That's where the treaty comes in."

"Treaty? You're just muscle. Nothing more."

"I strike fear into the hearts of the disobedient and have free reign to act in accordance with the treaty. There's nothing scarier than death."

"I wouldn't say that. If you believe your actions are morally upright, and you believe yourself to be the same, death isn't something that stops you from doing those actions. Have you never heard of a martyr?"

"Wait, this is considered moral?"

"No. I'm saying they think they're doing the right thing because they're fighting their colonisers. They're fighting for freedom."

"They're not fighting the Japanese. Those guys are Chinese."

"Wait, what? Why were you talking about Koreans hating the colonisers then?"

"I don't know," Takemi said, shrugging. "I wanted to sound profound."

"These people are crazy! They both have a common hatred for the Japanese but they decided to start fighting each other over race?"

"That's what gangs are like," Takemi said, shrugging once again.

Takemi pulled into another side road and parked up. Across the street from the driver's door, a grimy alleyway was housed by tall crumbling buildings that cast ominous shadows. Within the shadows, shouts of pain and the clashing of weapons echoed. According to Takemi's report, at least forty people were in a fierce battle within that narrow path.

"Alright, wait here," Takemi said, retrieving one of her daggers from underneath her coat.

"Wait," Yu-ra said, "what exactly is your plan?"

"Dole out justice."

"You're going to murder all of them? Forty people in a narrow alleyway?"

"Yeah, and?"

"There's forty of them. If more than a few of them decide that they want to take you out, they'll kill you."

"That's cute." Takemi chuckled. "As if these chumps could hurt me."

"Takemi," Yu-ra said, putting her hand on her shoulder, "it is not feasible to kill that many people."

"I don't need to," Takemi said, lifting her mask. "I just need to make an example of some of them. The rest will fall in line."

"And how long will that last? The reason you're still doing this job is because your solution only works short term. You're the one who said you want a way out."

"It's the most effective method of keeping the peace. All the leaders agreed on it."

"It may work effectively for turf wars, but what happens with more minor issues that you overlooked, when tensions get high over personal stuff and people react out of anger? And what happens when you're gone? Doesn't the whole system crash? They don't know who you are. You could just up and leave at any moment."

Takemi looked deeply into her eyes, staying silent for a moment.

"Then what's the solution?"

"I agree that your treaty somewhat works. Each gang gains something and has something to lose if they go against the treaty. But you need to apply that same concept to the infantries. What do they get out of it? And yes, they know what they lose. But if a situation gets out of hand like this, what they lose is so devastating that you'd lose hope for a way back to peace."

"So with a situation like this, they need a way out, some repercussions, as well as gaining something if they keep the peace?"

"Exactly!"

"So why don't we give their leaders the chance to hold their people accountable? And then each gang needs to give something up as a collective in order to keep the treaty intact. If they don't follow these instructions, the treaty is no longer valid for the gangs involved. None of them actually want war. It would be too devastating for them."

Yu-ra contemplated momentarily. Takemi was smarter than she gave her credit for.

"That sounds like it would work. Do you need back up?"

Takemi chuckled before turning on her voice modulator.

"Sorry, but I don't think you'd help much here."

Racing from the car to the alleyway, Takemi let out a fearful roar, garnering the attention of the nearest few gang members. She launched her two daggers into their clothes, pinning them to the ground, then leapt into the air blasting a flurry of kicks at the next nearest targets before landing on the ground. She must have yelled something, because a moment later, all the combatants in that alleyway dropped their guards and froze in place. Takemi walked through the crowd, the sea of fighters parting to make way for her. And within a mere five minutes, everyone had released their weapons from their grips. Yu-ra smiled. Takemi was growing.

# 17
# Who Killed Kim Cho-ji?

"That's the deal Ny-ron," Takemi said, pulling her car up outside of an apartment complex. "Each gang pays a fee to the Japanese for not being involved, and you hold those involved accountable. It's the only way to save your people."

"Which floor does he live on?" Yu-ra asked quietly, looking up at the rows of front doors across the two floors of the complex.

"Up there, number fifty-six," she whispered, pointing to the second floor, then returned to her phone call. "It doesn't matter if you don't care if they live or die. The Chinese have already agreed. So you'll agree too, otherwise it'll be you who my judgement falls upon."

Cutting the phone call, Takemi lifted her mask, turning to Yu-ra, and smiling with pride.

"Let's go," Yu-ra said, swinging the passenger door open with her boot, the cold air rushing in and wrapping around her ankles before she stepped out.

"I got his fingerprint by the way, this Byung-ho guy's," Takemi said as she exited the car.

"I know, stupid. Why would we be going to his place if you didn't?"

"Right. That makes sense," Takemi said as they made their way to the concrete steps to the second floor. "There didn't really seem to be anything wrong with this guy. I asked around. No one really had any issues with him. They all said he had a great work ethic." They two climbed the steps as Yu-ra continued to listen. "I don't get why you suspect this guy. You've barely interacted with anyone. You don't know him."

"I gave you my reasons."

"What, a discoloured jumpsuit? That's not much of a reason if you ask me?" she said as they reached the second floor.

"Not discoloured - bleached. I spoke to Kyung-tae. It's very common for criminals to bleach their clothes to remove DNA evidence."

"And what's wrong with my approach?" Takemi asked as she slid her mask back down. "I always get results. Five minutes with this guy and I would've gotten the truth, but instead we're sneaking around."

"If you want me here with you, you're doing it my way. End of."

"You go ahead. I think I left something in the car," she said, spinning on her axis.

She arrived at number fifty-six - Byung-ho's apartment. Yu-ra rapped her knuckles against the apartment door and waited a few moments. No response came. She knocked again, tapping the toe of her right shoe against the concrete as she waited.

*Drug dealing must pay well.* She eyed the welcome mat of the house. She never thought someone who worked for a drug-running gang would have such a homely place. Yu-ra heard a twang coming from the metal railing behind her as Takemi effortlessly hurdled over it. She held out a small piece of laminated plastic.

"Did you just go back down so you could jump over the railing?" Yu-ra asked.

"Maybe," Takemi said. "Here, don't smudge it,".

"I know," Yu-ra said, taking it out of her hands by the corners. "So I just push this against the sensor?"

"Yeah, the code is two-five-nine-four-three."

"How did you find… you know what, never mind."

Yu-ra pressed the fingerprint against the red light illuminating from the sensor and the metal cover above it popped up. She slid the cover upwards and dialled in the numbers. Yu-ra heard a click and pushed the cold handle down, swinging the door open. They crept in, leaving their shoes at the doorway. The layout of the living room was similar to hers, but this one much smaller, although maybe it looked that way because of all the furnishing filling up the space.

"By the way," Takemi said, sidling up to the kitchen counter. "They're rounding up a lot of the fresh blood, anyone that's joined within the last three years. You're lucky to have joined after it. It's a good thing you have me to vouch for you."

"Save it," Yu-ra said, holding her palm out. "Just get on with the task. I'll check the bedroom. You check all the cupboards."

Takemi sighed.

"What am I looking for?"

"Literally anything that can explain why his jumpsuit was bleached, why he could potentially have attacked Cho-ji, anything at all."

Yu-ra walked to the back of the room, into the hallway-like space and opened the door on her right. She peeked in to see the dull white walls of the bathroom. After creeping in, she checked behind the shower curtain. The bathtub still had soap scum around the edges, but there was nothing useful. She spun around, crouching down to check under the wooden cupboard underneath the sink. She filtered through the objects, finding nothing but regular cleaning items. Though there was an unusually large case of bleach - proof that it was a bleached jumpsuit she saw. She stood up, scrunching her nose as her face came too close to the hair covered sink.

*Money doesn't make you clean, I guess.*

She left the room and crossed the hallway to the bedroom which was furnished with just a king-sized bed, a bedside table, and a lamp that sat atop it. The bedsheets were bunched up on top of the bed. Rustling through the bedsheets, she found nothing of use. Where did he keep all his clothes? A floor-to-ceiling mirror built into the wall loomed behind her as she crept up to the bedside table and began rummaging through the drawers.

"You sure this is the guy that killed Cho-ji," Takemi called out. "I got nothing."

Yu-ra opened the bottom drawer. On top of all the underwear was a little plastic bag spattered with red droplet stains, half filled with blue crystals.

"Gotcha!" Yu-ra whispered, pumping a fist into the air. She scanned the room, looking for any other hiding spots. Looking back at the mirror behind her, a suspicion began to grow. Tiptoeing up to it, she pressed her palms against the surface and pushed left. It slid open, revealing a small wardrobe.

She shoved apart the rows of hanging shirts and trousers, revealing small red stains which littered the bottom of the wall at the back of the wardrobe. Her eyes followed them until they stopped at a dull white jumpsuit, the same one he was wearing when Yu-ra saw him first. And right beside it, held in a plastic Ziplock bag, was a knife stained with a dark red crust. The door creaked open and Takemi peered around the corner, pouting a little.

"You didn't answer me earlier," she whined. "I don't know what I'm doing. I hate this."

Yu-ra tossed the bag of crystals to Takemi as she entered the rest of her body into the room.

"You're finding our evidence, because this is definitely our guy." Yu-ra stood up and began pacing back and forth, tapping her finger against her chin. "Here's the scenario. Two packers have this genius idea to sneak out some of the drugs they're packing and make a little extra something on the side. But one of them uses some of it first, and he quite likes the high he gets. Disagreements lead to a scuffle."

"A scuffle, yeah?"

Yu-ra halted, directing her index finger at Takemi in an accusatory manner as her voice deepened in an attempt to mimic a menacing man. Unfortunately, it came out like a boy going through puberty.

"You will not destroy everything we have worked so hard for, you fiend!" She tucked her left hand behind her back and shifted her feet into a faux fencing stance, extending her right arm in front of her. "This day shall be your last, you junkie villain!"

"Why do they sound like nineteenth century Englishmen?" Takemi said, scratching her head. "You sound like a cartoon character."

"This is how they sound in my head, so get off my back." She huffed as she dropped her arm. "Anyway this guy pulls out a knife, does something he regrets and covers everything up because he knows the consequences."

"I don't know. These guys are usually pretty scared of me." Takemi shrugged. "I don't think they'd be able to let it get to that point."

"But they still get into race wars? Get over yourself. Just tell me what you think of the theory."

"Fine. Let's say I'm not part of the equation at all. Only then would I say it's feasible."

"We need to let Ny-ron know, before he hurts all those innocent… well, relatively innocent people."

Takemi tossed the plastic bag back to Yu-ra.

"Alright, let's head out then."

Yu-ra's left leg refused to remain still for the entire duration of the journey. Takemi parked her car across the road from the compound and Yu-ra dashed straight to the building, bursting through the door. She was met with a large forearm, from a bulky man with a buzzcut, stopping her in her tracks.

"I need to get past! It's life or death!" she said, trying to force past the barrier, but to no avail.

"You don't need to do anything. You know the rules. I need to pat you down." He grinned sadistically.

"You're not going to touch me." She hissed, successfully shoving his hand away. "I'm here to tell Ny-ron who killed Cho-ji."

"That's Mr Park to you, newbie."

"And that's Mrs Kim to you," she said, narrowing her eyes.

Yu-ra heard some footsteps approaching her from behind.

"Let her in. She's telling the truth," Takemi said.

The brawny man dropped his hands and bowed deeply, leaving an opening for Yu-ra.

"Apologies Cheonsa. I didn't realise she was with you."

Yu-ra rushed through the compound, back through the bowels of the restaurant and then up to the second floor. As she burst through Ny-ron's office, she was met with seven men lined up on their knees, their hands tied behind their backs which faced Yu-ra. Blood dripped from Ny-ron's knuckles, and beside him, against a wall, leaned a scarlet stained steel pipe. Ny-ron looked up from the men that were wrought with trepidation.

"What do you want? Can't you see I'm in the middle of something."

"I know who killed Cho-ji."

"Oh yeah, and how would you know that?" he said calmly, picking up the pipe that leaned on the wall which scraped along the ground as he ambled towards the first man in the line.

"Please," the man pleaded between short, quick breaths. "I have nothing to do with this."

"You better talk quick, girl, if you want to prove everyone else's innocence."

She raised her hands defensively, as if attempting to calm a rabid animal, and crept closer to them.

"It's Byung-ho, the packer. I've got evidence," she said, motioning to drop his weapon. "You can put the pipe down. I've got evidence."

At that moment, Takemi walked in, dragging a man with short straight black hair and a chubby figure by the collar as he thrashed about on the ground. It was the owner of the dull white jumpsuit. She tossed Byung-ho to the ground.

"She's telling the truth," Takemi said. "Hear her out."

Ny-ron dropped the pipe beside his potential victim, who fell to the ground, whimpering. Yu-ra lifted Byung-ho up onto his knees, holding him up by the arm.

"Where were you on the night Cho-ji died?" she said.

"What is this? I've got a foolproof alibi. I was taking care of my sick mother in the hospital," Byung-ho yelled. "Who the hell do you think you are to question me? You've been here barely a week and you think you can run things all of a sudden?"

Overly defensive at the earliest possible moment, one of the telltale signs that Kyung-tae told her about.

"Has Cho-ji ever done something that's really pissed you off, like maybe he stole some drugs and you just had to get them back by any means necessary? Maybe you'd go so far as to pull a knife on him?"

"I don't need to answer you, spade," he said, itching his thigh. "If you want to play detective, you joined the wrong line of work."

Takemi whipped her dagger out and pressed it against his neck.

"You're gonna answer her," she murmured in his ear, "or it's going to be your last defiant breath."

Byung-ho raised his hands up in defence.

"Okay, okay, relax. Look, I never had a problem with Cho-ji. Ask anyone, we were tight. One of my closest friends." Byung-ho itched his thigh harder, another telltale sign that he was lying.

Yu-ra held her hand out to Takemi.

"I gave you a chance to come clean," she said, as Takemi handed her the plastic bag containing the stained knife. "I found this buried in your closet. Wanna explain this? And don't lie, I can tell when you are."

"Okay, wait, I can explain," he blurted. "You were right, Cho-ji stole some drugs from the compound. I went to get it back from him but he wouldn't budge, so we got into a fight. It got really bad and I pulled a knife out for protection, and accidentally stabbed him. I was scared of what would happen so I hid the evidence."

Takemi pulled her dagger away.

"And what happened to the drugs that he stole?"

He began itching his leg once again.

"He had already used most of it. I put what was left of it back into production lines."

Yu-ra paused, watching Byung-ho's eyes bleed fear. But it wasn't Takemi he was afraid of.

"He's telling the truth," she said, turning to Ny-ron. "I know Cho-ji was my cousin, but he broke rules, and Byung-ho here was just trying to do right by you. I would consider the issue resolved. I'm not here for revenge."

Ny-ron dropped his weapon, waving away the seven men kneeling on the ground. They scrambled for the door.

"You're one smart cookie," he said to Yu-ra. "I may have a use for you after all."

"Please don't ever call me that again," she said.

"I need you to run a little investigation. Someone's been attacking our warehouses. Billions of Yen worth of product gone in one night. If you're as good of an investigator as you've already shown, you should be able to find out who stole it. If you do, I'll set you up for life."

Yu-ra pretended to take a moment to contemplate it.

"I'll do it."

"Isn't that my job?" Takemi cut in, stepping closer to him, her dagger still in hand, "Are you meddling in my work, Ny–ron?"

"Of course not, but you've already seen how helpful she can be. You've even worked with her more closely than I have."

"I'll give you that," Takemi said, tucking her dagger underneath the back of her coat. "She can continue to work with me. We need to have a meeting with your supplier," Takemi said and then pointed to Byung-ho, "to discuss what to do about this chump here. This'll put a stain on my reputation."

"Don't worry about that," Ny-ron said, picking his pipe back up off the ground. He brushed past Takemi's shoulder as he dragged the tip of the pipe along the ground with a high-pitched scratching, filling the silent room. "I'm a fair man, Byung-ho. I appreciate honesty." He crouched beside Byung-ho's face. "But who in the hell said you could think for yourself!" he barked.

"I'm sorry, sir!" Byung-ho cried. "I just wanted to fix things for you!"

"And you think you can fix my problems for me?"

"No, of course not, sir! I'm nothing more than your loyal subject!"

"And I appreciate that. But repercussions are in order," he said, tapping the pipe against Byung-ho's knee, "and I've determined that I'll be taking your leg."

"NO, WAIT, NO!" Byung-ho screamed as Ny-ron swung the pipe down onto Byung-ho's leg, his kneecap crumbling underneath the pressure, as he cried out in pain.

Yu-ra blocked her mouth with her hand as she turned away and muffled her squeal. A cacophony of bone yielding to the relentless force of the pipe reached her ears and she could feel her previous meal beginning to rise up her throat. She needed to get out. Now.

Yu-ra fled from the room and after a few seconds heard footsteps following her. She needed to get away. Away from everyone. Somewhere hidden. Somewhere no one went. The footsteps became fainter as she travelled deeper into the compound, down into a network of tunnels below the restaurant. Left. Straight. Follow the bend. Battling against the rising tide of her tears, she struggled to keep the glistening dew of sorrow within the confines of her eyes. She cut right. Left. Left again. Suddenly she found herself blocked by a dull grey steel door. There was nought but the sound of scratching at the base of the mysterious door.

"Is…" Yu-ra trailed off. Maybe there was some kind of rodent on the other side. But then the sound of sniffling came from behind the door. "Is someone there?" There was no response, but the sniffling became more overtly emotional, followed by the faint sound of crying. "Hey, my name is Yu-ra. What's yours?" The sniffling stopped, but still no reply came. "I can stay here as long as you want, if you need help. If you need a friend. To be honest with you, I'm trying to escape from this place right now. I'm in way over my head." Shuffling noises came from the other side, moving closer to the door. "Truth be told, I'm really scared right now and don't know what I'm even doing here."

Suddenly a weak feminine voice came from the other side.

"Do you know what happened to the other girl that was with me?"

"Other girl?"

"Kim Sun-jung."

# 18
# Warehouse

"Why did you even come with me?" Kyung-tae said as he pulled up to the latest warehouse that had caught fire. It was the fifth one.

"Lieutenant's orders," Woo-young responded as they got out of the car.

"Shut up, Woo-young. I'm being serious. Tell me why you're here."

"Do you want me to shut up or tell you why I'm here? You need to be clearer with your words." Kyung-tae cut his eyes at him as they arrived at the scene of the crime and Woo-young smirked in response. "So, your charm seems to come and go, then? You weren't so moody when you needed something from me."

Kyung-tae looked across the road as he was about to respond to Woo-young. A man stood there, taking in the scene. He looked familiar. Kyung-tae squinted slightly. Mr Choi? The man turned to leave and Kyung-tae rushed over to stop him.

"Sir!" he called, halting the man. "What are you doing here?"

"Kyung-tae?" Mr Choi responded as they met. "I was just passing by and I saw this. Reminded me of your case so I stopped and watched for a bit. It looks a little old. I thought you would have already investigated this scene."

"I have, but I think I missed something. So, I'm rechecking. In fact, we haven't even found any lighters at this scene yet."

"Have you got any significant leads on the owner yet?"

"No, but I know they're being ordered in bulk. I just don't know where they're going yet. The guy who makes them doesn't know himself."

"If they're being ordered in bulk, it means the guy is probably rich."

"Or he's buying them with the explicit intent to be used for arson. Like a calling card."

"I'll help you if needed – find out who's been buying the lighters?"

"No, it's fine, you go and rest. I'll solve this."

****

"So what exactly are we looking for?" Takemi asked, tossing some plastic litter she found on the concrete to her side as she stood up.

"Are you going to ask that every time we're investigating?" Yu-ra said, looking around the damp, ashy warehouse, and then up at the sixty percent missing roof. She kicked the blackened, wooden table leg at her feet.

"I don't know. Are you going to be a butthead every time I ask, butthead?" Takemi said, nudging her shoulder.

"Calm down, sassy pants, I was joking-"

"My pants aren't sassy. They're very fashionable," Takemi muttered.

"But isn't this your job? You should know what you're looking for."

"I've never really investigated arson. It tends to just be scuffles between runts, or a faction trying to move across industries. My job mostly entails making an example of them."

"I don't even want to know what that means. But speaking of, you need to help me with something."

"What's that?"

"There were two recent kidnapping cases. Two girls got kidnapped in one night, though there was no connection between the two girls. The first girl committed suicide. I found the second girl."

"Okay, so how does this involve me?" Takemi said as they traversed the warehouse grounds.

"Well, you won't be happy about this. I found the second girl being kept prisoner in the underground tunnels. Which means that someone from Ny-ron's gang was behind it."

"Oh-ho no they did not! They did this with me around? Who do I make pay?"

"You can't do anything about it."

"Why? This is exactly why my job was created in the first place."

"Because if you cause chaos within Ny-ron's gang, it will jeopardise our whole mission. All we need to do is get her out quietly. Who's going to make a fuss about it if they know they're dead if it gets out?"

"I guess that makes sense. So how do we get her out?"

"Just draw me a map of the tunnels and something to bust open a metal door. People won't notice me. I'll get her out."

"Let's get back to investigating."

Yu-ra pointed at a pile of tables on the far-left corner of the wide open room that looked as if they were smashed to pieces before they were set on fire.

"Start there. See if there's any evidence of where the fire started from. I'll start with the crates over there." She pointed to the centre of the room, at the crates that had clearly been pried open, seeing as the side panels were lying flat on the ground in front of it. "The underside of the panel is intact. They were broken into before the fire was set."

"Yes sir, master Yu-ra!" she cried, saluting her. "I'm at your service!"

Yu-ra's cheeks perked up, but she quickly dragged her hand down her face to stop herself from smiling.

"Hurry up and go, you idiot."

Yu-ra ambled towards the section of crates, looking around at the second floor decorated with scaffoldings and metal ladders. The pathways only had enough space for two to three people to walk in a line at a time. She spotted around six cameras dotted around the room. The warped wooden panels creaked and wobbled underneath her boots as she took her phone out of her pocket and tapped the torch button, burning away the shroud of darkness. As she searched, the voice of the girl who had asked about Sun-jung rang in her head.

*"I'll get you out of here,"* Yu-ra had responded to her. *"Give me some time to come up with a plan. I promise you I'll be back for you."*

"What was stored in these crates?" Yu-ra called out, directing her light towards the murky pools collecting in the pockets of the unlevel base. "Is this where they kept all their drugs?"

"This is the main location, yeah," Takemi's voice echoed back. "You know that deal we made?"

"Yeah. They were keeping all that here?" She eyed the crumbling black walls, not a trace of any drugs left in there, the damp beginning to rot the wood, overcoming her sense of smell.

"It's a prototype drug. They've not injected it into the mainline yet. But they've started testing it out with the Yakuza and Triad branches here."

Yu-ra walked back out into the room and turned off her torch, putting her phone back into her pocket.

"Hey, I think I found something," Takemi yelled. "Looks like some sloppy person dropped a lighter."

"Let me see," she said, beckoning her over. "By the way, where's the security room? Has anyone bothered to check the CCTV tapes?"

Takemi stopped in front of her and tossed her the greasy metal lighter. It slipped down the palm of her right hand a little before she stopped it with her left.

"It's up there," she said, pointing to the backroom on the second floor.

"What's this animal?" she said, rubbing her thumb against what was left of the engraving at the front.

"Looks like a bear to me," Takemi said, shrugging. "I dunno. It doesn't mean anything to me."

"So you're telling me that both the police and fire department searched this place and couldn't find this?"

"You'd be surprised by how much we get away with. Besides, it was buried pretty deep. They might have just overlooked it."

Suddenly, a clanging at the entrance door reverberated throughout the room. A shiver ran down Yu-ra's spine as her body involuntarily jerked back, causing the lighter to slip out of her hand. She reached out to grab it but it bounced off her palm clattering across the ground.

"Leave it," Takemi whispered in a harsh tone, seizing her wrist and yanking her across the room. They flew to the back of the room, pacing towards a mountain of smaller crates behind a toppled plastic table.

"I could have sworn I heard people talking in here," a familiar voice across the room echoed. Takemi pulled Yu-ra into a dive, landing them behind the crates with a skid. The friction tore a hole in her skirt and the arm of her cardigan, grazing the side of her thigh. The cold, wet, craggy ground poking her skin caused her body to stiffen. But the peeling skin on her thigh began to heat up.

"I didn't hear anything," an unfamiliar voice replied. "You're going crazy."

Takemi wrapped her open jacket around Yu-ra. She curled up a little underneath the jacket, Takemi's warmth transferring to her.

"It was so great for you to come with me. You are being extremely helpful," the familiar voice said monotonously. "A truly great detective you are, Woo-young."

*Wait, Kyung-tae? Is that you?*

"Like I said, boss' orders," the unfamiliar voice responded. "The lieutenant says you're so dumb that you'd probably cause another fire just standing in here."

There was a long pause between the two. Yu-ra analysed the mountain of wood in front of her, trying to find a gap she could see through. She shifted her whole body down, pulling away from Takemi's grip, a gap in the rubble seeming to open up. It was Kyung-tae, and he was scowling at the stout man wearing a goatee beside him, who was smirking back at him. Woo-young smacked Kyung-tae on the shoulder.

"Talk to me," Woo-young said. "What's the situation here?"

Yu-ra could feel a cramp starting to form in her neck from keeping her head off the ground. The tip of her scarf had soaked up a lot of the water from the ground, and some had seeped through her clothes.

Kyung-tae lifted his hand slowly moving towards their direction until he was pointing directly where they were hiding. Yu-ra's heart leapt out of her chest. Could he see them? Yu-ra yanked her head down and Takemi wrapped her arm around her tighter. Her heart thumped in her neck, the pulsing hushing Kyung-tae's voice.

"Over there," he said, before dropping his hand, "we found some methanol, same as the other warehouses. It's why the flame was invisible.

They came in with some sort of purpose, but there's nothing left here. This place is owned by a tech company, but there's no tech here - meaning that it was taken and the fire was a cover up."

"Okay," Woo-young said, "makes sense."

"The crates were pried open before the fire started, so that's most likely where everything was stored. But it would take a whole team to get everything out of here."

"You got that right. What did you find on the security tapes?"

"Nothing. They were lit up just like everything else here. Whoever led this job planned everything out."

"What I don't get is that each warehouse has been owned by an entirely separate company in entirely separate industries. So how is the arsonist choosing his locations?"

"Then work harder to find the connection."

Yu-ra lifted her head back up to see Kyung-tae staring at the lighter she had dropped.

"That's new," he said, marching towards the lighter and picking it up. "So, it was here."

"How did you miss something so obvious? The lieutenant was right about you."

"It wasn't there before. Someone has been here. Maybe..." he said before momentarily pausing, "maybe they're still here."

"What are you talking about?"

Kyung-tae shoved the lighter in his pocket.

"Shush!" Kyung-tae hissed before dashing towards the metal staircase to the side.

"Don't shush me, shit for brains!" Woo-young yelled.

Kyung-tae scrambled up the stairs out into Yu-ra's open view.

"Crap," she whispered as she clambered onto her hands and knees. "We need to move."

"Wait," Takemi whispered into her ear, keeping a vigilant eye on Woo-young, "okay now. Go, go, go."

They crawled around the boxes, until they were on the side that Kyung-tae wouldn't be able to see, and leaned their backs against them.

"Why the heck would he think we're still here?"

"Your husband's a freak, I can't lie to you."

Yu-ra looked up at Takemi's head, and then punched her in the arm, a loud pat echoing halfway through the room.

"Crap!" she said under her breath. She could hear Kyung-tae clang back down the stairs, the clicking of his heels getting closer to them. Yu-ra hugged herself into a tight ball, the thudding against the wall of her chest returning. His footsteps got closer still, the clicking entering within short proximity. Takemi pulled down her mask, tucking her other hand behind her back and crouching in a position ready to pounce. Her breath held still. She awaited the arrival of her husband's steps. Click-clack. Click-clack. Click-clack. The steps had arrived.

"Hey!" Woo-young called, "why is this water so blue?"

"It's reflecting the sky, genius," the booming voice above them replied.

"In case you didn't notice, it's awfully cloudy today."

Yu-ra dared to look up, seeing Kyung-tae's sharp chin pointing towards the sky.

"Damn, you're right."

"How did you make detective?" Woo-young said. "Are you seriously this dumb? I bet you're glad I came."

"You know, now that I think about it. I really *could* have done it without you."

Kyung-tae spun around and bolted back to Woo-young and Yu-ra let out a heavy breath of relief. She poked her head out from behind the crates to see Kyung-tae crouching down, scooping up the liquid into a glass tube and sealing it shut.

"What is it?" Woo-young asked.

"I've got a theory. Let's get out of here."

After a few moments, Yu-ra heard the entrance clang shut and took that as her cue to stand up and dust herself off. Thigh stinging from the dirty water getting into her graze, she checked her cardigan sleeve to see how big the hole was.

"This is one of my favourite cardigans." She sighed before they made their way to the spot that the two detectives were investigating. "What did they find?"

Takemi knelt down.

"It looks like they found some of the prototype drugs."

"Why do you keep calling it a prototype?"

"Because the guy who has been supplying it has been doing some wizardry on it. He's been giving it to us in batches. This latest batch is different. For some reason, it has a different effect on the user based on if it's in a liquid, solid, or gaseous state."

"How does that work?"

Takemi stood up, shrugging.

"Beats me."

"So the drugs weren't stolen," Yu-ra said, pacing around Takemi in small circles. "Whoever did this didn't want to sell the drugs; they set them ablaze."

"Why would they do that? They could have made billions from this."

"Maybe they're not after money."

"Then what are they after?"

"I don't know, but if Ny-ron owns any more warehouses, we should keep an eye on them. What I do know is that we have nothing to show Ny-ron."

"You've got nothing to worry about. He won't do anything while I'm around."

"Let's get out of here. I need to get home before Kyung-tae does, otherwise he might start asking questions," she said, lifting her sleeve up by the hole with one finger.

# 19
# Li-Na

Down in the bowels of the gang's headquarters, Yu-ra tapped on the steel door three times, paused, tapped two times, paused, and tapped three more times.

"Yu-ra!" the voice on the other side squealed, "you're back!"

"Indeed I am, girlie," Yu-ra said, as she took a device out of her pocket. "Stand back from the door. I'm getting you out of here."

Using the putty that enveloped the device, she shaped it around the door handle and started the five second timer. Yu-ra jogged a few metres down the grimy tunnels, and before she was able to turn back she heard a small boom, followed by the clanging of heavy metal hitting the ground. She turned back to see the metal door creak open and out stepped a petite girl with oily black hair, adorned in dirty, torn blue jeans and a blackened white t-shirt. Her arms were covered in scrapes, and her nails were jagged and dirty. She took a step away from Yu-ra after seeing the metal pipe that she was holding in her left hand. She had taken it with her reluctantly at Takemi's insistence for her protection.

"Don't worry," Yu-ra said, smiling. "This is to help me protect you."

Her right eye was slightly swollen, but her smile lit up the abyss that they stood in. She ran up to Yu-ra, embracing her so tightly that she began to struggle to breathe.

"Yu-ra," she cried, tears streaming from her face.

"Let's get you back home."

"Okay," the girl said, releasing her grip.

"You still haven't told me your name," Yu-ra said as they began to follow the secret escape route that Takemi had marked down on her map.

"Li-Na."

"Is that Chinese?"

"Yes."

"That other girl, Kim Sun-jung. You asked about her. She died. Suicide. I'm sorry."

"What," Li-Na said, lip trembling, "that can't be, she was the one keeping me hopeful that we would escape. When they came for her, those men, I overheard them saying that the police were on to them. After they took her, it was the only thing giving me hope, that one day the police would rescue me. But, then you arrived."

They turned right, then left, then left again. After a few moments, they heard footsteps and Yu-ra hushed Li-Na, gently pressing her against the wall with her arm. They slowly sidled towards their destination until the footsteps disappeared down a parallel passage. Continuing down the convoluted network of tunnels, they soon happened upon a steel door that Yu-ra had never seen. It had a little circular window like you would see on a submarine. She glanced into the window as she lowered Li-Na's head. Ny-ron was in there with a tall broad man who filled out his navy-blue suit, a tattoo peeking out from his shirt sleeve. Even his neck was thick and muscular. Fortunately, their backs were facing the door, so they didn't see her. Although, stranger than the man that Ny-ron was meeting, was the woman in a tight shirt and trousers who was beside him. She sported a black Kevlar vest on top of her white shirt. Suddenly, she turned towards the window, revealing her bewitching beauty. Yu-ra immediately collapsed her stature to the ground. Chun-mi? What was Chun-mi doing in a place like this?

"We need to get out of here fast," Yu-ra whispered before they zipped down their route.

The two girls continued down the tunnelled route, their feet pattering against the slick ground. Yu-ra looked at the map. A few more turns and they would be free. As they rounded a sharp bend, an unexpected collision jolted Yu-ra forward, her face meeting the broad back of a stout figure with an audible thud. As the man started to turn, panic surged through her veins. Her cover was on the brink of being exposed, and the consequences could endanger not only herself but also Li-Na. With determination coursing through her, she tightened her grip on the metal pipe she held. As the man pivoted to face her, she knew she had no choice. With a swift motion, she raised the pipe behind her head and unleashed all her strength in a single swing aimed at his face. The sickening crack of his nose breaking echoed in the tunnel as his head snapped back, crashing into the wall with a resounding thud before he crumpled to the ground. Yu-ra's pounding heart began to settle as she waited to see if he was still conscious.

"Okay," she said, "he's down. We're safe. Let's get out of here."

Eventually they found themselves beyond the confines of the compound and Yu-ra flagged down a cab for Li-Na.

"Go straight to the police station," Yu-ra said. "My husband is a cop, so don't worry. His partner was working on your case. They'll keep you safe."

With one last hug, Li-Na was away, finally embraced by the warmth of safety. After debating with herself for a few minutes, Yu-ra decided to recommence her descent into the labyrinth below them.

Arriving at the doorway she previously hid from, she found that the meeting with Ny-ron continued unabated. The steel door was too thick to hear through, but at the very least she could get some sort of evidence of Chun-mi being there. Yu-ra cautiously slid her phone till it was just barely peeking above the base of the window. The phone swayed side to side due to her lack of balance in her squatting position. She watched the screen as her finger aimed for the capture button, but just as she was about to snap a photo, Chun-mi turned…

Yu-ra dropped her hand. Did this woman have a sixth sense or something? Why was she always turning at the wrong moment?

Footsteps. They were coming towards the door. She needed to get out of there, fast. Yu-ra flitted away. Where was the best place to hide? Bathroom. She navigated the tunnels until she had arrived back at the restaurant and immediately dashed into the women's bathroom. Only the low humming of the air conditioning filled the room, so she entered the stall furthest from the entrance. She locked the door behind her and sat down on the lid. She sat for another half an hour, replying as best she could to texts from Min-ah in short bursts. She hated lying to her, but what could she do when she wasn't allowed to mention the case she was working on to anyone?

Yu-ra huffed as she stood up after another ten minutes, opening the stall door. Whilst standing by the sinks, she pushed forward on her hips and leaned back as far as she could to stretch out her stiff back. As she stood back up, the blood rushed to her head and she lost some balance as the world dizzied a little. She stood on her toes and pushed off the ground to stretch her legs before turning the sink on. Her phone began vibrating again, this time more frequently. She finished washing her hands and then turned her back to the room as she went to dry them. The door creaked open behind her as Yu-ra checked her phone to see some messages from Takemi.

"Well, if it isn't madame donkey face," came a familiar voice. "I never pegged you as the criminal type."

Yu-ra sighed as she put her phone back in her pocket and faced Chun-mi sullenly.

"I won't lie to you, Chun-mi, I did have you pegged as the criminal type. And would you look at that, here you are working for a drug dealing gang."

"Oh no, you have me all wrong. I'm just a bodyguard for a CEO. Whatever business he has here has nothing to do with me."

Yu-ra moved towards the exit.

"Yeah, whatever. If you don't mind, I'm busy."

"Busy hanging around that masked gentleman, right? I'm sure Kyung-tae is going to be happy he married an unfaithful spade."

Yu-ra couldn't understand why everyone thought Takemi was a guy. Sure, her voice was disguised and she was taller and more muscular than most women, but not enough to look manly.

"Yeah, he's loving it," Yu-ra said, moving faster towards the exit.

Chun-mi hopped in front of her.

"Where do you think you're going? Unlike you, I'm a very faithful person, and I don't appreciate Kyung-tae being played for a fool."

"Look, you have no idea what's going on here and I'd appreciate it if you just kept your mouth shut about this. I'm sure your father equally wouldn't like the fact that your boss has involvement in the criminal underworld."

Chun-mi flashed a smirk but then, almost as if her carefully constructed walls of composure crumbled instantaneously, furrowed her brow as her jaw locked. Yu-ra's wrist was snatched by Chun-mi, whose vicious teeth began to bare as she twisted it behind her back.

"Are you threatening me, princess?" Chun-mi said in a hushed tone in Yu-ra's ear as she yelped in pain.

Yu-ra tried twisting her wrist out of Chun-mi's grip, but it was to no avail. Her hulking strength was unbefitting of her delicate stature. The skin of Yu-ra's arm began to burn from the friction of their contact. Chun-mi began to cackle as Yu-ra yanked with all of the force she could generate, almost dislocating her shoulder. Chun-mi twisted her arm harder and, with her free hand, she gripped her scalp and slammed her head onto the counter, beside the beaming white sink. Yu-ra's vision went black for a few milliseconds before blurrily coming back, joined shortly by a ringing in her left ear as Chun-mi mumbled inaudibly behind her. With a painful cry, Yu-ra swung her leg back towards Chun-mi's shin but she dodged the easily visible kick. Chun-mi swept her leg out from underneath her and she fell to her other knee. A tear ripped down the side of her neck due to her head still being glued to the counter.

"Stupid cow," Yu-ra mumbled as her hearing came back.

"Woah," Chun-mi laughed, "you kiss your mother with that mouth?"

*She's too strong for me. How do I get out of this? Rile her up?* Yu-ra struggled in her grip some more before finally giving up and slumping down as far as she could. *No, she needs to think she's won. I'm not going to win in a fight right now.*

"Finally given up?" Chun-mi said. "That was easy."

"Please don't tell Kyung-tae," she muttered.

"What? Speak up, princess," Chun-mi sneered.

"Please," Yu-ra whimpered. "I'm begging you. I'm sorry for what I said about your dad. I'm done, I'll leave you alone. Just leave Kyung-tae out of this."

"Dear gods, how did you manage to convince Kyung-tae to marry a snivelling wretch such as yourself?"

"I don't know, maybe he just feels sorry for me."

"I knew it! You manipulated him! Kyung-tae always has been too soft."

Chun-mi let go of Yu-ra's wrist and Yu-ra fell back to the cold wall, her head slumped down.

"Will you let me go?" Yu-ra mumbled.

"Oh gee, aren't you fun? Relax. I've gotten bored. Besides, now I know that your relationship won't last."

Yu-ra propelled herself to her knees and looked up at Chun-mi with eyes on the verge of tears.

"Please," she begged, clasping her hands together, "you can't tell Kyung-tae. I'll do anything."

Chun-mi scoffed.

"Kyung-tae can handle his own issues. But, you can bet that I'll call on you when I need something."

With that, Chun-mi spun around and swiftly exited the room.

Yu-ra grasped the counter and heaved herself up onto her feet. Stumbling a little as she made her way to the exit, she pulled her sleeves over her hands and dabbed her eyes dry.

"Stupid cow," she muttered again as someone else burst through the door. It was Takemi.

"Hey, did you get my messages?"

"Yeah," Yu-ra replied matter-of-factly. "I got 'em."

"Who was that?" Takemi said, pointing to the door.

"How would I know?" Yu-ra said as she stumbled past her. "Let's just go report to Ny-ron."

"I don't think that's a good idea," Takemi said, following closely behind her. "He's not in the best of moods right now."

"Why?"

"I don't know. He had some meetings and he's been in a bad mood since."

"Well, I need to secure a better position with him, so I'm going to go report to him anyway."

The droning of the kitchens of the restaurant had become quieter than it was before, and everyone they walked past seemed on edge. Takemi began speaking to her about Ny-ron and the debrief they needed to do, but she became lost in thought, hearing not a word. What was she to do about Chun-mi's involvement? She couldn't tell Kyung-tae anything. What would Sung-jae do about it? As Yu-ra zoned back in, Takemi's words returning, they noticed that all the men who usually sat inside the office were waiting silently outside the doors. Yu-ra squeezed past them to the office door. Surprisingly, she wasn't met with any interference. After wrapping her knuckles against the wood, she waited a few moments before entering, Takemi close behind her. The moss-green sofas had been catapulted into the walls, the arms of the furniture broken off to the side. The rug from the middle of the office had been kicked up into a rugged pile, and shards of porcelain vases decorated the entire room. Ny-ron had his back towards them, his heavy breath causing him to heave up and down.

"What do you want?" he huffed.

"I-I have something to report," Yu-ra stuttered.

"And what's that?"

"It's about the warehouse-"

"And you may want to make sure you have good news to tell me," he interrupted, "you know, before you carry on."

Yu-ra glanced back at Takemi, who stood silently to the side.

"Y-yeah, so I don't believe your product was stolen," she said, stepping forward. "Whoever was in the warehouse set it on fire."

"What?" he said, turning to face them.

"The fire wasn't to cover their tracks. They just wanted to burn everything."

"And this is good news to you?" Ny-ron inched closer to her, and Takemi shuffled forward just a little.

"But!" she said, raising her hands in defence, "but, I can definitely find out who did it. And I'll bring them straight to you. We have a plan in place."

Ny-ron sighed.

"Ok. Keep up the good work. I knew I was right to put my faith in you."

"Thank you-"

"Because!" Ny-ron bellowed, causing Yu-ra to jump back in shock, "I trust my people! I let them work and they come back with results, because I'm a damn good leader!"

"Y-yes, you are," Yu-ra said. "In fact, we'll get out of your hair and get to work right away."

"And I appreciate it!" Ny-ron yelled, picking up the nearest object to him, a TV remote, and hurling it at the wall to his left.

"R-right, of course."

Yu-ra's temples began to pound profusely as she slowly began shuffling backwards until she had left the room and eventually the whole building.

# 20
# Training

Rain hammered against the back of Yu-ra's head as she arrived at the bus shelter enclosed by double glazed glass, a warm backdraft attacking her upon entrance. The heated room sat beside a sprawling boulevard that seemed to stretch on endlessly. She looked up at the electronic timetable - four minutes until the next bus. Rummaging through her pocket, she found her phone and dialled Sung-jae's number.

*"Hello,"* he answered.

"Hey, it's Yu-ra," she said as she reached for a cloth from her bag and dabbed the back of her scarf with it.

*"I have caller ID."*

"Right, yeah."

*"What do you need?"*

"I have some information, but it's delicate," she said, placing the now damp cloth back into her handbag.

*"What is it?"*

"There's someone I know that's caught up in this mess somehow."

*"Someone other than Takemi?"*

"There's this woman," Yu-ra whispered, checking over her shoulder, even though she stood alone, "and she's like a family friend of someone I know."

*"And how is she involved?"*

"I don't know for sure. I think she's just a bodyguard, but the guy she protects seems like a very important person."

*"What's her name? I'll look into it."*

"You have to promise not to be too hasty with it."

*"I won't blow your cover, relax. I have just as much invested in this."*

"I'm being serious, she's..." Yu-ra sighed, taking a moment before continuing. "She's friends with my husband."

*"I told you, I'll be careful. Just give me a name."*

"Her name is Choi Chun-mi. Her father is an ex-cop."

A long silence proceeded over the phone. As the bus pulled in, next to the stop, Sung-jae finally spoke.

*"I see. Don't worry, I'll handle it. Discreetly."*

"Thanks," Yu-ra said as she stepped out from under the bus-stop. "I've got to go. Bye."

Yu-ra cut off the phone as she climbed into the bus.

****

Down in the basement of the precinct, the spindly scientist tapped his foot anxiously at the doorway to his lab as he awaited the detective he had called. He couldn't wait to show him what he had found. Maybe he could scrap his current PhD and start a whole new one on this discovery. The one he was working on right now clearly wasn't going anywhere. At some point even he had to admit that. Two voices travelled down around the bend of the corridor.

"Assault and attempted kidnapping," one voice said, "three weeks. Captain asked me to sign him off."

"Three weeks?" an angrier, familiar voice said. Detective Kyung-tae.

"Two and a half actually. He confessed."

"So much for remorse shortening the sentence. Now all it takes is a half-assed confession," Kyung-tae said as they came into view.

"The law's the law," the detective with the goatee said. "Nothing we can do to change that. We're just enforcers."

"Ah, Mr Scientist," Kyung-tae said, as they arrived at the door. The scientist did his best to give a welcoming smile through his bushy beard, but they were clearly taken aback by it. Was it because he widened his eyes as he smiled? Were you supposed to do the opposite?

"Please, call me doctor, detective," the scientist said.

"But you said you haven't finished your PhD. How can I call you doctor?

Did you finish medical school?"

"No..." he said, his usual frown returning. He directed his attention to the other detective to change the subject. "Who are you? I only called one detective."

"Woo-young," he said, bowing his head, "he asked me to come. We've met before."

"I don't recall."

"Yeah, you were rude back then too."

"Very well," the scientist said, ignoring his comment and entering them into the lab, allowing them to sit at the table.

"This guy got back to you rather quickly," Woo-young said. "He must be good."

"Probably the new machines that have been installed," Kyung-tae replied.

"I can't believe you're actually talking to me about your case," Woo-young muttered, itching his scalp. "Boy, I do not miss the stone-hearted Kyung-tae."

The Scientist retrieved a small plastic bag of crystals and a vial of a faint blue liquid, then placed them on the table.

"These are the crystals you gave me a few weeks ago," the scientist said, "and this is the liquid you gave me to test the other day. What I've found is that they are, in fact, the exact same compound."

"I knew it!" Kyung-tae said, jumping out of his seat. "It's a drug, just one we've never seen before." Kyung-tae grabbed Woo-young by the shoulders and shook him aggressively. "When I got really paranoid outside of that warehouse and passed out, it wasn't because of fumes. I was high!"

"Wow, you really are opening up to me," Woo-young said, unfazed by the shaking, "A bit too much."

"I was just thrown off because my blood-test came out clean."

"I was wrong. I do miss the old Kyung-tae," Woo-young said.

"Of course it's a drug," the scientist cut in, "look at them. What else could you possibly use fine crystals such as this for? Are you a dimwit?" He looked at Woo-young. "Is he a dimwit?"

"Yes, very much so," Woo-young replied.

"Do you have more to tell us or not?" Kyung-tae said.

"Sorry, I was being facetious," the scientist said. Suddenly Kyung-tae nodded, seemingly deep in thought. It was as if he didn't understand the word that just came out of his mouth. "The exciting part is how the properties of the substance change depending on their state. They literally have different effects on your body depending on the state that you ingest them in. Like a three-in-one drug, in a sense."

"Okay, but how does that help me with my investigation? I just need to know that they're the same thing."

"Is it not part of your job to know the entirety of what you're dealing with?"

"Sorry, I was being facetious," Kyung-tae said with his head down, glancing up repeatedly to see if anyone had reacted to his use of the word.

"What?" the scientist said.

"Do you even know what that means?" Woo-young said.

"He really is a dimwit," the scientist said to Woo-young.

"That aside," Kyung-tae said, clearly trying to change the subject as quickly as possible, "since it was a drug, that means the warehouses didn't serve their advertised purposes. The drugs burnt up with the warehouses, leaving them in both a gaseous and liquid state."

"Okay, so the warehouses were fronts," Woo-young said. "We need to look into the companies that own these warehouses."

"That'll help us get ahead of the situation. They must be shell companies."

"Fair enough. Get a warrant to look into these companies. Seize everything they've got; financial statements, employment documents, everything."

"That's actually why I brought you. I need you to handle that end of the case." Kyung-tae put his hand in his pocket, then took something out, placing it on the desk - the lighter they had found in the warehouse. "I think this is the biggest clue. It looks custom made. So, I can trace it back to its owner."

"I'll see if I can help, but I still have my own open cases."

"Woo-young, you're the only one here I trust to get the job done."

Woo-young sniffed a few times.

"You really have changed," he jested. "I guess marriage softened your heart. I'm proud of you…partner." Woo-young pretended to wipe a tear from his eye.

"What about me?" the scientist said with a quivering lip. "I can help you. You trust me, don't you?"

Kyung-tae stared at him for a few moments before suddenly jumping out of shock, scaring both the scientist and Woo-young.

"Crap, I'm late."

"For?" Woo-young called as Kyung-tae rushed towards the door.

"Date night!" Kyung-tae called back, as he exited. "I can't believe I actually just said that out loud."

****

As Kyung-tae heaved up the concrete steps of his apartment, he silently thanked the subway system for getting him home in ten minutes as opposed to his usual twenty-five. He thumbed the fingerprint sensor and the metal cover popped open. After dialling in his code, he unlocked his front door. He kicked his shoes off as he stepped inside and hurried into the living room. A candle was lit on the coffee table in front of the sofa, diffusing the scent of mango and passionfruit around the room.

"Assalaamu-alaikum," came Yu-ra's voice.

Kyung-tae's heart hopped, but he made no sound.

"Walaikum-assalaam," he said. "Where are you?"

Yu-ra poked her hand in the air from behind the sofa and waved.

"Down here."

"Oh. Hey. Sorry I'm so late. I'll be ready in ten."

"Yeeah," she squeaked, "about that. I can't go."

Kyung-tae paused.

"Oh. Ok," he said, slipping his coat off and tossing it onto the arm of the sofa as he meandered towards the bedroom to get changed. As he passed her, she propped herself up on her forearm.

"Aish," she groaned. Kyung-tae glanced back to see her lightly massaging the side of her neck. Yu-ra cut her eyes up at him. "Are you not going to ask why we can't go out?"

Kyung-tae stopped and turned around.

"Oh, right. Is it because you strained your neck?"

"Well, yes. But that's not what I asked, is it?"

"But you just confirmed the reason you can't go out. I just said it differently."

"No, you didn't. You haven't used the words 'why can't you go'. You haven't asked 'what's up'. You haven't said 'what's wrong'." She winced as she propped herself up further. "You haven't even asked if I'm okay."

"Oh," Kyung-tae said, rubbing the back of his neck. "Sorry. I'm just going to quickly get changed."

Kyung-tae rushed off into the bedroom, throwing his blazer, shirt, belt, and trousers onto the cool grey bed sheets. He opened up the wardrobe on his right and rummaged through until he could find his matching navy woolly shorts and sweater. He slipped them on and rushed back out of the bedroom, forgetting to close the wardrobe doors behind him. Yu-ra had her arm over her eyes when he came back out.

"Hey," Kyung-tae said.

"What?" she grumbled.

Kyung-tae itched the back of his head.

"Uh, get up for a second."

"Aish," she whispered, "alright, I'm going to bed," she said as she pushed herself up straight, wincing the whole way through.

"No, wait," Kyung-tae blurted. He slid onto the seat beside his wife and held his hand up near her neck. "May I?"

She nodded and Kyung-tae lifted up the tail of her scarf, feeding his hand underneath. Why was she still wearing her scarf in the house? He analysed her skin closer. Was her skin slightly darker underneath her scarf?

"Ow," she said as Kyung-tae lightly pressed the side of her neck. The muscle was overly firm and burning hot, and her cheeks were reddened. He pressed his fingertips down a little more firmly, causing Yu-ra to twitch.

"Sorry," he said, lifting his hand away.

"It's fine."

"Ok."

Kyung-tae pressed his fingertips down harder and began massaging her neck in circular motions.

"I'm really sorry about this. I don't like throwing screws in the cogs so last minute. You were probably really looking forward to it. I was, for sure."

"It's fine, don't worry about it. I'm not really fussed."

Yu-ra slowly turned her head towards him.

"I really hope you're just being polite right now."

"Look that way," Kyung-tae said, pointing straight across from him. Yu-ra turned and the muscle in her neck became tougher. "I was just being polite, of course. You ruined my whole night."

"Your lack of intonation makes your sarcasm elite. I will give you that," she said as Kyung-tae inched closer to her and hung his free arm around her shoulder. He paused, then shifted even closer to her. Using his free hand, he lightly held the side of her face, and with his other hand, began to massage her neck more aggressively. "Ooh, that helps so much," she said, "thank you."

"No problem." Kyung-tae could feel the muscle had softened a little already. "So how did you hurt yourself?"

"Just studying in a stupid position for too long."

"How long is too long? Something like this feels like you would have been in that position for hours, which is just a really dumb thing to do."

"Thanks for your input. It's really helpful," she said in a dry tone. "And yes, it was a few hours because I fell asleep in that position."

"Ok. You want to take your scarf off, by the way?"

"No," she blurted, "don't worry, I'll do it later. It's not uncomfortable."

"Oh. Alright."

"Who taught you how to massage this good? Have you been doing this with other girls before me?"

"Yes, of course. You'd be naive to think you're the first woman I've given a massage to."

Yu-ra slapped his knee.

"Ya!"

"I meant my ma, you weirdo. You know how much she used to work when I was younger. I had to."

"Ok, that's a good answer. I'll let you off."

Kyung-tae got up and walked over to the kitchen area. As he kneeled down, he pulled open the bottom draw and dug out a pain relief patch. He tore it open as he went back to the couch. Sliding the patch out of the packet as he sat down, he carefully peeled off the backing sheet and discarded it onto the coffee table. He placed a large square plaster over her strained muscle and pressed down firmly, making sure not to leave any pockets of air.

"Thank you," she said. "I've actually got one other request from you."

"Depends what it is," Kyung-tae said as he put his arm around her shoulder and she sank into his embrace.

"Oh."

"I'm kidding, ask away."

"Can you teach me a few self-defence moves?"

"I guess it did depend on what it was. No, I can't. Not now, anyway."

"Why?"

"You just hurt yourself, I'm not going to spar with you."

"Not sparring, just some general self-defence."

"It's still strenuous activity, and you just hurt yourself."

"That's a fair point, but I raise you this - what if someone like that Li-feng guy comes after me in the future and you're not around. I can't just go clocking people in the nose. I'm not you."

"Li-feng is in jail. How many thugs do you interact with on a daily basis? What do you do in your off-time?"

"I'm a part-time vigilante. I'm currently working undercover in the criminal underworld to unearth all their secrets."

"Naturally."

"I'm being serious. I want to learn self-defence. Not to use it, but just to make sure I'm safe if I need to be."

"And that's fair, but can it not wait until next week?"

"No. Look, we've got all this free time because our date got cancelled. Let's use it productively."

"Well, you can't. I don't want to end up hurting you. I want you to come with me to dinner at Mr Choi's next week."

"Woah woah woah," she said, shifting back from Kyung-tae, flicking her hands up in defence. "I'm not going to their place."

"What? Why?"

"I..."

"Yu-ra, you keep doing this. Just say it straight. What's wrong?"

"Jinmu's lovely and I know how much he means to you." She sighed heavily before continuing. "But I genuinely cannot stand Chun-mi. Nothing you say can change my mind about that."

Kyung-tae analysed her eyes, to the point that she couldn't maintain eye contact with him. It did seem like they had an awkward interaction at their wedding, but how could that possibly cause such an issue? If she put a strain on her relationship with them now and he let it slide, it would continue throughout their marriage. Which, in turn, would strain his relationship with them. How could he solve this?

"I don't know what's going on between you and Chun-mi, but she's family too. I promise you, she just wants the best for us. Besides, I'm pretty sure she's working so might not even be there."

"Like I said, nothing will change my mind. She's a terrible person."

"I've known her for a very long time. Please just trust me. If you take the time to get to know her, and I mean really try, you will like her, and she will like you. Put everything that's happened behind you and start again. It's never too late."

"Is this really that important to you?"

"It really is."

"Why though?"

"I told you why."

Yu-ra sat up on her knees, directing all of her attention to her husband.

"No, but really, explain it to me, because I don't get it."

Kyung-tae sighed.

"Okay. You've got a brother, right?"

"Right."

"Two parents."

"I see where you're going with this, but you not having both parents shouldn't change what you think about yourself. It certainly doesn't affect how I see you."

"Wait, I'm not done," Kyung-tae said, placing his hand on her knee. "You have cousins and aunts and uncles, right?"

"Yes."

"Well, I've got my mother. That's it. And by Allah's will, the Chois were put in my life. And they became my family."

"You've got me now, too."

"I don't think you're understanding what I'm saying."

"No, I do. You have a very small family, but it's very tight knit and they mean a lot to you. I just wanted to say that I'm part of your family now, too."

"And I appreciate that."

"I won't change my mind about Chun-mi."

"Yu-ra-"

"But, I will come."

"That's all I ask."

"On the condition that I get some kind of… bargaining chip."

"Fine, what do you want?"

"YES!" Yu-ra shouted as she jumped up. "Ow," she whined, rubbing her neck as she sat back down.

"Anyway, bargaining chip. I'll come on the condition," she said, holding up a finger, "that you teach me some self-defence."

"You're really stuck on this self-defence thing, aren't you?"

"Just the basics. I'm making it easy for you."

"And what are the basics?"

"Things like how to get out of a grip, how to dodge a punch. If someone grabs my wrist, twists it behind my back and slams my head on a counter, how would I get out of that?"

"Oddly specific, but sure, I can teach you. But I reserve the right to stop as soon as your neck pain gets worse."

"Deal," she said, shaking his hand lightly.

"But we've also got to go down to your parents this weekend. Your mum has been calling."

"No can do. You've already used up your bargaining chip to get me to go to one dinner."

"Yu-ra, it's your parents. Why would I need a bargaining chip?"

"I'm genuinely swamped. This one dinner is all I can make. Over the next couple of weeks. I'll see if my schedule frees up."

"Alright, let's just get started."

Kyung-tae stood up, moving to the backside of the sofa. Holding onto the corner of his recently departed seat, he easily shifted it anti-clockwise a fair amount. Yu-ra, still seated on the other side of the couch, turned to him, raising a brow.

"What are you doing?"

"Making space," Kyung-tae said, before sliding over to her side of the couch and pushing clockwise. It was a little heavier than the other side, but not by a whole lot.

"Let me get off first!"

Kyung-tae paused for a moment, just barely letting on a smile. Suddenly dropping to his knees, he hunched over and clutched at his side.

"I wish you would have told me that earlier," he groaned. "My back gave out while I was pushing you."

"Are you calling me fat?"

"Officer down!" he cried.

Yu-ra got up off the sofa, hands on her hips in dismay.

"You just watch, I'm gonna kick your ass."

"You can't kick a man when he's down."

Yu-ra walked around the back of the sofa and tugged at Kyung-tae's arm.

"Get up, you baby."

"Alright, alright, I'm getting up." Kyung-tae chuckled as heaved himself up off the laminate floor.

Kyung-tae motioned his arm, directing Yu-ra into the space across from him.

"Okay, so first thing's first," Kyung-tae said. "This is self-defence. The first rule - if you can run away, you run away."

"Yeah, yeah, makes sense," Yu-ra blurted, hopping back and forth between her left and right foot. "Let's do this - I'll run a scenario by you and you tell me how to react."

"I really think it will be more effective if I go through the generic scenarios."

"Okay, teacher Kyung-tae, you know best."

"We'll start off with…What are you doing with your feet?"

"I don't know," she said, still hopping vigorously. "I'm just amped up, I guess."

"Anyway," Kyung-tae started, as he inched closer to her, "we'll start with wrist grabs." Yu-ra put her hands up to her face in an amateur fighting stance. "Let's just always assume the person is a lot stronger or bigger than you, just to make things efficient. You can put your hands down by the way," Kyung-tae said, reaching for her left wrist.

Yu-ra dropped her hands, allowing her left arm to fall into Kyung-tae's loose grip.

"Oh, right."

"Can you see the place where my thumb meets my fingers?"

"Yeah."

"That's where my grip will be the weakest. Therefore, that's your escape route."

Yu-ra nodded.

"Mmhm."

"Now try and pull your wrist out of my grip."

Yu-ra yanked her arm back, but Kyung-tae tightened his grip and easily kept her in place.

"It didn't work."

"Exactly."

"So how does this help me?"

"Well, the reason it didn't work is because the flat part of your wrist was facing the escape point, so I had a lot more surface area to work with."

"So what do I do? Use the side of my wrist?"

"Exactly! You're a fast learner."

"Thanks," Yu-ra said, grinning.

"So the aim of the game is to always weaken the grip as much as possible before you try and escape. Step one, twist your wrist so that the side of your wrist is pointing to the gap."

Yu-ra twisted her wrist in response.

"Next, you want as much leverage as possible. You don't just yank, because they're a lot stronger than you." Kyung-tae let go of Yu-ra. "Grab my wrist, the same way I did." Yu-ra took a hold of his wrist. "Tighter," Kyung-tae said.

Yu-ra followed suit.

"Yes sir, teacher, sir!"

"To get leverage, walk towards them, and then you use your body as leverage by leaning back so that you have more power in your pull." Kyung-tae inched closer to her, twisting his wrist accordingly. "Now when you pull, use your other hand to help and slice your elbow in the direction of the escape point, kind of like a Muay Thai strike."

He gripped the top of his wrist and leaned back slightly, sliding his wrist out of her grip easily as he motioned his elbow up towards her face.

"Okay, okay, I got it," Yu-ra said as she bounced between her feet again. "My turn."

Kyung-tae gripped her wrist relatively loosely. Yu-ra followed the steps she was taught.

"Twist," she said as she twisted her wrist, "get closer." She crept closer to him. "Lean. And pull." Yu-ra leaned back and pulled. She didn't escape the grip so she pulled harder. Just barely managing to pop her arm out of his grip, she lost her balance and fell backwards, throwing her arms out towards Kyung-tae. He quickly grabbed her arm and pulled her back up to stability. "Thanks," she said. "Oh right, Muay Thai slice. Let's go again."

"I'm going to make it more realistic this time," Kyung-tae said, taking up her wrist and tightening it into a fairly strong hold.

"I got this," Yu-ra said, attempting to escape again. Twist. Closer. Grab and lean. Pull and slice. With a pop, she slipped out of his grip. She instantly reacted by jumping up and down.

"Woo!" she squealed, clapping rapidly, "I did it!"

"You'll need more practice, obviously, but you did. Well done."

"Thank you, teacher sir!" she said, calming her body down.

"I've got a lot more to teach you, but we can practise every day. I think you'll pick it up quickly enough."

Yu-ra began hopping between her feet again.

"Alright let's do some more practice," Kyung-tae said.

"Okay," Yu-ra said, "but first what do I do if someone - let's say this pretty okay looking guy-" Kyung-tae scrunched his face momentarily at her comment. "Insinuates that I'm fat?"

"Woah, woah, woah!" Kyung-tae waved his hands in dismissal.

"Should I do that karate move you did?" Yu-ra cut in. "Go straight for the nose?"

"No! Of course not!" Kyung-tae said. "Wait, that's not the point."

"It isn't?"

"No! Did you say 'pretty okay looking'? Are you serious?"

"Why are you offended? I never said I was talking about you."

"I am a professional detective, Yu-ra. You can't hide things from me."

"So what you're saying, and you've made this abundantly clear, is that you actually were insinuating that I'm fat?" Kyung-tae paused. He needed to choose his words carefully. "Well," Yu-ra said, "silence speaks volumes."

Kyung-tae smiled.

"I will choose to withhold any comments."

"Ya!" Yu-ra blurted.

"Relax, we need to practise your defence more."

"You better watch your behind," Yu-ra said, putting her hands back up in a fighting stance. "This is what you're gonna see when you least expect it." Yu-ra began jabbing at the space in front of his face, pulling back at the last second. "Pew, pew, pew," she said with each punch.

"Woah there, you're going to take my head off," Kyung-tae said as he backed away slightly, but Yu-ra followed him.

She began swinging her legs aimlessly in his general direction and he effortlessly side-stepped her amateurish kicks.

"Haiyaa," she said with each kick.

"What are you doing?" Kyung-tae laughed. "You were the one who wanted to learn self-defence and now you want to fight me?"

Suddenly, she started hopping on her left foot, her other leg in the air but tucked in close to her. Hopping closer to him, she snapped her foot out at him.

"WAAA!" she bellowed.

"When did you become a Taekwondo expert?" He chuckled as he slipped her kick. "Guess I have to stop going easy on you."

Kyung-tae began throwing his own faux punches, breathing out with each expertly thrown jab. Yu-ra dipped her head away from him.

"Oww," she said weakly, gripping her neck. Kyung-tae's smile dropped and his heart sank momentarily.

"Sorry, sorry! Are you okay?"

"Yeah, yeah, I'm fine," she said, not convincing Kyung-tae at all, "But let's go back to practising self-defence to be on the safe side."

"Oh, right!" Kyung-tae blurted. "There's a few more grips I wanted to show you."

They both moved back into the centre of the open space. Kyung-tae took up her wrist once again. "Actually, before we start again. What does facetious mean?"

# 21
# My Dinner with Jinmu

*I'm sorry I had to do this in this way. I wish I could have told you in person but I can't handle another fight right now. I need to follow through on my decisions and stop letting Dad control me. You can tell him I've left, just don't show him this. I'm moving away to study, so you won't see much of me. I'll contact you again when I'm all set up.*

\- *Sung-jae*

Kyung-tae tucked his white shirt into his slacks and then fastened his belt. After rolling his sleeves up to his elbow, he observed himself in the bedroom mirror, fixing any loose strands of hair into place. He scoffed. When did he become so obsessed with his appearance?

Upon entering the living room, he discovered Yu-ra sprawled on the floor, yet again in a hoodie and sweatpants, rolling about.

"What are you doing?" Kyung-tae whined. "We need to go soon and you haven't even gotten ready yet?"

She pulled her hood down as she stopped her rolling.

"Woah! You clean up nicely, sir."

"And you don't."

"Rude."

"Go clean yourself up and get dressed, young lady."

"Okay, okay," she said, rising to her feet, "just let me show off to you a bit first."

"Show what off?" Kyung-tae said, raising a brow.

"Get ready for your jaw to drop, teacher Kyung-tae."

Yu-ra prepared herself, lightly bouncing on the balls of her feet. With a sudden burst of energy, she bounded towards the couch, seizing the headrest and effortlessly swinging her legs over to the other side. Releasing her grip, she landed gracefully on the floor, seamlessly transitioning into a fluid front roll before springing back onto her feet in front of Kyung-tae. With a quick wink in his direction, she elegantly descended, executing two smooth backward rolls before regaining her footing with ease.

"Well done!" Kyung-tae said, clapping. "I'm proud of you."

"Oh, I'm not done just yet," she said, flashing a smile.

With a swift movement, she threw her hands behind her, landing them firmly on the kitchen counter. With a powerful push, she propelled herself into a spinning motion over the counter, her legs twirling in the air.

"Hey, wait!" Kyung-tae called out, fearing she might hurt herself. But then, Yu-ra tucked her legs in at the last moment, landing graciously on the other side.

"Ta-da!" she said, extending her arms out like a gymnast.

"Wow…" Kyung-tae said, rendered slack-jawed, "colour me genuinely impressed."

"Okay, now let me show you how good I've gotten at those grip escapes."

"Later," he said, tapping his watch. "We seriously need to go."

"Ugh." She scoffed. "Fine, give me twenty minutes."

****

*You can do this, Yu-ra. It's just a few hours. Surely, you can hold your tongue for that long.*

She stood a few paces behind Kyung-tae as she watched him ring the grand doorbell of sterling silver. A red light on the bell's camera lit up and Kyung-tae pressed the doorbell once more. After a few more moments, the faint shuffle of feet behind the door became apparent. Almost simultaneously, as the door flung open, the automatic gate behind them slid open and a sleek white coupe pulled into the driveway. The humming engine cut off and out stepped Chun-mi with her perfect hair tied up in a bun, a few loose strands fashionably hanging out of the front. She took off her Kevlar armour, revealing her gleaming white blouse, and tossed it into the back of her car. Yu-ra's attention was suddenly pulled away by Kyung-tae tugging her arm.

"Oh! Sorry," she said, nodding at Jinmu. As she glanced down, she noticed some white fluff clinging to her honey-coloured dress. Quickly brushing her skirt down before turning, she greeted Chun-mi too. She didn't want to give her an ounce of space to make her usual comments.

Yu-ra trailed Kyung-tae into the expansive hallway, slipping out of her shoes upon entry. Unzipping her puffy coat, she gently nudged Kyung-tae, who was engrossed in light conversation with Jinmu. After meeting her gaze, he relieved her of the coat, hanging both of theirs on the nearby rack.

"Wow, you look amazing, girl," Chun-mi said with a smirk.

"Thanks," Yu-ra said bluntly, following Kyung-tae into the spacious living room. She glanced over her shoulder at Chun-mi, who slid the door closed behind her. "Your sarcasm won't get me today, because I genuinely look stunning."

Kyung-tae flicked his hand behind him, tapping her on the arm.

"Hey, stop it," he whispered as he leaned over to her.

"Sorry," she whispered back.

"Wow, where did that come from?" Chun-mi gasped, hand over her chest. "I meant it with all my heart."

Yu-ra hoped that Kyung-tae would see through this obvious act.

Ignoring Chun-mi's response, Yu-ra finally gazed upon the decor of the room. Rather than modern paintings, three of the walls were adorned with black and white banners consisting of different vegetation, as well as a few proverbs. The most notable one read - 'the smart hawk hides its talons'. Is that why Chun-mi was so two-faced? The last wall of the room was replaced with glass panelled sliding doors. In the middle of the laminate flooring sat a very low wooden table filled with a plethora of dishes. Around the floor of the table sat six legless, cushioned chairs. Jinmu led Yu-ra and Kyung-tae to their seats, while Chun-mi approached a spacious, ajar cabinet nestled in the room's corner. It was filled with pictures of a beautiful young woman who had many similar features to Chun-mi. Yu-ra tapped Kyung-tae on the side as she watched Chun-mi kneel down and bow her head to the ground.

"Whose memorial altar is that?" she whispered.

"Her mother's," Kyung-tae whispered back.

"They're not going to expect us to pray to it, are they?"

"No, it's been a while since I started refusing. They should know you wouldn't either."

Chun-mi stood up and walked over to her seat, across from Yu-ra who sighed quietly to herself.

"So, what took you so long?" Chun-mi said, clearly gawking at Kyung-tae.

"We got here on time," Kyung-tae said, raising a brow. "What do you mean?"

"She means this invitation has been extended for quite some time," Jinmu interrupted as he passed around a tray of starters. Yu-ra watched Kyung-tae, hoping he wouldn't make reference to her.

"Oh right," Kyung-tae said, glancing at Yu-ra for a moment before beginning to fill the dishes in front of the girls with food. "We've just been really busy for a while. There was a lot of furnishing to do for the house."

Yu-ra breathed a sigh of relief as she began to eat.

"I'd love to see it some time," Chun-mi said, accepting a full dish from Kyung-tae.

"It's not really guest ready, yet," Yu-ra cut in, still chewing her food, "but this food is lovely, Jinmu. Did you make it all yourself?"

"No. This is all Chun-mi," he said, sipping water before continuing to speak. "It's not my place to be in the kitchen."

Chun-mi smirked at Yu-ra.

"Oh my God!" she said, clapping her hands over her mouth. "Thanks so much, sis. You made my day. I was worried it wouldn't be good because I've never made it vegetarian before."

Yu-ra rolled her eyes. Did she really just inadvertently compliment that witch? Kyung-tae tapped the side of her leg.

"Yeah." Yu-ra sighed. "You're welcome."

"I think it's clear," Chun-mi said in a honeyed voice, looking back at Kyung-tae and brushing her hair behind her ear. "I'm prime wife material."

Was that spade trying to flirt with him? The audacity of this woman! Glaring at her half full bowl, she quickened her eating pace, her cheeks becoming fuller and fuller.

"You'd need someone that could take a punch then," Kyung-tae laughed, "otherwise it would end very quickly."

"Oh, I've got someone in mind," she said in a soft voice. Yu-ra scrunched the side of her dress up in her fist to stop herself from scrunching her face as she looked at Chun-mi.

"I hope it's the same person we discussed," Jinmu interjected.

"Yes, father." Chun-mi rolled her eyes. "It is."

"Actually," Jinmu said to Kyung-tae. "I'd like to discuss that with you at some point."

Pausing his eating, Kyung-tae returned his gaze to the rest of the party.

"Me?" he said, a perplexed expression clouding his features. "Why do you need to talk to me about it?"

Yu-ra lightly tossed her metal chopsticks onto the table with a huff. A little bit of food which had clung to the ends of the chopsticks broke off and flung across the table, a piece landing on Jinmu's clothes. Was it Jinmu? Was he pushing the idea that Chun-mi deserved to be with Kyung-tae? Or was he just in agreement with her? Either way, there was no way she was letting them get in the way of her marriage.

"Oh," Yu-ra said, realising everyone's gaze had honed in on her. She fumbled about, grabbing the chopsticks back as soon as possible. "Sorry."

"I see table manners aren't a big thing in your religion," Chun-mi remarked. "That was quite rude, Yu-ra. Considering we're feeding you and all."

"Chun-mi," Kyung-tae said firmly, narrowing his eyes at her. Though Chun-mi fluttered her eyes at him

"It's fine, don't worry about it Yu-ra," she said with an upturned nose. "I'm sure it was just an accident."

Remaining silent, Yu-ra began to subtly stuff her face with food, not even finishing what she was chewing before putting more food in as her cheeks swelled up like a chipmunk.

Suddenly the doorbell rang and a confused expression morphed onto the features of Chun-mi and Jinmu. They both stood up and left the room, leaving Yu-ra and Kyung-tae alone.

"What was that about?" Kyung-tae said, nudging her side.

Yu-ra calmly placed her chopsticks down at the side of her dish before shooting a glare at him

"Are you kidding me! Chun-mi is clearly trying to flirt with you."

Kyung-tae placed his hand on her knee.

"Yu-ra, come on. I know you're more mature than that. She's just comfortable around me because we've known each other so long."

"No, that's not what it is," she whispered harshly. "I'm pretty sure that Jinmu doesn't approve of our marriage either. And that's fine, not everyone has to, but they make it so obvious."

"I admit that he didn't at first," he said, holding up his hand in defeat.

Yu-ra shot the back of her hand into his shoulder.

"See, I'm right!" she said, a little too loudly, to her unfazed husband.

"But," he said firmly, shaking her knee with the hand that he already had on it, "he was much more against me being Muslim. That was hard to deal with. This - he just didn't want me marrying someone I don't know well."

"Well he must want you to marry Chun-mi," she said, crossing her arms, "but clearly you don't know her that well."

"Enough, Yu-ra. Please drop it."

Yu-ra could hear the sounds of a group of footsteps coming back towards the room.

"We'll talk about it after," she said abruptly, shoving his hand off her knee.

"Mr Choi always trusts me to make the right decisions. Why do you think he came to the wedding?"

As the door slid open, Yu-ra heard Jinmu conversing with a familiar voice. Her curiosity piqued, prompting her to turn around. As Kyung-tae jumped up out of his seat and rushed towards this new guest, Yu-ra's eyes widened at the sight of Prosecutor Sung-jae standing there. He was at least three inches taller than Kyung-tae. The two clasped hands and hugged shoulders in a macho fashion.

"Hey, man," Kyung-tae said, patting Sung-jae on the back, "we missed you at the wedding. How've you been?"

"Yeah, sorry about that," Sung-jae said, pulling back. "The job's the job, right?"

"Don't I know it," Kyung-tae said, "oh right, this is my wife." He gestured towards Yu-ra, who stood up and then waved to him.

"N-nice to meet you," she said, stumbling for her words, though Sung-jae didn't seem surprised to see her at all.

"You too," Sung-jae said, "I'm Chun-mi's older brother, in case you didn't already know."

"Ah," Yu-ra said.

"Sit, sit. We're still eating," Kyung-tae said, gesturing to the table.

Everyone reconvened at the dinner table but Yu-ra quickly sat in Kyung-tae's seat, which was met with a quizzical look from everyone. She nodded to the side in a gesture to Kyung-tae. He followed suit, sitting beside her, and then began piling food into a bowl for Sung-jae.

"How long have you guys been here?" Sung-jae said as he took the dish from Kyung-tae.

"About forty minutes," Kyung-tae said.

"That better have been your fourth bowl then, Chun-mi."

Chun-mi looked at her barely dented food.

"It's my first," she said, in an annoyed tone.

"What's the point of being rich if you don't eat properly?" Sung-jae responded. "I bet I can eat two servings in the time it takes you to finish that one."

"Alright," Chun-mi said, "when I win, I'm adding it to the chart of favours I have stored up. And I have a reason to cash in now," she said as she smirked at Yu-ra.

"Pfft, I'm literally the world's fastest eater," Sung-jae said, nudging her in the side. "Ready? Go!"

The two siblings suddenly began to stuff their faces at an alarming pace.

"There he goes again," Jinmu grumbled. "You're going to get indigestion, you idiot."

Sung-jae ignored him and somehow began to eat even quicker.

"Don't encourage him, dad," Chun-mi said between bites.

Peeking at her phone underneath the table, Yu-ra checked the message she had received from Min-ah. Kyung-tae leaned over to her, whispering in her ear.

"Put your phone away," Kyung-tae whispered in her ear as he leaned over to her. "You said you would make an effort."

Yu-ra let out a sigh, slipping her phone into her pocket before fixing her gaze on Chun-mi, who was busy stuffing her face. An idea sparked in her mind – this was the ideal moment to inject a bit of amusement. Amusement in the form of outing Chun-mi's involvement in crime.

"So Chun-mi, you're a personal bodyguard then? Who is it that you guard?" she said.

Chun-mi put her bowl down, gulping down the food which filled her chipmunk cheeks.

"I'm not slowing down for you," Sung-jae said to Chun-mi, as he continued to ravage his bowl.

"Grow up, Sung-jae," Jinmu said firmly. "Let them talk."

Ignoring Jinmu's comment, Sung-jae continued to eat.

"Park Dae-myeon," Chun-mi said as she swallowed her last bit of food.

"Who?" Yu-ra asked, leaning in.

"You don't know him? The CEO of Park Pharmaceuticals."

"Oh, no way! As in the biggest pharmacy brand in the country?"

Why would someone that rich have a connection to the biggest gang in Seoul? And why was Sung-jae so quiet about it?

"Chun-mi has done well for herself," Jinmu said, just barely revealing a smile.

"So, what's he like?" Yu-ra smirked, unconsciously leaning in further. "He seems kind of shady, if you ask me."

Chun-mi seemed unfazed by her comment, but Sung-jae put his bowl down and raised a brow at her.

"What's got you so interested in her boss?" Kyung-tae said.

"She works for the leading drug company in the country. Why wouldn't I be?"

Chun-mi glanced at Jinmu who nodded at her.

"To be fair," Chun-mi said, "he's a very interesting individual. He's currently working on this new medicine that treats different diseases based on whether it's taken in solid, liquid, or gas form."

"Oh," Yu-ra said, "Is that even poss-"

"How far has he gotten with this project?" Kyung-tae said, cutting her off. "Has he cracked it?"

"Very far. He's running trials right now."

"Interesting," he said, "and your boss, do you trust him? How much do you know about him?"

Wait, was that it? Had Yu-ra done enough? Was Kyung-tae now suspicious of Chun-mi?

"Trust him? I don't trust anyone, you know that. But like I said, he's very interesting. He's a real chain-smoker though. I hate being around him."

"Interesting in what sense?" Yu-ra asked, hoping to get more out of her than him smoking like a chimney.

"He's let it slip about his political aspirations," Chun-mi replied, "which is rather unconventional for a pharmacist."

"Political aspirations?"

"He has this misplaced notion that if he's rich enough, he could run a campaign to become a party leader and become Prime Minister. He often tells stories of his time in the military, so he could have some sway in an election, if I'm honest."

"So money is his motivator," Kyung-tae said.

"This is to do with your arson case, isn't it?" Jinmu asked.

"The warehouses that burned down - they were filled with this substance that has different chemical properties depending on its form. And I'm betting that if I trace everything back, I'll eventually find that his company owned the warehouses."

"Are you saying he might be involved in criminal activity," Chun-mi said, her eyes wide with fear. Boy, she was a better actress than Yu-ra herself.

"Potentially," Kyung-tae said, "but don't worry, you won't be caught in the crossfire."

"But am I in danger?"

"You? In danger? As if," Kyung-tae laughed, achieving a giggle from Chun-mi too. "Is he smart?"

"Yeah, he's smart," Chun-mi said, "but guess what - he's Pro-independence," she said, bellowing with laughter. Kyung-tae chuckled a little too.

"What's wrong with that?" Yu-ra asked innocently. "Everyone's entitled to their own political beliefs."

"Nothing," Kyung-tae said. "There's just no way that he'll ever be voted in like that."

"You're joking, right?" Chun-mi said, smirking. "Everything is wrong with that."

"All I said was that he's entitled to have his own political ideology," Yu-ra mumbled, thinking her point would pass by unnoticed.

"Anyone who is pro-independence is naive," Jinmu said, not bothering to look up from his dish. "They saved us during World War Two and created an economic era unheard of."

"They're heroes. Right, Sung-jae?" Chun-mi added, digging her elbow into his knee. In an instant, Sung-jae's entire body recoiled from Chun-mi, causing hot soup to spray from his mouth, drenching Yu-ra's face and dress. With a startled squeal, Yu-ra reeled back in disgust, while Chun-mi's laughter echoed through the room as she doubled over in stitches.

"Shit," Sung-jae blurted.

Squinting one eye open, Yu-ra picked up the blurry napkin that was in front of her.

"Are you a complete idiot, Sung-jae?" Jinmu bellowed as Yu-ra began dabbing her face with the napkin.

"Are you okay?" Kyung-tae said, a stir in his voice. Picking up his own napkin, he began dabbing part of her dress.

"It's fine," Yu-ra said bluntly, getting the last of the saliva off her face, "just show me to a bathroom please."

"Sorry, Yu-ra!" Chun-mi called out, her voice still subtly full of glee. "It was an accident,"

"I'll show you where it is," Sung-jae said, jumping to his feet.

Sung-jae led her out of the room, guiding her through a sleek, vast kitchen lined with counters, into a small corridor which held a washing machine and, next to it, a bathroom.

"Just through here," he said, raising his hand to direct her.

"Thanks," she said in a monotonous tone, "and thanks, for the apology."

"Right, sorry," he said, rubbing the back of his head. "I'll just be out here."

As Yu-ra entered the bathroom, the toilet lid obediently flipped open, greeting her with a faint whir. The pungent scent of bleach enveloped her senses as she took in the sleek surroundings. The walls boasted a pale silver hue, while the shower enclosure featured sliding glass panels and a built-in shower head with adjustable settings. The sink, though wide, was surprisingly narrow in length, illuminated by soft sky-blue lights from below. Yu-ra reached for a hand towel from the wall-mounted railing, then activated the tap, watching as water cascaded effortlessly into the basin.

"So impractical," she scoffed at the sink, as she put the towel underneath the water for a few seconds. Dabbing all the stains that were beginning to accumulate profusely, after ten minutes she decided that the stains wouldn't come out.

*There goes ten thousand yen down the drain. Well, at least it got me out of that pointless conversation.*

Naturally, it seemed inevitable that she would end up being shunned once again. Countless past experiences should have ingrained that lesson long ago. With a resigned sigh, she hung the towel back on the railing to dry before retracing her steps to the corridor outside. Pausing briefly before venturing into the kitchen, she caught snippets of an ongoing conversation. Curiosity piqued, she discreetly peeked through the slightly ajar door.

"I'm not some idiot," Chun-mi hissed. "I know what I'm doing."

"Really?" Sung-jae said in a calm tone. "Then why are you still here?"

"Is that all you see me as, dad's puppet? It's called being a good daughter. Who else is going to look after him, if not me? You've made it clear that you won't be around."

"Is this why you haven't been answering my calls all week? Just to force me to come here?"

"Yes," Chun-mi said, shrugging. "I finally had something to get you and dad in the same room, so I used it to my advantage."

"He doesn't need someone to take care of him. And when he does, he needs to be put in a care home. I mean seriously, Chun-mi!" he whispered harshly, as his hands began to tremble at his side, his jerky mannerisms causing his glasses to slip down his nose. "After how he raised us, do you really think he deserves our care?"

"He taught us how to take care of ourselves. As far as I'm concerned, that's the job of a father. And ours is to take care of him in old age."

"And that being at the cost of our mental health and childhood is fine with you?"

"Oh-ho-ho, now it all comes out! You've become a little pansy, haven't you?" she said as she punched his arm. "Is this your new girlfriend talking?"

"I made the decision to leave long before she came into the picture."

"Whatever. My point is that I get paid a lot of money to be a bodyguard for this guy, and I'm very good at the job. Anything else has nothing to do with me."

"Even with everything you know about this guy? What he did? What he took from you?" he asked, crossing his arms. Chun-mi ignored his question.

"I'm taking this guy down, Chun-mi, through proper channels. This includes every single person he's worked with. Just be clear from the firing zone when I do."

The door creaked as Yu-ra leaned forward and the two sets of eyes darted towards her.

"Yeah, didn't do much good," Yu-ra announced, glancing down as she burst through the door, brushing her dress with her hands, "but it's fine, I'll sort it out at home."

Chun-mi walked off, returning to the dining room.

"Ah okay," Sung-jae said simply before turning to leave as well.

"Wait," Yu-ra called. "You know whose wife I am, now. And seeing as how he's supposedly tight-knit with your family, the least you could do is let me out of this crap deal. I'm not even sure this story is worth it anymore."

"I-I can't," Sung-jae said, looking away sheepishly. "Takemi won't comply without you, and I know her well enough to know that any other form of coercion won't work."

Yu-ra leaned one hand on the counter and one on her hip.

"You're kidding me, right? What's stopping me from telling Kyung-tae right now? Would you really put him and his wife in harm's way?"

Sung-jae pushed his glasses up the bridge of his nose.

"I would."

Yu-ra sighed.

"Your whole family is out to get me," she muttered as she shoved past Sung-jae.

"We're really not," he said, following closely behind. "Chun-mi was hired to do a job, and she's doing it. That's not a crime."

Before Yu-ra could open the door in front of her, Sung-jae called out to her.

"Hey, wait!"

"What?" Yu-ra said, pausing her movement.

"Something big is about to go down, and I have a feeling I know what. I need to stop it - using the law."

****

Yu-ra and sung-jae entered the dining room and took their respective seats.

"You okay?" Kyung-tae whispered, placing his hand on her back.

"Yeah, fine," she said, shuffling in her seat to find a more comfortable position.

"Right, where were we with our conversation?" Chun-mi said with glee, rubbing her hands together sinisterly like a cartoon villain.

"We were discussing the naiveté of one who believes in Korean independence," Jinmu said, mindlessly clearing his dishes away.

"We don't need to continue with that conversation," Yu-ra said, with a nervous smile.

"I'll take those," Kyung-tae said, hopping out of his seat and stacking all the empty dishes. Yu-ra watched Kyung-tae, suddenly feeling a longing to get up out of her seat.

"Do you need help with that?"

"I've got it. You sit and talk," he said, carrying all the dishes off to the kitchen.

"I'm curious about your ideology, Yu-ra," Jinmu said, as Yu-ra kept her eyes on Kyung-tae until the moment he left the room. "What makes someone believe in independence?"

"Well, to start, who's to say that we wouldn't be this well off without them?" Yu-ra said innocently.

"Oh, you really are naive," Jinmu said with a tone that wasn't condescending, but rather filled with concern for Yu-ra. "Our people would have split into factions, a civil war would have likely occurred. Not only did they save us from that but the invasion from the Russians too. I thought you were highly educated, Yu-ra. I can lend you some history books, if you would like?"

"No need," Yu-ra said, smiling awkwardly.

"They didn't just bring us peace through security. They also brought us peace through religion."

"Shintoism?" Yu-ra said, mindlessly waving her hand in dismissal. "They don't even follow that religion themselves. It's more like a cultural tradition."

"And what makes your religion so much better than ours?" Chun-mi snapped.

"I didn't say that," Yu-ra said. "I was just saying that Korean people follow Shintoism more than Japanese people, which is where the religion originated from. Does that really make sense?"

"So you're saying that Shintoism means nothing," Chun-mi snapped, "because we don't follow it the same way they do in Japan?"

"No, that's not what I was-"

"You're either disrespecting my religion or you're disrespecting Japan. Which is it?"

"I'm not explaining myself well," Yu-ra babbled, "Forget it. I'm sorry."

"No, no, no. Explain yourself then. Which is it?"

"Chun-mi," Sung-jae said firmly. "She's not trying to cause offence."

"I'm just defending my beliefs. What's wrong with that?"

"There's nothing wrong with defending yourself," Jinmu said staunchly, gathering all eyes back on him, "and the moment you start believing there's something wrong with it, is the moment you get yourself in trouble."

"So what's the problem here?" Chun-mi said, glaring down Yu-ra. She truly only concealed her two-faced nature from Kyung-tae.

"I wasn't bashing your religion or Japan. I was simply saying that in Japan, the religion has lost the meaning of what made it a religion. They forced this religion onto this country and then left it behind. It wasn't something that we chose, individually and free from harm, to start following."

"And yet, that is meaningless in the face of what this religion brings to people," Jinmu raised his voice, in a tone filled with awe, as if he were giving a sermon. "Did you know that there's this concept in our religion - that once you pass, if you have achieved a truly extraordinary feat, you can ascend and become kami?"

"You can become a god?" Yu-ra asked, taken aback. "That brings you peace?"

"My wife, she watches over us in kami form."

Sung-jae stood up abruptly and then strode out of the room.

"Sorry for your loss," Yu-ra said shortly after Sung-jae's exit.

"The point is," Jinmu added, "our country would be in the gutter if they didn't save us. The least we could do is keep traditions and religion alive."

Kyung-tae walked back in, rolling his shirt sleeves down as he came back to the table and sat down

"I just meant that all we are is a colony to them. And in this day and age, they need us more than we need them. We have a sound enough structure to provide for ourselves."

"I think it's less about us needing them," Kyung-tae said. "It's just not a good idea, economically, to detach ourselves from them and the rest of the empire, short and long-term. Our currency would crumble."

"Exactly," Jinmu added. "I'm all for us having independence if it would actually lead us to prosperity. But it won't."

"Personally, I disagree," Yu-ra said, "I think we have a stable enough economy to become independent. And Japan wants us to be reliant on them."

"So, you're actually pro-independence?" Chun-mi said. "I thought you were just playing devil's advocate."

Yu-ra tapped Kyung-tae on the side.

"What's your take on this?" she asked, hoping he would calm down her opposition. She had already had enough of these conversations for her whole lifetime. She didn't want to start it up again.

"I'm inclined to agree with them. Look how advanced our country is compared to the rest of the world. We're only behind Japan in terms of technology. We're in an era of peace that we've never seen before."

"Even though you deal with crime day in and day out?"

"Sure, crime occurs, but the rate is lower than it's ever been." Kyung-tae placed his hand on her knee again. "I think you're the only one who has this opinion, and I don't think you're changing anyone's mind soon. Maybe just accept that."

A lump formed in her throat as she realised having Kyung-tae nearby had not softened the blow of everyone being against her; it had only served to make it worse.

"I need to use the bathroom again," she mumbled.

# 22
# Hijab

After using the bathroom, Yu-ra tried to rush the night along as best she could. Unfortunately, it still took her another hour to achieve, after feigning a sudden oncoming of her time of the month, which Chun-mi profusely offered to help with. They arrived home a short while later, in succession to a silent drive. She slipped off her shoes and undid her hijab, tossing it onto the sofa arm. After untying her hair, she flopped onto the sofa and breathed out a heavy sigh, lying her arm across her eyes. She heard Kyung-tae open and close the bedroom door on her left. He was behind her. How did she not hear him walk across the room? Five minutes later, the same door opened and closed.

"You alright?" Kyung-tae said, harshly breaking the tranquil silence.

"Yeah. Fine," she said, still laying her arm across her face.

"You sure?"

"Yes!" she said with a huff, dropping her arm to her side.

"You certainly don't sound it."

"Oh you can tell, can you?" she said, finally looking away from the ceiling and at him. Her icy stare softened a little after seeing him wearing the pyjama set she recently bought him.

"I'm…confused," Kyung-tae said, itching at the corner of his forehead. "Would it not be easier to just say what's on your mind instead of me trying to figure it out?"

"You know, you might be right."

"So what's bothering you?"

"You already know."

"I do?" Kyung-tae paused to ponder for a moment. "Oh! Chun-mi!"

"Not even just her," Yu-ra exclaimed with an exasperated breath. "The whole night was a disaster!"

"Yu-ra, you can't be serious. In what way was it a disaster," Kyung-tae said, walking over to her side and sitting on the arm of the couch.

"You really couldn't see it? Even with that whole argument about independence?"

"What was wrong with that discussion?"

"What was wrong with it? I didn't want to be part of it in the first place."

"But you defended the viewpoint. Isn't it their prerogative to ask you to elaborate?"

"They were the ones being narrow minded. All I wanted to say was that people are allowed to have their own viewpoints."

"But I agree with them. And they're also allowed to defend their own viewpoint, so I'm still not quite seeing the issue here."

"Again, my issue was that I didn't want to be part of the conversation. I asked them to stop the conversation and they dragged me back into it."

"I still don't get it. You're your own woman. If you don't want to take part, nothing is stopping you from sitting quietly. Besides, what's so bad about being part of the conversation? If anything, you opened up their mind to the opposing view at the very least, even if they don't agree with it. I mean, you certainly opened up my mind somewhat."

"Believe me. I really did not make them more open minded. I've had enough of these conversations to know."

"Either way, I don't understand why you think this means they dislike you."

"Did you not see the way they talk down to me?"

"Not really, no."

"You're kidding, right? Chun-mi has been a horrible person to me since the day I met her. Jinmu's nice and welcoming, but he says some very condescending things sometimes. And not on purpose, I think he might genuinely believe I'm stupid."

"He does not."

"Sung-jae is somewhat bearable. But even he won't let me..."

"Won't let you what?"

"Never mind. The point is, Chun-mi, and probably Sung-jae too, has something against me. And if they don't, it's worse, because that means that's just who they are as people."

"I don't see how Sung-jae could possibly have anything against you. He just met you today. And I haven't seen Chun-mi be anything but welcoming to you. What I have seen - and I've seen it a lot - is women generally act very cold towards her. I'm guessing I know why. But you have nothing to be worried about."

"Oh please, get over yourself. She's a two-faced twerp. That's why you haven't seen it. And all those women are probably just as justified as I am."

"Yu-ra, please don't speak about her like that."

"There you go defending her again."

"I'm trying to be unbiased. I shouldn't defend you just because you're my wife. And either way, I'm asking you not to backbite because that's wrong."

"Don't defend me then! I can stand up for myself. The least you could do is listen to me."

"I am listening to you."

"No, you're trying to debate me. Listen to me." Kyung-tae paused, looking over his shoulder at her, then looked away. "I know you can't see what Chun-mi is like," Yu-ra said, feeding her hand through the gap between Kyung-tae's arm and torso, and then wrapping her arm around his, "but that's because she's different around you. And those kinds of people aren't people you should be around. They only care for themselves. Their envious behaviour will seek out and destroy anyone else around you."

"Sounds like you're speaking from experience. You've dealt with people like that a lot, then?"

"I used to be one of those people."

"Oh." Kyung-tae hesitated. It seemed like he wanted to say something, but didn't know how.

"Back in high-school I had this friend, Si-yu - a truly amazing friend," Yu-ra said, leaning her head on Kyung-tae's arm, "someone who stood by me even when no one else would. You wouldn't believe how hard it was to be the only Muslim girl in my year group, and only one of four Muslim girls in the whole school. To have your whole identity mocked day in and day out. To be an outcast, even to the unpopular girls. T-to…" Yu-ra trailed off, a lump forming in her throat, "to have your hijab yanked from your head in front of the whole class just to appease their curiosity. But as I grew older, I found that people get smarter in hiding their Islamophobia. It becomes much more subtle so that they feel they can justify it to themselves that they are moral people. Soon they'll introduce laws that ban us from covering up. And they'll label it freedom."

Kyung-tae slipped down from the arm of the sofa into the space in between them.

"When I was about fifteen - I had somewhat of a crisis in faith," she continued, as Kyung-tae removed his arm from her grip and draped it over her shoulder. She looked up at him. "God knows how, but it happened. Si-yu didn't really understand it, but she tried to. The problem was - all her advice was coming from someone who didn't agree with Islam in the first place. Maybe it was because of my mum forcing everything on me. Or maybe it was my dad's lack of presence when it came to teaching me about Islam. But at a certain point, I felt like I had had enough. I would pretend to be the shy and modest Muslim girl at home. But the moment I left the house, I would tear off my hijab. And why wouldn't I? I didn't see the point of it. You can be modest without wearing a hijab, and you can be immodest while wearing one."

"Yeah, I guess," Kyung-tae said, looking over to her, "but it's an obligation on you. Does it truly matter if you see the point?"

"Are you being serious?"

"Sorry, I'm not trying to be rude or insensitive to your struggle. I'm just trying to understand what was going on in your head."

"Maybe it mattered to me, maybe it didn't. But do you see where I'm coming from?"

"Yeah I do. Not everyone with a hijab is modest and not everyone without one is immodest."

"When I took it off," she said, leaning her head on his chest, "I was well and truly free. I felt it anyway. Free from living up to any expectations from my family, free from any obligations to God, free to just be… me. Guys would flock to me in droves, now that I wasn't some enigma for them to hate. I was loud, and goofy, and pretty."

Kyung-tae laughed quietly.

"As if you weren't pretty beforehand."

Yu-ra looked up at him earnestly, her eyes almost beginning to well up.

"It didn't feel like I was." She turned away from him, blinking furiously to wash away any tears that were trying to escape her ducts. "People liked being around me all of a sudden. And it was insane what they would do for my attention, as if I was their queen. Who knew women could control men so easily? And by controlling the men, I controlled the women too. If something didn't go my way, I would manipulate people until it did. I wasn't hurting anyone, so what was the problem?" She turned back to Kyung-tae, his eyes fogged with a mist like a window in a crowded room as he rubbed her shoulder. "I forgot all about Si-yu, by the way. We drifted apart because she didn't get along with my newfound friends. And without that unimportant little headscarf I left the house with every morning, that constant reminder of the meaning of modesty dissipated. My morals loosened every time my hijab did."

Kyung-tae pulled away from her a little.

"What do you mean by that?"

"I became a bully - that's the only way I can phrase it."

"Oh."

"Those other Muslim girls in school," Yu-ra said, beginning to well up again. Her words became tangled in the fabrics of the bunched-up hijab she tossed to the side. It was as if the scarf was tightening around her throat. But this time, she couldn't stop the tears from escaping as a single droplet raced down her cheek, "the way I was treated, I did the same to them. Because I fell away from Islam, I tried to pull others away too." Kyung-tae sat in silence but shifted a little closer to her. "And the pure-hearted Si-yu, from afar, knew what I was becoming. So, she tried to step in." Yu-ra wiped her eyes, in an attempt to stop the river of tears now flowing down her cheeks. She waved her hands in the air, as if she was showing apprehension to some imaginary thing in front of her, "Ohh, but little old Yu-ra wasn't having it. She was on top of the world. Who was Si-yu to try and drag me down? The moment I became popular, she walked away."

Yu-ra slumped her shoulders, her head drooping with them. "So I made an example of her. I kicked and I punched her. I insulted her. And I did all of this with an audience. I ruined the rest of her high school experience. And I realised that I had become something I had always hated. I didn't have any influence with other people. I didn't control them. They controlled me - I was vying for their approval - and my lack of God consciousness made it easy for them to prey on my weak will. I never could fix my friendship with Si-yu, even after years of trying."

"Yu-ra…" Kyung-tae whispered.

Yu-ra looked back at Kyung-tae, smiling with her eyes.

"I'm not that person anymore, alhamdulillah."

"I know."

"But I know what that person is capable of," she said, relaxing her face, "and she is capable of a lot worse than what I described."

"Yu-ra, I completely understand what you're saying. And I know you're not that person," he said, rubbing her shoulder. "That was all a part of the journey to become who you are today. And if anything, isn't that the most beautiful thing ever? When the whole world is against you and you defy them, saying 'no, I will be who I am and wear my hijab proudly, for Allah and Allah alone!'"

"When you put it that way…"

"But I need you to trust me. Even if you're right about Chun-mi, please give me the benefit of the doubt. She is a good-hearted person. Maybe she just needs a little time to warm up to you."

Yu-ra's heart wrenched. After all that, Kyung-tae was still taking Chun-mi's side? Even if he knew Chun-mi for ten years longer than her, it still hurt.

Yu-ra slipped out of his warm embrace and stood up from the sofa.

"I'm beat. I'm gonna head to bed."

"Hey, one more thing. Your mum invited us down for dinner tomorrow. She said she's cooked a whole feast."

"I'm not going," she said slumping over as she dragged her feet towards the bedroom.

"Wait," Kyung-tae said, stopping her in her tracks. "Why do you keep doing that?"

"Doing what?" she said, turning around.

"Every time your mother asks us to come over, you always have an excuse. Why?"

"I'm not going because I don't want to go. End of. Go by yourself if you care so much."

"Yu-ra, enough of this friction with everyone. We need to go visit your parents."

"Then you'll have to drag me there. Otherwise, drop it."

Kyung-tae watched her in silence momentarily as she turned and dragged her feet once more.

"I'll head in soon." Kyung-tae said.

"Take your time."

# 23
# The Last Samurai

Kyung-tae poured over the eight camera screens in front of him, as he tossed the empty bag of dried fruit into the makeshift bin beside him. His behind wiggled in its seat until it found more comfort. However, being in the back of a small undercover police van, that was near impossible. Only upon rubbing his hands together did he realise the biting cold. Leaning over the passenger's seat to his side, he grabbed the heat pack from his bag of supplies. With his free hand, he scrolled through the contact list on his phone.

*Oh God, I've never found stakeouts more boring than this. What's happened to me?*

He clicked on Woo-young's name. *Ring ring…ring ring… click-*

*"Hello,"* came Woo-young's voice.

"Hey," Kyung-tae said, "I've got a deal for you. The deal of the century."

*"Whatever you've got, I'm not interested."*

"Wait! Allow me to awe you with my investigative prowess before you decide."

*"Why?"*

"It's about my case."

*"You do know I'm working my own cases, right?"*

"Sure. Anyway, I looked into those warehouses. I was right. There's a network of shell companies forming this web of sorts. The connections between the warehouse companies are sparse. Anyway, all these companies can be traced back to one business…" Kyung-tae paused, waiting for Woo-young to respond.

*"Are you trying to build tension or something? Just say what you want to say. When did you get so theatrical?"*

"When did you get so…" Kyung-tae trailed off as he attempted a retort but his mind ran blank. "Shut up."

*"Nice one. You're like a poet of our generation."*

"Look, it took a lot of work, but I traced it all the way back to Park Pharmaceuticals."

*"Oh wow, that's a big company. I guess those warehouses were probably insured. Maybe that's why you didn't get wind of it straight away."*

"Exactly!"

*"Sounds like you've got a doozy of a case on your hand. Good luck with that."*

"There's four more warehouses owned by companies under Park Pharmaceuticals. I set up cameras near each of them. I've got nothing from the past week."

*"Okay, and?"*

"You wanna- wait hold on," he said, as a van parked up near the warehouse but then shortly after drove off. "Sorry, thought I had something. Anyway, you wanna help me stake them out?"

*"Oh, no way. Spending the night in a cramped van with nothing but conversation with you? I wouldn't wish that on my worst enemy. Besides, remember that case I was assigned with the missing girls?"*

"Yeah."

*"The girl just randomly showed up at the police station."*

"What? How? Why?"

*"I don't know. Apparently she's been free for a few weeks and chose not to report to police until just now. But she's refusing to tell me why. It's weird."*

"That is weird. What possible reason could she have for not going to the police immediately? Anyway, let me know what happens," Kyung-tae said before hanging up the phone.

So, Woo-young was out, who else could cure his boredom? He scrolled up to his favourited contacts. *Ma…Spouse…* Yu-ra!

*"Assalaamu 'alaykum, what's up?"* came her voice a few seconds after ringing her.

"Wa'alaykum salaam. Just calling…"

*"Sure… and the reason is?"*

"You know, just to see how things…"

*"Yeah, things are fine."*

"I'm staking out again-"

*"Can I call you back? I'm kind of in the middle of something at the moment. But I'll call you as soon as I'm done."*

"Oh. Yeah, of course. That's fine," Kyung-tae said, but a pang in his chest told him that it wasn't. He had a million things to say to her, but simply settled for - "see you later."

Yu-ra wasn't as talkative as she usually was recently, and for the life of him, he couldn't figure out why.

Kyung-tae sighed as he put his phone back into his pocket. Noticing the cold metal of the lighter in his pocket, his thumb mindlessly traced the engraving.

****

"So, what makes you think the arsonist is going to hit here tonight?" Takemi said, lifting her mask from her face.

"It's not that I think it," Yu-ra said, turning off her phone and stowing it in her pocket before shifting her gaze back to the warehouse through the windshield of Takemi's car. "Ny-ron just moved sixty-five percent of his remaining product to this location."

"So? No one would dare steal it. He's got an army transporting it."

"But he's showcased the location to the whole world. And he doesn't realise it."

"And that's..." Takemi hesitated, as if unsure of what she was saying, "good for us."

"Yes."

"Ohh, I get it. Yes... Of course."

Yu-ra retrieved her phone, positioning it on the dashboard with its top leaning against the window. The camera was poised toward the warehouse, primed to capture any moment instantly.

"You know," Takemi said, closely observing what she was doing, "you might as well explain it again anyway. You know, just so you can feel useful."

Yu-ra glared at her.

"What?" Takemi said innocently.

"The arsonist can't pass up an opportunity this good. He knows exactly where the drugs are, and he doesn't know how long such a huge portion will be stored in this one place for."

"So it's bait!"

"Well done!" Yu-ra said, clapping in faux glee.

"Thanks, I do try my best."

****

*"I don't fully understand,"* came Chun-mi's voice over the phone. *"How exactly do you think my boss is involved in your case?"*

"Put simply, he owns the warehouses that burned down," Kyung-tae replied.

*"Wouldn't that make him the victim?"*

"But it just doesn't make sense. How can he be researching something so uniquely similar to the substance I found?"

*"I don't know. It doesn't seem that hard to believe."*

"Rule one of detective work - there's no such thing as a coincidence."

*"I get enough of this from my dad, thank you very much."*

"Maybe the substances I found are remnants of his failures."

*"A warehouse full is more than a remnant."*

"But if he didn't want those remnants out on the streets, he's got a motive to burn it. Plus there's the whole building insurance thing."

*"Insurance?"*

"You know, get a big payout, use the insurance money to start a political campaign."

*"Okay, so why don't you just book him now?"*

"I arrested the owner of the tech firm. He admitted to illegally storing the substance straight away. I've got nothing on the arsonist though. And if you ask me, he crumbled way too fast. I think he was set up to take the fall for that." Kyung-tae held up the damaged lighter, inspecting the gold emblem. "I open this blockade and all my answers come flooding through," he mumbled.

*"What blockade? What are you talking about? You realise I'm not sitting in front of you, right?"*

"You said your boss is a chain-smoker."

*"Yeah, he even gets custom lighters made."*

"What? Why have you never told me this before?"

*"I didn't think you would care."*

"I care a lot. What do these lighters look like?"

*"They're gold, with the insignia of a bear engraved in them. He left in a rush ten minutes ago, wearing some weird outfit. I can check his office and show you."*

Gold lighter with an engraving? It was him. It had to be. Everything was starting to make sense. There was conclusive proof that Park Dae-myeon was the arsonist. He just needed photo evidence of his lighters. Kyung-tae pointed his phone at the lighter in his hand and snapped a picture, sharing the image directly to Chun-mi.

"Check your messages."

*"Yes! Exactly like-"*

Suddenly something moved very quickly across the corner of the bottom left screen. A dark figure stopped behind a tall industrial sized bin, obstructing the view of it from the warehouse cameras, but not Kyung-tae's. A few moments later, the shadowed figure gracefully flipped over the bin and zipped across to the camera screen above it. It sidled towards the back entrance of the warehouse, where one heavy set guard stood. The mysterious figure, who was taller and broader than the guard, grappled him from the neck and dragged him away to the shadowed side of the building he came from. Kyung-tae tossed his phone to the side, not even bothering to hang up on the still-chattering Chun-mi. Twisting his way into the front seat of the van, he switched on the ignition and slammed his foot on the gas, speeding off in the direction of the warehouse he was just watching.

****

From the corner of Yu-ra's eyes, a broad but acrobatic figure, very similar in stature to the man Chun-mi was with when they met with Ny-ron, weaved its way through the sightlines of the cameras and the guards. Her hands shook with glee just before she pressed the record button on her phone.

"I capture this and my position is cemented with Ny-ron," she said.

"Oh-ho, I'll do you one better," Takemi said, a cheery grin sprawled on her face. "I'll bring him to Ny-ron myself!"

Takemi opened the window beside her.

"What? No!" Yu-ra cried. "What the heck are you doing? We don't even know who this guy is."

"I'll see you in five."

Takemi winked just before pulling her mask down. Slipping her hands through the window, she gripped the roof of the car, then pulled her whole body through.

"WAIT!" Yu-ra shouted out of her window at the sprinting Takemi before slapping her hand over her mouth after realising that she had possibly just alerted anyone nearby to her presence.

****

The van skidded to a halt, a few metres away from the back of the warehouse. As Kyung-tae rushed off towards the entrance, something moved in the corner of his peripherals. Was there someone in the silver sports car that was parked across the road? Brushing the thought away, he continued sprinting to the now unguarded door. A strong wind blew the door into the wall with a thud. As he entered the building, a harmony of screams was trying to escape. Was this arsonist burning buildings with people in? He had to catch him quickly. The air smelled like normal air. Good. He still had time to stop it.

CRASH!

The shattering of glass echoed. Kyung-tae dashed into the next room, his steps clanging against the metal walkway, as he observed two masked figures below him scrambling over each other at the centre of the concrete plains. There were two of them? Which one was trying to set the fire? Or was it both of them? Did they have a fight mid-way through their arson?

Through a labyrinth of scaffolding, Kyung-tae could make out four unconscious men lying around the room, and three more were dragging themselves towards the front exit as dark red liquid gushed from their thighs. Large, opened crates were distributed throughout the room, and thick, unvarnished wooden tables at its heart. Each was adorned with neatly arranged plastic packages containing crystals.

Hurrying to the nearest unconscious person to his left, he repeatedly slapped their face in a desperate attempt to rouse them. Despite the effort, there was no response. He slapped him harder. Still no luck. He needed to get these people help, but first, he needed to apprehend the brawling men downstairs.

"Hey," he called over to the men dragging themselves across the ground. Met with the gaze of every set of eyes in the room, he shouted, "call an ambulance!" as he vaulted himself over the railing in front of him. Upon landing, he raced towards the ongoing brawl, not bothering to ensure if the men would comply with his request.

The broad figure was veiled in black, adorned in a tight cotton jacket held closed by a heavy black rope, and a pair of trousers that were loose around his thighs and tied up around his calves. On his face sat a black mask with gold highlighting the features of the sharp nose, baring teeth, and devilish horns protruding from the skull. It was a mask reminiscent of those that samurai would wear to guard their faces but also instil fear into the hearts of their opponents. It was as if his outfit was reverent of both ninja and samurai. The broad man was scrambling away from the slim figure who leapt at him, causing both to tumble over. His forest green mask held no features, bar a few deep cracks, reminiscent of traumatic scars. He wore a simple outfit, comprising a lengthy hooded cloak layered over a plain white sweater. The fabric tore as the samurai seized his collar, hurling him away with a forceful knee strike. With a swift motion, he flipped himself onto his feet.

Slowing his pace as he came closer to them, Kyung-tae contemplated the possibility of one of them trying to stop the other from setting the fire. No. There was no time to think about it. He needed to act now. Worst case scenario, he could take both of them.

He dashed towards the samurai, who was studying his downed foe, unaware of the charging detective. Kyung-tae soared through the air, propelling his right foot at his opponent's head. Yet, the samurai effortlessly ducked the kick, then swept him off his feet the moment he landed. Pain crackled through Kyung-tae's back as he crashed to the ground, slick with a viscous liquid that coated his jacket. Rolling to his side, Kyung-tae witnessed the scarred man duck a flurry of the samurai's punches. The scarred man spun onto his knees, firing his elbow into the back of the samurai's knee, forcing him down, and then trapped him in a headlock. As he seemingly tried to tear the samurai's head from the rest of his body, Kyung-tae yanked him away from the samurai but he broke free from Kyung-tae's grip and rolled back onto his feet. With a small distance between the three combatants, they each assumed a distinct fighting stance, poised for the impending clash.

The scarred man threw a barrage of punches at Kyung-tae and he parried and countered with his own punches. In the midst of this, the samurai also launched his own flurry of punches towards the scarred man, yet still, he managed to block and parry both attackers simultaneously. With a powerful leap, the scarred man drove the sole of his boot into the samurai's shoulder and then swung the same boot, delivering a crushing blow to Kyung-tae's cheek, who spun out and crashed, spiralling across the ground. Agony pulsated through every colliding muscle group and Kyung-tae struggled to catch his breath as he watched the fight continue.

The samurai lunged at the scarred man, who swiftly ducked under his grasp and fired an elbow into his abdomen. The scarred man rolled underneath the samurai's legs and then vaulted onto the nearby table, springing off its side and landing squarely on the samurai's shoulders. Finally catching his breath, Kyung-tae plunged back into the fray. Meanwhile the scarred man seized the horns of the samurai's mask, wrapping his legs around his throat to choke him into submission. The samurai thrashed about, wrestling to gain a firm hold on his foe. With a powerful grip on his cloak, he effortlessly hurled him over his shoulder and through the very table he had vaulted off moments ago. Splintering wood exploded in all directions, as the scarred man crashed down. The samurai then unleashed a relentless barrage of blows upon him.

As the scarred man's frantic struggles gradually slowed, Kyung-tae barged into the samurai's side, but only managed to drive him away two or three paces. The samurai cocked his head eerily yet remained motionless. What was he doing? Kyung-tae readied his stance, fists raised defensively. Then, the samurai simply pivoted, striding purposefully toward the rear exit.

Kyung-tae finally understood. The samurai's job was complete; stop the arsonist - the unconscious scarred man.

As he walked away, Kyung-tae noticed that his build was identical to Chun-mi's boss. He was wrong. Park Dae-myeon was trying to stop the arson, not start it. It definitely made more sense than Kyung-tae's theory. But that left one question - why was he storing the drug in his warehouse and why was he so desperate to protect it?

****

Yu-ra paused her recording, returning her phone to her bag. They had been in there for a while. Something must have gone wrong. Who was that guy that ran in after them? Takemi was surely in trouble

****

"Wait!" Kyung-tae called out to the samurai, stopping him in his tracks, but nothing more. "I know who you are." He turned around, taking a few steps towards Kyung-tae. "Detective Oh," he continued, holding up his badge. "You'll have to return with me to the station. I have some questions regarding your company and the substance you're storing in these warehouses. Stay right where you are," Kyung-tae said as he kneeled down beside the stirring arsonist, taking a zip-tie out of his back pocket, "and thank you for your help with this case."

The samurai turned around again, taking a few steps towards the exit. Kyung-tae quickly rolled the scarred man onto his stomach, loosely holding his wrists in one hand. And with the other, Kyung-tae bound them together. Hopping back onto his feet, he jogged up to the samurai.

"Hey, wait," he called, "if you walk away now, you're admitting guilt. And like I said, I know who you are. You achieve nothing by leaving."

Kyung-tae placed his hand on the samurai's muscular shoulder, but over his own shoulder, he could hear movement coming from his detainee. Looking back, the scarred man was back on his feet, uncuffed, with two daggers in hand.

Suddenly, the air was ripped from Kyung-tae's lungs as a brute force slammed into his abdomen. Whipping his head forward, he caught a glimpse of a fist flying into his jaw, sending him crashing to the ground. As his chin pulsed and his temples pounded, a warm liquid began seeping from his teeth, filling up his mouth. Kyung-tae rolled onto his side and spat a mouthful of blood onto the ground. Glancing up, he watched as the scarred man charged at the samurai, who readied himself in a simple karate stance.

The scarred man swiped his right dagger at the samurai, aiming for his abdomen. The samurai parried with such a force that the dagger escaped his grip. But, the scarred man drove his remaining dagger into his opponent's shoulder. Damn it. He was going to kill him.

Kyung-tae pushed through the pain flooding his skull and raced over to the fighters. Without a glance, the scarred man swung his arm back at him. Kyung-tae ducked it, gripping his wrist and flipping him over his shoulder. He held him down, clutching his cloak, and the man's mask scratched at Kyung-tae's knuckles as he punched it once, twice, three times. His knuckles left blood stains on his mask. The scarred man gripped his wrist, wrapping his legs around his arm, and used his feet to throw him to the ground. He twisted and yanked, threatening to rip his arm from the socket. As Kyung-tae's muscle began to tear, he failed to hold in his escaping cry of pain.

He flailed about, scanning his nearby surroundings in an attempt to find something to help him break free. The samurai was standing once again, the dagger still jammed into his shoulder, with a dark liquid seeping through his clothes. Was he going to help? The samurai stuck his hand into his inside pocket, rummaging around, then pulled out a small metallic object. The scarred man's other dagger made its presence known beside him. He noticed the tip of that small metallic object in his grip was now alight. The samurai was the arsonist.

Kyung-tae snatched the dagger beside him, and blindly swung it at the man that had him in an armbar. Luckily he managed to stab him in the thigh, releasing the grip he had on Kyung-tae entirely. The scarred man cried out as he rolled about, holding onto his thigh. Kyung-tae propelled himself to his feet. Charging at the samurai, he attempted to knock the lighter out of his hand, but he swiftly dodged him. Kyung-tae then parried a heavy punch from the samurai's other arm, and shot his foot into his abdomen, causing him to stumble. Before he could regain his balance, Kyung-tae axe kicked the lighter out of his hand.

A dagger whipped past his ear and straight into the samurai's other shoulder. Grunting in pain, with a dagger trapped in both of his shoulders, he stumbled and fell to his knees. The scarred man hobbled over to them as fast as he possibly could with blood spurting from his thigh. Not bothering to remove the protruding daggers, the samurai readied himself for his opponents.

"Sorry about your leg," Kyung-tae said over his shoulder as he shifted into his Taekwondo stance.

Both Kyung-tae and his newfound ally swiped at their brawny foe. But the samurai ducked the scarred man's punch and parried Kyung-tae's at the same time. The samurai slammed his boot into the scarred man, flipping him onto his back, and then followed it up with a decisive knee driven straight into Kyung-tae's gut. The blood still sitting on his gums spluttered from his mouth. His ally spun into the air slamming his heel into the samurai's skull a thundering crack echoed across the entire complex. Then he hurled his elbow down into the samurai's skull, causing his mask to split. Kyung-tae dashed at the samurai, slamming his shoulder into him and wrapping his arms around his wide body. He pushed with all his might, but only managed to gain two steps. The samurai tore him off, flinging him to the side. He skidded across the ground, as a throbbing spread down the arm he had landed on. Kyung-tae swiftly flipped himself upright. The scarred man managed to get a powerful kick into the samurai's side, but the retreating leg was captured. The samurai launched his fist into his chest. Before he had the chance to collapse, the samurai gripped his mask and tore it off, tossing it away like garbage.

Kyung-tae flicked a broken table leg into his grasp with his shoe. Catapulting it at the back of the samurai's head, a deep thud echoed as it connected. The samurai released the leg he had captured, staggering forward as he did. After closing the distance between them, Kyung-tae sprang into the air. He wrapped his hands around the back of the samurai's neck and launched his legs past him, yanking him to the ground during his own descent. Kyung-tae kickflipped himself up, then raced over to his newfound ally, lifting him by the arm. His ally was no longer faceless. Nor was it even a man! How was she so strong? Through the bruised and bloodied face, he could see young eyes. This woman couldn't have been any older than Yu-ra, maybe even younger than her. What was someone so young doing trying to catch an arsonist? Who was she?

Suddenly, the young woman shoved him aside as the barrelling samurai came charging towards them. But, still within reach of the samurai, Kyung-tae caught a powerful punch to the side of his face, shocking his jaw and sending him tumbling across the ground once again. The young woman, on the other hand, effortlessly ducked the behemoth figure and used his own momentum to fling him over her shoulders. She flipped then launched her boot into his mask as a crack thundered through the room and split it into two pieces. The samurai's hands shot onto his face, as he held the mask together. He swung his legs into the woman's, sweeping her from her feet and sending her crashing to the ground. The samurai rolled onto his front and scrambled towards the exit. He barged the door open and raced off into the night. With not a moment's hesitation, the young woman scurried after him, exiting the building a few moments later.

As Kyung-tae stood up his phone began to ring. He answered as he rushed towards the exit.

*"I've got some important news,"* came Woo-young's piercing voice. Kyung-tae moved his phone away from his ear slightly. His pounding skull made Woo-young's voice unbearable.

"I'm a little tied up right now," Kyung-tae shouted.

*"You're not going to like this. Li-Na finally spoke about her capture. She didn't want to speak up at first because her father is a known criminal, so she just has a habit of being secretive."*

"Can this not wait?" he said as he shoved the warehouse door open, a cold wind blasting him in the face.

*"Kim Sun-jung. She really was kidnapped with her."*

Kyung-tae immediately halted in his tracks.

"What?" he whispered.

*"It couldn't have been suicide. According to Li-Na it didn't fit her character at all. They separated them and that's when Sun-jung died."*

"What?" he repeated, in an even softer tone.

# 24

# The Cache

Kyung-tae yanked the door of his van shut. As he slipped his phone into the slot on the top of his dash, blue lights projected onto his window, highlighting the road ahead of him. Slamming his foot on the gas, he sped off down the blue paths directing him towards the police station.

How? How could she claim that Kim Sun-jung was with her? And how could the kidnappers make her commit suicide with absolutely no signs of struggle whatsoever? And why in the world would they keep the other girl alive if they were going to kill Sun-jung?

A ringing tone ejected from the speaker system, breaking through the sounds of nothing but the revving of the van.

"Answer," he said, causing the ringing to stop, but a high-pitched beeping continued.

*"Hey, Nancy Drew,"* came Chun-mi's voice, exacerbating the pounding in Kyung-tae's skull.

"Who?"

*"Well I was going to call you Sherlock Holmes, but I'd say you're a lot cuter than him."*

"What are these names you keep saying to me?" Kyung-tae said, screwing up his face.

*"You're not very well-read, are you?"*

"Guess not," he said as he skidded around a corner. "What do you need? I'm in a rush."

*"Well don't be. I've got good news for you!"* she said with glee.

"Can it wait?" he said as he finally clipped on his seatbelt to silence the persisting beeps of the van.

*"You were right about my boss. You're a genius! He was fumbling around the office, with blood seeping through his shirt-"*

Chun-mi's voice seemed to fade away as he saw a sleek silver car speeding beside him. Through the passenger's window, he saw a familiar green mask. He could tell from the clothing and hands besides the ally he made, that a woman was driving her to wherever they were going. Suddenly, Chun-mi's piercing voice rang back through his ears.

*"Are you listening?"*

"Sorry, what?" Kyung-tae said, turning away from his window and speeding up even more. "I got distracted."

*"I said you were right about my boss. I found this weird mask that had been cracked down the middle, and a stash of those lighters that you had shown me. I've sent you some pictures from his office. He's definitely the arsonist you were looking for. If you want, I can help keep him here until you arrive to arrest him."*

"Look, I'm a little busy right now. I'll call you back when I'm free."

*"Oh,"* Chun-mi said softly, *"That's-"*

Kyung-tae cut off the phone as he continued down the directed route. As the roads became more familiar to him, he swiped away the navigation system and the blue light disappeared.

As Kyung-tae finally made his way back into the main station, there was an odd silence spread throughout the building. All staff had met in the conference room, a long room filled with white tables and chairs, and a large aisle down the centre. It was strange that he hadn't been notified about any meetings. Though the pounding in his skull had subsided somewhat, the soreness in his jaw still remained prominent. Thankfully, he hadn't seen any visible injuries since he had cleaned out his mouth. After wrapping his knuckles against the door, he poked his head in.

"Hi," he said in an uncharacteristically meek manner. The whole room had fallen silent, but the most surprising thing was that Captain Kim wasn't leading the briefing. Superintendent Murakami was; a short, greasy man with bushy eyebrows who sat in his office at all times and only dealt with the Lieutenant - and he had a fire in his eyes.

"WHO THE HELL ARE YOU?" he bellowed.

Sliding the rest of his body through the doorway, he squared his shoulders and saluted

"Detective Oh Kyung-tae, sir. Do you not know who I am?"

"Of-of course I know, you idiot," he stuttered, "but this begs the question OF WHERE IN THE HELL HAVE YOU BEEN?"

"I was caught up with a case, sir."

Murakami stamped his foot.

"Do you even know what's going on right now, you little weasel!?"

"No, not really."

Suddenly, the Superintendent slammed his boot into his podium causing it to crash to the ground. Then, as if a child throwing a tantrum, pounced on the knocked over podium and aggressively jumped on it repeatedly, the wood of the base splintering. Striding over to Kyung-tae, he glared up at him as Kyung-tae directed his gaze to the ceiling in response. Luckily, Lieutenant Kim finally decided to step in.

"Sir, he's here now. Let's just carry on with the briefing and get this situation under control."

The superintendent walked back over to the podium and kicked it once again.

"Someone pick this shit up!"

Kyung-tae rushed over and lifted it off the ground, making sure it stood steady before scanning the room for an empty seat. There. At the back of the room behind Woo-young. After quickly making his way across the room, he slipped into the seat.

"Nice entrance," Woo-young whispered to him.

"Shut up," Kyung-tae whispered back.

"To repeat myself, for a certain someone," Murakami said, narrowing his beady eyes at Kyung-tae, "all of your cases, EVERY SINGLE ONE!" he bellowed, "are being put on hold until we sort out this situation."

"What?" Kyung-tae whispered. "That's not right. How does he expect us to just drop everything? Does he not understand how important time is in our job?"

Kyung-tae moved to stand up, but Woo-young put his hand out, turning his head slightly.

"Don't. We've already had this conversation. He's not budging."

"You've got your teams," Murakami said, "and you've got twenty four hours to find the guns that were stolen."

"Guns?" Kyung-tae whispered as he leaned forward slightly.

"A guy in a mask broke into a military base," Woo-young said, tilting his head towards his partner. "They ransacked it and stole a cache of guns; pistols, shotguns, assault rifles, a whole cargo's worth."

"That's crazy. Anyway, I need to talk to you. I need your help finding these kidnappers. Where did you find your girl?"

Woo-young turned all the way around to face Kyung-tae.

"You can't go after them? Can you not see it's all hands on deck right now?"

"What's your point? I've got more important things to worry about. You guys have it covered."

"You think Murakami will let you get away with that?"

"He'll be none the wiser."

"Hey!" Murakami called out, "we got a problem back there?"

"No, sir!" Kyung-tae called back, standing up firmly and saluting. "I was just saying that I will give it my all for this case. I will get these guns back to you as soon as humanly possible."

"Shut up and sit down," Murakami responded.

"Yes, sir!" Kyung-tae called before sitting back down.

After the briefing had ended, Kyung-tae walked with Woo-young to his desk as he had been attached to his team. After bugging Woo-young for five minutes straight, Kyung-tae had found out that his kidnap victim had been sent home. Kyung-tae could almost feel his blood bubbling up.

"Why?" he said through gritted teeth. "She escaped a kidnapping and you think she's just safe all of a sudden?"

"She didn't escape. She said a pretty woman in a scarf rescued her."

"Who?"

"She didn't know her name. At least that's what she said," Woo-young said, shrugging. "But that's beside the point. In what way do you think this is my choice to make? Our team is waiting. Can we just put a lid on this for now?"

"Are you serious? A girl died. Under my watch. I couldn't give a crap about these guns. What are they going to do? Shoot up the whole country?"

"No, what will happen is some random gangbanger will try and rob a store, or a bar, or a casino. And things will go sideways, and he will shoot the place up. Causing people to die."

"The military will crack down on it. They've got far better technology than we do. They can handle it in half a day. Why are we wasting all our resources just so Murakami doesn't get chewed out."

"You really need to gain some perspective," Woo-young said, beginning to walk away.

"I need to gain perspective?" Kyung-tae said, grabbing Woo-young's shoulder and pulling him back. "You're putting the reputation of some guy who doesn't even do his job over a murder victim. How is it our fault that the military couldn't protect their base?"

"When did you get brave enough to speak out against authority?"

Kyung-tae dropped his hand from Woo-young's shoulder.

"When I realised they don't give a damn about the people they're meant to protect. I don't care about the guns." He jabbed his finger into Woo-young's shoulder. "I don't care about the arsonist burning down drug warehouses." Jab. "I care about the girl that was murdered." Jab. "And the girl that was kidnapped." Jab. "And stopping it from happening to anyone else. And here I was thinking you were someone who stands up for what's right."

Suddenly, Woo-young shoved Kyung-tae, sending him crashing backwards into the desk. Silence, and all eyes in the room, fell upon them.

"What did you just say to me?" Woo-young hissed. "Why don't you the hell get off your high horse and stop acting like you care about anything other than what affects you?"

"I don't," Kyung-tae said firmly, lowering his voice so that everyone would turn their attention away from them. "If you knew anything about me, you'd know that everything I do is selfless."

"Yeah, coming from someone who only communicates with his colleagues when he needs something. You're so selfless." Kyung-tae paused, no response coming to fill his blank mind. "You know what," Woo-young continued, turning away from Kyung-tae, "do whatever you want. Just don't involve me in it."

As Woo-young stormed off back to the briefing room to meet his team. Kyung-tae paused, his heart beginning to sink. How could someone call him, of all people, selfish? He was someone with a lot of insight. And he didn't just keep that insight to himself; he would offer sound advice when people had issues - advice that could pretty much solve all their issues. He didn't have to do that, but he did because he was selfless. How hard was he working to rectify Yu-ra's issues with her family. That was nothing but selfless. No. Of course he wasn't the issue. Woo-young just wasn't open-minded enough. Kyung-tae looked down at the desk next to him. There was a folder with the name of the kidnapped girl, and next to it, Kim Sun-jung's autopsy report.

*Screw the guns,* he thought as he sat down at the desk and flicked them open.

# 25
# Arsonist

At the edge of the bustling restaurant kitchen, Yu-ra sat at the bottom of the staircase which led to Ny-ron's office, awaiting her appointment. She found herself surrounded by a cacophony of culinary activity. A mouthwatering scent of steak fat being rendered on a skillet, the briny aroma of seafood being grilled, and the sweet smell of onions caramelising filled the room. Her attempt to collect her thoughts became an arduous task as the clattering of pots, the chefs' rhythmic chopping of vegetables, and the sizzling symphony from various stovetops relentlessly invaded her consciousness. The heady aroma of spices and simmering sauces wafted through the air. Amidst the orchestrated chaos, Yu-ra's contemplative silence was drowned out, her inner musings rendered inaudible against the backdrop of a kitchen in full swing.

Takemi was currently having a private meeting with Ny-ron. Yu-ra asked her not to mention the samurai, but Takemi had been awfully quiet since she got back into the car with her. She hadn't so much as lifted her mask since then. So, who knew if she would comply?

Maintaining a low volume, Yu-ra held her phone to her ear, listening in on Takemi's meeting.

*"I'm telling you now before it gets to you through some other means,"* came Ny-ron's voice, a trace of worry infiltrating his tone.

*"What did you do?"* Takemi said, her voice still weak, though barely noticeable through the voice modulator.

*"It goes against your rules. But I'm telling you now, because you're my friend and I trust you."*

*"They're not my rules. I'm just the new enforcer."*

Even if Takemi wanted to enforce those rules, it didn't even sound like she could at that moment. Though she doubted anyone else had noticed that.

*"Do I have your word? I'll make it worth your time. How does five million*

*sound?"*

The conversation quieted for a moment and the guards at the door began to eye Yu-ra suspiciously. She turned away from them and walked a few paces further away from them. Takemi's weak voice returned.

*"Tell me what happened."*

*"Where to start..."* Ny-ron trailed off.

*"Start with why you need me to look the other way."*

*"I kidnapped some girls."*

*"You did what?"*

*"I figured I could sell them on the market. I've been working closely with an expert and she says there's a lot of money to be made. Money that we need if my silent partner is to ever see his plans come to fruition."*

*"Are you stupid?"* Takemi said, with a now much stronger voice. *"Do you think the Japanese just pick any old girl off the street and make tons of money? A lot of work goes into their business."*

*"I know. I put in the groundwork."*

*"And how did that go?"*

*"Well, you know that waitress chick I was dating? She tipped me off about a girl that nobody would miss, and that expert I mentioned tipped me off about the other one, but..."*

*"But?"*

Ny-ron paused before chuckling awkwardly

*"But, it turns out that people did miss them. Maybe more work goes into this than I thought."*

*"You're damn right it does!"* Takemi shouted, then lowered her voice. *"What happened with the girls? If they've been sold off, maybe I can look the other way this time."*

Look the other way? Was she actually putting the mission before her reputation? Or was it only because she wasn't in any condition to enforce the rules?

*"Yeah... about that,"* Ny-ron said. *"My girl also tipped me off that a cop was looking for one of them. So I dealt with it. Made it look like a suicide."*

*"So what's the issue?"*

*"The issue is the other girl. She escaped."*

*"For God's sake, Ny-ron!"*

*"Look, the police are a non-issue. You know how useless they are. I need you to keep this from getting out. But I also need you to keep looking the other way."*

*"Keep? This is a one-time thing."*

*"My partner thinks I'm useless and, according to his bodyguard, doesn't trust me with anything. But he's the useless one. His own bodyguard doesn't trust him to make sound decisions. She knows we need this money more than he does."*

Bodyguard? Was he talking about Chun-mi? That would all but confirm that her boss was Ny-ron's partner - his supplier. Though it was clear that there was major tension between the two and that they didn't communicate often. Was Chun-mi going behind her boss's back to work with Ny-ron? Chun-mi was more evil than she thought. With two law enforcers in her family, she still worked with scum like Ny-ron. Sung-jae surely must have already known who the supplier was. He just needed evidence that Yu-ra still had yet to collect. He did say he wanted to use the law, after all. Maybe her journalistic skillset was more important to the mission than she realised. But why couldn't he ask Chun-mi to help if he now knew who she worked for? The world spun as she became plagued with an onslaught of questions she desperately needed the answers for.

*"Ny-ron! Look what happened. You can't do this again!"*

*"I know the risks this time. I'll put in the work to make sure this goes smoothly."*

*"Ny-ron!"* Takemi yelled, pain littered in her voice. *"These rules are here for a reason. It's my job to make an example of you. Do you know how much this complicates things?"*

*"Cheonsa, you're my brother. I know how difficult this makes things, but only if other people know - which they don't. You're everything to me, brother. I trust you with my life. I've never met a person better, which is why I chose to tell you. Please don't betray my trust."*

Suddenly the phone cut off. What happened? Did his battery die? Or did he cut the call himself? A few moments later, the office doors flung open and Takemi hobbled out, the same way she hobbled in twenty minutes ago. One of the guards beckoned Yu-ra back over. As she came closer to Takemi, she shot her a quizzical look so that she could find out if everything was okay. Still clutching at her ribs, she passed her in silence. The hum of the kitchen quieted as she entered the office and the doors closed behind her.

*So Ny-ron is scared of his business getting out, but what if they already found out? A samurai attacking a gang that stepped on their turf? Considering the enforcer comes off as biassed towards them, it makes sense for them to take it into their own hands.*

Vases that were previously on display were now shattered, the shards littered across the room. Sofas were tossed to the side, a show she was used to seeing by now. Ny-ron's jittery hands found the comfort of his pockets, his naturally confident stature now withdrawn as he stood in front of his long mahogany desk. Alone in the room with Ny-ron, a circumstance she hadn't encountered before, she was no longer under any protection. She was on her own.

"What have you got for me?" he murmured.

"Sorry?" Yu-ra said.

"I said what have you got," he said louder, but still quite softly.

"We kept an eye on one of your warehouses. It's one guy - pretty big build, wears a samurai mask."

"Samurai?"

"I only saw him from afar. I don't know what went down in the warehouse, but it never was set on fire."

"You've proven yourself quite useful to me."

"Thank you."

"I'll take it from here," Ny-ron said, waving her away with the back of his hand.

"Sorry," Yu-ra said, stepping forward, "if I may?"

Ny-ron paused, then nodded.

"I have a theory, and it may need your input."

"Go on."

"This person dresses up like a samurai, right? So they probably have an inclination to historical Japanese culture."

"Okay, so?"

"So they're most likely Japanese. But they must also have some kind of vendetta against you…" She paused. "Us," she said in an uncertain tone.

"And who would that be?"

"Well, this is what I need your input for. My personal theory is that the Japanese have some reason to attack your product. It could be one person acting on their own accord, or it could be the leaders sending a person undercover so that they have plausible deniability."

Ny-ron paused, raising his hand to his chin and leaning back against his desk. After a few moments of contemplation, he spoke.

"Your theory makes sense."

"So do I have your permission to continue investigating?"

"Investigating how?"

"We infiltrate the gang," Yu-ra said, raising a finger. "We find out what they know." Yu-ra raised another finger. "We find out if there is any such vendetta." Another finger. "We look for the arsonist's outfit." She raised a final finger.

Ny-ron paused again. Suddenly he leapt from his desk, bouncing on his feet, his confident aura returning.

"Oh, yes! Yes! This is great!" He rushed over to Yu-ra, squeezing her by the shoulders and sending a shiver down her spine. "I could kiss you!"

Yu-ra shoved him away as hard as she could, sending him back two steps.

"Please don't."

"You go investigate. Cheonsa will be your in. He can roam the gangs freely. Find out what you can but I need you to keep an eye on Takemi too."

"Why?"

"Just do it. There will be extra compensation in it for you."

"I want to meet your supplier."

"What?"

"That's my compensation. Let me meet your supplier."

Ny-ron contemplated again.

"Fine, I'll speak to him about you today. But no promises."

Yu-ra agreed and left the office shortly after. Takemi was then called into the office once again, and after five minutes returned, ready for them to go meet with the Japanese gang. As they left the building and walked towards the car, Takemi had told her that Ny-ron called her back to help with the investigation, offering a large sum of money if she helped.

****

The sun had just barely begun to set, as a shower of rain thrashed against the windscreen of Takemi's car which was parked outside of a dimly lit karaoke bar. Since the day that Yu-ra stopped Takemi from killing that Japanese gang member, they had been tailing him, keeping a close watch. Karaoke didn't seem like a place that you would expect a gang member to go to for fun. A seedy underground bar was more fitting, especially considering the seediness of the gang's business. Japanese graffiti, consisting of modern inspired designs of samurai, cherry blossoms, and Shinto shrines, painted the slick walls. Puddles beside the car reflected the artwork. Yu-ra's nose crinkled up as she internally critiqued the work - it was as if a child had finger-painted the walls.

Yu-ra turned to Takemi. Head laid against the window, her breathing had become noticeably heavy in the silent car. She still had yet to remove her mask.

"Wait here," she said. "I'll handle this."

"What?" Takemi said, struggling to lift herself away from the window. "I'll be in and out in three minutes with all the information we need."

"Look at yourself. If I can tell you're injured, so will they. At least with you not there, I can use you as a threat."

"I can do this," she said, pushing herself up straight, but audibly wincing.

"What are you trying to prove? And to whom?"

"I can do this…" Takemi said, quieter.

Yu-ra eyed her, dumbstruck at her stubbornness.

"You're going to stay here, or I will punch you in the ribs," Yu-ra said and Takemi shifted her body so that she was entirely facing her. Suddenly, Yu-ra threw her fist at Takemi. As she flinched back in pain, Yu-ra stopped her hand before it reached her. "I know you're too slow to stop it right now."

Without letting her respond, she rushed out of the car. Splashing through the puddles, she distorted the reflected art underneath her feet. As she entered the building, she made her way down a narrow staircase, at the bottom of which were two corridors on either side of her, leading to private karaoke rooms. She followed the corridor in front of her. Electric pop music playing in the main hall grew louder, and as she got closer, so did a whiny female voice singing the song. Through the doors of the main hall, she recognised that the whiny voice belonged to the skinny woman in a revealing silver dress.

Booths around the room had groups of people conversing and drinking. Tall circular tables, dotted around the room, also had groups congregated around them. After arriving at the bar to her right, she leaned onto the counter and tapped three times to get the bartender's attention. After an off-handed comment about never seeing someone like her in there before, he directed her towards her target. Sat at the other end of the bar, sipping a drink from a short circular glass, which held a large ball of ice, was the man she saved from Takemi. In front of him sat a singular cigarette planted in an ashtray, smoke still escaping from the butt.

"Hey, Ken!" she called out.

He put his drink down and tilted his head towards her. The scarf must have tipped him off because he instantly recognized her, stumbling off his stool and stepping away.

"Woah, woah, woah," he said, holding his hands out. "I don't want any trouble."

"Don't worry," she said, backing away slightly. "I'm just here to talk."

"How do you know my name?"

"I told you we'd keep an eye on you."

"I haven't said a single word to anyone," he stuttered. "I promise. I said what you told me to"

"I know." She nodded slowly in an attempt to reassure him.

"Then what do you want?"

"I just need some information."

"Where's Cheonsa?"

"Outside. You're safe…" She paused. "For now." That would make her sound more menacing.

Ken slowly moved back to his stool and Yu-ra found a seat beside him, requesting a glass of water from the bartender. He placed a tall glass of ice in front of her and then filled it with water from a two litre plastic bottle.

"What do you want to know?"

"I'm looking for someone; I believe one of your employees."

Ken's eyes were darting around the room, looking anywhere but in Yu-ra's eyes, as if he didn't believe her about Takemi.

"Name?" he said in an uneven tone.

"I don't know. But he wears a distinctive mask," she said before sipping her water.

"Why is Cheonsa outside?"

"What?"

"He could get this information very easily. He's a neutral entity, and pretty much has free reign here."

"Look, you owe me your life. Give me this information and we can call it even."

Ken breathed out a sigh of relief, as if she had just saved his life at that very moment.

"Sounds like a fair trade. What does this mask look like?"

"It's a black Oni mask, with gold highlights." She spread out her shoulders and hunched her back slightly to make herself look larger. "He's quite broad, wears this almost ninja-like costume with the mask."

"Wait, I actually know who you're talking about," he said, sitting up straighter than he had the entire time she was there.

"Great!" Yu-ra beamed, dropping her arms. "Who is it?"

"I don't know."

"You just said you did," she said, cutting her eyes at him

"He's not one of us."

"Then how do you know him?"

"He sold us some guns recently."

"Guns?"

"Pistols, nothing much more than that, but a lot of ammunition to go with it. We had to shell out quite a bit. Boss thinks it set us back years."

*Where could he possibly have gotten a hold of guns?*

"I don't get it," Ken said. "The way Cheonsa acted around you, I don't think anyone has ever seen him act so rash."

"What are you talking about?"

"And the control you had over him… I think the boss was right."

"The boss?" A sudden realisation hit Yu-ra. "You told them," she whispered.

"I did," he said, smirking. "So, Cheonsa cares about you."

Yu-ra paused, how could she turn this in her favour? She couldn't have them thinking Takemi had a weakness. Or perhaps being Takemi's weakness gave her even more protection, since she was willing to kill for her.

"Yeah, he cares about me," she said, squaring her shoulders. "So I would be very worried if you had any ideas of getting any closer to me."

"Hey now, relax." He chuckled. "Look, I don't know who this samurai is. He must be an outsider."

"Do you have any way to contact him? If you wanted more guns, for example?"

"He didn't leave a business card, if that's what you're asking."

"Look, this guy has been destroying our product, and now he's also selling you guns? Something big is about to go down. I would be worried if I were you."

"If Cheonsa cares so much about you, why isn't he here, making sure you're safe?" Ken itched at his forehead. "Does he not know what this place is?"

"Like I said, he's just outside," she replied, sipping her water again.

Wrapping his knuckles against the countertop, Ken gained the attention of the bartender. He gave a simple nod, to which the bartender put down the glass and rag he was drying it with. The bartender put his fingers into the corners of his mouth and whistled in a shrill tone. Suddenly, the entire room fell silent, all eyes honing in on Yu-ra, as well as all parties around the room simultaneously standing up. Yu-ra's heart began to pound in her ears, a shiver running down her spine as she began to break into a cold sweat. Everyone… Everyone in the bar was a Japanese gang member. And she had no one to protect her.

"If Cheonsa had any sense about him, he would be here to protect you. Unless…"

"Unless?" Yu-ra said, subtly sliding herself off her seat. Her clothes had begun to stick to her back from the sudden oncoming of sweat.

"Unless there's a reason he can't be here. Maybe a fight?" he said, standing up from his seat, "an injury? It can't be any other business. He would prioritise you."

"I can call him right now, if that's what you want?" Yu-ra bluffed, "but like I said, I think we should be worried about what this samurai is up to."

"I don't get worried, that's the job of my boss. I just do as he says."

"Well, tell him that he should be then." Yu-ra backed away, but was then met with the bartender's arm blocking her path. Her heart almost leapt out of her chest as her quick breaths shortened further. "Maybe then we can put our resources together to get this crap sorted."

"Give Cheonsa a call then, if he can come in and confirm it with the boss, we'll take you seriously."

Yu-ra huffed.

"I don't have time for this right now. If you have no leads, you're useless to me."

"The only lead I can give you is that he came with a girl in body armour. If you find her," he said, clapping his hands together and dropping to his knees as he looked up at her, "please send her back to us. I'm not even going to lie to you, I didn't believe in the idea of love before I saw her. But now I know what it feels like, and I love it!" he yelled, jumping to his feet again.

*Attractive girl in body armour, sounds awfully familiar. Chun-mi.*

"Thanks," she said, with a furrowed brow.

"I think this makes us more than even."

"Yeah, whatever," she said, turning around to walk away, but met the bartender's arm yet again. Turning back around, she breathed out softly, trying to gather her thoughts. What's going to get her out of this situation? Using Takemi as a threat wasn't working. But without Takemi, there was nothing stopping these gangs from going at each other's throats. Yu-ra was sure that neither gang wanted this, which must have been exactly why someone like Takemi was there in the first place.

"You've met my boss, right? Park Ny-ron."

"The guy with the anger issues, sure."

"Well," Yu-ra said, flashing a small smile, "he's also extremely racist." She began to pace back and forth between the minimal space between Ken and the bartender, with her hand on her chin. "I mean, he's just itching for a reason to start a war with you guys. And believe me I'm more than enough of a reason."

"Don't worry." Ken chuckled. "We're letting you go."

Yu-ra stopped in her tracks.

"Then let me go then."

"My boss just wants to confirm something with you first; something that the samurai told us."

Yu-ra crossed her arms, leaning her weight towards one hip.

"And then I can walk out of here?"

"You have my word," Ken said, bowing.

"What did the samurai say?"

"It was about your boss, actually. He's trying to make a move on our turf. We hear two girls went missing, and it was his doing."

Yu-ra's eyes shot open and her breathing became heavy again.

"What?" she whispered. How in the world did the samurai know this?

"And," Ken said, slowing his speech as the corners of his mouth began to prick up, "apparently he has no plans of stopping there."

If the Samurai was a Japanese gang member, how would he know that? And if Kyung-tae was right and it was Chun-mi's boss that was committing arson, what did he gain from telling the other gang? Control over the gang? Maybe he didn't want a partner and wanted to take over? Was this his ploy to oust Ny-ron? Was he setting him up and using the insurance money for a political campaign like Kyung-tae thought? But why wasn't the money enough? What good was being a gang leader if you're already leading a country?

"Ok, you can go." Ken chuckled.

"What? But I didn't say anything."

"I've got what I need."

"The samurai was lying," she blurted. "He doesn't know what he's talking about. Takemi would stop him."

"Who's Takemi?" he said, raising a brow.

"Who?" Yu-ra said, itching the base of her neck, "sorry, I meant Cheonsa. I was just thinking about someone else."

"You can go," he said, nodding to the bartender who then dropped his arm.

"I'm being serious. I have a very close relationship with Ny-ron. He's done no such thing."

"I believe you." Ken smiled. "Now off you go. Otherwise the boss might change his mind."

Yu-ra straightened herself up.

"Okay, I'm going," she said, before turning around and, in as subtle a manner as she could, rushed out of the room.

# 26

# Trapped

*My time in the special ops unit is going well, but the things I've had to do… it feels strange. I want to keep doing those things. My sergeant praises me endlessly after each mission. But it feels different than when you used to say you were proud of me. If I told you what I've been doing, would you still be proud? I'm not so sure you would approve of my lifestyle anymore. But I still continue. And I still feel… What do I feel?*

\- *Letter #29*

Yu-ra placed two steaming porcelain cups of green tea on her sparkling kitchen counter, sliding them over to Sung-jae and Takemi. They each sat at a stool, two idle seats laying between them. Yu-ra sat down across from them, pulling the sleeves of her cardigan over her hands, before nervously rubbing them together. She was uncomfortable with the situation she had arranged, but it had gotten to a point where it was necessary. And even worse was that Kyung-tae could be back from work at any moment. Takemi held the cup of tea in her hand, but she still had her mask down.

"So," Sung-jae started, before taking a sip from his steaming cup but then immediately sputtered it out. Putting his finger in his mouth to feel the roof, he winced. "Shit, that's hot."

"Don't swear in my house," Yu-ra said firmly, narrowing her eyes.

"Sorry," he replied instantaneously, wiping his hand across his mouth to clean any spittle. "So what did you call this meeting for?"

Yu-ra paused for a moment before deciding what to say.

"I know how important this case is to you. It's important to me too. If I could write a story on how intricate the criminal underworld is in this city, I would become a hit journalist… But I-" Yu-ra hesitated, then gestured to Takemi. "We need to get out."

"No can do," Sung-jae said, holding out his hand.

"No, you don't understand - I think our cover is blown."

"Well, when the case is over and done with, I'll make sure you're relocated to someplace safe."

What? Did he just dismiss the entirety of what she had just said? He must not have heard her right, surely?

"Our cover is blown," she repeated. "We're both in danger."

"Yes, I heard you. And I will ensure your safety and privacy upon the closure of this case."

"What?" Yu-ra said, venom beginning to drip into her tone.

"I can't let you go yet."

"What don't you understand about our cover being jeopardised?" Yu-ra shouted as her composure collapsed.

Sung-jae turned to Takemi.

"Do you want out?"

"No," Takemi grumbled.

Sung-jae turned back to Yu-ra.

"Well, there you go."

"What do you mean there you go?" she snapped. "Takemi is a grown woman. She can make her own decisions and she made it. What do you even need me for? Takemi has every connection you need. I literally hold no value to you."

"You're right," Sung-jae said, then pointed to Takemi, "but you hold value to her."

"What's that supposed to mean?"

"Don't," Takemi said, gripping her cup tighter.

"No, please continue," Yu-ra said, feeling something bubbling inside of her, rising up.

"I-" Sung-jae hesitated. "Who do you think got you involved in the first place?"

"What are you talking about?"

"I said don't," Takemi growled, squeezing her cup tighter.

"I'm saying she's the one who wanted you to be part of this in the first place," Sung-jae said. "Do you really think I'd involve some random citizen for no reason at all?"

"Is this true?" Yu-ra said to Takemi, who remained motionless. The bubbling that had built up reached her surface. She slammed her fist on the countertop, sending a shock through her fingers and a cramp in her palm. "Take that damn mask off," she screamed, "and tell me what he's talking about."

Takemi hesitated, then slid her mask off her face, placing it down on the table.

Her face was slightly swollen in some parts, particularly her half-closed right eye, which was blackened on the bottom lid. The scarring on her cheeks looked as if it had healed a fair amount since she had received them. A half-healed gash traced the contour of her lip. Takemi stared at her with frigid eyes but Yu-ra's gaze softened somewhat.

"He's telling the truth," Takemi said, finally. "I found you on purpose…Got you involved on purpose. It had nothing to do with Sung-jae."

Yu-ra narrowed her eyes, her stare hardening.

"Why?"

"I can't…" Takemi's head dropped. "I can't do this without you."

"You can't do this without me?"

Takemi lifted her head.

"You've got to focus on the benefits though. How hard has it been for you to find someone willing to hire you? You'll be guaranteed a job after this. If not in journalism, you'll definitely be offered a job in law enforcement."

"You can't do this…without me?" she seethed.

"Yeah, it's a compliment if you think about it," Takemi mumbled.

"So, you go out of your way to get me involved in criminal activity, then you jeopardise my safety; and your reason is that you can't do this without me?"

"...Yeah. I need you. And I won't work for him without you."

Yu-ra analysed her, seeking any minutia of remorse in the depths of her eyes. But nothing returned.

"Well you're going to have to. You're the one who chose this life. Deal with the consequences of your actions. I'm done with you."

"What's that supposed to mean?"

"It means if I ever see your face again, I'll get you arrested for murder."

"Well, like I said, I'm not doing this without you."

Yu-ra turned to Sung-jae.

"And you, as a man of the law, are okay with this?" she said, almost foaming at the mouth from anger. "You would just allow me, a law-abiding citizen, to walk into hostile territory?"

"I don't think you understand me," Sung-jae said, "so let me make this crystal clear to you. I. Do not. Care."

"And if I die, and you have to answer to Kyung-tae, what then?"

"He doesn't know about this. And if you die, he'll be none the wiser about our connection."

"You both make me sick to my stomach," she said, a churning in the pit of her stomach causing a faint reaction in her throat.

"Why don't you look at the bigger picture here!" Sung-jae yelled, slamming his cup on the desk, causing Yu-ra's heart to jolt and tiny pieces of porcelain to splinter across the table as a crack split the side of the cup. "What the f-" Sung-jae paused momentarily and took a breath. "Do you even realise what it would mean if I can dismantle these gangs? Organised crime would crumble throughout the entire city. I would be heralded a hero. *You* will be heralded a hero. Could you imagine that?"

"If I survive that is."

"My point being that this case is more important than the safety of one measly woman."

Yu-ra shrugged off the fact that he just called her measly.

"You can't make me stay. And if you try, I will tell everyone about what you're doing. This investigation hasn't been sanctioned. You'll be in trouble."

"What kind of relationship do you think we have?" Sung-jae said. "You don't get to make demands of me. I own your life right now. You're going to see this thing to the end. And if you don't, all of your personal information;

your address, university, friends, family, husband, it will all become public information. Kyung-tae won't be able to protect himself, let alone you, from that."

Yu-ra shot a searing glare at Sung-jae, her eyes ablaze with intensity. Suddenly, Takemi launched her chair to the side, crashing against the far wall, the impact of which caused one of its legs to snap off, leaving a splintered aftermath. She charged at Sung-jae, gripping him by the collar and yanking him off his chair.

"You won't do any of that," Takemi hissed, "and if you try, I will come for you."

Sung-jae chuckled.

"You're joking right?" he said before scoffing. "You're not joking."

"No," Takemi seethed.

"Look at you," he said, smirking. "You can barely stand up straight. And you think you're going to stop anything?" Sung-jae grabbed the lapel of Takemi's jacket and shoved her away. A scream escaped Yu-ra as Sung-jae rammed his boot into Takemi's chest, sending her crashing into the stool behind him, shattering it into pieces. Yu-ra's blood pumped in her ears, and her breathing became extremely heavy.

"GET OUT!" she shrieked. Sung-jae and Takemi paused, looking towards her. "Get out of my house," she said, rushing over to Sung-jae and pushing him towards the door, "get out of my house, the both of you. And don't ever come back!"

As Sung-jae allowed himself to be guided by Yu-ra, he stopped her as he reached Takemi, and then he lifted her up off the ground, pulling her with him towards the door.

"There's no escape for you, Mrs Baek," Sung-jae said as he opened the front door and proceeded to walk out, pulling Takemi along with him. "Just follow through on your promise."

Yu-ra soon found herself nestled in the solitude of her room, her blanket tightly wound over her head, enveloping her in a bubble of darkness. Her thoughts erupted into a swirling tempest, a deluge of ideas of what to do in her current situation crashing against the shores of her consciousness. The weight of her responsibilities enveloped her, the ceaseless torrent of contemplation leaving her breathless. Like a kaleidoscope, fragments of thoughts danced before her, forming an intricate mosaic of concerns and ponderings. Doubts clung to her mind. Anxieties whispered in her ear. And a flurry of emotions threatened to drown her in their tumultuous current. Her yearning for a moment of tranquillity brought her to one fundamental conclusion which she could not escape - she needed to get help. She needed Kyung-tae.

****

Kyung-tae glared at the looming laboratory that was lit up like a phantom in the darkness. Stray raindrops splattered into his eyes as he read the giant neon letters protruding from the tower's roof. *Park Pharmaceuticals.* Its facade was constructed of predominantly reflective glass panels and the lighting fixtures cast a soft glow around the sharp edges, which enhanced the building's modern allure. More rain began to dapple his cheeks.

"He's definitely here?" Kyung-tae spoke into his phone as he dropped his gaze to the entrance of the building.

*"He's in the next room,"* Chun-mi replied.

"Alright. I'll see you in a few minutes."

*"Are you sure he's the guy? I get the drugs thing, but how does this translate to a kidnapping?"*

"Honestly, I have no idea. But I've been racking my brain since I found out it wasn't a suicide." The rain began to pour down in torrents, hammering down on him.

"And then the obvious thing smacked me in the face," he continued. "I found his drugs at the scene of the crime. I also looked into her autopsy report again. There were traces of the drug in her bloodstream. It must have pacified her, which is what made it look like suicide."

*"What did the rescued victim say?"*

Kyung-tae could just about hear her voice over the rain as he rushed under the glass shelter protruding from the entrance.

"Like I said, I've done all the investigating I need to," he said, slicking his hair back to get the wet clumps out of his eyes.

*"Yeah, you're right. There's no point speaking to her."*

"Just be on standby. I may need your help to bring this guy in."

*"Didn't you bring anyone with you?"*

"I don't need their help."

*"But you're asking for mine?"*

Around the corner, wheels of a vehicle were fighting to keep friction against the slick ground. After a few seconds, the revs of the engine closed the distance from him and a sleek jet-black car with tinted windows skidded to a halt in front of him. Kyung-tae eyed it with caution. His suspect was inside the building, so who was this? Rival gang members? But why would a rival gang attack a guy who was destroying his own product? He could be working with them. Or it could be his distributor coming for recompense. After all, he was destroying every product that he manufactured to be sold. The car door popped open and a pair of worn black combat boots stepped out, followed by a man decked out in SWAT gear. Kyung-tae raised his gaze, until he met the eyes of the officer. It was difficult to see through the deluge of pelting droplets, but as he stepped closer, Kyung-tae realised it was none other than his partner - Woo-young. What was he doing there?

"What do you want," Kyung-tae called out as he slipped his phone away. "You finally here to help? The tactical gear may be a bit much, but I respect your dedication."

"I'm not here to help," he called back as he arrived under the shelter, raising his voice just barely over the enraged beads hailing down above them. "I'm here to give a warning from Captain Murakami."

"You told him?" Kyung-tae, much to his surprise, yelled.

"We've got a lead on an arms deal. You can come with us to help-"

"No."

"Or you'll be suspended with no pay."

"I'm not going anywhere with you."

"Then if you don't drop this case and leave right now, I will be taking you in."

Kyung-tae stared intently then jabbed his finger into Woo-young's shoulder.

"Give it." He jabbed him again. "Your best." Another jab. "Shot."

Woo-young swung his fist but Kyung-tae effortlessly manoeuvred around it. Slipping behind his partner, he slithered his arm under Woo-young's and then pulled it up to his throat. Kyung-tae tightened his arms together, strengthening the headlock he had secured him in. The immediate floundering of Woo-young's body was met with the doors of his car popping open, followed by four men in the same tactical gear that was under his grip. As the team of boots drummed towards him, both Kyung-tae's jaw and grip tightened, causing him to begin grinding his teeth. Woo-young flailed even more violently. How dare he? That's what being his partner was worth? He didn't trust him enough to go on his own? The storm thundering down on them had personified inside him. A scream pounded at the walls of his skull, threatening to destroy the facade of calmness he worked so hard to maintain.

"Let him go!" shouted the first man to arrive at their feet. Kyung-tae paused momentarily before the troops slipped their batons out from their holsters and then he shoved Woo-young to the ground. Woo-young rubbed his throat as he gathered himself. Kyung-tae gritted his teeth as he made his way back towards his car, balling his fist as tight as he could, his nails beginning to dig into his skin.

"Where are you going?" Woo-young shouted.

"Home," Kyung-tae yelled back.

"Hey," Woo-young called, "if you're not coming to help, then you're suspended."

# 27
# A Marriage Story

Yu-ra had just finished sweeping up the splintered wood of the chair that Takemi had broken as Kyung-tae entered the house, clothes clinging to his skin. As he trudged through the house, he left behind a miniature flood in the trail of his footsteps. Yu-ra hadn't bothered to hide the chair but Kyung-tae had paid no attention to it. Maybe it was due to the clumps of drenched hair that obscured his vision. Or maybe he didn't care.

After Yu-ra had mopped up the water that tracked through her house, Kyung-tae exited the bathroom in a fresh jumper and trousers, his hair dry and fluffy, held back with a headband. Yu-ra eyed him. How should she tell him about Sung-jae? Start from the very beginning? Kyung-tae's drooping shoulders and sluggish walk to the couch emphasised his weary countenance. Maybe it wasn't the wisest decision to unload all of her concerns on him at that particular moment. Maybe right now, her job was to be there for him.

"Hey," Yu-ra said, walking over to the couch, "you okay?"

"Well," he said, looking up at her. "I'm going to be spending a lot more time with you, so I guess so."

"Are you on holiday?" she said, placing her hand on his shoulder.

"Nope. Got suspended," he said nonchalantly.

"What happened?" Yu-ra asked, sitting beside him.

Kyung-tae sighed.

"Remember that girl that committed suicide in one of my cases?"

"Sun-jung?"

"Yeah. It turns out that she was actually kidnapped with another girl called Li-Na. And if she was kidnapped, that means she didn't commit suicide after all." Yu-ra turned to him, but stayed silent. "So I retraced my steps, and the most important factor to the case was that they left behind evidence at the scene of the crime - the same drugs that Park Dae-myeon is formulating. In fact I have definitive evidence that he's the one behind my arson cases. I went to arrest him but I was stopped by my partner… Said he would arrest me if I continued with what I was doing and suspended me for not joining his investigation."

"What? Yu-ra said, furrowing her brow. "That makes no sense. Why would they stop you from doing your job? And how does he have the authority to suspend you?"

"He was just the messenger."

"Oh."

"Yeah…"

"And why didn't they want you arresting criminals, again?"

"A military base was raided and a lot of guns were stolen. They want all hands on deck. Because clearly all our other cases mean nothing."

"Hang on," Yu-ra said, a whirlwind rushing her thoughts as she began to process everything Kyung-tae had just said to her.

He thought that Dae-myeon kidnapped Sun-jung, but that wasn't true. It had nothing to do with him. It was Ny-ron who did. Kyung-tae was wrong. He was following the wrong trail. And if he saw it through, it would hurt him even more. She needed to help him.

"You okay?" he asked, examining her bewildered expressions.

"I-I need to tell you something. I want to help you."

"What do you mean?"

"I don't think Dae-myeon has anything to do with the kidnapping."

"O-okay?" he said, cocking his head in puzzlement, "but how are you able to decide that?"

"You won't like what I'm about to say, but you have to see it objectively and listen to what I'm going to tell you, okay?"

"I'm always objective, come on Yu-ra. It's me."

Yu-ra breathed out softly.

"I think Chun-mi was involved in orchestrating the kidnapping of Sun-jung."

"Oh for God's sake," he muttered, "again, Yu-ra? Really?"

"This isn't about my grudge," she said, jumping out of her seat, "although now it's clearly justified. I'm not pulling this information out of thin air. It's actual insider info. I've been working undercover in a gang. I'm ninety-nine percent sure that Chun-mi convinced the leader of this gang to kidnap at least one of those girls. I know this because I'm the one that got Li-Na out of there." As Yu-ra continued, Kyung-tae's face became more and more contorted. And slowly, anger began to flush his eyes, something she had never seen before. "And yeah, Dae-myeon is probably supplying the drugs, but the drugs alone are probably enough to cover his political campaign. Why would he need to commit arson?"

Kyung-tae remained silent for a few moments as his eyes flickered left and right before settling, his expression returning to normal.

"Are you being serious?"

"Deadly. I've been working with the gang that sells those blue crystals."

Suddenly the rush of anger flooded his eyes again.

"You are being serious. What's wrong with you?" he yelled, causing Yu-ra's heart to leap as she subconsciously took a step back. "Why would you get involved with a gang?" This was the first time Yu-ra had so much as heard Kyung-tae raise his voice. Kyung-tae's head fell to his palms. "How did you even get involved?"

"It's not my fault. Do you think I did this of my own accord? I'm a journalist, not a criminal."

He looked up at her.

"So is this about your journalism?"

"Partly. It'll help me get a job."

"That's not an excuse, Yu-ra!" he shouted, jumping out of his seat.

"Let me finish! I didn't get a choice." She huffed, flinging her hands down in exasperation. "The Choi family are evil. They're all out to get me. Chun-mi has been attacking me since the day I met her. I've physically seen her have meetings with a gang leader. Sung-jae trapped me in this deal and won't let me out even after having my cover blown! I wouldn't be surprised if Jinmu hates me too!"

"What Chun-mi's boss does has nothing to do with her," he said, walking over to the kitchen counter with his back turned to her. "He's obviously been supplying drugs to the gang. That's most likely what the meetings were about. And are you really going to attack a man who's basically been in recovery mode since the day after our wedding?" He finally turned to look at her. "And wait a minute, all of this is happening and you never once thought to tell me earlier so I could help you?"

"You really think I didn't think of that? That's the first thing I thought of, but Sung-jae threatened you!" She cried, as her vision began to blur slightly from the salty water building up in her tear ducts.

"Why would Sung-jae threaten me? He's known me since I was a teenager."

"He didn't know you were my husband, and when he found out he resorted to just threatening me!" The water from her ducts glistened her eyes.

"Look how emotional you're being!" he yelled, finally looking over at her. "You think the Choi's are evil masterminds because you can't take the time to forgive them and move past how you met."

"What do you mean I'm being emotional?" she said, pacing to the opposite side of the kitchen counter and throwing accusatory fingers at him. "If you took a step back to look at the situation, you'd know that they clearly have a vendetta against Dae-myeon at the very least. I mean Jinmu is probably..."

Jinmu... Very pro-Japanese. Similar build to the samurai. His family have some sort of vendetta against Dae-myeon. And a military connection for guns.

"What?" Kyung-tae scoffed disdainfully.

"Jinmu - I think he's the samurai. The samurai who sold the guns to the Japanese!"

"Yeah, the guy who couldn't beat two guys with a knife almost killed both me and that scarred girl," he mocked. "And this is me being emotional, right?"

Yu-ra slammed her palm onto the counter, a shock running up her forearm, though she refused to react.

"Yes! Take a moment to think about what I've said!"

"That's not being emotional. Being emotional is not forgiving your own parents. I mean, what kind of person gives up on their parents?"

"What?" Yu-ra uttered, taken aback. "What the hell does that have to do with anything?"

"It has everything to do with it. Just because you have issues with your family, doesn't mean you have to drive a wedge between mine," he said, and Yu-ra's head shuddered in disbelief at his statement. She opened her mouth to speak, but before she could Kyung-tae continued, "You know every time they call me, I have no idea what to say to them because you refuse to go and see them!"

"I'm being emotional? You have no idea what my mother put me through growing up! Things that will be ingrained in me for life."

"And cutting them off is going to fix all those issues, isn't it? Because she's going to be here forever, right? So, who cares if you don't forgive her?"

"At least I've done something to try and achieve happiness, rather than dwelling on all of those issues!"

"Is that your metric for success in life? Chasing happiness? Happiness is fleeting and will never last. Chasing it is just like any other addiction people have. Why don't you spend your time chasing something worthwhile, like fulfilment? Being content with whatever happens in your life and making the best of it?"

"Yeah, you're right," she scoffed. "You really are emotionless."

****

The two argued back and forth for a few more hours, tracking into every room of the house. All manner of minor annoyances caused the fight to be prolonged.

"You're barely at home as is!" Yu-ra would shout.

"And you are?" Kyung-tae spat back. "How many times have you come home after midnight and I just let it go to give you your privacy?"

Soon they would be onto another topic.

"Leaving my family behind?" Yu-ra would say. "I invite my brother over all the time!"

"And when he does come over, the mess he leaves behind is foul! Why am I cleaning up after him?"

Kyung-tae didn't know why he would bring up such minor irritations, but he felt it was time to finally get everything off his chest. He needed her to see how unreasonable she was being, otherwise this marriage would never work out.

"Why did you even need to work undercover?" Kyung-tae asked, following her out of the bedroom and back into the living room. The argument had come full circle. "For a job? I provide enough."

"Oh congratulations!" Yu-ra said, clapping sarcastically, "you really are just like everyone else. You think you know exactly what I'm going through and what I deserve. Am I not allowed to dream? Can I not choose to be a driving force for good at the very least until I'm ready to have children?"

"But there are other ways to do good. Why does it have to be investigative journalism?"

"Are you serious? Do you only listen to half of the words I say?"

"I am listening. And I do know what you go through. You think I don't experience discrimination from my own people too? I wasn't born into this. My mother and I had to oppose our families to become Muslim. All we had was each other. And here you are choosing to cut ties with your family. It's disgraceful!"

Kyung-tae must have hit a nerve with that last sentence because Yu-ra's red eyes became inflamed with irritation. But he was done giving her excuses. It was time for her to grow up and clean the hate from her heart.

"With all due respect, you have no idea what it's like to be a Muslim woman and you never will. We don't get a choice in whether or not we show our Islam."

"Why does everything have to always be a gender war? Can we not just work together and love the differences we have? It's not about it being a choice. No one can force you to wear it. But you still do. And maybe the reason you have these thoughts is because your mindset is wrong from the get-go?"

"For God's sake, what are you talking about now? Are you saying I have an impure intention for wearing the hijab?"

"No. You already told me about your journey back to hijab. Clearly you don't. But you've become fixated on the idea of wearing it because you have to and the benefits you've found from wearing it. There's nothing wrong with that. But you've forgotten about the foundation, which is loving Allah with all your heart, more than anything this life can provide for you."

"Are you saying I don't have that love?"

"No, don't twist my words. I'm saying you may have forgotten that before anything, that comes first. I love my ma with all my heart and I would drop everything for her and I don't complain because of that love. That concept should be tenfold when it comes to Allah. And why would you want to disobey Him when you love Him that much? Would you make your hijab more fashionable just to make it more beautiful in the eyes of other people if you truly love Allah? Would you want to hide your Islam?"

"NO! But we don't get a choice in whether or not we can. People don't assume you're Muslim, so you can walk the streets freely, not having to be scared of being attacked for your religion."

"But I wear my Islam proudly. I fought hard to have people accept that this is my belief and I will never shy from it. You should too. It's not our job to water Islam down for them. Why should we apologise for their misconceptions of us?"

"I do wear my Islam proudly. You're not understanding my point. The discrimination you face and the type I do are two entirely separate things. I don't just face physical and verbal islamophobia all the time, I'm also attacked by my own Muslim brothers and sisters. Just because I have to display my Islam, I'm inspected under a microscope wherever I go. Any imperfection is made into a show for everyone to see. Oh look, this sister is flawed. Let's publicly shame her. That'll help fix her flaws!" She cried sarcastically, through furious tears.

"I agree with you. They're wrong for that. Those discussions should be private. But surely, you realise that there's a responsibility to those who have to display their Islam. The moment they decide to wear a hijab, because no one can force them, they have to realise that they automatically become representatives, whether they want to be or not. And again, if you love Allah, isn't it one of the most beautiful blessings in the world to get to be a representative of this religion?"

"And why can I not choose to be an inspiration to people who want to be career women? Obviously I want to have kids in a few years. We already had this discussion before we got married. But for now, I don't care how much discrimination I face. Why can't I be allowed to have that drive to prove everyone wrong? Why does everyone always have to know better than me?"

"I'm saying that it's not worth your time! When the whole world is against you. Why are you so desperate for their approval? That! That is your emotional response!" he said, jabbing his index finger in her direction. "You getting involved with a criminal empire to prove you can do a job is an extremely emotional response."

"And why are you so desperate to be a cop? Why are you so desperate to save kidnapped women that you would jeopardise your entire livelihood?"

"I have to. It's my duty as a police officer to protect and serve, and if I don't act quickly, people will die. I don't want that on my hands."

"This is you being emotional!" she yelled, clapping her hands together at each word, "refusing to see things objectively. Being incredibly brash to the point where you get kidnapped girls killed? Who are you to tell me about being content with what happens in my life when you act like this?"

"What did you just say?"

"I'm the one that saved Li-Na! The leader of the gang I was working with secretly kidnapped both of them. The only reason they killed Sun-jung is because you made it obvious that you were on to them."

"What?" he muttered, his eyes flickering back and forth as he processed the implications of what she just said. She couldn't be telling the truth, could she? How could it be his fault? If he waited, she would have died anyway, right?

"I mean you wouldn't even look at that autopsy report. Well I did! And if you had bothered, you would have known that the drug was found in her system ages ago!"

"That's not..."

"Ha!" she exclaimed, "I'm being emotional because I don't want to talk to a woman who put me through hell? Why do you think I even married you? It was just an escape from her. That's it! I never wanted to get married this early. I had to fight it twice already before you came along. And clearly it was a mistake because you refuse to take my side in any situation, some husband you are." She scoffed.

A sharpness pierced his heart and a flood threatened to burst through the dam of his tear ducts. How dare she say that, as if it was his idea to approach her?

"Well, the feeling is mutual. I only married you because of my ma! The difference is that I realised that I treated her poorly and married you to make amends."

"Oh, so that makes you morally superior, does it?"

"Yes!"

"And here we are, the arrogance of the man who thinks he's better than everyone!"

"No, the opposite actually. I can see that I'm not superior to everyone else, which is why I can forgive them."

"You know what - since you're obviously so superior to me, I'm done." After briefly disappearing into the bedroom, she reemerged, coat in hand,

and made her way to the front door. "Clearly I'm beneath you. So, you can stay here by yourself. Don't call me, because I won't answer!"

"Where are you going? What do you mean you're done? We haven't come to a resolution to this argument?"

"It means I'm done with you," she said, without even facing him. "We're done."

"What does that mean? Are you divorcing me?"

"I don't know, just leave me alone!" she hollered before slamming the front door shut behind her.

Kyung-tae dragged his feet to the couch, pausing momentarily before his legs buckled, sending his back sinking into the cushions. His hands shot to his face and the torrent that threatened the barrier of his eyes earlier finally burst through and tears streamed down his cheeks. Despite his futile attempts to stem the flow with incessant wiping, the tears continued to cascade, as if emerging from an endless spring. With each passing moment, the relentless stabbing in his chest only grew in size. He rubbed his eyes with increasing desperation, until he could almost feel the thinning of his skin under his touch.

"AHHHH!" he cried out, as he finally gave up, his hands falling away from his still watering eyes.

# 28
# Reality Check

Kyung-tae blinked, coaxing his weary, puffy eyes to open. The dim room gradually sharpened as his vision adjusted to the darkness. Slipping himself off the couch, the fatigue in his muscles became more prominent. A shrill bell pierced the air, prompting Kyung-tae to reach for his phone. The harsh glow of the screen stung his barely opened eyes. It was Mr Choi. Why was he calling at such an odd hour? Oh. It was only nine in the evening.

"*Hello,*" came Mr Choi's gruff voice.

"Hey, sorry, but I'm kind of busy right now. Can I call you back?"

"*This won't take long,*" he said in his usual monotonous voice. "*Chun-mi told me the good news. But she said she hasn't heard from you and she was expecting a call.*"

"Something came up," he replied before Mr Choi continued. He walked over to the kitchen and poured himself a glass of water.

"*I know I don't say this enough,*" he said, in what sounded like a strained voice, "*but I just wanted to say how proud of you I am. You're not just an amazing detective. You're also an honourable man. You put everything into the case you're currently working on and you don't get distracted by anything else until it's closed. It's an admirable quality.*" Kyung-tae went back to the couch and sat down before sipping his water. "*You don't know the whole story of why I was so against Chun-mi working for that man. But I'll tell you now.*"

"You don't have to tell me anything you don't want to," Kyung-tae said.

"*No, you should know.*" Mr Choi paused for a short while. "*He was involved in my wife's murder.*"

"I thought you arrested him?"

"*I did. He went through the usual rehabilitation and got out within a few years. I always knew he was scum, but he convinced everyone around him that he had changed. In fact, when he started up his business, he almost convinced me too. But thanks to you, we can finally prove he should never have been released. He'll never see the outside of a prison ever again."*

Kyung-tae sat silently for a while as Yu-ra's voice rang through his head. How could Mr Choi be an arsonist? Just because he had a vendetta against this manufacturer?

"I actually got suspended," Kyung-tae said. "I believed he was the one that kidnapped Sun-jung. I went against everyone just so that I could get him. But I'm done. I need a break." He sighed.

*"Ah yes, I hear that the other girl was rescued."*

Just because he saw Mr Choi at the scene of one of the crimes, didn't mean it had anything to do with him.

"Yeah, she's safe."

Just because Jinmu had ties to the military, didn't mean he was the only one with the capability to steal the guns and sell them. Dae-myeon fit into all of these too. As well as the fact that it was all but confirmed that the lighter was Dae-myeon's.

*"Good for you. It's a good thing she was rescued when she was. If her existence was found out from the other gangs, it could have led to a gang war. You have to take Dae-myeon down. If he would kidnap a girl once, he'd do it again. And that's going to start everything up again."*

What? How did he know that Li-Na was kidnapped by a gang? The only reason he knew was because Yu-ra told him. Li-Na never included that in her statement.

"How…" Kyung-tae paused, pondering momentarily. Something was wrong, but he couldn't let it be known that he was suspicious yet. "I've got to go. Something's come up with Yu-ra."

****

Yu-ra waited for the owners of the house in front of her to arrive at the entrance as she kicked her boot at the concrete below her. Heat still emanated from her rosy cheeks. Her nose was sore from excessive wiping, and her eyes were slightly puffy. Logically, she felt as though she should have called Min-ah and stayed with her, but strangely this was where her legs carried her.

A few moments later her father opened the door. Yu-ra instantly fell into his embrace, holding onto him tightly as she pressed a tender kiss to his cheek, feeling the slight rasp of his bristly beard against her chin. As she pulled back, she found a bright smile engraved on his cheeks and she couldn't help but smile back at him.

Slipping off her shoes, she was enveloped by the cream walls and warm lighting of the hallway and then the living room. As her mother entered from the kitchen, she greeted her simply, from a distance, to which her mother responded in kind. Yu-ra sat on the edge of the couch that was situated on the far edge of the room, flush against the wall.

"So, what did you do this time?" her mother said, arms crossed. "There must be some reason you visit now. It's because you need something, right?"

"For God's sake," Yu-ra muttered, pushing herself off the sofa. "You can't leave me alone for one second, can you? How are you, Yu-ra?" she said as she brushed past her mother, entering into the corridor and then her old bedroom. "It's nice to see you, Yu-ra. I missed you, Yu-ra. So nice of you to ask!" she called as she slammed the door behind her.

Yu-ra nestled among the plush animals atop her bed, cocooning herself with the warmth of the blanket. The comfort began to settle in, but ten minutes later, a gentle knock echoed through the door.

"What!" Yu-ra moaned.

The door opened and Yu-ra lifted her head to see her brother standing in the doorway with a plate full of food.

"Eomma says you look thin and you need to eat," Hyun-woo said as he walked over to her and passed her the plate. "Where's Kyung-tae?"

"At home."

"Oh," he said before turning around and exiting the room, though he didn't close the door behind him.

As she began to eat from her plate, she heard whispering outside of her room, so she paused.

"Did you give her the food?" her mother whispered. "Is she eating it?"

"Yes," Hyun-woo moaned.

"Is she okay? Did she say anything?"

"I don't know. Ask her yourself."

"Useless boy," she said in a hushed tone before the sound of his head being slapped was heard.

"Ow!"

A few minutes later, her mother came rushing in with a glass of water.

"Here," she said, "you're going to choke if you eat that all without water. It'll help your skin too."

Yu-ra accepted the glass then took a timid sip.

****

Kyung-tae rang the doorbell of Jinmu's residence. No response. He rang again. Nothing.

Ring. Ring. Ring ring ring. Ring ring ring ring ring.

It was just after ten pm. There was no way that no one was home. After slamming his boot into the door, he began to hammer the side of his fist against it. Finally, Jinmu arrived at the entrance with a grim look on his bruised face. Where did he get those bruises from? Kyung-tae wanted to interrogate him; trick him into admitting the crimes he had been perpetrating. Yet, abandoning all formalities, Kyung-tae seized the fabric of Jinmu's shirt and propelled the startled figure down the hallway without a moment's hesitation.

The corridor bore witness to an unsettling dance of dominance, each step forward a battle between an unrelenting force and an immovable object. But the object felt weaker than normal and was able to be pressured into the living room. As they entered, Kyung-tae finally released his grip and shoved Jinmu back a few paces.

"How did you know about Li-Na?" Kyung-tae shouted.

"What are you talking about?" Jinmu replied nonchalantly.

"No one knew she was kidnapped by a gang apart from Yu-ra."

"You already know that Chun-mi works for that scumbag Dae-myeon."

"If she knew, why wouldn't she tell me? You all knew I was trying to find these girls."

Jinmu hesitated.

"Because-"

"Because you didn't care and you just wanted to burn all his warehouses in some kind of sick revenge plan!"

Jinmu's nose wrinkled at the statement Kyung-tae made and he remained silent for a while.

"You really think that little of me?" he said, finally breaking the silence. "Simply burning his stock and making him lose money is what you consider making him pay?"

"It's your fault!" Kyung-tae cried, shoving Jinmu back a few more paces. "You're the reason Sun-jung died! Not me!"

"You still haven't grown up, have you? Maybe you're not worthy of Chun-mi after all. I guess your mother was right to deny the proposals all along."

"What the hell has Chun-mi got to do with this? You knew about these girls, and where they were, and you said nothing to me! I could have saved them!"

Kyung-tae charged at Jinmu once more, ready to seize his collar. But Jinmu slipped his attack and retaliated by flipping Kyung-tae and slamming him down onto the low-risen table beside them.

"You naive little boy!" Jinmu bellowed as he backhanded Kyung-tae, a small stinging cut forming on his cheekbone. "I gave you every chance to save those girls!"

"What are you saying?" Kyung-tae cried as he struggled under his mentor's grip.

Jinmu held his left arm down, then twisted the wrist that hung off the edge. Kyung-tae flung his body about like a fish out of water as pain ran through his arm.

"I took you on a stakeout, knowing they would be returning for their drugs! I advised you to wait in the car instead of rushing off so that we could tail them back to their hideout! And when you were in trouble I allowed them to stab me just so they had a reason to escape and we could still follow them back. And your brash actions caused them to kill her out of fear!"

Jinmu slammed his hand down on Kyung-tae's wrist and a sickening crunch echoed throughout the expansive room. A searing pain shot through his arm as his muscles cramped up and waves of intense discomfort radiated from his wrist. Kyung-tae screamed out as a surge of disbelief shocked him. The pain faded momentarily as the world seemed to slow down. What was this feeling? Fear? He eyed Jinmu through his now watery vision. Who was this man that would so easily hurt him? As a mix of fear and helplessness washed over him. The pain of his injury began to set in once again and he cried out once more, his breath escaping him. Jinmu stepped back from him, allowing him to whimper to himself.

"I guess you're still in need of a lesson," Jinmu said as he took out his phone and rang a number. "Chun-mi. Take her."

Kyung-tae immediately halted his whimpering as Jinmu cut the call.

"Take who?" he yelled. "What are you up to?"

"You should go check up on your wife," he said as he turned his back to Kyung-tae and began walking away. "You can let yourself out. And don't worry. I didn't break your wrist."

Sitting up, Kyung-tae gently rested his wrist in the palm of his other hand, the pain of which had travelled all the way up to his shoulder.

"Hey!" he seethed, spittle flying from his lips as he struggled to control his breathing. "Despite what Chun-mi told me, Dae-myeon never served in the military. I'm guessing he also doesn't actually own a samurai mask. You stole the guns from your old military base."

"Your point?"

"That I'm going to take you in, one way or another. And you will serve a sentence for every single one of your crimes."

****

"What drink do you want?" Yu-ra said, nudging her younger brother before she clinked through rows of glass bottles on the refrigerated shelves of the brightly illuminated twenty-four hour convenience store.

"Just get me that strawberry soda," he said, carrying the basket of snacks to the till.

After they paid, the siblings strolled at a calm pace in the direction of their home, arms linked as she rested her head against her brother's arm. Keeping within the areas lit up from the streetlamps, Hyun-woo adjusted himself from the weight of the bag he was carrying. Maybe Kyung-tae could train her brother. He was a good teacher.

A few minutes into their journey, a sleek black sports car pulled up beside them.

"Go home, Hyun-woo," Yu-ra said, sighing. "I'm going to be gone for a while."

"Why?"

"Just go," she said, as Chun-mi stepped out of the sports car.

Hyun-woo followed the order and briskly walked off.

"It sure is a nice night for a stroll," Chun-mi said as she walked around the front of her car, "but what's an ugly cow like you doing out at this time of night?"

"You drove all the way down here for this?" Yu-ra said, raising a brow. "What do you want?"

"I'm here to take you back."

"At the request of who? I'd think that Kyung-tae is smart enough to not ask you for help."

"He is. Father's request. You know how it is."

"Whatever," she said, walking towards the car.

"Wait. Phone," Chun-mi said, holding out her hands. With a scoff, Yu-ra reluctantly handed over her phone. "Wait. I don't want your stink in my car." She clicked a button on her phone and the boot of her car popped open.

Yu-ra furrowed her brow as she pulled up her skirt slightly before folding herself into the narrow space of the boot.

# 29
# Kidnapped

The living area of the apartment that Chun-mi had taken Yu-ra to exuded comfort and style. A plush sectional sofa lay in one corner with a refined glass coffee table as the centrepiece. As her eyes wandered, her right hand lay confined within a plastic zip-tie, the other end of which was locked around the handle of the top draw of the marbled kitchen counter. Yu-ra found herself drawn to the muted colour palette that adorned the walls and furnishings - whites, greys, and gentle earth tones that whispered tranquillity. The thoughtful design spoke of a lifestyle that blended modern aesthetics with the comfort of home. Yet, all the lighting being artificial and lack of windows caused her to feel claustrophobic at the same time.

The front door creaked open and three figures entered. A stumbling one with a green mask entered first. Followed by an irritated Ny-ron. And finally, a tall man with a similar build to Jinmu entered. He was adorned in a formal shirt with the sleeves rolled up to his elbows, and smart trousers. A tattoo ran down his right forearm stopping at his wrist. Chun-mi's boss - Park Dae-myeon. Takemi collapsed onto the floor beside Yu-ra.

"Who's this?" Dae-myeon grumbled.

"She was my investigator," Ny-ron said meekly. "She thinks one of the Japanese was committing the arson."

"That's stupid. That Ken guy, he had no idea about it. Apart from the samurai."

"Hey," Yu-ra said, garnering everyone's attention. "I know it's very unlikely that you'll let me go, but I know who the samurai is. He's not a gang member."

"Your theories didn't pan out last time," Ny-ron said. "What makes you think we'll believe you this time?"

"Because I figured out who he is. And you have a much closer link than you realise. I'm even pretty sure that he's trying to frame you, Dae-myeon.

Planting evidence to make you out to be the arms dealer and the arsonist."

"And why would he possibly have reason to do that?" Dae-myeon said.

"Because then you get arrested with extreme prejudice. They have some sort of vendetta against you. His identity is my offering. Think about it."

Dae-myeon scoffed at her, simply shaking his head as he exited to the next room.

Ny-ron cuffed Takemi to the same handle as Yu-ra and followed Dae-myeon out of the room.

"What happened," Yu-ra asked, nudging Takemi.

"Ken. He ratted us out."

"Figures."

"I'm not sorry for getting you involved in this. We're going to take down an entire criminal empire and it'll be thanks to you, not me."

"I don't know why you're still talking to me, seeing as you no longer exist."

"You're the one who spoke to me first." Takemi sighed. "Yu-ra, I need you. I can't- I *cannot* do this without you. This was my only escape from prison."

"And why exactly is it my job to save you from your prison sentence?"

"The only reason I'm here is because I was tailing you and I saw his bodyguard take you. If I wasn't in the condition I'm in now, I would have intervened then and there."

"So you want a medal, do you? They didn't give you one for all the murders you committed in Taiwan?"

"I followed her back here and waited for them to leave. I just wasn't counting Ken ratting us out to them so soon. They got the jump on me."

"I don't need you to take care of me."

"Are you kidding me? You're tied up right now! How are you going to save yourself?"

Suddenly, Ny-ron came crashing through the door and slid across the laminate floor.

"You're done!" Dae-myeon bellowed as he came in and picked Ny-ron up from the ground. He then buried the sole of his foot into Ny-ron's chest, flipping him onto his back. "She's my bodyguard, not my damn advisor! I'm in awe of that empty space you have up there! It must really be a nice feeling to not have to think through your actions!"

"It wasn't my fault," Ny-ron wheezed. "Chun-mi was the one who convinced me. She said it would help with your campaign. And look what's happened. Our stock has burnt up and set us back billions!"

"You've had life too easy. I should have never helped keep you out of prison. When I get back, you better be gone. And you better run for your life, because I'm letting them know it was you. Out of the kindness of my heart, I will tell them that Cheonsa judged you guilty and dealt with you. I'll allow you to use this place for a few days until the commotion dies down."

As Ny-ron's chest heaved up and down, Dae-myeon looked down on him, his face wrought with disdain, before he left the building.

"Some brother you are," Ny-ron muttered.

Brother? Suddenly everything started to make sense - why everyone in the Choi family was after this gang and the Park brothers in particular.

After a few moments of catching his breath, Ny-ron stood up and wobbled over to Takemi. He yanked off her mask, flinging it to the side. Takemi's face was still lightly bruised.

"God damn spade," he scoffed before uncuffing her.

Takemi rose tentatively, her legs betraying her balance for a moment.

"I can help you, Ny-ron," she said. "I can get you back in charge. Everyone just needs to know that I'm in your corner. They'll have no choice but to comply."

Ny-ron smirked.

"That won't work," Yu-ra murmured before raising her voice. "I told you, fear is not a good motivator. If they lose trust in your unbiased nature, they'll turn to scheming to take you out. And once you're gone, Ny-ron is next."

"So what's your solution, O great Yu-ra?" Takemi cried, throwing her arms in the air.

"We need a scapegoat. Someone who can take the fall for Ny-ron. Someone who we can claim we've taken care of."

"And who would that be? Dae-myeon, I presume?" Ny-ron smirked.

"No, there would be too many repercussions to that if they find out that he's your brother. I've got a better idea."

"And who would that be?" Takemi asked.

"Chun-mi, Dae-myeon's bodyguard. She's the one who convinced you in the first place, right? All the more reason she deserves to be dealt with."

"She's right, Ny-ron," Takemi said. "It's a far better plan than any one of us could think of."

"I promise you, Ny-ron," Yu-ra said, "things will return to normal with time, and this will all just feel like a bad dream one day."

A smile began to bloom on Ny-ron's face.

"We'll protect you," Takemi said, stepping closer to Ny-ron. "I promise you that much, brother."

Suddenly, the grin on Ny-ron's face dissolved and his skin flooded with a fiery hue. Veins visibly throbbed in his neck as his inflamed eyes tunnelled towards Takemi. Nyron grabbed her then launched her back into the counter that Yu-ra was still cuffed to.

"Ny-ron," Yu-ra yelled, "stop! We're trying to help you!"

But Ny-ron clearly couldn't hear her as he charged at Takemi like a bull that could only see red. Takemi, though clearly a lot slower than normal, used the counter as leverage and flipped out of Ny-ron's reach. The underside of the drawer dug into the backside of Yu-ra's forearm as Ny-ron yanked it open, threatening to snap her wrist. She muffled a cry of pain as Ny-ron hastily rummaged around the cutlery and eventually retrieved a large knife.

Yu-ra wrapped her legs around Ny-ron's ankle, causing his balance to fumble as he tripped backwards into Takemi's arms, who in turn heaved him over her shoulder, slamming him face first onto the ground. Takemi fell with him but rolled onto one side and gripped the arm that held the knife. She tore it from his grip and tossed it across the room, clattering with each bounce.

"Takemi, give me the knife you idiot!" Yu-ra shouted.

"Sorry!" she called, rolling away from Ny-ron and chasing after the knife she had just released.

However, moments before Takemi reached the weapon, Ny-ron grabbed from behind and hauled her to the ground. But he didn't let up there. Gripping her from the collar, he lifted her up and slammed her against the door. A punch to the gut snatched blood from Takemi's insides and she sputtered it over Ny-ron's face.

"YOU DARE CALL ME BROTHER?" Ny-ron screamed, launching Takemi into the side of the counter. A bone crunching noise shot across the room as Takemi cried out.

"Ny-ron, stop!" Yu-ra shrieked as she leapt to her feet, pulling the kitchen drawer open with her. Turning her back to the scuffle that was occurring behind her, she mustered all of the force she could and relentlessly attempted to rip the drawer from its hinges. With each yank, the cutlery inside clattered about, and half of it leapt from the drawer, clanging across the ground.

Suddenly the sound of punches and kicks and cries disappeared and all that echoed throughout the apartment was Yu-ra's strained huffs and the thuds of the drawer being opened and closed. Yu-ra halted, fearing the worst outcome as she slowly returned her gaze to the two combatants. As her eyes fell upon her childhood friend, the sight of a blade sliding out of Takemi's abdomen sent a chilling shock of disbelief down her spine as she froze in place momentarily. Takemi vomited blood before collapsing to the ground.

The clangour of the knife zipped through the room after slipping from Ny-ron's grasp. His gaze was intensely fixated on his hands before an abrupt sense of urgency propelled him out of the room.

"Watch them!" he called out to someone as he rushed away.

Yu-ra's eyes were still fixed on Takemi, bleeding out on the ground. Her heart sank and her knees finally began to wobble. Then they tremored. And finally, they gave out as she collapsed into the same position as Takemi.

# 30
# Kyung-tae and Yu-ra

*You won't be happy about this, but I've deserted my post. Things were going fine. I completed my mission in the same way I completed every mission. My squad were cheering for me. So I figured I would make them cheer even more this time. But I took it too far. My sergeant turned on me. And the blame for every single mistake our squad made, every single unsanctioned mission that our sergeant sent us on, was placed on me. I was looking for you for a short time. But I think I found my calling. I have this new job, and these people accept me for who I am. I get respect and I get honour, like I used to. Besides, I don't want to be a burden to you.*

\- *Letter #37*

The organised chaos of the accident and emergency room permeated the air like a palpable force. Nurses were rushing various patients on gurneys, with now sullied sheets, through the corridors and the scent of antiseptic flooded Kyung-tae's nasal passageways.

A man in a white coat that had been prescribed to him arrived and closed the blue curtain behind him, shutting away the blur of bustling activity but not the noise that came from it.

"It's fractured," the doctor said as he slid his pen through his thick, frayed hair and into the space above his ear and placed his clipboard on the small table beside the headboard of Kyun-tae's bed. "I'm going to start applying a cast now, but it will take a few weeks to heal completely. So no strenuous activity, okay?"

Kyung-tae suddenly realised his gaze was still stuck on the blue curtains behind the doctor and he shook himself into an alert state.

"Sorry what?"

"I said I'm going to put a cast on your wrist," he repeated as he began to position Kyung-tae's wrist gently into the correct position he needed.

Kyung-tae allowed the doctor to do his work as he called Chun-mi again

- the tenth time in the past twenty minutes, after hours of trying to get through to Yu-ra herself. Or was it the eleventh? Once again, there was no answer.

As the doctor applied a synthetic padding to Kyung-tae's injury, he called the next most useful person on his list - Sung-jae. Within a few moments, he answered.

*"Hello."*

"Where's Yu-ra?"

*"What? Why would I kn-"*

"I don't have time for your crap, Sung-jae. I know you coerced Yu-ra into working for you. Luckily, I don't have time to deal with you right now. Jinmu's done something with her."

*"Jinmu?"*

"Her family doesn't know where she's gone, all they know is that she said she would be gone for a few days. Her best friend knows nothing about it whatsoever. And Chun-mi's involved. You would obviously have some way of tracking her. I know you're not that stupid." Sung-jae remained silent for a moment. "Please, please, PLEASE tell me you're not that stupid!"

*"The operation was off the books. I didn't want any records of anything. The only one I was tracking was Takemi, out of necessity."*

"Who's Takemi?"

*"A woman who worked within the gangs. She wore a green mask."*

"And where is she?"

*"I don't know. Her chip went offline. It was powered through the emission of electrical signals from her brain, so either she's dead or the chip was removed from her neck."*

"And what about any historical data?"

*"I'll check. I'll call you back in a few minutes."*

As Kyung-tae awaited Sung-jae's call, the doctor began moulding the cast to fit the form of Kyung-tae's hand. His leg refused to stay still, vibrating up and down.

"Will you hurry up?" he shouted at the doctor who hopped back a little in response.

"I'm sorry, but it takes time to make sure this sets in the correct position, otherwise your bones could heal incorrectly."

When the cast had almost dried, the doctor began doing his final checks. Kyung-tae's phone rang once again.

"Where is she?" Kyung-tae blurted as he answered.

*"I can't find anything,"* Sung-jae said in an urgent tone. *"It's all gone. I can't find any of the evidence I had built. I can't find the entirety of my tracking data. It's all gone!"*

"What do you mean, it's gone?" Kyung-tae yelled, smashing his boot into the bedside table which collapsed to the ground, causing the doctor to reel back in shock once again. "I swear to God, Sung-jae, if anything happens to her, and I mean even a scratch, I will burn your entire life to the ground."

*"This isn't my fault. This is my father's doing. Why do you think I left home in the first place?"*

"Once your scumbag father is behind bars, I will be coming for you next. You can damn well bet on that!"

*"Kyung-tae-"*

Kyung-tae cut off the phone and, leaping from his seat, yanked open the curtain.

"Wait!" the doctor called, "the plaster hasn't set completely!"

Kyung-tae ignored him as he carefully dashed through the chaos of the emergency room.

****

Takemi had dragged herself across the laminate floor to Yu-ra's side, painting a trail of blood from the initial position that she had collapsed in. All the while, the skinny, greasy looking man that Ny-ron had left behind watched at the doorway with beady eyes. Takemi nestled her head on Yu-ra's lap.

"I'm going to get you out of this," Yu-ra whispered in her ear as a tear dripped from her face onto Takemi's cheek. "Kyung-tae will find us and I'll get you to a hospital. You just need to hold on a bit longer. Please."

"Yu-ra." Takemi strained. "I still don't feel sorry for getting you involved."

"Forget about that. We can talk about it later. You need to conserve energy."

"No, you need to listen to me, while I'm still able to tell you." Takemi rummaged around in her coat pocket, retrieving a thick pile of envelopes that had been held together with an elastic band. "Here. These are half of the letters I wrote to you when I was in the military."

"I never received any letters from you."

"They were never sent."

"Takemi," Yu-ra murmured, wiping another tear that had dripped onto Takemi's face, smudging the blood that was on her cheek, "who writes letters in this day and age?"

Takemi smirked momentarily.

"I don't feel sorry because I don't feel anything… for anyone. I keep trying. I really do. But it's like…like nothing changes inside me when I see someone get hurt. Nothing changes when I hurt people. When I see people crying, when I see people who I know are innocent being gunned down and tortured, I'm still empty inside. I don't feel angry, I don't feel sick, I don't feel horrified, I don't feel guilty. I'm just apathetic."

Yu-ra sniffed the mucus that was beginning to drip from her nose back up and then wiped her nose with her cardigan.

"Stop opening up to me as if it's the last time you'll ever speak to me."

"I didn't run from the military. And I never once felt any particular way about what they made me do. In fact they loved me. I was a special OPS leader. I simply kept doing the things that made them praise me. It's just that one time I went too far, and then they turned on me. Used me as a scapegoat for every evil thing they ever did. They chased me out."

Yu-ra brushed Takemi's hair back with her free hand.

"When we get you stitched up, you'll never have to go back to the military. You'll never have to do any illegal work whatsoever. You can stay with me until we get you back on your feet."

Takemi smiled at her.

"Hey, I think I just felt something. It was like a little stir in the left side of my chest. What is it?"

"Sounds to me like it's a bit of hope. Hold onto that feeling."

"No, I don't think it's that." Takemi chuckled. "But I think I finally get why I was so desperate to have you around."

"And now you don't need to worry about it anymore, because I'm not letting you leave me ever again."

"When I'm around you, I still do what I think will get me praise. But the difference is that when you praised me, I felt like it was because I was becoming a better person. More human. And you're the only one who cared about making me into a better person too. The moment I did something wrong, others would leave or turn on me. But not you. That's why I wanted you back with me. It's your defining trait - You never give up on anyone."

"You could have just called me, you idiot." Yu-ra sniffled. "I would have invited you to my wedding if I knew you were around. We could have gone back to having a normal relationship."

"Yeah, maybe you're right." Takemi chuckled again, but more weakly than before.

For the first time, a tear formed in the corner of Takemi's eye which then dripped down the side of her face.

Yu-ra continued to brush her hair as she quietly sang her favourite ballad in her ear.

"I remember this song," Takemi said. "We used to sing it in the school on rainy days, pretending we were in some kind of drama."

And slowly but surely, the heaving of Takemi's chest settled, becoming lighter and lighter. And, finally, ceased altogether. A million needles pierced Yu-ra's heart and, as the panic set in - the panic that she was all alone with no one left to help her, and that she had spent her life pushing everyone away - her breaths became the frantic fluttering of a caged bird, desperate to break free.

The beady eyed man at the door grew a sinister smile as he must have realised that Cheonsa was finally dead. There was no longer an entity to hold him accountable for his actions, nor any other criminal in Seoul.

The man removed his jacket as he unsettlingly shuffled towards her. With each predatory step his smile grew more sinister, as if he'd had a sickening new idea. Yu-ra gently placed Takemi's head against the ground and then stood up, her hand still bound to that same drawer. Before the man had time to process what she was doing, she flung the drawer open and grabbed the first knife she found.

Unfortunately, the man lurched at her before she could threaten him. He seized her leg, causing her to thrash about as she tried to pull herself back to the counter. Managing to slip off a shoe, he more aggressively grasped at any part of her he could. Yu-ra ungracefully flung her legs about and somehow caught him in the chest with a forceful kick. He fell backwards, tripping over the edge of the coffee table and subsequently crashing through it.

Yu-ra whipped the knife into the space between her wrist and the zip tie and then sliced it off. She turned back around to see that the now enraged man had found his footing. Yu-ra swiped the knife at him as he launched himself at her. He ducked it, seizing her wrist and then he tried to jerk her towards him. Yu-ra twisted her wrist and, using her other hand for support, tore it away from his grip. Utilising the shock he felt from her being able to escape his grasp, she plunged the knife into his left shoulder and then rammed her shoulder into his abdomen, causing him to tumble backwards. He slipped over the trail of blood, head slamming into the exposed leg of the broken coffee table during his descent. Body now limp, a pool of crimson seeped from the back of his head, spreading through the room and soon mixing with the blood that was already there.

# 31
# Blood Brothers

Gingerly, Yu-ra inched her way across the floor of the apartment towards the man that had attacked her, meticulously avoiding the pools of blood that had saturated the room. She cautiously slipped a hand into his trouser pocket, with a pulse that had still not calmed since earlier, luckily discovering a phone. After turning it on, she pressed the man's right thumb against the screen and it unlocked. She swiftly entered the number of her parent's residence and her mother answered a few seconds later.

"Assalaamu 'alaykum Eomma," Yu-ra blurted. "I don't have-"

*"Where have you been? Why did you leave your brother alone?"*

"EOMMA!" Yu-ra yelled. "I don't have time right now. Can you give me Kyung-tae's number? I don't have my phone on me."

A few moments of more bickering and then searching later, her mother read out Kyung-tae's number and Yu-ra wrote it down before cutting off the phone.

Upon dialling Kyung-tae's number, the persistent ringing stretched endlessly. Each successive ring heightened the pace of her pulse. And as her brain hyper focused on the sounds, they grew louder and more intense.

Ring Ring.

Ring RING.

RING RING.

Finally, a welcomed silence replaced the incessant chiming.

*"Hello,"* came his voice.

His beautiful, soothing, sweet, and caring voice. The only voice in the world that she cared about hearing in that moment. The voice that momentarily washed a sea of tranquillity over her. As her tears began to trickle out once more, that momentary calm escaped her.

"Kyung-tae-ya!" she wailed.

*"Yu-ra!"* he cried before she could get any more words out. *"Where are*

*you?"*

"I don't know, some apartment."

*"Okay, just stay on the phone. I'm going to track it and come get you. Are you safe?"*

"I think so."

*"If you're not, hide somewhere. A cupboard, wardrobe, lock yourself in the bathroom, anywhere that you'll be safe until I get there."*

Yu-ra's voice trembled as she struggled to articulate her words through a veil of tears.

"Kyung-tae-ya. There was a man that attacked me," she said, her voice escaping through rapid breaths.

*"Did he hurt you?"* he said, his voice laced with worry.

"No. I'm fine, I promise, you don't have to worry." She sniffed. "But I made him hit his head on a table leg. I think I might have killed him."

*"Check his pulse."*

Yu-ra placed her fingers on the left side of his throat, shallow thumps tapping against them.

"I think I feel it, but I'm not sure."

*"I'll check when I get there. Just stay on the line."*

****

Kyung-tae had finally arrived down the street from the location of the signal, but it wasn't the apartment complex he had envisioned. In fact it wasn't an apartment complex at all. It was a towering warehouse with two brawny men standing guard at the front door. How was Kyung-tae going to get through safely? As he closed in on the location, he ducked behind a nearby car, in close enough proximity to the guards that he could hear them.

After a few minutes of watching and contemplating, a few people had arrived at the entrance. One of the guards spoke to them in a foreign language and, after replying in the same language, they let them in. The language sounded familiar. He was certain he had heard it before…

That was it! It was the same language that Yu-ra spoke. Though he had only heard her speak it on a few occasions.

"Yu-ra," he said into his earpiece. "There are some guards blocking the way. I need your help."

*"What can I do?"* she replied, clearly confused by his statement.

"I think they're speaking Korean. Whatever they say to me, I need your help in responding."

*"Ok, gotcha."*

Kyung-tae walked up to the two men confidently, refusing to let his expression falter. The two men greeted him in Korean, and then seemingly asked him a long question.

*"They're asking you a riddle,"* Yu-ra said. *"You're driving a train with no brakes. There are five people stuck on the track. You can choose to divert the train to another track, but there's one person stuck on there. What do you do?"*

One of the guards then spoke to him more aggressively than before.

*"They're asking what's taking so long. You ready? Repeat my exact words…"*

As Yu-ra spoke, Kyung-tae repeated word for word, though in an uncertain tone.

"Jeoneun sokdo-reul nohyeoyo."

Suddenly, the guards erupted into belly laughter and one of them began patting Kyung-tae on the shoulder, causing him to recoil slightly, a shiver running down his spine in anticipation of a fight. The guard patting him spoke again.

*"He's saying that he likes you."*

Kyung-tae smiled nervously as the guard stood to the side to allow him to enter. However, before he could, an incredibly large group of people arrived at the scene. There must have been at least twenty men. They all looked Japanese. The man leading the charge called out to the guards.

"Where's Cheonsa? Is he in there with you?"

"You're not allowed to be here," the guard said calmly as the horde arrived at the doorstep, "so you better hope Cheonsa isn't here with us."

"We've got business with Ny-ron, so you better let us through or we'll force our way in."

"If you had an appointment, I would know about it," the guard said, unfazed by the man's previous comment.

Suddenly, the man, followed by the rest of his crew, charged at the two guards, easily overpowering them and breaking through the front doors.

"Guess I didn't even need your help," Kyung-tae said as he seamlessly mixed in with the crowd of men, using the commotion to hide his presence.

As the gang began causing a ruckus inside the warehouse, kicking over tables with meticulously arranged piles of packaged crystals and throwing various workers to the ground, Kyung-tae continued to follow his tracker.

"By the way," he said, "what kind of riddle was that? It sounded more like an ethical dilemma."

*"I didn't know how to explain it. They essentially say something random each time and see if the person can respond in a way that even slightly makes sense in the context."*

"What did I say?"

*"You said...'I speed up',"* she said, sounding as if holding back a giggle.

"That's...dark."

Kyung-tae soon found himself in an underground labyrinth of tunnels. He continued down the grimy narrow pathways.

Talking. Kyung-tae heard men chattering around the corner so he slipped his back against the wall and waited. One sounded angry at the other but they were speaking Korean, so he couldn't understand. They were clearly in a rush because they jogged straight past Kyung-tae without even realising he was there.

After they passed, Kyung-tae continued on his path and eventually arrived at a door. But it looked different from the ones he passed by on the way. It wasn't a heavy duty steel door that looked like it would be used to keep prisoners in isolation. It looked like a normal apartment door. The dot on his tracker was just on the other side.

Kyung-tae knocked timidly.

"Yu-ra," he whispered against the door. No response. "Yu-ra," he whispered again, but louder. There was a shuffling behind the door and then, moments later, it flung open.

Kyung-tae's eyes widened as his whole world seemed to stand still. Silence. Not even the sound of flowing air entered his ears. Everything in his vision blurred. Everything but his wife. And he absorbed her. Her tired eyes and her twitching red nose. The adorable way her upper lip rested above her teeth. Her rosy cheeks and the dimples that formed as a mesmerising smile bloomed across them. His knees wobbled as all the adrenaline from his body began to drain. Gazing intensely upon her skin, he recorded all the beautiful imperfections that he had never taken notice of before. And in that moment, he decided that never in a million years would he change even a single imperfect detail about her.

Before his legs had the chance to give out, he wrapped his arms around her waist as he guided her back into the apartment, stopping just short of the still wet trails of blood. Yu-ra reciprocated with a hug of her own, laying her arms over his shoulders. Kyung-tae closed the gap between them further as he hugged her tighter and tighter.

A tear he had been fighting to keep back broke through his tear duct and trickled down his cheek. After the first one broke free, a cascade followed, and he was helpless to stop them.

What had this woman done to him? The last time he remembered crying before he met her was at his father's funeral. His knees finally buckled and he guided Yu-ra to the floor with him, her rear landing on the sticky trail of blood.

"Crap," he said, pulling her away from the blood and hugging her tighter. "I'm sorry."

"Don't be," she muttered, nestling her cheek against his neck, the heat of which gently caressed his skin. "I hated this skirt anyway. Worst skirt I've ever bought. It's so unbelievably ugly. I can't believe you let me buy this. What were you thinking?"

"I'm sorry." He chuckled lightly. "I'll buy you a whole closet full of dresses when we get out of here."

Yu-ra's wet cheek tickled his skin as she nestled her head more deeply.

"Takemi, she's gone," she said as her breaths became more rapid and a tear dripped onto his exposed neck. "I was her best friend. Her only friend. And because of me she died. She only came here to save me and the only reason I was here was because I kicked her and everyone else out of my life."

Kyung-tae looked over at the body of the battered and bruised young girl that was bleeding out, and a pang attacked his heart. Besides her body, open letters were strewn across the ground, droplets splattered over quite a few of them. Were they tears?

"I met her once. Fought her, even."

"What?"

"In a warehouse. I saw her brawling with Jinmu. Eventually I realised she was on my side. She was strong. Really strong. And I get a sense that you were a part of her strength, maybe even the whole. I relate to her in that sense."

"I'm not a strength," she said, her scarf lightly scratching at his skin as she shook her head. "I decided that I was the only person worthy of forgiveness, when really she just needed someone on her side. I'm arrogant. I'm selfish. I'm hypocritical, for God's sake."

At that moment, Kyung-tae didn't know what to say. These were the exact words that he wanted to hear from her last night. But it didn't feel the way he thought it would. It wasn't a nice feeling at all, hearing her say those things about herself. It hurt, as if something was clawing into his heart.

He didn't have an all-encompassing solution to the emotions she was going through. So, he hugged her tighter. Maybe all she needed right now was…

"I'm listening. Say what you need to say."

"I'm sorry I said those things to you. I know you're just always trying to help."

"No, don't apologise. I was wrong and I need to accept that."

"But you weren't. If anyone is going to change my relationship with my family, it's going to be me. So I have to take responsibility for that. And I said some really horrible things to you, so I do need to apologise."

"As did I. And things that were probably far worse." Kyung-tae pulled back from her and brushed her cheek lightly with his thumb. Then, with his sleeve, patted her cheeks dry. "To tell you the truth, the only reason I spoke to you initially really was because I wanted to make amends with my ma. But I was a complete idiot for even suggesting that it was the reason I married you."

"I lied too. I was forced to have meetings with suitors twice before you. And they were disgusting people. But then I met you, and all our values aligned. And I could see from a mile away that you were a good man."

"Yu-ra, I fell in love with you a long, long time ago," Kyung-tae said as he analysed her breathtakingly hazel eyes. "That's why I married you."

"You know I've been racking my brain, trying to figure out what particular moment I decided that I wanted to marry you. But, I've been coming up blank every single time."

"Thanks," Kyung-tae said bluntly. "Not like I'm pouring my heart out to you or anything."

"Shut up for a second and listen. There wasn't a particular moment because every time I met you, I remembered a story I heard."

"It better be a good one." He pouted.

She smiled a little before she continued.

"There was once this successful businesswoman. She inherited her wealth, but after her second husband died, she continued to trade. The problem was that she was hindered by the fact that she was a woman. It wasn't safe for her to travel and trade by herself. She had heard of this shepherd, a young inexperienced man who her sister had hired to graze her flock previously. And when it was time for the young man to collect his wages, he had asked the other shepherd to collect his too as he felt too shy to go."

"I feel like I've heard this story somewhere before. But, I can't remember where."

"You'll figure it out. Anyway when the business woman's sister heard what the young shepherd said, she praised him endlessly. Now, when the businesswoman hired people, they would always cheat her out of her money. So, she hired this young shepherd, knowing he was an honourable and honest man, even offering him fifty percent of the profits."

"Wow, that's generous."

"She sent her servant with him and upon returning, the servant praised him for the care and concern he had shown, and the honesty in his dealings. And so, after hearing all these things about him, the businesswoman fell in love with him. When she sent another servant to find out if he would be interested in marrying her, he said 'why would she want me?'"

Kyung-tae chuckled lightly.

"What a response to a proposal."

"You see he was an orphan and poor, so he didn't think he had any worth. It wasn't his status that made the businesswoman want to marry him. Plenty of suitors came to ask for her hand. She was worth a lot. Though, she would turn them all down. You see, this young shepherd, she fell in love with his character. And when they got married, she supported him through all his difficulties. He went through difficulties we couldn't even imagine. But he grew to be the greatest man who will ever walk this Earth."

"Ah," Kyung-tae said, smiling softly. "I remember now."

"I married you because you embodied those same characteristics. I've never met a man more purehearted than you. As much as you like to believe that Jinmu is the one that made you that way, he isn't. You're nothing like him."

Another tear trickled down Kyung-tae's face and he pulled Yu-ra close to him again. He hugged her tighter and tighter until he could no longer maintain his balance on the side of his thigh and they fell into a lying position. Placing his free hand under her head, he whispered in her ear.

"I don't want to move yet. Can we stay here for a while?"

"Of course."

"Yu-ra, I don't want you to ever think that you could possibly be someone's weakness," Kyung-tae said as he looked over at Takemi's lifeless body again. "You need to promise me. Because I promise you, there's not a single person on this planet that wishes you weren't a part of their life."

"Okay, I promise."

Kyung-tae pulled back from her and gazed into her eyes.

"Yu-ra, every time I pray, I thank Allah that he blessed me with you. Even when I was scared you would leave me, I still thanked Him for putting you in my life. Because I'd rather you were in it for a short time than not at all."

Suddenly, Yu-ra pressed her soft, warm lips against his, tenderly embracing each other as a shock ran down his spine and the hair on the back of his neck stood on end. Just as quickly as she had kissed him, she pulled away. But those two seconds; they felt like a thousand.

"Sorry," she said, clearing her throat.

"What for?" Kyung-tae replied as a radiant smile unexpectedly illuminated his face with an infectious joy.

"I just realised we've never kissed before and I felt a sudden urge to kiss you."

"I see."

Yu-ra itched her cheek.

"This…isn't appropriate for our current situation."

"You're right," he said, struggling to contain his still beaming smile. He kissed her gently on the forehead. "Let's get you out of here."

As Kyung-tae helped her to her feet, brushing down her skirt for her, he contemplated how they would get out of the building. Considering Yu-ra had been attacked, it was safe to say that her relationship with the gang had been thrown out the window.

"What happened to your hand?" Yu-ra said, looking at the cast Kyung-tae had on.

"Fractured my wrist. Don't worry about it. It'll heal."

Yu-ra gazed upon Takemi's body for the first time since Kyung-tae had arrived.

"We need to take her body. She doesn't have any family, and I don't want her to be cremated."

"Okay, but it looked like a commotion might break out in that warehouse," he said as he went to pick up Takemi's body. "We're going to need a way out of here safely."

****

As the couple navigated their way back down the path that Kyung-tae had followed, the sounds of shouting and the clanging of metal became louder. A pungent aroma stung their nostrils and an acrid scent filled the air. After a few moments, the source of that scent was made clear as grey wisps invaded the air. And, as they arrived closer to the commotion, the environment became more familiar to Yu-ra, even through the thickening smoke.

"Wait!" she squealed, then slapped her hand over her mouth. "Sorry. I know where we are."

"You do?" Kyung-tae said, carrying Takemi in his arms.

"I know the tunnels on the other side like the back of my hand."

"Okay! Let's go!" Kyung-tae affirmed.

"Issue is, we have to go back through that warehouse to get to the tunnels on the other side. You had to walk down some stairs as you entered the warehouse, right?"

"Yeah."

"The warehouse floor is on the same level as the tunnels. There's nothing underneath the warehouse."

"Okay, don't worry. We'll figure it out."

At the scene of the commotion, hordes of men swarmed the ground floor, their clanging metal pipes were a discordant symphony that reverberated around the space. There were two groups of men, separated by an empty aisle. Japanese on one side and Chinese on the other. Toppled tables created barriers around the edges of the room, and mountains of narcotics blazed in makeshift bonfires, casting an eerie glow that danced around the room. Kyung-tae and Yu-ra ducked behind the tables, out of the line of sight of the rioting men and the fearful Koreans scattered across the room. The resonant clanging gradually subsided, eventually coming to a lingering silence as a broad, well-kept man in a suit strode proudly up to a platform at the front of the room. Behind him followed a woman in a body armour and a man with fiery copper hair and a thin scar. His shoulders were hunched and his body was turned from the others, a shell of his former self. As Dae-myeon stood at the platform, a megaphone in his hand.

The couple crept further down the room towards the back end of the crowd as a squad of Koreans gang members entered the room and formed a wall in front of Dae-myeon. Yu-ra pointed at the hollow man at the back of the platform.

"That's Ny-ron, the gang leader," she whispered. "Well, second in command now. He's the one who kidnapped Sun-jung and Li-Na. In that apartment, Dae-myeon said he would tell everyone what Ny-ron did."

As Yu-ra glanced at Kyung-tae, she found that his jaw was tightening. Surely his hands would be balled into fists if he had not been carrying Takemi.

"Okay, let's get you out of here first," he said. "I'll report this and come back with a squad. This looks like it could break out into a serious fight. We're going to need help to stop it."

Suddenly a deep voice boomed across the entire complex.

"I'm sure you all have many questions," Dae-myeon echoed, "number one being who I am. Well, I am here to answer."

"I'm still not convinced that Chun-mi is all bad," Kyung-tae said, "and please let me explain first."

"I'm listening," she replied.

"I know her, and I know that she would do anything to impress her father. She never knew her mother, really, so there's no reason that she would work for Park Dae-myeon. Not for revenge, nor out of apathy. She still has principles. But the hatred Jinmu has for this man, I'm sure he'd even use his own daughter to further any plans he has."

"I am the new leader," Dae-myeon boomed once again. "I control your supply, and without me the gang will crumble into nothingness. You need not worry about Ny-ron any longer. He handed over the reins willingly. Nor need you worry about Cheonsa."

Suddenly there was an uproar in the crowd.

"Where's Cheonsa? Bring him out!" they chanted.

"People, calm down, please. I am enacting what Cheonsa wishes. The man who was involved in orchestrating any human trafficking has been dealt with severely and is no longer with us."

Wait. That's not what he said in the apartment? They must have come to a different conclusion about what to do after they left.

"That's not good enough," a Japanese man called out. "The police arrested ten of us since your man stepped on our turf. They've been on the lookout for us because of you!"

"And where's Cheonsa to confirm this?" another voice yelled.

"Yeah!" the crowd chanted in affirmation.

"They kidnapped one of our own, too!" A Chinese man called out.

"Please!" Dae-myeon bellowed, "I have not finished what he ordered me to do. And I do not wish to be at the mercy of his wrath!" The crowd quieted. "Cheonsa ordered that I offer a year's worth of supply for free. It will set us back more than one year, but that's how important making amends is to us!"

"You're lying!" a voice in the back echoed. "We know that Ny-ron was the one who orchestrated the kidnappings!"

How did they know that? Did Jinmu tell them when he sold them the guns? And where were those guns? There wasn't a single one in sight.

"We want his head on a spike!" another voice called out. The whole crowd erupted into a chaotic mob, screaming for Ny-ron's head.

Kyung-tae pulled Yu-ra along the back of the crowd and onto the other side of the room, using the chaos for cover. They had to keep low, otherwise she would have stuck out like a sore thumb.

"How are your knees not hurting?" Yu-ra whispered as he hobbled with Takemi's body in front of her.

"They are," he said simply.

Yu-ra looked across the room, at the jittery man who was shrinking away behind Chun-mi.

"I don't know who told you that, but it isn't true," Dae-meyon said, his demeanour subtly losing the pride that filled his face.

"Bring Cheonsa out now!" a voice called.

"He needs to make an example of Ny-ron in front of us!" another voice called.

Suddenly Ny-ron's previously anxious figure underwent a remarkable transformation, manifesting a burst of frenetic energy. His hunched shoulders reverted to being squared with determination as he darted past Chun-mi and shoved Dae-myeon out of the way. The rapid movements seemed to emanate from an unspoken urgency, a silent plea etched on his furrowed brow.

"Cheonsa's dead!" Ny-ron cried. "He betrayed us!"

Dae-myeon's face had reddened and his nostrils flared like a bull. Clutching Ny-ron by the shirt, he spoke words that no one else could hear. Unexpectedly, Chun-mi kicked Dae-myeon away from Ny-ron. Filled with rage, Dae-myeon charged at Chun-mi, who effortlessly dodged him and then launched her right heel into the back of his head. Dae-myeon collapsed and Chun-mi placed the same foot on his back to keep him down. There was no way he was the samurai. He fumbled around like a complete idiot.

"Speak your mind, Ny-ron," Chun-mi said.

"Cheonsa killed your people without repercussions!" Ny-ron cried out. "He was working with a spy, protecting her. But he's been dealt with. I killed him. And I did it to protect us all. He knew too much and was too untrustworthy. And we were stupid for ever trusting this neutral entity without knowing their identity!"

During Ny-ron's speech, an eerie silence had settled like a heavy fog. Chun-mi removed her foot from Dae-myeon's back and he scrambled to his feet. The silence hung in the air as everyone in the room contemplated what this meant for them. Neither Yu-ra, nor Kyung-tae, nor anyone else in the room knew what would happen next. Their entire system was held together by this one entity. Yu-ra knew of no one else with the skillset to take up that mantle. The room, filled to the brim with people, had become a canvas of suspended breaths and expectant stillness.

BANG!

An explosion ripped through the silently still air. Suddenly, Kyung-tae slipped Takemi's body to the ground and pulled Yu-ra lower, sheltering her with his own body. After a few moments, they lifted their heads to see the crowd with their heads ducked. Yet one man stood still in the middle of the crowd. Arm extended, towards the front, and a gun in hand. Yu-ra's eyes darted to where Ny-ron was. Under his right eye, where his scar once lay, was now a gaping hole. Half of the eye had been torn asunder and blood trickled down his cheek, like a singular scarlet teardrop that he had been holding back. And as those walls broke down, finally allowing him to let it out, Ny-ron sank to his knees, then gracefully tumbled to the ground. A fallen leaf in the wind of mortality.

# 32
# Escape

BANG! BANG!

The man holding the gun in the middle of the Japanese crowd collapsed to the ground, relinquishing his grip of the weapon. Park Dae-myeon stood in the mirrored position of the man who just fell, a similar gun extended from his body. As the shock was gradually worn away from the faces of the gang members, the warehouse became a turbulent cauldron of chaos, their frenzied footsteps echoing amidst the stacks of crates like war drums. A symphony of gunfire and clashing of metal pipes echoed through the screams of war. Dae-myeon ducked his head and rushed away with a smirking Chun-mi. A bullet exploded through the table that Kyung-tae and Yu-ra were hiding behind, whipping past his ear.

"I need to get you out of here," Kyung-tae said, lifting her up and shielding her from the chaos that raged beyond him. "I'm going to have to leave Takemi behind for now. It's too dangerous to be slowed down. I promise you we'll come back for her."

Yu-ra looked at Takemi, then at Kyung-tae longingly.

"I-we can't leave her. Please."

Kyung-tae hesitated.

"Okay," he said, picking Takemi's limp body back up, "where do we go?"

"This way," Yu-ra said, pulling him along by the jacket as she guided him away from the tumultuous storm of bullets.

A gang member came crashing through the tables in front of them, halting them in their tracks. And the man who sent him through the table spotted Kyung-tae, charging at him. Kyung-tae quickly turned to Yu-ra, and in one smooth motion dropped Takemi into her arms and spun his leg backwards in the air, his heel just managing to catch the attacker's jaw. As he fell to the ground, Kyung-tae took Takemi's body back off Yu-ra, who was struggling to hold her up.

As they escaped the room, with more and more gang members crashing into the barriers, his wife directed him down a labyrinth of corridors.

"You know," Kyung-tae said, "since there's so much chaos, we could just brute force our way out the front. How likely is it that they would care about two random people escaping?"

"No, it's too much of a risk. I've explored these tunnels when I helped Li-Na get free. We won't get caught by anyone."

"Okay. I trust you."

The roaring of the battle behind them quietened. Yu-ra dragged him along a maze of grimy concrete tunnels, and the weight of Takemi had begun to seriously strain his wrist. It was as if his hand was attached by a single string and that string was being yanked on. Only the sound of their quickening breaths and pattering footsteps could be heard as they continued. But then the pattering came from somewhere else other than their own feet. They slowed down, listening attentively. Other people were running. As they made their way down another few corners, the source of the footsteps was made clear.

"You've got enough ammo to take down an army. It doesn't matter whether or not you all have guns!" came Dae-myeon's voice, and then his figure, along with Chun-mi's, came into view. "You break down their front doors and drag them onto the streets! From their houses, businesses, whatever!"

"Jinmu must have sold guns to all of the gangs," Kyung-tae said. "He wanted this war. Why is Chun-mi still with him?"

"Better question," Yu-ra said. "Why is he still allowing her to be around him?"

"We're coming out on top of this," Dae-myeon cried. "I don't care if we no longer have clientele. They all die!"

"What's the plan?" Yu-ra said, as they followed a few metres behind them, using the corners of the walls for cover. "We going to take him down first? Maybe the war will end if they don't have a leader."

"No, you're my priority," Kyung-tae said. "I'm getting you out of here safely, first."

Dae-myeon and Chun-mi's footsteps got further and further until they disappeared entirely.

After a while they arrived at what looked like a large restaurant kitchen. Stainless steel pots, pans, and utensils hung on the walls. Industrial sized stoves spread out beneath them. In the centre of the room, sat a stainless steel countertop, around which a number of staff in white uniforms were rushing around. Though it wasn't the organised rush of kitchen staff working. It looked like the rush of people in fear. Suddenly, they stopped, observing Kyung-tae and Yu-ra, and then rushed through the kitchen doors out to the restaurant area.

"We should probably get out of here as soon as possible," Kyung-tae said.

However, as they made their way towards the exit the staff went through, three men burst through that door. An older man with lines etched around his eyes and two younger men who looked more athletic. Through the gaps between the men, Kyung-tae saw people cowering underneath tables. The couple walked backwards a few paces and the men followed.

"That's the spy!" one of the men said, pointing at Yu-ra.

"Yu-ra, go grab me one of the woks," Kyung-tae said as he placed Takemi's body on the countertop.

Yu-ra whipped one of the woks from the wall and then slid it across the counter. Kyung-tae picked it up with his unfractured hand.

"I'm going to go get those civilians to safety," Yu-ra said as she dodged the three men who charged at Kyung-tae.

"Don't do anything dangerous," Kyung-tae called, as he slammed the back of the wok across the face of one of the younger men, sending him tumbling to the tiled floor. "I'll be there in a minute or two."

The older man swung a fist at him, to which Kyung-tae effortlessly dodged, retaliating with another clang of the wok to his head.

The final man then pulled a knife from underneath his jacket, smirking at his foe. The man knew that if he got close, Kyung-tae could be rendered immobile. The two men on the ground also had found their footing. Causing all three men to reveal a smug look on their faces.

Using all the force he could muster, he launched the wok at the man with the knife. It connected at the centre of his forehead with a thud that echoed through the room. Utilising the shock that the other two showed, he snapped the back of his foot into the older man's face. After the kick connected, his head smacked into the side of the counter and he collapsed. Without a split second of waiting, he front-kicked the last man in the stomach. As the man bowed, succumbing to the pain, Kyung-tae roundhouse kicked him, sending him flying into the industrial fridge beside them. Before the men had the opportunity to rise or wake, Kyung-tae lifted Takemi from the counter and rushed out of the room.

****

Beneath the rows of rectangular wooden tables, on the opposite side of the bar area of the romantically lit restaurant, Yu-ra lifted another civilian woman up. Her knees and her thighs were starting to ache from all the squatting she was doing. Small pockets of flames licked at the air as the acrid smell of smoke filled the room. Groups of men wrestled around fires, slamming each other into tables and punching each other's guts. Narrowly dodging the brawling men, Yu-ra managed to guide the fearful woman out an exit at the side of the building.

Suddenly, Kyung-tae burst into the room. Like the robot he was, he scanned the room, searching. When his eyes locked with Yu-ra's, a grin spread across his face. He rushed across the aisle between the tables. Blocked by piles of scrapping men, and unable to dodge them with ease due to having Takemi in his arms, he leapt onto a table and bolted past them.

"Let's get out of here," he said as he arrived at Yu-ra's feet.

"There's two more people we need to get out of here," Yu-ra said as she pointed at the brawls, "but they're right in the epicentre."

"Okay, I'll get you an opening," Kyung-tae said, placing Takemi by the door. "You get them out safely."

Kyung-tae flew back into the centre of the room. As if floating, he leapt into the air and kicked off one of the brawling men, using the leverage to bullet his boot into the other man and effectively split them apart. Yu-ra used this opportunity to dash back into the room and guide an older man from his hiding place beneath a table. Within a few seconds she had raced him over to the exit. As Yu-ra, heart pounding, sped back into the centre of the room, she saw a rush of gang members clawing at her husband. He had leapt onto a table, using the high ground to keep them at bay. Luckily this gave Yu-ra another opening as she spotted the last civilian teenager crawling out from underneath the table. Yu-ra helped her up and guided her away from the commotion.

As she retraced her steps down the aisle, several men careened into her line of sight, tumultuously colliding with tables on the opposite side. Kyung-tae had resorted to firing powerful kicks at them, probably due to his injured hand. As the teenager finally escaped, Yu-ra spun back around.

"Tae-Tae, let's go!" she yelled.

Kyung-tae heeded her command after landing one last powerful kick which propelled one man into the crowd, causing them to crumble. Kyung-tae raced over to his wife and picked up Takemi's body.

"After you... Yu-Yu," he said uneasily.

As they raced down the empty streets, only one thought filled Yu-ra's mind. Peace. Finally a moment of tranquillity. A moment to breathe. A moment to just be. The wind rushed her ears as she tried to keep up with Kyung-tae. How was he so fast even when carrying Takemi? As her mind became clouded with thoughts again, she realised that the once familiar hum of the city had changed. It now roared in the night. The air crackled with tension as they came upon a scene. The once orderly streets now played host to an unbridled war, riots breaching the city's veins. Furious flames escaped the buildings surrounding them, casting an eerie glow on the unfolding mayhem. Bullets cascaded through the battlegrounds and bodies littered the dead man's land. No way to tell whether they were civilians or criminals. It was as if the very ground beneath their feet trembled with the reverberations of shattered peace. The trembling increased tenfold as a wave marched in step towards them. Sharp metallic vibrations punctuated the air with a discordant rhythm. Over the horizon, a subtle glow of city lights highlighted rows of tactically clad officers, banging on their riot shields. Thus, a special assault team marched onto the battlefield.

# 33
# Crackdown

*What the hell is going on recently?* Woo-young thought as he pounded on the bulletproof shield he held in front of him with his baton. *A military base gets raided and the guns are spread that quickly?*

A torrential rain of bullets thundered and the sharp coppery smell of blood surged through the air as the squad spread out amongst the warring street.

"*Sure would have been useful to get our own guns,*" one of the SAT members said through Woo-young's earpiece.

Woo-young, along with four of his men, all clad in blacked out tactical gear, advanced into a crowd of men and women hiding behind a makeshift barricade on the side of the street. Every now and then, they would peep their heads out to fire on the opposing side. Approaching the first gang member he saw, Woo-young slammed his boot into him, sending him tumbling to the ground. As he tumbled, Woo-young brought his baton down on the man, each blow meeting resistance with a resounding thud. He continued to strike the man, his mouth contorting at every impact, his cries silent through the tumultuous discord rampant in their surroundings. Eventually, the opposing force diminished entirely, his body falling limp. Woo-young's eyes flicked away from his downed victim and he moved on to his next target.

However, after the first man went down, the crowd took notice of the assault team and redirected their efforts to their new foes. Across from the expansive avenue, the other members of Woo-young's squad were facing a similar assault. Some members took to firing on the police officers, their bullets either catching their riot shields, or catching their own members. As some bodies fell, other bodies rose to meet the challenge of Woo-young's team. At least twenty gangsters charged at them, slamming themselves into the riot shields in an uncoordinated manner, yet still forcing the squad back.

Before the squad managed to arrange themselves in formation to keep the attackers at bay, a horde of gangsters managed to scramble over them, suffocating them underneath their shields and blocking out the rays of light from the streetlamps.

A powerful force crashed into Woo-young's back, pushing him further into the crowd that was hammering down on his shield.

"We're spread too thin!" he called through his microphone. "We need to regroup!"

Flailing his baton and shield about haphazardly, he scrambled to gain some leverage. Managing to find a trickle of light gleaming through, the suffocating air began to ease. The horde, like zombies that could not attain any other thoughts, continued to attack.

"Form up!" Woo-young cried. "Back to back!"

As Woo-young inched backwards, attempting to locate his team members, the crowd seemed to thin. The light slowly returned and the air lightened. Suddenly, members from the horde were torn away, and through the now gleaming light stood a man in navy sweatpants and a matching hooded jacket, with a white cast around his left hand. Woo-young's partner smirked at him.

"Need some help?" Kyung-tae mouthed across to him.

"What are you wearing?" Woo-young shouted, scrunching his face as he lifted the guard in front of it. "You dress like a normal human outside of work?"

"Pass me your gear." Kyung-tae said, arriving in front of him. He slipped his wounded arm into the handles of Woo-young's shield and took up his baton. "Get your men in order. I'll give you an opening."

As Kyung-tae charged at what was left of the crowd, Woo-young watched him bash his baton into the skulls of the three gangsters to his right, using the shield to keep the other side of his foes at bay. Rushing back away from the makeshift barricades, he gathered his squad back up. A few moments later, Kyung-tae arrived to return Woo-young's equipment. And as the officers retreated, the zombified members returned their short attention spans back to their natural opposition. Some of them, running out of ammo, resorted to rushing dead man's land and even managed to reach the other side.

Kyung-tae tossed his baton back to Woo-young and then slipped the shield off his arm.

"Thanks," Woo-young said, catching his equipment.

"I've got to get my wife somewhere safe," Kyung-tae said. "You got this covered?"

"I'm good. Besides, you're suspended anyway. You have no authority."

Kyung-tae chuckled at him and then flew off into the night from whence he arrived.

Woo-young's team of ten managed to organise themselves in a huddle a safe distance away from the fighting.

"What the heck are we supposed to even do?" Min-jun, the youngest member of the squad, said. Though it was hard to distinguish each member with them all wearing identical helmets. "They've got guns and we've got sticks! We're ten men up against at least fifty! And that's what's left of them!"

"The priority are the civilians," Woo-young said. "If we don't have enough firepower to take them down ourselves, we'll have to let them thin themselves out and only go in to rescue people."

"Yes sir!" the team chanted.

"I can see at least five people that look like civilians on this side," he said as he pointed out men and women who were cowering behind improvised blockades, struggling to find openings to escape. He then pointed to the civilian nearest to them. "He's first. We go in two separate teams."

"Yes sir!" they chanted, arranging themselves in their previous teams.

"My team, on my six," he said, lowering his face guard as they followed him towards the cowering civilian.

As they inched closer and closer, the tautness that gripped his civilian's features seemed to dissolve from his face. And a light ignited in his eyes.

BOOM!

What was that? Woo-young's gaze darted around the streets. It didn't sound like a pistol. Rather it reverberated with the weighty and formidable tone of something much more powerful. Woo-young's sight returned to the man he aimed to rescue. But that rescue was no longer possible. Blood spilled from his lips and the left corner of the base of his abdomen had been torn apart, a gaping hole left behind. As the tramping of synchronised footsteps arrived behind Woo-young, a group of identical soldiers wrapped in an honourable khaki fabric, their trousers tapered down at the boots. Their shoulders bore the patch of the rising sun emblem, a sign of their national allegiance. Woo-young turned to a figure wearing the leader's patch, and time slowed as the man gestured, first left then right. His men spread in unison and lowered their firearms. With a final drop of his arms, the troupe opened fire…

Like a forest being mercilessly cleared, the bullets bulldozed over anyone without protection or cover. Helplessly watching on, the pandemonium of noise seemed to become more uniform to woo-young as screams of anguish perished.

Woo-young's senses returned to him, his blood boiling as he turned back to the leader's neutral expression.

"What in God's name are you doing?" Woo-young cried. "We had this under control! We can take care of our own problems!"

"Clearly not!" the leader bellowed as he shoved him back an arm's length away, "and don't you dare talk down to me like that again, you dog! We come here to save you from your own crime and this is the appreciation we're shown by you lowly people!"

"Our problems? You're the ones who let your bases get raided!" Woo-young shouted, shoving him back.

In a fit of snarling rage, the leader launched a front kick into Woo-young chest, propelling him to the ground.

Woo-young's eyes darted around, his heart clenching at the sight of civilians cowering on the ground, their barricades wearing down. Some, becoming aware of their impending demise, impetuously scrambled from their hiding spots, only to be unrelentingly torn to shreds in the very spot they stood, their blood painting the battlefield.

"These aren't only criminals that you're killing!" Woo-young cried, looking up at the leader. "You're killing innocent civilians!"

He looked back again, the civilians who remained in hiding resorted to praying in tears as their barricades diminished and were finally released of their fear as they were mowed down by arrays of metallic shards.

"You raise savages in this country," the leader said, lifting him up from the ground, "as far as I'm concerned, we're helping remove the filth from your society. Send your men home. You're done here."

****

Kyung-tae and Yu-ra turned another corner on their journey to the morgue. And yet again came across another battlefield. Who knew the criminal network of Seoul was so widespread? A similar scene to what they had just happened upon with Woo-young was displayed in front of them. Kyung-tae handed Takemi back over to Yu-ra again.

"I'm gonna get those civilians out and then we leave, okay?" Kyung-tae said, after which Yu-ra reaffirmed him.

Racing towards the closest civilian, he lowered his head below his arms. As if that was enough to protect him from the flying bits of metal, ready to shred him apart.

A gang member spotted him, and then swung their melee weapon at his head. Kyung-tae ducked into a roll, and then sprinted away, not bothering to check if the attacker was following. The civilians were more important.

But as Kyung-tae drew closer, the sound of clinking bullets became the rattling of gatling shells. Almost there. Almost there.

BOOM. BOOM. BOOM.

The civilian in front of him was ripped apart and Kyung-tae instinctively dived backwards. This was too dangerous. There was nothing he could do. And he needed to focus on his number one priority; getting Yu-ra to safety.

****

The cold clinical room chilled Yu-ra's fingertips. The white-tiled walls and pervasive anti-septic scent attempted to mask the morbid reality of the morgue. Dim overhead lights cast a muted glow on the room. The hum of refrigeration units echoed as Yu-ra slid the shelf supporting Takemi's body into its unit. She softly clicked the door, and with a sigh then leaned her back against the surface. On the other side of the regimented rows of stainless steel tables, Kyung-tae watched her with a soft eye.

"Woo-young just called me," he said. "The military units I saw, the ones gunning people down, they sent them home. As if they're trying to hide any trace of their failure." Yu-ra nodded, but stayed silent. "She must have been really special to you." He sighed.

"She was," Yu-ra muttered, with a downcast expression. "I used to show it, but not so much recently. I treated her like crap."

"I'm sure she didn't feel that way."

"She did," she said. Kyung-tae opened his mouth, but then stayed silent for a moment. "And I deserve everything that I have coming to me. I didn't even really internalise the fact that she upheld an entire system of peace all on her own."

"All you can do is do right by her. If you never make the same mistake again, wouldn't she be proud of you?"

A smile momentarily peeked at the corners of her lips.

"Yeah."

"I think our next step is to get you home safe," Kyung-tae said, walking over to her side of the room, then leaning back against the unit beside her, "but after that, I have no idea where to go. The fact that these guns got out, the Japanese elections next year are going to be all over the place. Someone has to take the blame."

"They'll just shift the blame to the Koreans. They were spread in our country, after all."

"Racism will skyrocket," Kyung-tae said, pulling his hand down his face in exasperation.

"The racism is already there. People don't need a reason to be hateful, but they'll latch onto anything they can to justify externalising it."

"But wouldn't that then lead to rioting? For them to blame us without justification. They don't actually know who raided the bases. We don't need to tell them."

"Who are people going to believe? One of the most powerful countries in the world or one of their colonies? In fact the general population of this country will believe them too. Even if it is one man who caused this chaos, they'll think the collective punishment is justified."

"Then we need to prevent that from happening."

"And how do we do that?"

"Well, our first step is to end this war. There are countless civilians out there that will be caught in the crossfire."

"And how do we stop a war?"

"I...don't know," Kyung-tae said, raising his hands to his hips.

"Well then...let's brainstorm," she said, pushing herself away from the refrigerator door. She moved over to one of the steel tables and took a seat on the tabletop. Kyung-tae followed suit and sat beside her.

After half an hour of a back and forth discussion of both plausible and insanely implausible scenarios, Yu-ra finally arrived at a solution.

"I've got it!" she said, clapping her hands. "I can organise a peace treaty. The gangs want peace. They just don't have a reason to stop the war and if one of them comes out on top, they own the entire underground scene."

"How the heck would you organise a peace treaty?"

"I have contacts." She smirked at him.

"Okay hotshot, that obviously makes things so much clearer." He pouted.

"Don't get jealous."

"I'm not."

"That's what they all say."

"Who's they?" Kyung-tae whined. "Why do you and ma keep saying that?"

Yu-ra shrugged.

"There's no need to be jealous just because I'm more important than you, crybaby," she said, ruffling his hair.

"Don't call me that," Kyung-tae said, brushing his hair back into place in an exacerbated manner.

"Ok, sorry crybaby."

Kyung-tae tilted his head towards her, his eyes bearing an enduring fatigue.

# 34

# Sometimes, Even a god Must Stoop to Conquer

From the depths of the infernal flames roaring in the streets, as the onslaught of bullets subsided, a figure emerged, adorning a fearsome black and gold Oni mask. He strolled peacefully through the bloodstained battlefield. Through the valley formed from the hills of flesh tinged with the sickly hue of death, empty shells of what used to contain human souls. The screams, cries, and thunderous roar of battle still rang in his head as his nostrils were filled with the acrid scent of smoke, and the metallic tang of blood. In reality, there was but an eerie silence, broken only by the occasional groan of the wounded and the pattering of his feet into puddles of blood and rainwater. A winner had been determined in this battle. But, that win would be a futile moment. This battlefield was their final destination.

As the samurai approached the groans, he drew his katana with a whispering sound, the blade emerging from its sheath like a slumbering dragon awakening from its lair. He placed the blade against the throat of the wounded combatant, a subtle smile growing underneath his mask. With a smooth stroke, the blade glided through the combatant's jugular, like a chainsaw through flesh. And the sanguine stream spurting from the body's throat stained the samurai's boots as he advanced to the next survivor.

Oh to be a soldier again. In the heart of war, with war in the heart of him.

# 35
# Treaty

"So what made you choose this as the location?" Kyung-tae said to Yu-ra as he observed the serene site from their bench.

They sat at the heart of a park, where walking paths converged like the veins of a leaf. As Kyung-tae put his arm over Yu-ra's shoulder, they admired the centrepiece of the park - a single majestic Sakura tree stood fiercely, and lonely. Emerald carpets of grass surrounded the pathways and centrepiece. And upon these carpets sat resplendent statues dotted around. Petals drifted lazily in the air like delicate confetti, a few landing on Kyung-tae's lap.

"Neutral ground, easy escape, not open to the public at this time, a lot of cover if needed," she said, pointing to the statues. "Also the tree is really pretty."

"You think like a policeman," Kyung-tae said, chuckling.

"You think about pretty trees?"

"Shut your face," Kyung-tae said, gently resting her head on his shoulder. "You ready for this?"

"As ready as I can be."

"Breathe easy. I'm here too, remember?"

"Are you one hundred percent okay with this deal?"

"We all have to make sacrifices for the bigger picture. Besides, just because I won't arrest them now, doesn't mean I can't find more evidence against them later and lock them all up."

After a few minutes of sitting quietly together, a gruff voice came from behind them.

"Well, ain't you two cute?" Kyung-tae turned to see an annoyingly familiar bald head. It had to be him, didn't it? "Last time I saw you two, you could barely touch each other," Li-Feng said.

Neither Kyung-tae, returning his gaze to the tree, nor Yu-ra, responded to his comment, choosing instead to remain in silence. After a few moments, Yu-ra stood up to greet the peevish figure who had arrived at their bench.

"You can't possibly be the leader of the Chinese," she said. "What kind of gang leader does his own dirty work? I assumed you would have told your boss and he would show."

"My boss ain't very trusting, but I'm a trusted ambassador," he replied, fixing his jacket in a pompous manner.

"Ambassador's a big word, well done," Yu-ra said, clapping sarcastically.

"You should be happy I'm here. You saved my daughter. I need to return the favour somehow."

"Li-Na was your daughter?" Yu-ra asked, raising a brow.

"Yeah."

"She's too nice to be your daughter."

"Just remember," Kyung-tae said, looking over his shoulder at them, "I'm right-handed. I can still break your nose."

"I take it back, you two ain't cute. You're annoying as hell."

Yu-ra returned to her seat next to Kyung-tae, and Li-Feng stood in silence a few feet away while the couple had quiet mundane conversations between themselves. Ten minutes later, two Japanese men arrived. One with a buzzcut who must have recognised them based on how quickly he pointed them out, and another older man beside him. The older man had slicked back grey hair, but a black goatee beard and a red dragon tattoo running up the side of his neck.

"Ken," Yu-ra said, nodding at the man with a buzzcut. "I take it this is your boss."

"I don't appreciate being spoken about in third person, girl."

"And I don't appreciate being called 'girl', but we make do with what we have."

"Everyone here?" Ken asked.

"We're waiting on one more," Yu-ra replied. Though, right on cue, Park Dae-myeon arrived at the scene, his usual sharp look having become a more dishevelled one. His shirt was untucked and his sleeves rolled up, revealing the forearm tattoo he had - a bear, the same type that was engraved on those lighters.

"Surprised he turned up," Kyung-tae said. "Didn't think a call to his office would be enough."

"I gave an offer he couldn't refuse."

"Which was?"

"He started a war over the death of his brother. I promised him the identity of the man who orchestrated his murder. The samurai."

"Just be careful of him," Kyung-tae whispered. "He seems on edge."

All the necessary pieces were in one place. It was time to start the peace negotiations.

"So..." Yu-ra started, "we all want peace, but the figure that kept the peace is no longer with us. However, that doesn't mean that we don't still have the ability to keep the peace ourselves."

"But why've I gotta keep peace?" Li-Feng butted in. "They tried to traffic my daughter!" He pointed at Dae-myeon and then to Ken and his boss. "And that's their business in the first place!"

"We've clearly all been wronged by the Koreans," the Japanese boss said. "Isn't the obvious solution to wipe them out and make peace with the Chinese?"

"You've also wronged us!" Dae-myeon blurted. "Your people killed my brother without permission! Why the do you think this war started in the first place!"

"Woah, woah!" Yu-ra called out, "you guys need to relax. We're here to make peaceful negotiations. All of us have done something wrong, but clearly we need to find a way to move past it."

"And how in the hell do you think I can just move past the murder of my brother?" Dae-myeon shouted.

Kyung-tae stepped in front of Yu-ra, holding his arm out to shield her.

"Lower your voice," he said. "Like she said, these are peaceful negotiations, and she's here to help you. So you better appreciate it and find a way to make peace."

"Who's this punk?" Dae-myeon sneered.

"He's a cop," Li-Feng said.

"What?" Ken's boss bellowed, whipping out a gun from behind his back and pointing it at Kyung-tae. "What the hell are we doing with a cop at our meeting?"

Simultaneously, Dae-myeon also pulled out a gun, pointing it in the same direction. Kyung-tae blocked Yu-ra from their line of sight. He could easily take both of the weapon wielders down in a short time period, but he wasn't sure that he could do it without any collateral damage. So, what was the next best action?

"I'm here because my wife is going to be the person that saves you and all your people," Kyung-tae said, "and she's the only reason you're not going to jail."

"And if we kill you both, right now?" Dae-myeon asked.

"Well, for one thing, that won't happen," Kyung-tae said. "And if anything happens to my wife, it'll be the end of you."

"You're not doing a good job of convincing us," Ken's boss said.

"The only reason we allowed you to keep your guns is so that you could feel safe," Yu-ra said.

"Not only will I arrest the man who burnt down the warehouses, the one who orchestrated the kidnapping of those girls," Kyung-tae said, "I also won't arrest you."

"Ok, so we torture the information outta you and then kill him." Li-Feng said, "not that I'd do that to you. I still ain't returned the favour to your wife. After that though…"

"You guys are no match for him, believe me. But if you manage to negotiate peace, I will have him locked up for life. I promise you that. I'm sure you have men in prison to do your bidding. And as a plus, everything I hear is off the record. No information said here today will be used against you and I won't come for any of you."

The men contemplated Kyung-tae's words, and after a few moments, both men put their guns away.

"Get that in writing and we have a deal," Ken's boss said.

"Already done," Kyung-tae replied.

"So, are we finally ready to begin?" Yu-ra asked, stepping out from behind Kyung-tae.

****

Yu-ra jotted down some notes on her phone from her seat as she led the meeting. Kyung-tae opted to sit beside her silently, only occasionally stepping in. She guessed he had enough trust in her to handle the situation herself. None of the other parties could bear sitting next to each other, so instead chose to stand. It was Li-Feng's turn to make known his grievances.

"What the hell even is this?" Li-Feng said, throwing his hands in the air defiantly. "I thought we were here to end a war, not have a damn therapy session. This is why women don't belong in the workplace."

"I am hosting this meeting," Yu-ra said, "and we will run it as I see fit. Dae-myeon and Kaito had their turn, and now it's yours. We need you to voice your grievances, and what you want out of this deal in order to make it fair for every party involved. We follow the structure and order I have set so that these negotiations don't break down."

"I don't understand what half those words mean, girlie. But fine, I'll do your little roleplay."

"Go ahead then."

Li-Feng rattled off his concerns, stating his frustration towards his daughter almost being trafficked, his inability to understand the need for peace because he "finally gets to fight without any repercussions", and how the Koreans broke the laws of the underground without consequences.

"So," Yu-ra said, after finishing her notetaking, looking up at the meeting participants, "as far your daughter is concerned, and the general lack of consequence, Ny-ron has been killed, which would have been the consequence anyway. The root cause of the issues has been dealt with and we cannot push the blame to Dae-myeon because he had no awareness of the situation."

"So what, then?" Kaito, Ken's boss said "We just tell everyone to go home and go back to the way things were?"

"No," Yu-ra said. "We can't go back to the way things were."

"So what do we do?" Dae-myeon said, through tired eyes.

"Your system was set up to fail in the first place. How can you rely on one person to keep three gangs in check? What happens after that person dies? Do you just find another person to replace them?"

"This gang is just a means to an end," Dae-myeon said. "It was never meant to last forever."

"And what did you do before Cheonsa? Because these gangs have been running long before she came around."

"She?" Ken said, mouth left agape. He was ignored by everyone as they continued the conversation.

"We were pretty much at war the whole time," Kaito said, "though we managed to maintain our own separate strongholds."

"The set up we had only worked because of Cheonsa," Dae-myeon said, "an all-powerful neutral entity to keep us in check. And we had no overlap to cause friction. It was very beneficial business wise."

"Then the solution is this," Yu-ra said. "I'm going to write up a contract, stating that no one has to suffer for the events that occurred as no one alive was at fault. We revert back to the old ways, because you never will find another person to replace Cheonsa. She was unique."

"Wait a sec," Li-Feng chimed in, taking a step forward and holding his index finger up as if he had just had a genius thought. "We just said we were always fighting before Cheonsa, right? So, like, how does that even count as peace, ya know?"

"Let me finish," Yu-ra said. "You will all need a monetary motivator to make peace. And everyone was involved in some sort of wrongdoing, therefore, everyone must give up something and everyone must gain something."

"Woah woah woah," Li-Feng called out, "I ain't giving up shit, spade."

"You better watch your mouth, old man," Kyung-tae finally spoke up, "or I'll make sure your injuries are permanent."

"Don't cause more friction," Yu-ra said, slapping Kyung-tae's knee.

"Sorry," he replied.

"Yeah, you better be," Li-Feng muttered, though he withdrew himself.

"Back to my solution," Yu-ra continued, "you all have a somewhat similar goal – money. Why don't you all work together?"

"I'll never work with the Japanese," Dae-myeon said. "What do you take me for? A dog?"

"You're exactly that!" Kaito shouted. "You're here to serve the Japanese, and that's it!"

"And this is exactly what we're not going to do," Yu-ra said with a huff, slapping her knees as she stood up. "If we're going to make peace, we need to be willing to make changes. The main one being that we're going to divide turfs, the benefit being that you all get to make money from all avenues, you won't be limited to one."

"Yeah, good luck selling narcotics." Dae-myeon scoffed- "You'll never find a product to compete with mine."

"Exactly," Yu-ra said, "which is why you're going to work together and all sell the same product."

"What?" Dae-myeon seethed, "and how do you figure that?"

"No, she's got a point," Kaito said. "We divide up our properties. We all sell the same stuff, everyone gains monetary value. The only thing is what do we do if someone tries to step over the line. It clearly didn't work even with Cheonsa, so it's even more likely to happen."

"I don't need your bloody trafficking business. My drugs make enough for my plans."

"Then we add another clause," Yu-ra cut in. "Something that you want that no one else wants."

"Like what?" Li-Feng asked.

"You want to be a politician," Yu-ra said to Dae-myeon. "If we guarantee you the votes of everyone left in each gang, across the whole of Seoul, that will stack up to quite the amount. It will pretty much guarantee you success in this district at the very least."

Dae-myeon contemplated her idea for a few moments.

"That's good enough for me."

"So back to the question of people who break the rules," Li-Feng added. "What do we do?"

"It needs to be severe enough to be a deterrent," Yu-ra said, "but not something that starts with violence. That will just lead to another war."

"What if we cut that group out of the deal?" Kyung-tae said. "They break the rules and they no longer are allowed to trade. All their properties are divided up amongst the remaining groups, it won't start a war because two groups benefit and only one loses out. So the losing party wouldn't risk a fight…theoretically."

"That sounds," Li-Feng started, stroking his chin thoughtfully, "feasible."

"Where on earth is he getting all these big words from?" Kyung-tae whispered, nudging Yu-ra who then shrugged.

Kaito agreed too. Dae-myeon stood silently, his right hand resting behind his back.

"This all sounds like it could work," he said, his gaze cast towards the ground and his shoulders shuddering, "but there's one problem… I loved my brother!" he cried.

He snatched his gun once more, this time aiming it fiercely at Kaito, his eyes blazing with an intense redness. Kyung-tae had already begun dashing towards Dae-myeon, as if he had already predicted the scene, and then dived into him. As the two grappled, hurtling towards the earth, Dae-myeon fired off two blasts from his chamber. Fortunately, Kyung-tae's lightning reflexes meant the two bullets tore through the air, colliding with the Sakura tree and chipping off a few pieces of bark. Kyung-tae ripped the gun from his grip and tossed it to Yu-ra.

"You're going to agree to this treaty," Kyung-tae said in a gruff tone as he held down his much bigger opponent, "otherwise I'll take you in right now. And believe me, that won't be good for your political career considering everyone thinks you turned over a new leaf."

Dae-myeon struggled under his grip for a moment before giving in.

"Fine," he said, defeated.

"I can't believe I used to think you could possibly be the samurai," Kyung-tae said, getting up off the ground.

# 36
# Psyche

Tucked away amidst the towering skyscrapers as the midday sun warmed the once serene setting, now scarred by debris, smoke, and fallen soldiers, Chun-mi sat at a small round ivory plastic table. Lush greenery formed a tranquil garden surrounding the rooftop seating area. She crossed her legs as she leaned back, occasionally sipping her coffee as she watched the unassuming civilians. Even knowing what went on last night, what was currently going on, they continued about their indifferent lives. Continued with their idle chatter, laughing and being overly affectionate with each other. Unbeknownst to them what her father had to sacrifice to make this city a safe place.

"Why would you pick a place like this to meet?" came her brother's voice from behind. She turned towards him, nodding in greeting.

"Because I want to relax," Chun-mi said, stretching her arms out. "My job is finally done. I no longer have to work for that scumbag."

"And this was all worth it to you?" Sung-jae asked, taking a seat across from her. "Do you even know how many innocent people died… Are still dying?"

"And yet we're all better off for it," Chun-mi said, taking another sip of her hot coffee. "Sacrifices need to be made for the greater good."

"You sound just like dad." Sung-jae scoffed. "Are you that desperate for his approval?"

"Is that not a good thing? Stop acting like you're any different. I know you're using Kyung-tae's wife for your undercover operation. We both have the same goal - take out the scumbags that murdered our mother and ruined our family. And we'd all do anything to see our goals through, even allow innocent civilians to get caught in the crossfire."

Sung-jae stayed silent for a moment, his eyes downcast.

"You're right." He sighed. "I let dad's influence stay with me, even after I left."

"The only difference is that he understands that his plan has a finality to it. Yours will lead nowhere useful. You already know he tried that route."

"But when he tried, he was an abusive drunkard," Sung-jae seethed. "At least I can retain my sobriety and a clear head while I work."

"Look, we can argue about this all day. You've given up on dad, that's fine. Go ahead and leave again. I'm done trying with you, but we've achieved what we wanted to achieve. Now just leave us in peace. I'll take care of dad from now on."

"Take care of him?" Sung-jae said with a puzzled expression. "You don't know…"

"Know what?" Chun-mi said, raising a brow.

"I care about dad just as much as you, maybe even more. I know who he used to be, back when he had mom."

"And where exactly are you going with this?"

"Dad's lost it!" Sung-jae asserted, slamming his hand on the table. "Have you spoken to him recently?"

"Will you relax? I spoke to him last night. He's fine."

"Have you spoken to him since? He's not fine."

"Just because he's not fine by your standards, does not mean he's not fine."

"The war has ended Chun-mi!"

"What? Since when?"

"I don't know but everyone who was fighting just suddenly stopped. Your plan failed."

"That can't be true. Why the hell would they stop fighting?"

"I don't know but they clearly made peace. Imagine what that's going to do to dad. He's been working on this for years. All of it, all of it flushed down the drain in one night! It was probably the only thing keeping him sober all this time."

"He gave up drinking the day you left, idiot. He stopped because of you."

"Which also happened to be the same time he started planning this! Listen to what I'm saying Chun-mi. Years of his life have just been wasted. What do you think is going through his mind right now?"

"I don't know, so just tell me!" she yelled, garnering the attention of the other customers.

"He's lost it, Chun-mi! He's gone absolutely insane, and we need to stop him!"

****

Bodies. Bodies and limbs everywhere. Strewn before the crimson-soaked samurai. His sword was permanently stained with his deeds and his clothes were physically heavier from the saturation of blood. The sun shone a light on his actions from the previous night. The mountains he formed in the plethora of streets.

No, wasn't he on the battlefield? Cloaked in the darkness of the night, he watched the chaos of the warring gangs unfold on the street below. How did he get there? Perched atop the corner of a two-storey building, the samurai crouched in absolute stillness. He watched and waited. Waiting for his cue. Waiting for a winner to emerge.

"Stop!" called out a voice from one of the gangs.

"Stop!" called another voice from one of the other sides.

"We're retreating!" called a voice from the third side.

The clashing of metal pipes, shattered bottles and bullets gradually diminished, and the combatants began to disperse in all directions. Why? Why weren't they fighting? Why? Why?

No. He wasn't perched atop a rooftop. He actually *was* in the midst of the battlefield. The mounds of rotting flesh around him hit him like a hammer bashing in his skull.

A rustling in the wind. What was it? Was there a survivor? The samurai scanned his surroundings, his eyes darting back and forth. But not another person stood.

"How the hell did you find me?" came a male voice. "Go grab the kids and hide," it said. But where? Where was it coming from? "Ji-yun, are you listening to me? Go!"

The samurai looked down. He wasn't standing on a scarlet drenched street. He was standing on wooden floorboards. And a Korean man in a bloodied and torn shirt lay on the ground propping himself up on his hands. A woman in a nightgown stood at the doorway, frozen.

"You survived," the samurai said. "Why?"

"W-we stopped fighting," he stammered. "We've formed a peace treaty so that no one else dies. I-isn't that a good thing? Why are you here?"

"You survived," the samurai muttered again, stepping closer to the man. "Why?"

"I-I just told you. Please, I have a wife and kids. They need me to provide for them."

"You survived," the samurai said once more, bringing his blade to the man's throat. "Why?"

And with one single stroke, tore away any life that remained in the man. His wife, finally able to move, screamed a hellish shriek. She stumbled backwards, and the samurai locked eyes with her.

"You survived. Why?"

"Survived what?" she wept, trembling at the knees. "I wasn't part of anything that my husband was involved in, please! I have kids to take care of!"

"You chose to marry a miscreant. You chose to have children with it. And now must suffer the consequences." Tears began to stream from her eyes as the samurai closed in on his prey. And he breathed his last statements, "Be at peace, child. In your next life, I will be the subject of your worship."

# 37
# Lure

"Are you not going to tell us where you're holding the meeting?" Sung-jae asked, sitting upright on the L-shaped couch.

After the afternoon sun dipped below the horizon, casting a warm glow upon the rooftop of the apartment complex, Kyung-tae and Yu-ra rendezvoused with Sung-jae and Chun-mi. Dimly lit automatic bulbs, strung across the roof, offered a subtle illumination, contrasting with the bustling city below. Despite the urban commotion, a sense of calm pervaded the rooftop. Potted plants adorned the edges while white recliner seats adorned the opposite side. The wooden floorboards of the patio-like rooftop creaked underneath Kyung-tae's shifting feet. The couple chose to stand a fair distance away from the Chois, maintaining their position near the exit.

Kyung-tae scoffed at Sung-jae's remark. Who did they think they were to even ask that?

"What?" Chun-mi said, reclining beside her brother. "You don't trust us?"

Neither Kyung-tae nor Yu-ra responded.

"Fine," Sung-jae said, taking his glasses off and placing them on the plastic table beside him. "You have plenty of reasons to not trust either of us. But we're on your side."

"Can you really say that about her?" Yu-ra said, nodding at Chun-mi.

"*It* has a name," Chun-mi said, narrowing her eyes.

"What?" Yu-ra huffed. "Do you just hear whatever you want to hear? I said *her.*"

"Look, we all want the same thing," Sung-jae said, "to help our father. Because that's what he needs - help."

"I'm here to arrest him," Kyung-tae said. "Nothing more, nothing less."

"And that's fine," Sung-jae said. "We've agreed to that."

"I just want to help." Chun-mi sighed, sitting up straight. "I didn't realise how bad it had gotten for dad. We need to stop him."

"Fine," Yu-ra said bluntly, "but that doesn't mean we're telling you where the three leaders are waiting for us right now."

Chun-mi checked her phone.

"He'll be here in a short while," she said, "can we quickly run down the plan once more? I need specifics."

Kyung-tae sighed once more, but then began narrating their scheme. Their scheme to lead him to a confined space, using Chun-mi to lull him into a false sense of security. The meeting to sign the contract was the bait. Kyung-tae knew Jinmu couldn't resist having all the pieces in one location. The two men would be hidden away ready to overpower him while his defences were down. Then they would call in to have the police arrive while they watched over him. They couldn't have the police ready because Jinmu was too smart for that. It had to be a surprise.

"Got it," Chun-mi affirmed.

Fifteen agonising minutes had crept by, each second heavier than the last. The oppressive silence hung in the air like a shroud, a palpable weight pressing down on them all. Kyung-tae was sure they could practically feel the weight of the impending decision bearing down upon them, a decision that would irrevocably alter the fabric of the Choi family. Kyung-tae's heart hammered in his chest as he grappled with the enormity of what lay ahead. The thought of severing ties with those he once considered family gnawed at him. With each passing moment, the distance between them stretched farther, a chasm of uncertainty and regret. But it was time. Time to end the relationships which held him back and prioritise the people who truly cared for him. He could still forgive them, but not to a point with which he could maintain contact with them. There was no longer a need to rebuild that bridge.

Suddenly the wind rushed by Kyung-tae's ear. His heart skipped a beat as a looming figure momentarily eclipsed the fading light. Then, as swiftly as it had arrived, the figure descended in front of him, the air fraught with an eerie stillness that seemed to swallow all sound.

Jinmu had arrived, but where was the warning? Chun-mi hadn't mentioned anything. Why did he not come up the stairs through the entrance?

Jinmu was still garbed in his battle-worn gear, with a thick crack traversing the centre of his mask. Though this time, equipped with more weaponry. He swept Kyung-tae off his feet, flipping him onto his back with a thud.

"Chun-mi," Jinmu said. "I take it that you know your role."

Chun-mi hesitated momentarily, then stood up, crossing the rooftop towards the couple.

"Yes, father."

With lightning speed, Chun-mi seized Yu-ra's arm and hauled Yu-ra towards her.

"Chun-mi!" Kyung-tae roared, as he rolled onto his feet, "don't you dare!"

Time slowed as Yu-ra's gaze reached Kyung-tae, ridden with fear. Chun-mi's arm collided forcefully with Yu-ra's abdomen, eliciting a sharp cry of pain from her. As Kyung-tae bounded towards the two women, he noticed Chun-mi's arm remained firmly planted at its point of impact, propelling Yu-ra relentlessly toward the door behind her. His outstretched arm neared Chun-mi, almost grasping her, but a powerful force tore him away from her. Helpless, he could only watch the scene play out as Chun-mi launched his wife through the doorway into the stairwell of the apartment complex. The force that had torn him away from protecting his wife thrashed him against the ground, a shock cracking into his tailbone.

Jinmu's grip was snatched away from Kyung-tae, giving him the opportunity to find his footing.

"Dad, stop!" Sung-jae's voice came. "We're trying to help you."

"Help me?" Jinmu scoffed. "You're the one who abandoned us, and now you want to help?"

As Kyung-tae flipped onto his feet, he heard a few grunts of pain coming from Sung-jae. He spun around to see a territorial dance between father and son, each throwing their own expertly placed punches, and equally, each parrying the onslaught of attacks with precision. It was as if they fought with the same mind.

Kyung-tae charged towards the exit once again but a kunai whipped past his ear, the pointed blade slicing through the air and planting itself deeply into the door. Jinmu slammed into his back, propelling Kyung-tae face first into the door beside the kunai.

"ARGHH!" Kyung-tae bellowed, swinging his left arm back blindly towards Jinmu. He effortlessly caught Kyung-tae's injured arm. Leaping to the air, Sung-jae wrapped his arms around his father's head, fortunately interrupting him before he could do any serious damage. Sung-jae planted his feet on the door and then launched himself over Kyung-tae's head, tearing Jinmu down to the ground with him. Kyung-tae watched as the pair struggled for dominance on the ground, but neither could gain leverage so they each opted to gain some distance from each other and returned to their feet.

"Fine," Kyung-tae said, loosening up his shoulders. "If that's how you want to play it, then that's exactly what we're going to do. But I promise you, if my wife isn't safe when I'm done with you, jail will no longer be an option for you."

With Kyung-tae to the left of Jinmu, and Sung-jae to the right, they simultaneously charged. He balled his injured hand into a fist and hurled it at Jinmu's face, just as Sung-jae flung his boot towards the same area. Jinmu deflected the kick, but just as he was about to do the same for Kyung-tae's punch, Kyung-tae abandoned his attack. He ducked low and drove his opposite fist into Jinmu's stomach, causing him to double over with a grunt. Kyung-tae slammed the side of his left arm into Jinmu's head, knocking him towards Sung-jae who followed up with a roundhouse kick to the head sending him crashing into the couch.

Kyung-tae dived headfirst into his downed foe, gripping onto Jinmu and, utilising his momentum, vaulted himself across to the other side of the couch, carrying his opponent with him.

"ARRRGHH!" Kyung-tae cried as a tear ripped into his left shoulder from the weight of Jinmu. He catapulted Jinmu into the railing at the side of the roof with as much force as he could muster.

"Kyung-tae!" Sung-jae called out as he dashed towards them, indicating that Jinmu was on the brink of tumbling over the railing.

Kyung-tae grabbed onto Jinmu's wrist, attempting to yank him back to his feet, but his overwhelming weight caused Kyung-tae to be pulled with him. Bracing his feet against the railing, he used it as leverage to just barely haul him back onto the roof.

Suddenly, the foe he had saved from severe injury whipped the back of his fist into Kyung-tae's cheek, flipping him onto the ground. A pulsing formed in his cheek as he rolled to his feet, observing father and son trade blows once again. As Kyung-tae raced back into action, Jinmu caught Sung-jae with an elbow to the jaw, followed up with a front kick to his stomach which launched him to the ground. Kyung-tae rammed his boot into the back of Jinmu's knee, and then, grabbing onto his head, vaulted himself into the air. He jetted his legs past Jinmu and spun around mid-air to face his opponent, yanking him to the ground and smashing his mask in the process. The shattered mask splintered across the roof.

Kyung-tae rolled backwards onto his feet, and then lifted up Sung-jae as Jinmu too found his footing. His eye bore a bruise and blood trickled from his lips. But worse than that, his eyes were empty. Devoid of life. Soulless.

Jinmu unwound a rope from his hip, a dagger tied to the end of it. He began twirling it in the air, ready for his opponents to advance.

"Ready?" Kyung-tae asked, readying his fists once more.

"Yeah," Sung-jae replied.

Jinmu whipped his roped dagger at Kyung-tae as the two charged at him. Weaving underneath the weapon as it shot past his head, and then again when Jinmu yanked it back to retrieve it. The tormented samurai whipped his dagger across the rooftop once more, this time at his son. It caught him in the left shoulder eliciting a cry of pain, but Jinmu didn't care. Instead, he slammed his foot down onto the rope, slinging Sung-jae face first into the ground. Retrieving the roped dagger, Jinmu began twirling it in the air once more. And, once again, fired it at Kyung-tae. Parrying it with his cast, Kyung-tae then grabbed the rope while he had the opportunity, causing it to wrap around his arm multiple times. An intense battle of tug of war ensued as the two opponents struggled to retrieve the weapon. Kyung-tae leaned back, attempting to gain extra leverage, but Jinmu was too strong

"Sung-jae!" Kyung-tae called out.

Leaping to his feet and racing over to Kyung-tae's side, Sung-jae grabbed onto the rope too and they both hauled Jinmu towards them. As Jinmu slowly inched closer to them, Kyung-tae slammed his foot down onto the rope, causing him to tumble in their direction. Kyung-tae swung his leg backwards, hammering it into Jinmu's face.

****

"Chun-mi, stop!" Yu-ra cried as she blocked a punch from her side. Unfortunately, that wasn't all Chun-mi had in store for her as she hurled a barrage of punches at her sides, seventy percent of them catching her in the side or the face. Pain reverberated throughout her body.

"Cry all you want," Chun-mi sneered, as Yu-ra inched back towards the slender, gleaming staircase of the narrow hallways, dangerously close to the edge of the step. "You know how to make this stop. What happened to that mouth of yours? No more sass?" Chun-mi continued bombarding her. "I guess you only get mouthy when you think you have Kyung-tae to protect you."

The pain in her body began to subside as her blood began to boil. In an instant, Yu-ra ducked her head and fired her fist into Chun-mi's abdomen. The sheer shock from Yu-ra fighting back meant she was unprepared for the hit and doubled over. Utilising the moment of freedom, Yu-ra hurled another fist towards Chun-mi's head. But before she could make contact, Chun-mi seized her wrist.

"Still got some fight in you, then." She smirked, as her grip tightened. "I guess it will at least make this more fun.

Yu-ra twisted her wrist and, using her other hand for leverage, drove her elbow towards Chun-mi, simultaneously yanking her hand from her grip. The complete shock froze Chun-mi in place, allowing Yu-ra's elbow to collide with her cheek. Chun-mi wobbled to the side and Yu-ra spun behind her. She rammed her shoulder into her back, sending her flying down the top flight of stairs, crashing into the pristine wall at the end.

"Will you stop!" Yu-ra shouted down the staircase. "What do you even get from this?"

Chun-mi pushed herself up off the ground, her eyes an infernal blaze. She charged up the staircase, but Yu-ra sprung herself over the railing, though maintained her grip. She then quickly lowered herself down to the second flight of stairs, bracing her knees as she let herself fall a short distance, the impact running up her shins.

"When did you get so limber, you spade?" Chun-mi shrieked as she vaulted over the railing.

"Your dad is going to prison regardless of what happens," Yu-ra called out as she sprinted away from her down the stairs. "The only difference is that your family will be broken forever and you'll have an unsatisfying life, led only by your desires and your endless amounts of money. What is it that you even want?"

Chun-mi managed to grasp the end of Yu-ra's scarf, jerking her back to the ground

"I want everything that's yours, you cow!"

"You don't know what you want!" Yu-ra yelled as she held up her arms for cover while Chun-mi pummelled her defences. Her tender forearms pulsed with pain. "You've lived your whole life thinking all you ever wanted is what your father wants for you! You think you belong with Kyung-tae?

You'd never fit with him. You don't know anything about him. Why would you even like him?"

Yu-ra smashed her boot into Chun-mi's shin, toppling her to the ground. Pushing herself back up, Yu-ra once again began vying for escape down the staircase.

"Oh I'm done with Kyung-tae," she screeched down the hallways as she began chasing Yu-ra once more. "He'll never accept me knowing I'm going to be the cause of your death!"

"You're throwing your life away for your dad's plans!" Yu-ra shouted back. "Why? So your father can get revenge for a woman you never met?" Chun-mi vaulted over a few of the staircase railings until she landed in front of Yu-ra. She fired her foot into Yu-ra's stomach, ripping the air from Yu-ra's chest as she was sent crashing into a piece of artwork that hung against the wall behind her, knocking it off its hook.

"Where are they?" Chun-mi roared as she stepped closer to her.

"Why are you wasting your time avenging a dead woman." She huffed. "Instead of protecting the parent you have right now?" Chun-mi stopped in her tracks. Was Yu-ra finally making sense to her? "You'll throw away the rest of the time you have with him? For what?"

Chun-mi gripped Yu-ra's collar, raising her fist to her cheek. Her eyes blazed an intense fury.

"Where are they!?"

"If you don't want to live like this," Yu-ra said softly, "you have to be the one to take the first step. Because our parents sure as hell never will, so it's on us to do our best. Because we still have the drive to make change. And we have to take responsibility for who we are."

Chun-mi's fire seemed to dissipate, and her eyes softened.

"Where are they?" she murmured.

"If this is what you want," Yu-ra said, placing her warm hand on Chun-mi's ice cold one, "I'll tell you. But there's no coming back from this."

****

Jinmu thrust a punch into the side of Sung-jae's knee, destabilising him. Another punch propelled into his stomach and then he fired an uppercut into his jaw, hurling him onto his back. Struggling to close his injured hand, Kyung-tae jabbed at Jinmu, to which he easily ducked, so Kyung-tae swung a low hook at him, catching him on the cheek. He stumbled back and Kyung-tae shot a front kick towards Jinmu, but he seized his leg and yanked him forward. Before Kyung-tae could react, Jinmu flipped Kyung-tae onto his shoulders and launched him across the roof, crashing into the recliner chairs. Jinmu bounded across the rooftop and then catapulted Kyung-tae into the railing, a sharp pain radiated throughout his spine as he suddenly lost control of his breathing. Unable to move, his body began to slump. But Jinmu held him up by the collar and pounded his fist into Kyung-tae's face.

Sung-jae wrapped his father into a headlock, ripping him away from the defeated Kyung-tae. Jinmu flipped Sung-jae over his shoulder and onto the ground. As Chun-mi burst through the door, Jinmu drove his elbow into his downed son, extracting a painful yell and a blood-filled cough. Then, restricting his movement with his knees, began relentlessly pounding at his face.

"DAD!" Chun-mi screamed, "DAD, STOP!" But Jinmu either couldn't hear her or chose not to listen, continuing his ruthless barrage. "DAD!" she cried, racing over to her father's side and pulling at his arm. Jinmu flung the back of his hand into her, spinning her on her axis and to the ground. He returned to his endless attack on the almost catatonic Sung-jae.

"Jinmu, stop!" Kyung-tae bellowed, finally regaining his ability to move as he pushed himself to his feet. "That's your son! You really think this is what your wife would have wanted?"

"Dad!" Chun-mi cried again. "I know where they are!" Suddenly, Jinmu halted his attack, looking at Chun-mi with those soulless eyes of his. "I know where the meeting is, let's go. They're at Diamond Residences, the apartment complex that Dae-myeon owns. Apartment 2B."

Without so much as a confirmation nod, Jinmu fled the scene, opting to vault over the railings rather than taking the stairs.

Chun-mi crawled over to Sung-jae who was coughing up blood onto the wooden panelling.

"Where's Yu-ra?" Kyung-tae said, watching as Chun-mi lifted Sung-jae into a sitting position. His ears were ringing and he could barely hear her response.

"She's fine," Chun-mi said. "I didn't hurt her." Kyung-tae approached the exit but then paused as Chun-mi spoke again. "Kyung-tae, I'm sorry. I'm sorry for following through on my father's every order. For how I treated Yu-ra undeservedly."

"This isn't the time. We need to go stop your dad."

"I know you're never going to speak to me again after this, so I need to tell you now. I had it mixed up in my head that we belonged together because that's what my father had planned for me. But the truth is, I've never liked you that way. To be totally honest with you, I find you repulsive. You're too... weak for me."

"Yeah, thanks."

"I'm bad with words, but you know what I mean."

She was right. That family no longer had a place in his life. So, holding it over her did nothing for him.

"Consider yourself forgiven." Kyung-tae said, before leaving the scene to go and find his wife.

# 38
# Family Business

Yu-ra eyed her husband as he sped the four of them through the streets of Seoul, towards Diamond Residences. She managed to clean him up as much as she could, as did Chun-mi with Sung-jae, his head resting on her lap, but the bruising on his cheeks was quite severe compared to Kyung-tae's. Yu-ra's heart lurched knowing how much pain Kyung-tae was powering through.

"Why don't we call the police now?" Yu-ra asked, "get them to surround the building?"

"We don't even know if he's there yet," Chun-mi said, as she brushed Sung-jae's hair with her hand.

"Besides that," Kyung-tae added, "he's unhinged right now. There's no telling the amount of damage he'll do if he feels trapped. He'll lash out and I can't put any more innocent people in harm's way."

"Tae-tae, I know you won't like this," she said softly, "but I want to help you take him down."

Kyung-tae glanced at her.

"No, it's too dangerous," he said bluntly.

"Look at yourself," Yu-ra said in a trembling voice. "You're on the brink of collapse. I can't sit back and wait for you to not come back to me."

"I know you're worried about me, but we have Chun-mi this time. You'll just hinder me if you're there because I won't be able to stop worrying about you."

"Tae-tae, please," she said, placing her hand on his shoulder.

"Yu-ra, he'll use you against me. He doesn't care who he hurts as long as he achieves his goal."

"I promise you, if it gets too dangerous, I'll run for safety. Immediately."

Kyung-tae sighed.

"Immediately?"

"Immediately."

Kyung-tae contemplated for a moment.

"Wait, no, no, no. That's stupid. Yu-ra, you are not doing that. I'm your husband. I'm meant to keep you safe."

"What am I meant to do then? I don't want to be useless."

"Hey! Don't ever say that about yourself. Just make sure the police arrive on time. The moment we've confirmed his location, and we've got him locked down, call them. Make sure they know that he's the one who distributed the guns. They'll come quicker."

"Okay," Yu-ra said, lightly squeezing his shoulder, "just promise me you'll come back to me."

Kyung-tae chuckled.

"I'll always come back to you."

"Promise," she said with a stern look.

"May Allah protect me and bring me back to you."

"Ameen."

Kyung-tae skidded the car to a halt outside the imposing building, a modern marvel of architecture amidst the urban landscape. Its sleek glass facade reflected the surrounding cityscape, shimmering under the white hues of moonlight. Upon entering the lobby, they were greeted by an opulent marble foyer adorned with contemporary art pieces and designer furnishings, but no people. Even the concierge desk stood unaccompanied. The building must have been emptied by Dae-myeon after they left.

As they traversed the marble floor, their footsteps echoed in the eerie silence, punctuated by the shocking sight of blood spatters staining the pristine surface. Jinmu was on the site.

"Chun-mi, take Sung-jae up the elevator. He still looks a bit worn out," Kyung-tae said, as he grabbed onto Yu-ra's hand. "We're taking the stairs."

Chun-mi and Sung-jae split off, as Kyung-tae raced up the elegant staircase to the second floor with Yu-ra close behind him. Apartment 2B's door stood ajar, openly vulnerable.

"Crap," Yu-ra muttered as Kyung-tae released her hand, dashing into the apartment.

As Yu-ra reached the door, Kyung-tae dived into Jinmu, wrenching him away from a trembling Dae-myeon, paralysed on the ground. His face had been slashed from the base of his left eye, down to the right side of his jaw and blood began to trickle down from various points along the laceration.

In the midst of the luxuriously stylish apartment, lined with floor-to-ceiling windows along the back wall, the centre of which held up a grandiose television, Kyung-tae and Jinmu wrestled each other on the ground. Beside the sleek kitchen area that was situated to her right, she noticed the two bodies that had been ferociously mauled, their entrails littering the scene. She raced over to Dae-myeon's side, as the stately chandelier above them illuminated the horror of Jinmu's actions.

Arriving at the scene, Sung-jae and Chun-mi leapt at the two on the ground, but Jinmu kicked himself off Kyung-tae, with a powerful thrust, and the two slid across the ground in opposite directions. Kyung-tae spun his legs in a circular motion, using the momentum to regain his footing, but stumbled slightly upon standing.

Chun-mi launched herself into a flying kick. Jinmu blocked, forced back a few steps, and she flung the back of her leg at his in a low sweep. Dodging it, Jinmu lifted himself into the air and drove his knee down on Chun-mi, crashing her into the ground. Immediately flipping himself to his feet as Kyung-tae charged towards him, he spun himself into a powerful back kick targeting Sung-jae, sending him colliding with Dae-myeon. Jinmu gripped Kyung-tae and hauled him through the doorway, continuing the fight where Yu-ra could no longer see.

Chun-mi chased after them as Sung-jae regained his, shaky at best, balance.

"Sung-jae," Yu-ra said before he could race off, "look at him."

"Yeah, I have," Sung-jae replied. "He's a monster."

"No, really look. It's like he's in survival mode. He's been consumed by his need for revenge and the rage he's carrying. The reason he's so dangerous is because he's being pumped with adrenaline and his natural instinct for survival is making him do anything he sees as necessary."

"What's your point?"

"You need to get him out of that. Once he's come to his senses, you can outwit him or reason with him. He wants a way out of this, he just can't see it clearly."

"Call the police, and some ambulances," he said as he dashed off, back into the heat of battle.

****

Kyung-tae smashed through the door of apartment 2A, tearing it off its hinges and bringing the door with him as he slid across the ground. The room was identical to 2B but mirrored. The same potted plants in the corners of the room. The same spacious floor plan. Everything. He rolled back onto his feet as Chun-mi launched a powerful kick into Jinmu's back, sending him into the apartment too. Tumbling towards Kyung-tae, Jinmu ducked low and rammed his shoulder into Kyung-tae's chest, sending him crashing into the large TV behind him, the screen painfully splintering into his back.

Chun-mi sprang into the air, wrapping her legs around Jinmu's neck, and using the force of her weight, pulled and tugged at him in an attempt to take him down. Jinmu maintained his stability, and slammed Chun-mi into the countertop at their side. Lifting her up, he slammed her down once again. Chun-mi drove her elbow into the crown of his head but he continued to repeatedly slam her against the counter. Leaping to his feet, Kyung-tae dived at him, grasping him in a headlock and tearing him to the ground as Chun-mi released her grip from him. Jinmu effortlessly flung Kyung-tae to the side as Sung-jae arrived at the scene.

"Dad, stop!" he cried, "please!"

But of course, Sung-jae's pleas held no weight.

Leaping onto the counter, he thrust Chun-mi away with his boot. As Kyung-tae and Sung-jae stumbled towards the counter as fast as their pain-ridden bodies would allow them, Jinmu sprang at the glass chandelier, ripping it off its hinges and bringing it plunging towards his three foes. Sung-jae dived at Chun-mi, knocking her out of the way as Kyung-tae launched himself in the opposite direction. Sparks zapped in all directions as the glass smashed into hundreds of pieces, large and small, cutting at the exposed skin of any individual they met.

"We need to end this!" Kyung-tae yelled. "Everyone grab him!"

As all three of them bolted towards him, Jinmu hurled his body back onto the counter, sliding across it and finding a stainless steel pan with which he catapulted at Kyung-tae's head. Just managing to dodge the projectile which thwacked into the wall behind him, Kyung-tae was met with Jinmu's boot slamming into his cheek. His kick was weaker than usual. Even through Kyung-tae's pounding headache, he could feel the change in impact of the hits. They were wearing him down.

Managing to regain his balance, he saw both Sung-jae and Chun-mi receiving the same action as Jinmu spun effortlessly on his hands, propelling his legs in all directions like the blades of a fan. Sung-jae's chest heaved up and down as he struggled to get back to his feet. He coughed some blood to his side before he forced himself back up. Kyung-tae raced over to the steel pan that was thrown at him and launched it at Jinmu, who then deflected it with his agile kicks. Sung-jae dived at his legs, but Jinmu flipped backwards off the countertop and then tripped back into the stove, before returning himself to his feet and spitting some blood to his side.

"Dad!" Sung-jae strained, "you need to give yourself up! I'll help you get a lower sentence, I promise."

Chun-mi flipped over the table firing an axe kick into Jinmu. He blocked with his forearm but his arm gave in, and as she fell, Jinmu slammed his other fist down into her chest, flinging her into the countertop. Kyung-tae vaulted over the counter, spinning on his hands and thrust the back of his heel into Jinmu's head. He quickly regained his balance as Kyung-tae landed next to him, and he slammed Kyung-tae's head into the counter, making his temples erupting in a volcano of pain. Jinmu threw him to the side, Kyung-tae's vision fuzzing as he lost control of his limbs.

****

"What are you doing?" Yu-ra shouted as Dae-myeon finally found his ability to move, pulling a gun from behind his back.

"I'm going to end this," he growled, marching towards the door.

"No the hell you're not!" she yelled, picking up the nearest object she could find, a vase at the centre of the coffee table to her right.

She catapulted it at Dae-myeon's head, shattering it into pieces and knocking him onto the ground. As she raced towards him, he spun around snapping his gun towards her and freezing her to her spot.

"Don't."

****

Jinmu sprang into the air, split kicking his two children, and as he landed, thrust his fist into Kyung-tae's chest, sending him back a few paces. But then Jinmu fell to his knees with a grunt.

"Dad!" Sung-jae called as he found his footing, "I…" Jinmu forced himself back to his feet and then flew into a spinning kick, cracking across Kyung-tae's jaw, spinning him on his axis. He pounced on Kyung-tae then grappled him into an armbar, yanking at his injured wrist. "I…" Jinmu flipped him onto his back and continued pulling, a tear ripping down his entire arm as he cried out in pain. As Jinmu finally managed to snap his cast in half, Kyung-tae lost all control of his breath, at the brink of hyperventilating from the pain coursing through his body. "Dad, I forgive you!" Sung-jae yelled.

Suddenly, Jinmu stopped, staring into blank space with eyes still catatonic.

"Nothing can justify what you put us through, dad," Sung-jae continued, "but you never did anything that's too far to come back from. And I forgive you."

Jinmu fell back away from Kyung-tae who then stumbled to his feet.

"Gra-," was all Kyung-tae's breathless body could produce. "Gra…Grab him!" Kyung-tae bellowed, finally able to push through the pain and control his words.

All three of them bolted towards Jinmu. His children locked an arm each in a hold and Kyung-tae slid past them, wrapping his uninjured arm around his throat and pulled him down to the ground with as much strength as he could muster through his mounting pain.

Jinmu thrashed about maniacally underneath their grasp, like a shark who smelled blood.

"Dad," Sung-jae said, struggling to keep his grasp as his eyes began to water, "I'll come back home, I promise. I won't leave you."

"Dad," Chun-mi said, as his thrashing calmed, "I just want my family back."

"Jinmu," Kyung-tae said calmly. "You've made mistakes. The only way to move past them is to pay your dues and ask for forgiveness. Wallowing in rage and self-pity will do nothing for you."

"Dad," Sung-jae said as life returned to Jinmu's eyes, his body falling into a stillness as a tear trickled from his bruised eye, "give yourself up. I promise that I'll stay with you. I will defend you until the day that you're free."

Falling forward from their grasp, Jinmu's body went limp. They let him fall to the ground and Kyung-tae held his wrists together with his unbroken hand.

"There's some zip-ties in my pocket," Kyung-tae said, nodding to Sung-jae, "grab one and cuff him."

As the sound of sirens began to holler in the far distance, just barely audible through the open windows, Dae-myeon arrived at the entrance. Sung-jae followed suit with his orders and tied his father up.

"You got him?" Dae-myeon said hurriedly. "What are you doing with him?"

"Police should be here soon," Kyung-tae said. "They'll be taking him in."

"Ah, good, good."

****

Yu-ra hurried into the kitchen area, scanning for a blunt weapon. Searching through the cupboards, she found a small but heavy pot to which she took up the handle. Racing to the exit, she yelled out.

****

"Kyung-tae!" Yu-ra shouted across the hall, "he's got-"

Suddenly Dae-myeon drew his gun, pointing it at Jinmu. Sung-jae sprang to his feet, sprinting at Dae-myeon. As Dae-myeon let off two rounds, Sung-jae collided with Dae-myeon.

****

*BANG! BANG!*

As Yu-ra reached the apartment across the hall, Dae-myeon bashed into the doorframe, knocking him unconscious with Sung-jae towering above him. Sliding into the apartment, Yu-ra surveyed the room. Where did the bullets hit? The room was already in a wreck. She glanced at Jinmu, his hands tied behind his back static on the ground.

"Y-Yu-ra," Kyung-tae whispered, holding his injured hand across his abdomen. He lifted it up, revealing the blood staining his broken cast. Blood seeped through his thick jumper as his lips reddened, a thin liquid trickling out. Coughing, he sputtered some blood across the floor as the grip Yu-ra had on her weapon relinquished, clanging against the ground. Her heart plunged as he fell backwards and she flew to his side, catching his head before it hit the ground. Kyung-tae looked away from her, teary eyed as the blood from his lips began dripping onto her exposed wrists.

****

Kyung-tae sensed an icy chill creeping into his fingertips, gradually numbing them as his wound burned hotter.

"Kyung-tae," she whispered, her voice trembling as tears dripped onto his forehead.

"At least I can't feel the pain in my arm anymore," he groaned.

"You said you wouldn't leave me," Yu-ra said, wiping the droplets from his head.

"No, I said I would come back to you." He chuckled weakly then coughed hoarsely. "I'm here aren't I?"

"I'll call an ambulance," Sung-jae said, pulling out his phone and rushing out of the room.

Jinmu, finally gaining some consciousness, rolled onto his back, observing the couple.

"K-Kyung-tae," he murmured.

"Don't," Yu-ra asserted, glaring at Jinmu. "Move him away from me."

Kyung-tae was expecting snarky remarks but, strangely, Chun-mi simply followed the command and lifted Jinmu from the ground, walking him out of the room.

"I didn't realise how cute you are when you get bossy," Kyung-tae said, grinning meekly.

"This is all my fault," she wept. "I told Chun-mi where the meeting was. I didn't check Dae-myeon for a gun, I let him escape the room. I-"

Through his already heavily beating heart, pangs attacked his heart.

"Yu-ra, Yu-ra, Yu-ra," he said, placing his right hand against her cheek, "didn't we make a deal that you would never blame yourself? This isn't your fault."

"I just told you why it's my fault, idiot."

"I'm bleeding out here, can you not make fun of me, please?"

"Stop making jokes," she whimpered.

"Yu-ra," he said, brushing her cheek, "blaming ourselves gets us nowhere. You taught me that. All it means is that we can't move forward."

"Ok, ok, I won't blame myself," she whined. "Just hold on until the ambulance gets here."

Kyung-tae's chest became heavier. He didn't know what would happen next and he was terrified. Terrified to a level he had never felt before. Had he done enough with his life? Had he made amends with everyone he needed to? Had he asked for enough forgiveness? His uncertainty with himself had never been so pronounced. But he couldn't show it, not in front of Yu-ra. That would only serve to make her feel worse. His job as a husband was to comfort her.

"If this is my time, there's nothing we can do, Yu-ra," Kyung-tae said. "The time I've had with you has been an endless blessing and we've both helped each other become better. Isn't that the most beautiful thing in the world?"

"Kyung-tae, I can't - I can't do this," Yu-ra said, her breath beginning to leave her. "Please, Kyung-tae."

"Yu-ra," he said weakly, "I'm so glad you found me."

Yu-ra kissed him on the cheek.

"I'm sorry I was so harsh with you. Please, forgive me."

"Harsh? As if."

"Kyung-tae."

"I forgive you."

Yu-ra kissed him on the cheek once more.

As Kyung-tae slowly closed his eyes, he could hear the quiet sobbing of his wife. The whimpering and every other sound quietened as his breath became more shallow. At least he could be sure that Yu-ra would be okay without him. That she would be able to live a fulfilling life, no longer allowing grudges to hold her back from who she could truly be. And that was enough for Kyung-tae. If that was his life's only achievement, he was content.

Before long, all sounds faded into silence, his breath slipping away as consciousness departed.

# 39

# Written by Baek Yu-ra

**Descent into the Underworld**

**A student coerced into the world of crime details her account.**

Baek Yu-ra, a journalism major at Maewha University, was recently found to have a former affiliation with an individual who later became associated with criminal activities. This fact, utilised by the prosecution, sent her on a two month long undercover escapade into the realm of crime syndicates. Her exclusive access into this clandestine domain enabled her to make numerous discoveries. These discoveries encompass the sequence of events that incited mass riots and street warfare within a single night, detailing those responsible for the theft and distribution of arms. Additionally, insights into the structure of the criminal underworld and its methods of maintaining peace, as well as its exploitation of the justice system, were uncovered.

**Abuse of a Weak Criminal Justice System**

Late one night, two months before the war that broke out on the streets of Seoul, I unexpectedly encountered an old acquaintance, only to later learn from the prosecutor who apprehended us that this individual was implicated in criminal undertakings. More precisely, she served as a mediator within the realm of lawlessness. The revelation of a text, owned within each syndicate, detailed the civility that had formed within an otherwise uncivilised world. This document conveyed that each gang would exclusively operate within their own industries, yet coexisted within the same localities. However, severe repercussions, including the imposition of the death penalty, awaited any who dared breach these rules.

Through the same prosecutor who employed me, and leveraging a connection I maintained within the present police force, I meticulously gathered and scrutinised a wealth of arrest reports. Presented below are a select few summaries, among many, all exhibiting a consistent pattern spanning the past twenty years. I have opted to highlight a few arrests made by one police officer in particular, during his active years: the decorated soldier and retired senior detective, Choi Jinmu. All sources are listed at the end of this article.

Park Dae-myeon: Renowned for his cutting-edge pharmaceutical laboratories, Park Dae-myeon carries a shadowy history. However, the public embraced his display of contrition when he was acquitted of his manslaughter charge. A two-decade-old report reveals that he was initially accused of the murder of Choi Soo-yeon, the late wife of Choi Jinmu. Park subsequently provided a written confession for manslaughter, reducing his sentence from life imprisonment to a mere decade. Moreover, by maintaining exemplary conduct and demonstrating seemingly genuine remorse, Park was granted early release after serving just five years of his sentence. As evidenced in numerous recent articles, it was discovered that he had been manufacturing and supplying a new form of drug to the syndicate operating within the narcotics industry. Park has since been arrested and is currently on trial to determine the length of his sentence.

Kim Cho-ji: A member of the Korean gang, arrested eight years ago for the distribution of narcotics. His admission of guilt resulted in a reduced sentence of six months instead of twelve. However, inconsistencies in the reports indicate that the initial arrest was of one Park Ny-ron, the younger brother of Park Dae-myeon. Yet, the confession of Kim Cho-ji promptly absolved any accusations against Park Ny-ron.

Zhang Mei: A Chinese gang member who was apprehended for the illicit provision of loans and ties to an underground gambling operation. Thanks to a confession, she completed her sentence expeditiously, serving just three months. Despite being a repeat offender, she consistently received the same sentence. Interestingly, each arrest began with a different suspect.

There are countless other reports which coincide with this same pattern of discrepancies and abuse of a lenient justice system. Has this loophole gone unnoticed? Certainly not, as the criminals of Seoul have undoubtedly taken note. There was once a period during which the Korean republic opposed the merger of judicial systems. Following twelve years marked by recurring case resolutions, Choi Jinmu retired from the police force.

It remains unclear when Choi Jinmu first began conspiring to incite a gang war. However, two months ago, a series of seemingly unrelated events orchestrated by Choi culminated in the eruption of such a conflict. Following the establishment of a truce between the gangs, Choi Jinmu was arrested and is now on trial, represented by attorney Choi Sung-jae. In light of the extensive evidence gathered against numerous members of Park Dae-myeon's gang, resulting in multiple arrests, a special task force has been formed with the primary goal of disrupting and eradicating all gang activity in Seoul. Detective Lim Woo-Young has been appointed as the acting commander of this task force.

*Turn to page 7 for the full story*

****

**Loss of Identity**

During our schooling, we were educated that Japan's annexation of Korea in 1910 was intended to protect us from external threats. With limited literary and historical sources contradicting this narrative, few records of that period have survived. However, I have always been in possession of some conflicting sources, including the diaries of my great-grandmother, which shed light on the reality of the situation. These entries recount how the Japanese authorities conducted book burnings and implemented re-education camps. Yet, some families across the country succeeded in safeguarding a handful of tomes.

Written exclusively in Korean, these texts can only be translated by a select few individuals in the present era. They all express a distinctly anti-colonialist perspective and represent a pivotal moment in history, marking the final period when such sentiments could be openly articulated, the final period when our indigenous language was openly spoken, and the final period when the flaws of the judicial system listed above were absent. These texts have been in existence since pre-colonial times, yet they have not been represented in the media or journalism landscape.

**Lessons**

So, what do we take from this? What use are these historical documents and the extensive display of a corrupt judicial system? Well, to understand that, we need to ask ourselves, how did it get to this point? From a generation fiercely battling for freedom, to a subservient one who would shun their own for wanting independence and safety for their people.

Our judicial system has been showcased as highly effective through the ninety-nine point seven percent conviction rate, yet this has not lowered crime rates, nor served as a deterrent to would-be offenders. This pro-colonialist ideology has been perpetuated by the media we voluntarily consume and the propaganda we are force-fed. The ideology then gives rise to the mindset that Japan has saved us and improved our lives in all aspects. If they can do no wrong, then the judicial system cannot be faulty, even if it is working against us. We begin to lose everything special about ourselves. We lose our cultural identity but our generation won't care because life is easy for us and we would rather create superfluous problems for ourselves. Superfluous problems to distract us from the people unjustly suffering and dying due to corrupt systems.

Numerous instances highlight the judiciary's failure to serve the populace. Individuals such as Choi Soo-yeon, whose untimely demise remains without true justice. Individuals such as detective Oh Kyung-tae, who devoted his life to safeguarding the innocent and was willing to sacrifice everything for them. And then there's Choi Jinmu, who endured the loss of his wife and was subsequently plagued by a flawed system throughout his career, prompting him to take matters into his own hands to rectify the city's rampant corruption. When you combine a brilliant detective, abundant free time, and the belief that he will ascend to godhood through remarkable achievements, you create an individual who will relentlessly pursue their objectives, sparing no effort to achieve them.

This all started with a deficiency of integrity in our education system, our media and especially our journalism. When we manipulate words to obscure the reality of situations, moulding the mindset of our people to fit a predetermined narrative, we reduce ourselves to subservient zombies who parrot only the sanctioned thoughts endorsed by our government. When we censor anyone with an opposing opinion, subjecting them to dehumanising attacks, we obstruct the avenue to independent thought

And in a society devoid of free thinkers, how can we champion true justice ever again?

# 40
# Epilogue

Yu-ra carried a tray of mini-cakes through the corridor and into the living room of her parents' house, placing it onto the coffee table in front of Kyung-tae's mother. Sitting on the couch beside her, Yu-ra wrapped her arm over her shoulder.

"I made these especially for you," Yu-ra said, kissing her on the cheek.

"You're just great at everything, aren't you?" she said, smiling as she pulled Yu-ra closer to her.

"How are you feeling?"

"I'm okay. More importantly, how are you? That article must have gotten you into a lot of trouble."

"I got the job actually," Yu-ra said, grinning ear to ear. "I'm the only one who has any insight into what went on that day last month. Set me leagues above everyone else. People are finally starting to think for themselves and be open to different mindsets. It's why it got leaked to the public in the first place. And it's not like they can hide the evidence. It's been spread online. People would actually riot if I didn't get the job."

"I'm so proud of you," she said, picking up one of the cakes from the tray. "I've got even more reason to brag about you to people now." Yu-ra chuckled as Kyung-tae's mother took a bite of her cake and swallowed before continuing. "When do you start?"

"Next week is my induction process."

"What about university? You haven't finished your final year, right?"

"Yeah, but I've just got a few assignments left. I don't need to be in for that, so it won't really detract from anything. I'm already on track for a top grade."

"Yu-ra, Yu-ra, Yu-ra," she said, with a glint in her eye, "journalist extraordinaire."

"EOMMA!" Yu-ra yelled.

"Oi," Kyung-tae's mother said, grimacing with her hand to her ear, "you're gonna burst my eardrum."

"Sorry," Yu-ra said before pressing her hands over her guest's ears, "EOMMA! Hurry up and join us!"

Yu-ra's mother calmly entered the room, carrying a tray of hot drinks.

"Why are you yelling, you stupid girl?" she said, placing the tray on the coffee table next to the cakes. "Did I raise you to have manners like that?"

"Come and sit down," Yu-ra said. "She's your friend, not mine."

Yu-ra's mother followed suit and the three girls spoke for a short while, predominantly about Yu-ra and the big changes that would ensue in the near future. Though Yu-ra upheld her lack of worry, knowing she would always have a supportive family.

The doorbell rang, breaking their conversation, and her father passed through the living room and into the corridor leading to the front door. Moments later her father returned to the living room with a gift bag.

"What's that?" Yu-ra's mother asked.

"Gifts," he replied simply as he examined the contents of the bag.

"From who? And what in particular?" Yu-ra's mother replied, rolling her eyes.

"Men for you," Kyung-tae's mother said, nudging Yu-ra's shoulder.

"Why are you nudging me?" Yu-ra asked with a puzzled expression.

"My son in law," he said, looking up from the bag, as Kyung-tae entered the room, his cheeks glowing as he grinned.

"Assalaamu 'alaykum!" he sang, before arriving at his mother's side, kissing her on the cheek.

"You're in a cheery mood," his mother said.

"I take it you got the promotion?" Yu-ra asked.

"I did," he said, walking over to Yu-ra and kissing her on the cheek. After standing back up, he looked at her father, who was eyeing him with a subtle disdain. "Sorry."

"Why are you apologising," Yu-ra said.

"Nothing. Anyway I turned it down."

"What? Why?" her father asked. "First you turn down being head of the task force and now this?

"We realised that he hates the job and I'm not comfortable with how unsafe it is," Yu-ra said. "We decided together that that's what he'd do. He won't have a difficult time finding another job and it's not like he was getting paid enough for the work he was doing."

"I have plenty of money saved up," Kyung-tae said. "I can take care of your daughter, Abeoji."

"If you're sure about this," her father said. "Just make sure you don't waste too much time."

"Yeah," Kyung-tae said, looking at Yu-ra fondly, "I'm sure."

"How's your pain?" he asked. "All gone?"

"My wrist has healed completely, but I still get pains in my hip every now and then. Though, it's nothing major."

"Appa," Yu-ra said, "come and sit down. You need to try some of this food I made."

"Oh, guess what," Kyung-tae said. "They thought it was a negotiation technique and even offered to move us to Kyoto. Provide accommodation and everything."

"And you didn't take it?" her mother asked, exacerbated.

"Why should he," her father spat back.

"It's not some utopia," Kyung-tae said. "We're happy here."

ISBN 978-1-916848-08-5

9 781916 848085

Literacy Club Publishing

Printed in Great Britain
by Amazon

62690383R00211